Cherry Grove

Susan X Meagher

Susan X Meagher

Cherry Grove

© 2007 BY SUSAN X MEAGHER

ISBN 978-0-9770885-8-4

THIS TRADE PAPERBACK ORIGINAL IS PUBLISHED BY BRISK PRESS, NEW YORK, NY 10011

COVER DESIGN BY CAROLYN NORMAN

COVER PHOTOGRAPH BY COLIN ANDERSON

FIRST PRINTING: JUNE 2007

Acknowledgements

I have had the privilege of spending many of my summer weekends on Cherry Grove. There are few better places to spend a warm, sunny day. It's the camp every queer kid longs for—and there's no age limit!

This book and my life are dedicated to Carrie, my partner in every venture.

By Susan X Meagher

Novels
Cherry Grove
All That Matters
Arbor Vitae

Serial Novels
I Found My Heart in San Francisco:
Awakenings
Beginnings
Coalescence
Disclosures
Entwined
Fidelity

Anthologies
Undercover Tales
Telltale Kisses
The Milk of Human Kindness
Infinite Pleasures
At First Blush

To purchase these books go to
www.briskpress.com

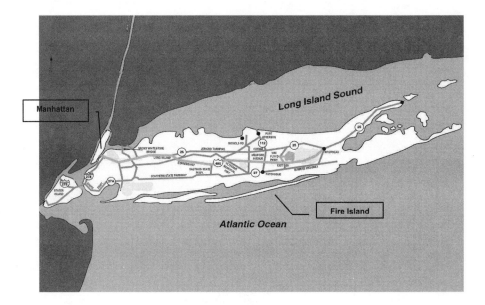

Fire Island is a barrier island about five miles from the south shore of Long Island. It's nearly thirty miles long, and less than a mile wide. Fewer than 500 people are permanent residents, but that population swells dramatically during the summer.

It's made up of many tiny communities, one of which is Cherry Grove. Ferries leave from two towns on Long Island to take passengers and supplies to the different communities on Fire Island.

Chapter One

I 've done some stupid things in my life, but this might be the winner. I stood in front of the wall of windows fronting the ocean, my skin prickling with fear. Dark, inky blue skies met the sea, merging into fathomless darkness. It was so quiet it was almost silent. I opened one door a little to let some sound in to drown out my racing heartbeat. The relentless swell and ebb of the waves usually calmed me, but tonight the ocean merely seemed like a convenient place to dump my body.

Stop it! You're being ridiculous! People do things like this all of the time. Have you ever known anyone to die from a date? No!

I closed and locked the door again, unable to stand the cold, wet breeze. Coming out here had made perfect sense from a practical perspective. But I wasn't feeling practical. All I could think of was how few people were in town. Almost nothing on the island was open, and when I'd arrived last week, I noticed that the little grocery store, the lifeline of the community, was only open for six hours a day. When the busiest place in town is open from ten to four, you're in a very tiny town.

So, why did I feel so vulnerable? Shouldn't the fact that there couldn't be more than fifty people in town make me as safe as I'd ever been? I know I must pass rapists, thieves, and killers every day at home, but being here, with almost no one, made me feel as if every noise were a threat.

I'd been slightly spooked all week, and even though I knew I was being ridiculous, I couldn't get over it. I was used to so much noise, such a constant rumble of people and cars and trucks and subways, that the silence was deafening.

I was, I'll admit, starved for human contact. It hadn't occurred to me that my cell phone would get such horrible reception. Thankfully, there was a phone in the house, but I had to pay long-distance charges for every call, and that made idly gabbing to one of my friends seem wasteful. I hate to admit how much WASP penury I carry in my genes, but when human contact seems like a waste of money, my frugality is hard to ignore.

Even though I was lonely, that was no excuse for doing something so foolhardy. Something so completely out of character that I felt disconnected from my real self. I didn't know why I'd done it, but I hadn't even paused when Gina...I *think*...no, I'm sure that's her name...when Gina suggested we get together tonight.

What sort of accent did she have? I'm not even sure how to mimic her, but she did something funny with the endings of many of her words. I'm no linguist, and I have to admit I wasn't focusing on what she was saying or how she was saying it, but there was something there. I might have been able to assess it if I hadn't been focusing on her mouth. And her lips. And her big, dark, deep-set eyes. My God, those eyes!

Entering my bedroom, I found a notepad and pen. Working quickly, I wrote a note to my housemates.

> *If I'm gone when you get here, it's not by choice.*

Oh, for Christ's sake. Don't be melodramatic. Just lay it out. I ripped the page from the book and started again.

> *I made a date with the woman from the ferry on Wednesday, May 4. Her name is Gina. I didn't have a chance to tell anyone where I was going, so if I'm not here when you arrive, she might have some idea where to find me.*

Is that clear? Oh, fuck, who cares? You'll be dead, and your picture will be on the front page of the *New York Post*. How titillating will the headline be? I suppose that depends on whether they've found my body. "Missing Gay Prof: History?" That should do it. Maybe I should add that to the note so I'm sure to go out with a bang.

Annoyed with myself, I took the note and put it in the refrigerator, knowing that my housemates would go there to put food and wine away before they even noticed I wasn't home. The edge of the paper fit neatly under the butter dish.

Maybe I should write a note to my mother. Oh, but then she'd think I *knew* I was going out with a killer, and she'd never be able to understand. I opened the fridge and took out the note, adding a quick scribble.

> *If you can avoid it, don't show anyone this*
> *note. Tell everyone, including the police, that I*
> *called to tell you I was going out.*

Pausing, I slammed the door closed, knowing that my addendum was stupider than the note.

Maybe I should call a friend or even my sister to tell her I was going out with someone I'd met on the island. But then I'd have to get into the details. How I didn't know her. How we'd spoken maybe twenty words—total. How special I felt to have such a lovely woman notice me, much less ask me out.

But I couldn't make myself do it. If Gina were coming over to kill me, telling someone she was coming wouldn't change a thing. The last thing I needed was more anxiety, and that's exactly what I'd get if I told my sister.

A strong, firm knock on the front door made me jump. I took a deep breath and started for the door, wiping my clammy hands on my khakis as I went.

She was even prettier with the warm, amber glow of the porch light on her olive skin. "Hi," I said. I knew my voice would quaver, and I'd decided to say as little as possible.

"Hi." Her voice was low and just a little raspy. Oh, God, I hope she doesn't smoke! She slipped by me and walked into the living room. "Very nice place." She looked around the room, and I could see her assessing the design and the furnishings. Maybe she thought I owned the house and she was gauging how much she could get for ransom.

"Just finished my first week," I said, even though I'm sure she knew. Gina looked like the kind of woman who kept track of people. And since taking the ferry was the only practical way to get to Fire Island, she probably knew just about everyone's business.

"A share, right?"

"Oh, yeah." I laughed nervously. "I could barely afford my piece."

"How many housemates do you have?"

For some reason, I blurted out, "Five," even though I only had three. I suppose I didn't want her to think I could afford a quarter share of such a big, beachfront house. I didn't want to tip the scale if she hadn't decided yet to kidnap or kill me.

"Have your own bedroom?"

"No," I said, even though I did. "I have to share."

Noticeably disappointed, she asked, "Is your roommate on the island?"

"Yes." I was proud of myself for this lie, but Gina looked decidedly unhappy.

"When will she be home?"

I glanced at my watch. It was eight thirty. "Midnight?"

Gina raised an eyebrow in question and then walked over to me, putting her hand on my waist. "We'd better get to it, then."

"Get to…get…what?"

Her hand slid to the small of my back, and without a bit of hesitation, she pulled me close. She smelled of the sea and fresh air and…herself. Nothing artificial or chemical. I looked into her eyes and opened my mouth to speak right when she tipped her head forward to cover my mouth with her own.

I felt for her shoulder, and when my hand wrapped around it, I pushed…very lightly. Her other arm went around me, and she held me tighter, kissed me harder. My body started to respond, and my anxiety rocketed when I felt the situation spin out of my control. I gripped her harder and pushed. "Whew!" I brushed my hair from my eyes as I staggered backwards. "That's a little...I didn't...I wasn't ready..." I gestured at her. "For that."

Gina looked at me, her dark eyes narrowed. "You weren't ready for what? We don't have a lot of time, right? So, let's get to the good part." She smiled then, and my heartbeat picked up. My God, how many teeth does she have? Forty?

Her smile, even though it was beautiful, was a little put-on. It wasn't quite authentic, and I could tell she wasn't happy with me. I walked to the sofa and sat down. "I'm not used to moving so quickly. I thought we'd just, you know, get to know each other."

She perched on the arm of the sofa, her warm leg pressed against my arm. "I'm Gina. I think you're attractive. I thought you wanted to get together."

"I do! I did. I'm just..."

"Not used to moving so quickly," she said. Gina turned a little so she could look at me more directly. "How often do you let complete strangers come to your home?"

Flushed, I stammered, "Not very."

"What about me made you want to get to know me?" she asked, staring at me with a blank expression. "My sense of humor? My brain? My love of kittens and puppies? What?"

"I don't know," I said, irritably. "I thought you were attractive."

"Right." She nodded. "That's what I thought about you, Hayley."

"Hayden," I corrected, peevishly.

"Right. Hayden." Her head tilted to the right, and she seemed to stare even more intently. "I'm gonna tell you the truth." She waited a beat, possibly to make sure I was listening. "I don't care if you have a nice personality. I don't care if you're smart or dumb. I don't care if you club baby seals to make fur coats. I'm only interested in your ass."

I jumped up and glared at her, but I could feel my cunt start to tingle. "That's crude!"

"No. That's honest. I came over to have sex. If you wanna go sit in a coffee shop and talk about the stock market or real estate or whatever it is you're interested in, go for it. But I'm not into that."

"What? You don't talk to women? You just have sex with them?"

She smiled again, and this time it looked sincere. Her eyes smiled along with her lips, and tiny wrinkles formed at the corners. Her voice took on a softer, warmer affect. "I talk. Once I know a woman, I talk a lot. If you'd turned me down when I said I'd come to your house, I might have had coffee with you. Gotten to know you. But you didn't. You wanted me to come over so we could dance around for a few dates, acting like we wanted to know everything about each other, and *then* have sex. Am I right?"

I swallowed. "Probably something like that."

"That's cool. If that's how you live your life, go right ahead. But I don't do that. You're probably only gonna be here for a few weekends, and I don't wanna invest a lot of time only to find out you're no good in bed." She stood and cracked her neck—loudly. "No hard feelings." Without hesitation, she strode for the door.

I jumped up and dashed after her before I had a moment to think. "Wait, Gina, come on, wait."

She turned and leaned against the front door, looking bored and a little tired. "What?"

"I'm gonna be here all summer. Not just weekends. So there's time to get to know each other."

That earned me another smile, and I felt a little shiver on the back of my neck.

"I'm glad. Maybe we'll do that. But I've had a long day. I'd like to have some good sex and a good night's sleep. But your roommate's coming home, and by the time we get down to it, you'll probably come up with some flimsy excuse why you don't wanna do it after all. I can tell you're not into it, so this isn't gonna work for me."

"She's not really coming home," I said, giving her a guilty-looking shrug.

She waited a second to respond, and when she did, she looked…disappointed. "I know. There isn't a woman here that I didn't bring to the island. I know where every one of 'em is." She cocked her head. "Why lie?"

"I thought you might push me to have sex, and I wanted an excuse."

A thoughtful frown caused her eyebrows to narrow. "In my world, we say, 'I don't wanna have sex.'"

"I think we're from different worlds. As a matter of fact, I'm sure of it."

"Me, too." Her voice had a sharpness to it that stung. She reached for the knob, and my hand reached out and covered hers.

"Your world sounds interesting. Tell me more about it."

Turning to face me, her warm, large hand cupped my cheek, and she lifted my face just enough so we made eye contact. The look in her eyes told me she meant business. "After we have sex."

I exhaled slowly and felt my eyes close briefly. "Okay. But can I get you some wine? Beer? I think I'd like a drink first."

She caught my belt loop before I could walk a step. "If you need to drink to do it, let's skip it."

"No. I don't want you to leave. I'm just not…"

"Used to moving so quickly," she supplied one more time.

I put my hand on her arm, holding on to her for a moment. Then, as if she knew what I needed, she wrapped me in her arms and held me. "Don't worry about it. Maybe we'll run into each other again." Then she kissed me on the top of my head. "Maybe we can even have coffee and talk. Do it your way."

I nuzzled my face into her neck and smelled her body again. She'd relaxed. Almost as if she were relieved we weren't going to have sex. Her body was soft and warm, and it felt wonderful to cuddle against her. I realized I wasn't a bit afraid of her now. I honestly felt safer than I had since I'd come to the island. I consciously tried to silence the critical voice that so often keeps me from doing what I want. When I felt Gina's hands drop to my ass and squeeze, I realized she was responding to my putting my hands under her shirt and stroking her muscular back.

I let my head drop back, and she kissed me gently. "I'll see you around, okay?"

Surprising myself, I put my hands on her ass and pulled her closer. "Don't go."

"Change your mind?"

"I hate to waste time," I said, smiling.

Her arms encircled my waist, and she held me tight again. It felt so damned good to have her hold me. Even though she was just an inch or two taller and maybe ten or fifteen pounds heavier than I, it was like being cradled. I felt so cozy that I was a little surprised when she bent her head and started to kiss me as if she were ablaze.

The shift was so dramatic that I didn't respond for a second. But I consciously shut off the voice that told me it was wrong to be vulnerable with a stranger. I just held on and tried to keep up.

Her lips were so soft, so sensual, that I would have sold state secrets to keep them pressed against mine. In moments, my knees felt wobbly, and I tried to guide her back to the sofa. But she didn't follow my lead. She just turned me a little and pushed me against the wall.

Gina leaned into me, and her hands slid from my waist to my breasts. Her touch wasn't rough, but it was very firm and decisive. Her confidence and strength allowed me to relax and give myself to her. My arms draped around her neck, and I started to kiss her, putting all of my pent-up desire into showing her how much I wanted her. It had been over a year since I'd had sex, and I'd forgotten how absolutely fantastic it felt to have another woman touch me as if she had to have me.

And there was no doubt that Gina was going to have me. Any way she wanted. I couldn't imagine refusing her if she'd opened the door and brought in a dozen circus clowns to help. And I hate clowns.

Her kisses grew hotter and wetter, and even though her tongue was safely lodged in my mouth, my nipples thought they'd been sucked long and hard. All I wanted was to have her get my clothes off and get me into bed. But Gina didn't show any indication that she was headed in that direction. She grasped my hands and spread my arms out, pinning me to the wall while she pressed harder into me. It was a difficult to take a deep breath, but I wasn't sure if that was due to her compressing my lungs or my panting.

She wedged her knee between my legs and pushed hard, making me cry out. "Come on," I moaned. "Take me to bed."

She pulled her mouth from mine for a mere breath. "Later," she whispered and then went back to driving me mad. My legs were shaking with desire. If she hadn't been holding me so tight, I would have fallen to the floor. But she was holding me. Hard and tight. Her hands were squeezing my breasts with such force that she took my breath away. But just when the pain began to feel like too much, a jolt of electricity hit my cunt. I don't know how she did it, but she knew just how much I could take.

I thrust my hips against her, trying to find something—anything—to rub against. She kicked at something, and then an object scraped across the floor. She grasped me by the waist, lifted me, and then settled me back onto her leg. I glanced down and saw that her foot was on an iron doorstop that I hadn't even noticed. I didn't spend any more time thinking about the décor, since I now had just what I needed. A nice, firm leg to hump.

I've never been much of a humper, to tell the truth. I've always needed a talented hand or mouth to get me hot. But I was nearly combusting from Gina's sure, firm hands and her hot mouth. Grunting with pleasure, I flung my arms around her neck and started to rock my hips. She growled, low and sexily, and slipped her hands under my shirt. Gina pinched my nipples hard—harder than I thought I could stand—but it was exactly what I needed. I held on to her with all of my strength while I snapped my hips, feeling the seam of my pants rubbing against my vulva.

We were both groaning and gasping. Sloppy, wet kisses interspersed with our fevered pants. She reached behind me, grabbed my ass cheeks, and lifted them, tilting me just enough to press my clit harder against her leg. I threw my head back, hitting the wall so hard that I saw stars. My orgasm seemed to rip through my body, hitting my breasts, cunt, and ass all at once. Everything tingled and pulsed in unison, while I whimpered and kissed any part of her my lips could reach.

She kissed me again, her touch so gentle and sweet that it felt innocent and almost tentative. Then she lowered me to the floor and lay beside me, placing my head next to her breast. Gina held me for a while, kissing my head and my face while I recovered.

I felt her fumbling with something and then sensed her attention wane as she moved around a little. She let out a heavy sigh and then settled back down. But her body was moving and jostling beside me. I lifted my head to see her hand in her open jeans, gently touching herself.

Puzzled and a little hurt, I turned to look at her. Her expression was so childlike and playful that I couldn't do anything but kiss her. She worked my tongue into her mouth and sucked on it as her body began to move a little more quickly. I put my hand on her breast and cupped it, teasing her hard nipple through her clothing. It didn't take her long to start breathing heavily and have a quiet, shuddering climax. "I couldn't wait," she said, kissing me again. "I was so turned on my pussy hurt." I tried to put my hand into her jeans, but she stopped me. "Not yet. Give me a minute."

"I just wanted to make sure it didn't still hurt. I could kiss it and make it all better."

"For that," she announced, her lips showing a sated smile, "we go to bed."

◈

I usually wake up, have a cup of coffee, and finish the paper before seven o'clock. This morning I woke up, felt for Gina, realized her side of the bed was cold, got up and peed, and then slept until eleven o'clock. I'd forgotten how relaxed good sex makes me. Apparently, great sex makes me nearly comatose.

Yawning and rubbing the bite mark Gina left on my shoulder, I shuffled into the kitchen, delighted to find a note on the table. My delight lasted for one sentence.

> *I was going to go get you some coffee, so I checked your refrigerator to make sure you had milk in case you use it. I know your asshole friend thinks I'm a dumb wop, but after last night, I really thought you might be different.*
>
> *It was really stupid to have me come to your house without knowing anything about me. But if you thought I was gonna kill you, you're stupider than me and your friend put together.*

I'm not hooked into the Mafia. But if I
were, I'd have you killed. I'm not kidding.

Good God! She wasn't supposed to see that note! My stomach was turning over so fast I was sure I was gonna vomit. I swallowed half a glass of water and called the one person I knew could help me think this through.

Dialing her cell phone, I breathed a sigh of relief when she picked up. "Dana, it's me. Got time?"

"Yeah. Sure. What's up, sweetie?"

"I did something so stupid last night, and I don't know how to fix it."

"Hayden, you sound like you're gonna hyperventilate. Now, calm down and tell me what's wrong. Just start at the beginning, baby."

Just hearing her voice helped calm me a little. "Okay. Here's what must have happened. I took the ferry to the island on Friday. Elaine was with me."

"Lucky you," Dana said dryly.

"I know she's not your favorite person, but she's the one who got this share organized. I wouldn't have been able to do this if it weren't for Elaine."

"It doesn't matter what *I* think of her, baby. *I* didn't sleep with her."

"One day, I'm gonna find some cretin you slept with and get my vengeance."

"Ain't gonna happen. I have very, very good taste."

"I'll accept that compliment." I took a breath while Dana laughed softly. "Here's the story. There was a great-looking woman driving the ferry. Tall, dark, really striking."

"Dark like me or dark like a white woman with a tan?"

"She's white, honey," I said, my laughter releasing a little more of the tension. "Apparently, she's Italian. Anyway, Elaine saw me ogling her and made a crack about her."

Her tone sharpened. Dana loved hearing things about Elaine that made her dislike her even more. "What kinda crack?"

"I don't recall exactly what she said, but it was something annoying. I just remember telling her to knock it off."

"So, the woman heard her, right?"

"No. At least, I didn't think she did. That's the weird thing. She was in the little place where the driver sits. A bat couldn't have heard Elaine."

"So, what's the problem?"

"The note she left strongly infers that she heard Elaine's comment."

"Note? Elaine insulted a woman on the ferry, and the woman sent *you* a note?"

I tried to think of how to put the situation in the best possible light, immediately deciding that wasn't possible. "I, uhm, was in town yesterday afternoon, and I saw the woman. Her name's Gina."

"And she gave you a note?"

"No! Let me get this out. Please." I wanted to mind-swap and have Dana know everything I knew, feel everything I felt. But I knew that wasn't wise, even if it was physically possible. You always have to be a little cautious when you talk to your ex. Always. "I talked to her for a few minutes, and I told her it'd be okay if she came to my house last night."

"So, she came to your house and blasted you for what Elaine said? That sounds odd."

"There's an extra detail. I had sex with her."

"Pardon me?" It was hard to shock Dana, but I was sure I'd done so.

"You heard me. I had sex with her. But before she came over, I wrote a note to my housemates telling them that Gina was coming over. I put it in the refrigerator."

I paused and could almost hear the gears grinding in Dana's head. "Have you been doing drugs, Hayden? I'm serious. Are you high?"

"No, Dana, I'm not high. I thought Gina was hot, and she must have thought the same about me. We hit it off and had sex."

"On the first date. You, Hayden Chandler, had sex with a woman on the first date."

"It wasn't really a date. Gina made that clear. She came to my house to have sex. Nothing else."

"It took me a month to get you in bed!"

At first, I thought Dana was teasing, but then it became clear that she was completely serious. Damn. I hadn't meant to upset her. "Honey, I was immature then. I was only twenty-three."

"You're only thirty now, Hayden." She sounded angry and hurt, and I didn't have a thing to say to soothe her. "Is this what you do now? Are you into sex with strangers?"

"No! Well, I guess I was into it last night. But that's the first time I've ever done anything like that. You know that's not how I am. Gina was just so…I don't even have words to describe her. She was so decisive, almost authoritative. But she had this adorably sweet smile that made me feel—"

"I get the picture," Dana said curtly. "So, what do you want from me?"

"I want you not to be angry with me. I shouldn't have called you. It's not fair to talk to you about things like this."

We were both quiet for a few moments, and I could picture her face. Her chin would be tilted up a little, and she'd be staring into space. Her lips might be pursed, or she might have a pen in her mouth, sucking on it contemplatively. "It's okay," she finally said. "We're friends. I want to be able to tell you the truth about my life, so I have to be able to handle the truth about yours."

My heart lodged in my throat. Dana was such a good woman. "Thanks, honey. I'm very glad you're my friend."

"I always will be," she said, her voice catching a little.

"I know that," I said, realizing that I did. It took me a second, but I stopped thinking of the bond we'd always have and asked, "What do I do?"

"One question. And it's a simple one. Why in the world did you leave a note in your refrigerator?"

"Simple question. But the answer's a little hard to pin down. I can only say that I was in a strange frame of mind."

"How strange?"

"Well, what would make me leave a note that said if I turned up missing, Gina should be the prime suspect?"

She was quiet for just a second, but I could tell by the way she was breathing that she was about to lose her temper. "Were you really afraid of her? If so—"

"No, I wasn't. I mean, I was, but only in the sense that my mind was working overtime. I've been reading too many murder mysteries."

Dana let out a long breath. "This whole thing sounds so unlike you, Hayden. And I mean *everything* about it. I think you should chalk this up to a momentary attack of lunacy and let it go."

"No. No," I said, a little louder. "I don't want to."

I could hear her grinding her teeth. I used to tease her that one day she'd lose the peaks and valleys from the abuse she gave them. "It's pretty obvious what you have to do. You find this woman and apologize. If you want to see her again, you get on your knees when you apologize."

"You're right. Of course, you're right. I just freaked out when I saw her note this morning. She sounded so hurt."

"Wouldn't you be?"

"I don't know," I said, because I didn't. "I might think the woman was just being careful. I might not take it personally."

"Sounds like she did."

"Yeah. Sure does. In the note, she referred to herself as a 'dumb wop.'"

"That's not good. Sounds like she's thin-skinned about her ethnicity. If she is, she might be too hurt to accept your apology. I wouldn't get my hopes up."

"They're not up," I said. "They're damned down."

❖

I trudged over to the dock just after noon. Actually, it's hard to trudge on the slightly elevated wooden boardwalks that pass for streets on the island. One of the charming things about most of Fire Island—and Cherry Grove, my little neighborhood, in particular—is that there are no roads; therefore, there are no cars. These narrow boardwalks crisscross the community, and the only vehicles are wagons, the red Radio Flyer being the wagon with the most cachet. Getting all of my things to the house via a wagon made for a child carrying her dolls wasn't the easiest thing in the world, but it made moving in a bit of an adventure. And since everyone is in the same wagon, so to speak, quite a few people offered to help. That's another great thing about Cherry Grove. Nearly everyone is friendly and helpful. But I had a feeling a certain ferryboat driver wasn't going to be among the friendly, and my stomach was clenched like a fist.

I wasn't sure if Gina was even working, but I didn't have any other way to get in touch with her. I made a mental note to remember to get the full names and phone numbers of any strangers I slept with in the future. Just my luck that I do it once and have to get in touch with the woman. Being easy isn't as easy as it looks.

A ferry pulled in right on time, but it was a much smaller ferry than the one I'd taken. I thought maybe there was another company serving the island, but then I spotted her in the...whatever you call the little place where the wheel is. Hmm, maybe a wheelhouse? Or did that die out with Mark Twain?

The island is pretty deserted until Memorial Day, and a Thursday mid-day passage obviously didn't appeal to many. Fewer than a dozen people got off, and not one of them was Gina. A rather unsavory-looking fellow helped the few people unload their things, then waved in Gina's direction, and walked over to the Grove Café. She was alone in her little nook, and the return trip to Sayville wasn't for ten minutes.

Regrettably, I had no reason to delay, so I walked down the dock and jumped aboard. The wheelhouse, or whatever it's called in this century, was up on the second deck in the very front of the boat. When I emerged from the stairs, she was sitting on one of the benches behind the wheelhouse. She didn't turn around, even though I knew she'd heard me coming up.

Her hair was windblown and looked a little curly. It was a misty, damp day, and she was wearing a fleece jacket and jeans. Her feet were resting on an open crate that held life preservers, and for some reason, I found her yellow, rubber rain boots improbably sexy.

I stood there staring at her from the side, spending a moment looking at the whole package. Her jacket was bright orange and tailored to her body, with navy blue panels on the sides that made her look lean and trim. She also wore a snug, French-cut, navy blue T-shirt with the ferry company name on her chest. Even though her skin was olive and her eyes were dark, she looked fabulous in blue. And whoever bought the shirts obviously wanted Gina to look good in hers, since it fit her like a glove. Her jeans, which hugged her thighs, were tucked into the calf-high boots, and she looked a little like a girl who was waiting for a big puddle to jump into. But she also looked like the sexy, aggressive, dominant woman who'd rocked my world.

I'm surprised she didn't hear my heart thudding in my chest, but she didn't turn until I sat next to her. "Hi," I said, my voice shaking.

Her head turned, and her dark eyes didn't register a single thing. Not surprise, not anger, not even recognition. "What?" She sounded bored and mildly annoyed.

"I wanted to apologize for the note I left for my housemates. I know it looked like I mistrusted you—"

"No." She closed the thick, hardcover book she'd been reading and tossed it next to her, making a hollow-sounding thunk. "Most people leave notes to their next of kin when I visit." She got up and went to the wheelhouse, latching a metal gate behind her. She was five feet from me, and anyone who got on would hear me, but I tried not to think of the potential embarrassment.

"Gina, please let me explain."

"Your note explained all I needed to hear. You and your asshole friend obviously think it's fun to play with rough trade, but your little WASP conscience got the best of you. You didn't want to actually tell anyone you were having some low-class dago over, but just in case you disappeared, you wanted to save other nice girls from the same fate."

Damn, I couldn't very well dispute that. It was far too close to the truth. I didn't think of her as a dago, but that was cold comfort. "My friend and I aren't alike, Gina. I was attracted to you. Not because you were rough trade or Italian or anything like that. I thought you were incredibly pretty and sexy. I'd never had a woman as lovely as you are show any interest in me, and I was flattered beyond belief."

She fixed me with a cold stare. "Don't be so flattered. There aren't many women on the island at this time of year."

I don't know why, but it didn't occur to me that she'd be cruel. After we'd had sex in my bed, she'd stroked my face and kissed my cheek so tenderly. Her body had been giving off so much heat that she'd thrown off the sheet and lain there naked, her skin glistening with sweat. Just before she'd closed her eyes, she'd taken my hand, kissed it, and held it over her heart as she drifted off to sleep. How could a woman who was so gentle last night be so calculatingly cruel this afternoon?

I couldn't speak, and I didn't want to give her the satisfaction of seeing me cry. Maintaining as much dignity as I could, I got up and descended the stairs. The tears started as soon as my feet hit the last step. My bad luck continued when the deckhand walked up to the boat as I was trying to get off. A large cabin cruiser had just pulled up in front of us to dock, and the waves were making the ferry jump. He held out his hand to help me off and said, "What's wrong, lady?"

"Nothing," I said, pulling away from him as soon as I could. "Nothing at all."

❖

I wasted the better part of the day crying and moping around the house. I loved being on the island, but it was taking me longer than I thought it would to get used to the quiet and the isolation. At home, I could walk to a dozen places to shop or chat or have a little nosh. Here, I could either sit alone in my big house or go to the café, the hardware store, or one of two bars. None of them appealed to me today, and it was now raining too hard to walk on the beach. So, I stared at my computer, the blinking cursor on the blank page reminding me with relentless persistence that I wasn't accomplishing a damned thing.

When the phone rang, I nearly ran for it. I didn't recall giving Gina this number, but she was a smart girl. Maybe she knew the owners. I was massively disappointed to hear my sister's voice. "Hi. I wanted to check in with you and see when you're coming down. It's been weeks, and Dad seems pretty low. Seeing you always cheers him up."

Second and third thoughts about having answered the phone raced through my mind, but it was too late now. "I haven't really thought about it, Karen. I haven't even been here a week, you know."

"I know, but you haven't been home since Easter."

"Easter was three weeks ago. That's not that long a time."

"It is when you don't get any visitors. You don't know what it's like for him. You don't see him often enough to know how sad he really..."

I tuned Karen out and let her vent for a little while. I've learned that a well-timed—or even a poorly timed—"uhm-hmm" lets her feel as if she's properly chastised me. I respect and love my sister, but I don't let her guilt-trip me. She's the self-appointed guardian and protector of our father, who, as near as I can tell, doesn't need or want either. True, Dad is obviously clinically depressed, and he needs medication. But he's fifty-nine years old, and he doesn't want any help. He's not a danger to himself or anyone else, so there's not much we can do. But that doesn't stop Karen. Since our mother and he divorced fourteen years ago, she's tried to take over for Mom. She won't listen to my firm belief that she's taking on a role that isn't hers to take. I might feel different if Dad wanted her checking in on him all of the time. But he truly doesn't seem to care.

"Hayden?"

"Yeah? Sorry, Karen, someone just sent me an instant message, and I was looking at my computer." That excuse nearly always worked when she caught me not paying attention. Thank God she was as addicted to her computer as I was to mine.

"Will you come this weekend? Larry said he'd take Dad's barbeque out of the garage so we could have a cookout. Please?"

Boy, she must have been on the warpath to have Larry agree to go to Dad's. My brother-in-law was a devoted golf nut, and he hated to miss a weekend round. "Sure. I'll be there. I'll come on Saturday morning, but I have to be back Sunday night."

"That's fine. It's not as long as I'd like, but it'll help."

If I thought my being there would lift Dad out of his depression, I'd move back to Philadelphia. But that's not going to happen, no matter how much Karen wishes.

Chapter Two

I felt like I'd been on one train or another for the whole day. The trip from Philadelphia to New York took two hours. After that, I had to wait almost an hour at Penn Station for the train to Sayville, which was a two-hour trip on the LIRR. Thank God I had my iPod.

The line for the Sunday evening ferry back to the island was short, but there was a delay at the ticket window. Great. Nothing like a glitch when you've been traveling five hours to go a hundred miles.

A woman in a motorized wheelchair was trying to buy a ticket, but the woman in the booth said the boat couldn't accommodate her. There was just one person in line between us, so I could hear the woman in the chair explaining that she'd called the ferry company before she arranged for her summer share. She was nearly in tears, and her companion was beginning to lose her temper. The woman in the booth was frustrated, but she was clearly only repeating what she'd been told—that the ferry couldn't accommodate people in wheelchairs.

The ticket seller finally picked up a walkie-talkie and called the boat. I heard Gina's voice crackle over the receiver. "What's up?" she asked.

"There's a woman here in a wheelchair, and she said someone from the company told her she could ride the ferry. But I've been told that's not allowed."

There was a pause on Gina's end. Then she growled, "I'll take care of it. Be there in two."

The woman and her friend moved aside, and the rest of us purchased our tickets. As promised, the ferry pulled in, and as soon as the engine shut down, Gina came bounding off. I moved off to the side, and thankfully, she didn't see me. She strode up to the woman and her friend, and Gina's stern expression melted into a warm smile.

"Hi, I'm Gina. Want to go to the Grove?"

I could see the relief on the woman's face from where I stood. For some reason, a chill ran down my back.

"Yes," the woman said. "I spent scads of money on a share for the summer. I'll go over on a raft if I have to."

"No need," Gina said. She was so calm and confident that I knew she'd handle the situation one way or another. She glanced at the people gathered near the boat and said, "Would everyone please board now?"

We all did as instructed. Then Gina walked alongside the woman and her friend, and they approached the ferry. I heard her ask, "Do you mind being picked up?"

The woman looked both stunned and disappointed. "You can't lift my chair when it's empty, not to mention having me in it."

"I didn't ask if you thought we could do it," Gina said. She'd moved to where I could see her, and I caught sight of her placid, reassuring smile. "I asked if you minded."

"Well, no, I guess not. But no one has ever picked me up. I'm worried—"

Gina squatted down next to her and whispered something in her ear. The woman looked at her and then smiled. "Go right ahead, then. But I'll hold you to it."

Upon hearing Gina's shrill whistle, two young men emerged from the boat. They were both tall and rangy, but neither looked particularly strong. "We're gonna give this lady a lift." She gave the boys explicit instructions that they seemed to understand, since they immediately put their hands where she directed. She lifted her chin, looked into the boat, and said, "Hayden, will you come here?"

Stunned, I got up and jumped off the boat, finding myself looking into those big, brown eyes.

"Will you stand in front of us and tell us when we're approaching the edge of the dock? We're pretty surefooted, but it's nice to have another perspective."

"Sure," I said, still amazed that she'd not only seen me, but also trusted me to participate.

The woman's friend said, "I can do that."

Gina smiled at her and said, "I'm sure you can, but Hayden's an employee. She's covered under our insurance."

"Oh, I see."

I was a little surprised at this development, but I tried not to look it.

"Okay, boys, on the count of three. One…two…three."

They picked up the woman and her chair, but it wasn't easy for them. They just had to move her a short distance, but the boat was swaying a bit in the calm harbor. "You're right at the edge," I said. I jumped onto the boat to help distract the woman, who looked terrified. "They do this sort of thing all of the time," I said. "I've seen them pick up a loaded refrigerator, and they didn't break an egg."

The ridiculousness of my comment made her look at me, and by the time she looked back down, she was safely on the deck. Gina and the two boys looked like they were about due for hernia repair, so I guided the woman and her friend to a wide aisle on the far side of the boat while the crew caught their collective breath. "Is this all right?" I asked. "Or would you like Gina to take you upstairs?"

The woman looked at the steep set of stairs in the center of the boat and laughed, and Gina walked over to us, her cheeks pink through her tan and big beads of sweat clinging to her hairline. "Everything okay? Do you need us to secure your chair?"

"No, it won't go anywhere," the woman said. "As you can tell, it's substantial."

"Yeah," Gina said, "I got *that* message. How often are you gonna leave the island? We'll get a ramp for you—"

The woman shook her head. "If you can lift me onto the boat in October, that's all I need. I'm not going anywhere."

Gina reached into her pocket and took out her wallet. She produced a business card and said, "Call me whenever you want to leave. It's not a problem. We should have a ramp, anyway. It'll be waiting for you in October."

"I'll call," the woman said. She wiggled her finger, and Gina leaned down and was gifted with a kiss on the cheek. "You're a doll."

"Nah," Gina said. Her cheeks flushed brighter, but she still looked cool and calm. "All in a day's work." Then she turned and dashed up the stairs. I noticed the word "PILOT" in big blue letters across the back of her tight, bright orange T-shirt and told myself to watch my nomenclature. It wouldn't do for an employee to call her the driver.

Since I didn't know what my job was, other than to look like an employee, I did what the boys did—went upstairs as soon as we left the dock. As I walked, I pondered this rather remarkable chain of events. I was still hurt and angry, but I didn't want to have a summer-long feud with the woman who was obviously *always* piloting the damned boat. I also hated to avoid people. It felt too fifth grade. But I was nervous when I got upstairs and Gina gestured with her head, saying, "Will you guys go below and make sure our special passenger is stable?" The older-looking of the two boys gave her a puzzled glance, but they left without further comment. "Come on in," she said, while lifting the gate.

I flicked the little sign on the gate that said, "Crew Only." "What's my hourly rate?"

She looked a little relieved, even though her eyes never strayed from the ocean. "Well, we're union, so it's pretty good. I'll give you an advance right now." She reached for a rubber-covered book and leafed through it, all without lowering her gaze. Finding what she was feeling for, she handed me two slips of paper, each of which said, "Free Round Trip."

I was on the verge of declining, but thought that might be rude. "Thanks," I said and slipped them into my pocket.

"I've got a couple of minutes after we dock. Wanna have a quick drink?"

I stared at her face and tried to remember how tender she'd been in bed. Maybe the asshole part was just a small segment of her personality. She was, without doubt, the most attractive woman I'd ever been out with. Even though we hadn't truly gone out, or exchanged full names, I still counted her as a date. Maybe she had other charms besides her looks and fantastic abilities in bed. And if not, those two were nothing to sneeze at. "Okay. You buy."

"I was planning on it." Her head still hadn't moved, but her lips curved into a small, satisfied grin.

◈

By the time we got the woman in the chair off the boat, we'd used the majority of Gina's break. She did receive another kiss, and she seemed happy and relaxed as we walked to the bar at the end of the pier.

"Why'd you ask me to help today?" I asked. "The woman's friend could have easily done what I did."

"Maybe. But I don't trust strangers with safety. I knew I could count on you."

I blinked in surprise. "Four days ago you said you wanted to kill me!"

She turned and showed a surprisingly shy smile. "Not because you were incompetent. I knew you were levelheaded and wouldn't screw around today. That means a lot to me."

"Huh. So, you'd rather work with someone you want to kill than a perfectly nice-looking stranger."

She smiled, her gaze starting at my chin and slowly moving up until our eyes met. My whole body felt a few degrees warmer by the time I was gazing into those dark brown eyes. "I didn't say it made sense. I don't always make sense." Looking away, she slipped her hands into her pockets. "I can be rash. Especially when my feelings are hurt."

We walked into the bar, and the bartender waved at Gina. She hustled over to us and said, "I know you don't have time for more than a cup of decaf."

"You know my schedule better than I do," Gina said, smiling at her with a gentle openness to her expression that I hadn't seen yet.

"Make it two," I said.

She nodded and went to pour. Even though we only had a few minutes, neither of us spoke while we waited. As soon as the woman delivered our coffee, I looked at Gina until she met my eyes. "Was that an apology?"

"What? Saying I have a temper?"

"Yeah."

She poured some cream into her coffee and stirred it slowly and contemplatively. "Kinda. I guess."

"In my world, we say things like 'I'm sorry' or 'I was wrong.'"

A slow, sexy grin appeared, and Gina said, "We don't live in the same world, remember?"

"No, I guess we don't."

I stared at the top of her head since she was apparently fascinated by the cream still swirling in her cup. I actually expected her to apologize, but it soon became clear that I'd be waiting a long time. "I apologized to you, Gina. I went out of my way to find you and let you know I felt bad. And I hadn't meant to hurt you. You went for the jugular with me."

"I know," she said quietly, still looking down. "And I did feel bad. I've thought about you every day. I've scoped out everyone who gets on the boat, hoping that I'd see you so we could make things right between us."

"I had to leave the island on Friday, so I walked down to The Pines to take a different ferry. But I was too tired to do that tonight."

She nodded, looking a little hurt. "I wondered how you got off the island without me noticing."

"You could have come over," I said. She nodded again, still not lifting her head. "So, here's your chance. Make things right. I'd like you to apologize."

She looked so uncomfortable that I almost told her to skip it. But for some reason, I needed her to say it. She finally looked me in the eyes and said, "I was mean. Intentionally. That sucks, and you didn't deserve it. You hurt my feelings, but I don't think you meant to."

"Thanks," I said. I'd expected a simple "I'm sorry," but I was beginning to learn that Gina didn't always do what was expected.

She checked her watch and said, "I've gotta go." Reaching for her wallet, she stood up and found a five-dollar bill. "Will you see me again? For…like a date?"

I leaned back and gave her a smile that probably looked more like a smirk. "A real date? Where we talk and get to know each other?"

"Yeah. Talk, drink wine, wonder if we'll like each other enough to fool around."

"Sure. That'd be nice." I stood up, too, and leaned in close to her. "But I know I like you enough to fool around. Why don't you come over later tonight?"

That earned me a surprised, but very pleased smile. She reached into her wallet again and pulled out a business card. "My full name and cell phone number. The police love to find little things like this at a murder scene. Gives 'em a thrill."

I ignored her comment while trying to pronounce her name. "Skog-na—"

"Sco-nya-mee-yo," she said. "It's not the easiest name in the world, but I like it."

"I like it, too," I said. I pulled out my own wallet and found one of my cards.

Gina took it and rolled her eyes after scanning it. "A professor?"

"Assistant professor," I said. "Much lower on the food chain."

"At least, I can pronounce your name," she said, smiling. "We buy supplies from a ship chandler." She touched my elbow to lead me outside. "If you want to know more about me, you can ask anyone who works on the island. Anyone," she emphasized.

I grasped her arm and squeezed it. "I think I know the important things. And I'd rather learn about you from you than strangers."

She put her hand behind my head and pulled me close. When our faces were less than a couple of inches apart, she said, "See you in a couple of hours." Her breath was warm, and I realized that she hadn't had a sip of her coffee. She smelled like bubblegum, and I smiled as she kissed me gently. "We'll stay up and talk."

"We'll see," I said, returning the brief kiss. "I'm still not sure you merit a real date. I might just want to have my way with you and send you packing."

Gina patted my cheek, not saying a word. But I could tell she didn't mind my teasing her. "See you soon." She turned and walked away, her hips swaying in a way that made me wish the last ferry run were in minutes, rather than hours.

❖

Luckily for me, the ferry stopped running early at this point of the season. Gina tapped on my door not long after eight. I'd showered, shaved my legs, flossed, brushed my teeth twice, clipped and cleaned my nails, and did a little maintenance on my eyebrows. She wouldn't find a speck of dirt on me, but I didn't mind if she looked real hard anyway. I was surprised to see that she also cared about how she looked. She'd either gone home or had another set of clothes on the ferry because she wore black jeans and a pumpkin-colored fleece pullover. This one didn't fit as snugly as the orange one, but it looked fantastic on her. The color was perfect for her skin tone, and the material made me want to hug her.

"Hi," she said, showing her teeth.

"Come on in." I took her hand and led her to the living room. "You look nice," I said. "Did you have time to go home?"

"Not really. But I had to. I spilled some fuel on my shoes, and I couldn't stand to smell myself."

"Wine?"

"Ah…" She looked around, perhaps trying to see the bottle. "What do you have?"

"Red. Is that okay?"

Her smile was inscrutable, but she nodded. "Red's my favorite."

I went into the kitchen to pour, and she followed me. As soon as I put the bottle down, she picked it up and read the label. "Is it all right?" I asked.

"Huh?" She placed the bottle back on the counter. "Sure. Fine." She took a sip, and I thought I detected a flinch, but she smiled and clinked her glass against mine. "To first dates."

"Nice," I said. "To first dates."

We went back into the living room, and she sat on the far end of the sofa. I took the other end, but sat with my back against the arm so I could put my legs up and be closer to her. "How'd you get here, anyway?" I asked.

"Took a taxi." She raised the glass, took more of a gulp than a sip, and then set the glass on the coffee table. "So, professor, tell me about yourself. You can start around…oh, 1981 or '82?"

I was going to follow up on her non-answer about how she got to the island, but decided to let it pass. She obviously liked to keep things to herself, and I doubted I'd be able to stop her. "I was born in 1978 actually, unless you meant you don't want to hear about my preschool years."

"No, no. I want to hear it all. You just look like you're in your mid-twenties."

"Thanks. I used to be, but I'm hurtling towards thirty."

"It's not so bad," she said, giving me an encouraging look.

"I'll give you a short version of my history to avoid boring you into an early grave. I was born in Philadelphia. I have one older sister, Karen. My dad teaches chemistry at a prep school, and my mom is now married to a nice guy who's a dean at Penn."

"Did you say he's in the pen?" Her eyes were sparkling with good humor, and I shook my head.

"No, but having a convicted felon in the family might be more exciting. Anyway, I went to the prep school where my dad teaches, and then I went to college at Brown."

"You went to a color?"

I found it wasn't always easy to know if she was teasing or not, so I gave her a half-smile and said, "It's a school in Rhode Island."

"Never heard of it."

"Well, it's there. I'm almost certain."

"You'd know," Gina agreed. "Then you started teaching?"

"Ah, no. I had to go to grad school." She looked interested, and I was now certain that she wasn't kidding. The woman didn't know you had to have a graduate degree to teach at a university! "I went to Dartmouth for grad school, and when I finished, I got the job at NYU. That was three years ago."

"Wow. You're almost thirty, and you just started to work three years ago?"

I nodded. "Sounds kinda old when you put it that way."

"It is old," she said, laughing harder than seemed appropriate. "I started working when I was eight."

"No!"

"Yes," she said, nodding enthusiastically. "I washed cars, cleaned offices, all sorts of things. I could go on all night, but I want to know more about you. Tell me about your family."

"Not too much to tell. My dad lives in the house I grew up in, and my mom and stepfather live near Penn."

"Where he works."

"Yeah. The University of Pennsylvania." I didn't want to insult her, but I couldn't tell if she was familiar with it. Many people have never heard of Brown, but Penn's pretty well known.

"Yeah, I know it. They have a good football team most years. Joe Paterno had some great teams there."

I cringed. "No, that's Penn State in State College. Penn is in Philadelphia."

"Mmm." She picked up her glass and drained it. "Colleges aren't my thing."

"Did you go?"

"To college?"

"Yeah."

"Nah. I knew everything I needed to know to do my job by the time I graduated from high school. I wanted to get busy and start working."

That was a unique perspective. I don't know many—make that any—people who know all they need to know by the time they're eighteen years old. "I guess there's no reason to go if you're not interested."

"Exactly. My mom wanted me to go, but she knew she was wasting her breath. She forced my oldest brother to go, and he got a degree, but he didn't think it was worth it."

"Where did he go?"

"Suffolk."

"Is that in New York?"

"Sure. You don't know it?"

"No, I don't think I've heard of it."

"Hah! I guess I *do* know a little bit about colleges. I know one you don't know."

I couldn't resist her smile. "I'm sure there are thousands of colleges I don't know."

"He said he basically wasted two years. Why bother?"

"Two years? He got a degree in two years?" Was that even possible? You'd have to take a heavy load every term, including summers.

"Yeah. It's a two-year school. He *finished* in two years, too. Most people don't."

Holy shit! She doesn't know the difference between a university and a community college. I didn't know if I looked stunned, but I was trying hard not to.

Gina continued. "I was never good at sitting in a classroom listening to somebody drone on about something I didn't care about." She must have realized what she'd said because she made a face and added, "I'm sure you're good at what you teach. What *do* you teach?"

"History."

Her eyes lit up. "My favorite subject. I would have gone to college if I could have just read history books."

I reached out and squeezed her knee. "You should have gone to grad school. That's all I did for years."

"Damn, that *would* be nice. What kinda history do you teach?"

"European. Ancient European."

"No!" She slapped her thighs. "I love ancient history."

I wasn't sure if she was pulling my leg or not, so I probed a little bit. "What do you like?"

"Roman, definitely Roman, but Greek's okay, too. I mean, you've gotta give 'em some credit for getting the ball rolling, right?"

"Right," I said, surprised and pleased that she was genuinely interested in my field. Of course, I couldn't imagine she'd gotten very far into it. Not many people do, even with a degree. Ancient history has to be one of the least popular majors in the country. "We'll have to compare our favorite books."

"Cool." She was so happy she was practically wriggling in her seat. "I'm really into Italian history from the fifteenth century on, but I've read some books in your area. I felt like I needed a good foundation, so I started with the Classics."

"All on your own?"

She gave me a look that seemed a little insolent. "Who else is gonna read for me?"

"Good point." She was touchy about school. That much was clear. Maybe she couldn't afford to go or didn't get into any place decent.

Without much of a segue, she changed the subject. "Tell me more about your family. What's your sister do?"

"She teaches, too. High school. Her husband is a sales manager for a drug company. He travels a lot."

"I wouldn't like that," she said without hesitation. "I'd never want a partner who was gone a lot. Wouldn't work for me."

"I don't think I'd mind," I said. "I'm so busy with school that it might be nice to have some evenings alone to catch up on things."

"We can agree to disagree," she said, nodding decisively. "So, that's it? That's your whole family?"

"Uh-huh. They're all in Philadelphia, and I'm all by myself in New York."

"Where do you live?"

"The East Village."

"In the city?"

"Yeah," I said, wondering where she could live that she hadn't heard of it. "How about you?"

"The island."

"You live here?"

She blinked and then laughed. "No. *The* island." When I didn't react, she added slowly, "Lawn Guyland."

"Oh!" Now I got it! She had a Long Island accent. I was embarrassed to admit this, but I couldn't tell a Brooklyn from a Bronx from a Queens from a Long Island accent, but now that I'd heard Gina's, I realized that some of my students spoke exactly like she did. It wasn't a particularly lyrical accent, but it somehow became her. "I don't know anyone who lives on Long Island."

She gave me a smile and admitted, "I don't know anybody who lives in the city."

Before I could censor myself, I nearly shouted, "No!"

"Yeah," she said, looking rather proud. "Everybody I know lives on the island."

"Nearly everybody I know lives in Manhattan or Brooklyn. It's not such a small world, is it?"

"I guess not. But it makes sense. I mean, who'd want to drive into the city just to hang out? I don't like to go outside of Suffolk County if I don't have to."

"That's the county Long Island's in?"

"There's four of 'em," she said, seemingly testing to see if I was kidding. "Kings, Queens, Nassau and Suffolk. But most of us only consider Nassau and Suffolk to be the real island. We kinda ignore Brooklyn and Queens. Don't tell 'em," she added, sotto voce.

"I've only been there twice," I admitted, my head spinning while I tried to figure out what she was talking about. "Just to get to the ferry."

"Well, I'll have to take you around some time. If you can't find it on Long Island, you don't need it."

I rather doubted that, but I wasn't going to argue. I also wasn't going to admit that all I knew about Long Island was that it was, in fact, a long island next to New York City. As a matter of fact, it might be part of New York City for all I knew. And I had no idea why she brought Brooklyn and Queens into the mix. But I wasn't going to ask Gina any more questions about the whole affair. She was obviously a little touchy when it came to her town—if it was a town. "Do you ever come into the city?"

"Oh, sure. I've been there a lot. I worked there for about six months."

"Really? Did you enjoy it?"

"I just worked. Went home as soon as I was done. I hated having to go that far to work, so no, I didn't. I left as soon as they found someone to replace me."

"But what about just visiting?"

"Just to visit? Probably six, maybe seven times."

"In your life?"

"Yeah. I've been to JFK a bunch. Does that count?"

"No, I meant coming into Manhattan to do something. Like go to a play or a museum."

"I went to Radio City for the Christmas show a couple of times when I was a kid. And a bunch of my friends drug me to Times Square for the Millennium. And I went to a couple of museums with my class when I was in school. So, I've been there." She stuck her chin out and said, "I've been to the city a lot more than you've been to Long Island."

She had me there. "Good point. I'm just one of those people who grew up wanting to live in New York. I've always considered New York to be Manhattan."

"We've got a hundred miles of island out here."

"A hundred miles? You can't be serious."

"Yes, I am. It's a long, long island. We've got nice places, bad places, mansions, slums, ocean views, views of your neighbors' bedrooms. You name it, we've got it."

"Is Long Island a city or part of—"

"Damn," she said, laughing. "You don't know a damned thing about it. How can you ignore a place this big that's right next door to you?"

"I don't know. I guess it's like New Jersey to me."

She flicked her hand as though she were swatting a fly. "I don't know anything about Jersey."

"Well, it's big," I said, teasing her. "And it's a state. And it's right next to New York."

Her smile was so lovely I barely heard her say, "True." And even though she'd only been there fifteen minutes, we'd been talking long enough. I wanted to feel those nice, strong hands on my body. Not so slyly scooting next to her on the sofa, I snuggled against her when she held her arm out. "Long Island has you. That's a lot." There was just one thing that I had to resolve before I could be intimate with her again. "Gina?"

"Hmm?"

"You didn't really pick me up because there weren't many other women on the island, did you?"

"No. Definitely not," she said. She gave me a gentle squeeze and kissed my cheek. "To be honest, I usually go for an Italian girl. I've never been out with someone with blue eyes or uhm, light-colored hair. But I'm really glad I branched out. You're special, Hayden. Real special."

I cuddled up against her and felt her chest expand and contract when she breathed. "I don't know what made you come up to me, but I'm damned glad you did."

❦

We didn't rock the house like we'd done the first time, but I think I enjoyed having sex with Gina this time even more. We were on an equal level now, and she seemed more interested in being close to me, rather than just giving me orgasms. It was almost two in the morning when we went to sleep, and it seemed as if I'd just dozed off when I heard her watch alarm beep in my ear. Of course, I didn't know what it was at the time, other than an annoying sound that made me whimper in protest. I was so confused that Gina picked up my head and pulled her arm away to shut it off. "Go back to sleep," she whispered.

I reached out and pulled her to me, starting to kiss her body. "Don't leave me," I murmured between kisses.

"I have to," she said. She kissed me firmly and then slipped out of bed.

"Are you the only employee? Isn't there some kind of law to keep them from working you to death?"

"That's a little dramatic," she said, her voice raspy from too little sleep. "Things calm down after Memorial Day."

I sat up and rubbed my eyes. "You work less when it gets more crowded?"

"Yeah. Summer employees. I just work the early shift after Memorial Day."

"What do you work now?"

"I'm the only pilot. I work the first run to the last."

"Every day?"

"Yep. Every day."

"Gina, you can't work those kinds of hours. You'll drop from exhaustion."

She found her clothes, and I woke up fully while watching her get dressed. I'd spent time preparing for her visit with my grooming, but Gina had spent time picking out sexy underwear. I don't know how long it had taken her, but not one moment had been wasted. I was willing to bet that no other ferry driver wore a melon-colored bra that made her breasts look as if they were on the verge of escaping from their flimsy confines. I might have been drooling when she shimmied into her matching panties and faded jeans. "It's not bad at all," she said, snapping me from my ogling haze. "I only make four runs on weekdays. It's just the early run that hurts. I only get five or six hours of sleep, but I can take a nap if I need one."

I covered myself with the sheet since the bed felt so cold without her. "I'm worried about you. Are you sure you're awake enough to drive that big boat?"

She finished dressing and walked over to me. She felt so warm and soft with her fleece brushing against my skin. "I don't have the big one. The little one's a cinch to pilot. When can I see you again?"

I liked that she didn't seem to doubt my interest. "Whenever you want. I'm here almost all of the time."

"Can I call you?"

"Sure. My cell phone's on the card I gave you, but I have to go down to the pier to get decent reception. So, leave a number where I can call you back. Call me soon, okay?"

"It's a deal." She kissed me tenderly, running her hands over my back while she did. "Now go back to sleep. It's not even dawn."

She let me go, and I flopped onto the bed. "No arguments. Now you promise me that you'll take a nap later, okay?"

"Promise." One more kiss, and she was on her way. I lay in bed missing her for a grand total of two minutes before sleep claimed me once again.

Chapter Three

I lay in bed early Friday morning, unable to sleep. The woman who lay next to me had thoroughly relaxed my body, but I was unable to calm my racing thoughts. Gina looked so adorably innocent when she was sleeping. As she had each time we'd slept together, she held my hand. That small gesture seemed more caring than having her enfold me with her entire body.

She was a very quiet, very still sleeper. Her mouth was always closed, something I wished I could accomplish. I always woke up with saliva on my pillow, and I could only imagine how attractive it was for a bed partner to watch me drool. But nothing escaped from Gina's lips. No drool, no heavy breathing, no snores. She closed her eyes, wriggled around for a few moments, and then fell asleep as if she'd been anesthetized.

We'd been together four times, and I liked her better each time we talked. There was no doubt I'd never had greater sex, but that wasn't what made me look forward to her visits. Getting to know her better had supplanted sex as my favorite part of the evening, and I hadn't expected that to happen. We'd only been able to spend about an hour talking during her visits, but that was enough to capture my interest.

During our first night together, I'd expected her to get up in the middle of the night and take off, never to reappear. But I was finding that she was much more complex and entertaining than I'd anticipated. So, my guilt continued to build as I watched her sleep. Because no matter how open-minded I claimed to be, I didn't want my housemates to meet her. I felt like shit for feeling that way, but that's how I felt, and lecturing myself about my weak moral fiber wasn't changing my feelings. My housemates were arriving on the late-afternoon ferry, and I wasn't going to invite Gina over until they were gone. I knew I was a bitch, but I knew I wasn't going to change my mind.

✦

I don't know how she managed it, but Gina slipped out of bed, showered, blew her hair dry, and put on the fresh clothes she'd brought with her the night before—all before I stirred. She sat next to me on the bed and gently stroked my arm. I could feel her weight on the mattress and smelled my soap and shampoo. I didn't open my eyes, but I puckered my lips, and she laughed softly as she bent to kiss me.

"Playin' possum?"

"No. I'm really half asleep. I don't know how you do this."

"Practice. Do you have any hair products?"

I half-opened one eye. "You smell like shampoo, so you must have found it."

"No, not shampoo. Other products, like gel or holding spray or something like that."

"Oh." I closed my eye. "No, I've never used anything that makes my hair look significantly better. Why bother?"

She didn't reply for a moment, but then said, "Hey, I don't think I'll have time to see you this weekend."

My eyes popped open. "Really?"

"Yeah. I work like a dog on the weekends. I wouldn't be any fun."

I stroked her arm, lingering on the definition along her bicep. "Take care of yourself, okay? I don't want you to fall asleep at the wheel."

"I'll be fine. Call you next week, okay?"

"Sure. Any time."

She stood up and looked at me. "Are you really gonna be here all summer?"

"Yeah. Full time. I'm gonna get my money's worth."

She laughed. "You don't have to teach summer school or anything?"

"Not this year. I'm working on a project, and I thought this would be a good place to write without my normal distractions."

"You're writing?"

"I just started. I've been grading papers since I got here. That'll teach me to assign papers in three classes."

"You writing about ancient history? If you are, I wanna read it."

"You're on," I said. "You can tell me if I'm hitting my target market."

"What's that? Ferry pilots?" She smiled, but there was a touch of uncertainty in her eyes.

"No. I'm writing for the general nonfiction market. Average people who probably don't know much, if anything, about ancient history."

I would have liked it if her smile hadn't looked so forced. "I'm your market. I'm as average as a woman can be." She glanced at her watch and started to back up. "Gotta go. I won't get my coffee."

I sat up straighter, waiting for a goodbye kiss, but one wasn't forthcoming. "Gina?"

She looked back at me as she turned for the door. "Huh?"

"Have a nice weekend."

"Thanks. You, too. Bye."

The front door closed quietly just a few seconds later. I'd only had a few hours sleep, and the sun wouldn't be up for a half hour, but I got up anyway. For some reason, I went to the front door, hoping to see her walking away, but she'd been too fast. I couldn't even hear her tread on the path. The island was silent, save for the gentle, calm drone of the waves.

❖

I'd just left the market late that afternoon, and I was close enough to the pier for my cell phone to actually ring. I found myself a little bit disappointed to see that it wasn't Gina, and it took me a second to sound as pleased to hear Dana's voice as I usually did. "Hi. What's up?"

"First, I called to see how things went with the ferry driver."

"Oh! Damn, I can't believe I didn't call you with an update. I'm a slacker."

"Sounds like things got patched up." She didn't sound as pleased as I thought she would. But I hadn't given her the update to tell her how cool Gina was, so I could hardly blame her.

"Yeah, they did. She finally accepted my apology and offered one herself. Even though it seemed like she didn't have much practice, I badgered her until she properly apologized."

"You should be proud of yourself," Dana teased. "A coerced apology is very satisfying."

"It was. I could tell she felt bad; she just didn't apologize very often. It's a good skill to have, so I feel like I've given her a gift that will keep on giving."

"Where do you stand?"

"Things seem fine. We've seen each other a couple of times, and I think she's pretty cool."

"That's great. Maybe I can meet her."

Ah, I knew she'd be supportive. "I'd love for you to visit. But I thought you were too busy to take any time off."

"I am. But I got a little research grant from the New York Public Library. It's not much, but it'll get me to New York and pay for my meals and a very cheap hotel for a week."

"Stay at my apartment."

"Your apartment, huh? Gosh, I never thought of that. It was just luck that I called you before I started searching on Priceline."

"Thank God. You know I'd be pissed if you paid for a hotel—whether I was going to be home or not. I don't have anything for the baby to sleep on, though."

"Oh, I'm coming alone. It'd be nice if we could have a family vacation, but Renée doesn't want to have to drag the baby around town without me. We'll come together when we both have some free time."

"Renée and Maya could stay with me. It's a little cold, but Maya would love the beach."

"Maybe later in the summer, if I make some progress on this journal article. I don't wanna miss seeing my girl go into the ocean for the first time."

"I hope you know I'll strangle you if you don't come out here for at least an afternoon. That's my price for the apartment. Non-negotiable."

"Maybe I should've started with Priceline," Dana said, the lighthearted tone of her voice telling me she was teasing.

"Come on. I miss you, and if you're any kind of friend, you miss me, too."

"I'm a damned good friend, Chandler. I'll be up to see your sorry butt. Just tell me when to come."

"Any time. Other than an hour or so to chat with Gina before we have sex, I don't have any other distractions. Come early, stay late."

"I think I'll go to New York next Monday. Can you send me the keys?"

"Sure. I'll even call my doorman and tell him you'll be there."

"Great. I'll probably drive out to the island at the end of the week and leave from there."

"You're driving?"

"Yeah, I think I will. It's only four hours."

"Then leave on Sunday afternoon and come here first. You can spend the night and head into Manhattan on Monday after rush hour. You don't wanna be on the LIE on Friday afternoon. Besides, you have to go nearly all the way to the city to get back to I-95. You'd be doubling-back."

"What's the LIE?"

"The Long Island Expressway. That's how you get into Manhattan."

"Well, aren't you Miss Know-It-All about Long Island. You don't even have a car. Are you soaking up driving directions just from being out there?"

"No, but I've heard it mentioned in traffic reports for as long as I've been in New York. Now I know where it is and where it goes."

"Gotcha. I think Renée will be okay with those plans. Can you send me directions?"

"Sure. And I'll send you a ferry ticket. I got a free one for sleeping with the pilot."

"Well, you're really coming up in the world, aren't ya?"

"Don't tease me, or you won't get the ticket. And I know you never turn your nose up at fourteen dollars."

"I don't turn my nose up at fourteen cents."

"I'm charged about seeing you, Dana. I'll even cook."

"Wow. You *do* miss me."

"Yeah, I do," I said. I knew she'd been able to hear the loneliness in my voice, so I added, "But I miss my housemates during the week, so don't feel too flattered." Damn, I was starting to sound like Gina. The difference was that Dana knew I loved her.

※

Gina came over on Thursday night, the first time I'd seen her since the previous Thursday. I hadn't called her, and she'd only called me late that afternoon. I'd been worried that she'd tired of me or that I'd offended her in some way, but when I opened the door, she looked happy to see me. She folded me into her arms and kissed me hard before she set foot inside the house.

I put my hand on her shoulder and leaned back in her embrace. "Miss me?"

"Yep. I missed all of you." She kissed me again, palming my ass while her tongue slipped into my mouth. She sure knew how to hit my accelerator. "Let's make up for lost time."

Her nimble fingers started to unbutton my blouse while she guided me into the house. By the time the backs of my calves hit the sofa, my blouse was off and my bra was being slid from my shoulders. I considered a minor protest, but then decided the leather sofa could stand up to any wear and tear we might create.

She pushed me down, after unzipping my pants and slipping them and my panties down my legs. I uttered a mew of complaint when my bare skin touched the cold leather. Gina stood in front of me and stripped, dropping each piece of her clothing to the floor, grinning at me like the devil herself. She stepped on my slacks, leaving them on the floor while she guided me onto my back. Then she gently settled her weight, partly on me and partly on the sofa. "Let me show you how much I missed this," she murmured, once again kissing all errant thoughts from my foggy brain.

※

We got into bed while I was still pulsing from my last orgasm. "You were on fire tonight," I said. I lay next to her, waiting for her to kiss me goodnight and take my hand. But she rolled onto her belly and sighed heavily.

"I told you I missed you," she said. She gave me a wolfish smile and then rested her hand on my shoulder.

I stroked her side, one of my favorite parts of her body. Her waist wasn't as trim as it looked in her clothes, a fashion trick I hadn't been able to figure out. She was almost boyish, but the delightful curve to her ass nearly screamed "woman." I loved to run my hand down her side, feeling the muscles she'd developed through years of physical labor, and then slide my hand down the steep curve of her cheeks. Invariably, I had to lean over and kiss that lovely spot, lingering on the dip on each side of her ass. I was just lifting my head after placing a soft kiss on her silky skin when something occurred to me. "Hey," I said, seeing that she was about to fall asleep. "Can you make a little time on Monday morning?"

"Huh?" Her eyes opened. "I've got…mmm…an hour—tops. That's not enough time to—" She shifted and patted my ass, letting her hand rest there.

"No, no," I said. "I don't want you to come here. I thought I could meet you at the café when you have a break. One of my closest friends is visiting me, and I'd love for her to meet you."

Gina rolled onto her side and stared at me for a second. I couldn't tell what was going through her mind, but she looked both pleased and puzzled. "Yeah, I could do that. Tell me about her."

"She's an assistant professor at Harvard…in Boston," I added, just in case Gina wasn't familiar. "Her name's Dana, and I'm the fairy godmother to her little girl, Maya." I got up, went to my dresser, and brought a photo album back to bed. Gina sat up and gave me her full attention. "This is me with Maya on the day she was baptized. Isn't she a doll?"

"You both are. Fairy godmother, huh?" Gina looked at me with…I'm not even sure what it was, but it made my heart skip a beat.

She took the album from me, dropped it to the bed, and took me in her arms. Pulling back for a moment, she looked at me again, her eyes searching mine for something. For what, I didn't know. We kissed while slowly falling to the mattress and then kept kissing until my heart felt as if it would burst. I wasn't sure what was going on, but I felt so utterly loved when she held me this way. She pulled away, stared at me with those beautiful dark eyes, and kissed me one more time. Then she lay on her back, tucked me up against her side, grasped my hand, kissed it tenderly, and laid it on her breast. Her warm hand covered mine, and I could feel her heart beating rapidly.

I snuggled up against her, feeling warm and protected and sleepy. Before I could begin to sort out what had just transpired between us, I was sound asleep.

⊕

On Monday morning, Dana and I sat at a booth at the café, waiting for the ferry to arrive. I was nervous, but I couldn't sort out what about the meeting was making me so prickly. I was either worried about what Dana would think of Gina or what Gina would think of Dana. Maybe I was worried about both of them. That seemed likely, since my stomach felt like I'd been drinking lighter fluid.

Dana was blithely sipping a cup of coffee, unaware of the somersaults in my belly. When the ferry horn blew, I practically peed my pants, but Dana merely glanced out the window. "She handles that boat well. How long's she been doing it?"

"Uhm …" I stared at her for a moment and then made a face. "I don't have any idea. She told me she's been working since she was seven or eight. I was kinda afraid to ask any more questions. She's so sweet I couldn't bear the thought of hearing about her working in a sweatshop when she should have been in grade school."

"You shitting me?"

"No. She told me she's been working since she was a little girl. But I honestly don't know much else about her work history."

Dana studied me for a moment. "It's hard to imagine you with a working-class woman."

"Thanks!" I know I sounded harsh, but I was steamed. "What's that supposed to mean? I'm too elitist to truck with plebeians?"

Dana unsuccessfully tried to hide her smile. "That wasn't what I was thinking, until that plebeian remark."

I stuck my tongue out at her, just to show I was a regular Joe.

"I was thinking," she said, "that you've never dated anyone outside of academia. That doesn't mean you're an elitist. It just means that you've always been attracted to people like you."

"That still sounds plenty insulting," I said. "Where am I supposed to meet women? My local bodega? The laundromat? And how many fry cooks have you been out with?"

"None. I've never dated anyone who wasn't in academia, either." She reached across the table and covered my hand. "Hey. It wasn't a criticism. Just an observation."

Looking into her big, brown eyes, I knew I'd overreacted. But just as I started to apologize, Gina slid into the booth next to me. "Hi," she said. She kissed my cheek and extended her hand to Dana. "I'm Gina Scognamiglio."

"Dana Little. Good to meet you. Although I did see you yesterday on the outbound trip."

"Oh, yeah? I wasn't scratching myself or doing anything embarrassing, was I?"

Dana laughed. "No. You were up there in the front, looking all businesslike. If you were scratching, I sure couldn't see you."

I could tell she felt comfortable with Gina. Sometimes, Dana was a little stiff, even formal with strangers, but not today. I started to feel a little more relaxed, but my startle response was still off the charts.

"Are you staying long?" Gina asked. She nodded when the waitress held up a pot of coffee.

"No. I'm going to Hayden's co-op in the city for a few days. I'll be riding back to Sayville with you in a while."

Gina shifted her shoulders and rubbed against me. "Hayden's co-op, huh? Is that a big vacation destination?"

"You obviously haven't seen Hayden's co-op," Dana said, right before she yelped and rubbed her shin. "Don't kick me!"

"Don't insult me," I said.

Gina put her arm around my shoulders. I liked that she was acting a little bit proprietary over me. "You two must have known each other for quite a while. Hayden's never kicked me."

"We met...damn, I guess it's been seven years, right?" Dana said.

"Sounds right to me. I was just a lonely girl freezing her butt off in New Hampshire, when Dana offered to warm me up."

Gina's eyes grew wide, and her gaze darted from me to Dana and back again. "You...you're...I mean, you were..."

Oh, fuck! I could almost see Dana's hackles go up. She always gets pissed off when people are surprised that we were lovers. I don't blame her, since it usually happens when someone thinks it's odd to see a white woman with a black woman. I hoped to hell that wasn't true of Gina. But I didn't know her well enough to know how she felt about black people or anyone else for that matter. "Dana and I were lovers when we were in college. We broke up when she moved to Boston." I didn't add that she'd gotten the job I would have killed for. I also didn't mention that she got an offer from Columbia, so she could have stayed with me in New York. Dana was staring at Gina, who was oblivious to her unease.

"That's something I'll never be able to understand. It's just not natural," Gina said. Her coffee had just been delivered, and she poured some milk into it. I was wondering how to slide out of the booth and run when she continued, "How can you be friends after you break up?"

She looked at me, and I let out a silent sigh of relief. "It wasn't easy at first." I snuck a look at Dana and saw that she looked relieved, too. "But we still loved each other. It just didn't make sense to stay together when we knew we'd be apart for a long time–maybe all through our careers."

"Mmm." Gina didn't say another word, but I could tell she wasn't satisfied by my answer.

"Things have worked out," I added. "Dana met a great woman, and they had that adorable baby whose picture I showed you."

"Your baby is a doll," Gina said. "I bet you miss her."

Dana smiled the half-grin she always made when she was about to say something sarcastic. "I won't miss the three o'clock in the morning feedings. Or the crying for no earthly reason. But yeah, I already miss my girls, and it's only been a day."

"What are you doing in New York?" Gina asked.

"Some research. The New York Public Library has some great resources on Harlem."

"Are you in history, too?"

"Yeah. I specialize in American History, unlike our friend here, who studies people who predate Jesus."

"I like history, too," Gina said, and now I could feel her body grow tense when Dana gave her a doubting look.

"Gina's a fan of Italian history," I said, somewhat defensively. "My guys were dead for hundreds of years before her guys were born. But we're gonna compare and see if we have any favorite books in common."

"I don't think Hayden and I have ever read the same book," Dana said while smiling at me. "We didn't have any of the same tastes. I guess opposites attract."

"Similarities can attract, too," Gina said. She didn't look defensive or seem tense, but there was a certain challenge to her statement. "I'm really looking forward to talking about some of my favorite Romans. As soon as I get some time off, we're gonna have a good, long chat." Her hand covered my shoulder, and she squeezed gently. Suddenly, I felt as if they were politely fighting over me! This stunned me since Dana had no damn right even to have an opinion on whom I slept with, and I didn't know Gina well enough for her to think I was her property.

"Where'd you study history, Gina? Maybe you went to a school where they didn't know how to hook you on the interesting stuff."

Now I was getting mad. I was certain…fairly certain…that I'd told Dana that Gina hadn't gone to college. And if she was trying to show her up, I was gonna do more than kick her under the table.

"I went to Bay Shore High," Gina said, her chin tilting up as I was learning it did when she felt challenged. "They didn't know how to hook me on anything. I study history on my own 'cause I like it. I've never needed anyone to tell me what I should read or what I should think about it. So, college didn't interest me." She gave me a sidelong look. "But if I could have had a teacher like Hayden, I might have actually applied to some schools."

"You didn't even apply?" What in the fuck was Dana doing? I'd never…ever…seen her acting so oddly. "How'd you do on your SATs?"

Gina pulled her arm away from me, and I could feel her straighten up. "Didn't take 'em. I wasn't gonna go to college, so why waste the money?"

"Didn't your parents give you a hard time? Didn't they want you to—"

"To what?" Gina asked. Her eyes were sparking with anger, and I was afraid she might…well, I didn't know what she might do, but I didn't want to find out.

Dana looked at her earnestly. "My parents didn't go to college, but from the time I was a kid, they saved and planned and worked to make sure I could. It was important to them that I didn't have to work as hard as they'd had to just to keep the family going."

Oh, now I got it. Dana was identifying with Gina in some weird way. Both from blue-collar families and all of that. But she was in over her head if she thought she and Gina were simpatico on the topic of higher education.

"My parents didn't go to college, either," Gina said. "But my dad never had to leave my mom so he could get a better job. You can work too hard or too little at any job." She put her arm around me again, and this time, she pulled me close. I didn't like being used to make a point, but I made an exception this time. Gina had Dana dead to rights, and I have to admit I was proud of her. Not many people blew Dr. Little out of the water so easily.

"I wasn't…I wasn't equating our situations," Dana said. "I just assume most parents want a better life for their children."

Gina gave her a sardonic smile. "I think good parents do. But having a title or a fancy job doesn't mean you have a better life. Besides, if everybody had a degree, it'd be just like graduating from high school." She chuckled, a quiet sound that seemed to my ears very close to mockery.

"A college degree *is* like a high school diploma now," Dana said. A kick that should have made her cry didn't stop her from continuing. "To stand out in the crowd, you need an advanced degree."

Laughing softly, Gina said, "You've been hanging around with the wrong crowd, Dana. Most people don't have degrees."

"I bet that 25 percent of people do."

"In the whole country?" Gina's eyes were sparkling now, and it was clear she was having some fun. "You think 25 percent of the whole country has a college degree?"

"At least." Dana's eyes had narrowed, and I knew she'd bet her mortgage payment if Gina would take her up on it.

"Fifty bucks," Gina said. She reached into her jeans and took out her wallet. Extracting two twenties and a ten, she handed them to me. "Hayden looks up the answer and pays off."

I could actually see the hitch in Dana's breathing. She hated, truly hated, to waste money. She didn't usually bet, not even the departmental football pool, but when pressed, she forgot how much she hated to lose money. "Fine," she growled. She took out an equivalent amount and pushed it in my direction. I knew it was probably most of her cash, since she never carried much.

"Guys," I said, "don't do this. It's not worth losing fifty dollars over."

"Yes, it is," they said in unison.

I didn't know Gina well enough to judge her resolve, but I knew Dana plenty well. She was in for the duration. "Fine," I said. "I'll look it up on the Internet."

"Make sure you use the census bureau's numbers," Dana said, scowling.

"I will. I took several courses in research methodologies," I said. "I'm not some freshman who thinks everything on the Internet is true."

"That's settled, then." Gina got up and twitched her head towards the ferry. "Time to go." She looked at me and said, "Why don't you come with us, Hayden? You can entertain Dana on the inbound and me on the outbound." She gave me that wolfish grin again, and I responded in kind without even thinking.

"Okay. I'd like to have a few more minutes with Dana." To slap her silly, I didn't add.

"All right. The boat leaves in five minutes." She put her arm around me and said, "No charge for you, Hayden." I swore I could hear Dana make a gagging sound, but I didn't turn around. There would be time to choke her once we were on the ferry.

✤

Gina left us after we climbed aboard. It was cool and very breezy, giving us a perfect excuse to stay on the main deck. There were fewer than thirty people on the boat, giving Dana and me the opportunity to chat in private. "What the fuck is going on with you?" I demanded, getting our chat off to a pleasant start.

"What?" She gave me that "What did I do?" look that had never worked with me. For a smart woman, she didn't learn very quickly.

"You know what." I was glowering at her, something that *had* always worked. Dana was one of those people who hated to be in trouble. She'd do just about anything to get out of the doghouse. Her fear of angering me led her to the truth. "So I didn't like your pickup. Why's that a big deal? You can't be serious about her."

Offended once again, I asked, "And why can't I be? Is there a rule that I have to avoid fantastic-looking women?" I saw her flinch and added, "Present company excepted."

Dana grunted something that my sharp hearing couldn't pick up. "This isn't about how she looks."

"She looks great, doesn't she?" I asked, like a child wanting peer approval for a new doll.

"She's not bad. A little butch for my tastes, but not bad."

I pinched her right above the knee, a place she was both sensitive and ticklish. "She's not butch at all, and you know it. She just has a job that you think of as traditionally male. Some feminist you are. And she's a lot prettier than 'not bad.' Admit it."

"Hayden, I don't like the chick, okay? If I liked her, she'd be much more attractive. But she rubbed me the wrong way, and that colors how she appears. I just see that smart mouth and those mocking eyes."

"And beautiful, thick, dark hair."

"She's got nice hair," she said, giving me one point. "And a great cut. But it's hard to notice with that smart mouth."

This was getting nowhere, and we were proceeding at a very rapid rate. I valued my friendship and my love for Dana too much to have her leave while she was angry. Gently, I touched her leg right where I'd pinched her. "Can you step back and tell me why you don't like her? I don't wanna go out with someone who's an asshole, and I'll admit my judgment is colored by her everything." I gave her a dopey smile, and I could see her begin to thaw.

"I'm not sure," she said thoughtfully. "I liked her at first, but she's so rigid. She acts as if she knows everything. Like you couldn't convince her of anything if she didn't innately believe in it. She seems like a Republican. Probably a rightwing Republican."

"No!"

"Yeah, that's it." She was smiling with glee. "She seems like the kind of person who'd vote Republican so she could keep her job driving this noxious, fume-belching boat." She waved at the admittedly noxious fumes. "Can we move? I'm gonna pass out."

I got up and followed her to the front of the main deck. It was colder, but the air was heavy with moisture and felt clean. "I don't think she's like that, but if she is, I don't want to know."

"She obviously doesn't care about the underclass," Dana said, looking triumphant.

"What?"

"Haven't you noticed her backpack? It's one of the ones they sell in Chinatown."

I stared at her for a second, wondering how Gina's backpack fit into the discussion. "So, she has a Chinese backpack, and your point is...?"

"No, no." She shook her head, clearly exasperated. "She has one of those forgeries. A knockoff."

"So, she has a knockoff. So what?"

"Hayden, do you have any idea what I'm getting at?"

"No. I couldn't have less of an idea."

"Okay," she said, now calm. "There's a billion-dollar trade in designer rip-offs. Many of the fake purses and wallets and sunglasses and watches are made in China. Gina has a big Prada bag, and there's no way she bought a real one. Hell, she's an idiot even if it is real, but she's an exploiter if it's fake."

"And why is that?"

"Because," she said, exasperated again. "It hurts the legitimate manufacturers, it hurts the people in sweatshops making the knockoffs, it hurts our economy because the stuff isn't taxed and there aren't any import duties paid, it creates this black market here where people can easily be exploited… It's wrong in every way."

"Fine," I said, now testy because of her lecture, "she's a horrible person who exploits people by buying a purse. I think I can live with that."

She made a face. "She doesn't just buy a purse. She buys a big, showy, Prada bag. No one would believe it was real. I hate people who have to act as if they have the money to buy these ridiculously extravagant things. It's consumerism gone mad."

"Dana," I said, trying to be patient with her. "I'm not going to stop sleeping with a gorgeous, nice woman because she buys a showy bag. I don't care if she wears a string of clear marbles and says it's a diamond necklace."

She let out a heavy breath. "This is just a summer fling?" Her expression didn't hide the hope that it was just that.

"What else? I'm chasing down jobs at Princeton, Yale, and Harvard. With luck, I won't be here in September."

"I'm pulling as many strings as I have," Dana said, now serious and clearly sincere. "We'd love to have you in Boston, and I know you'd love it."

"I know I would, too," I said, even though I wasn't sure Renée wanted me living right next door. Dana and I had made our peace, but the new girlfriend was never as happy about the reconciliation as the ex-lovers were.

Dana put her arm around me and kissed my cheek. "I'm sorry I was an ass. I'm not sure what happened, but I wanted to brain her by the time she'd been there ten minutes."

"It's not a big deal. You'll probably never see her again. And next time, I'm gonna be more invested in a woman before I introduce her to you. Then you'll have to be nice."

Dana grunted her agreement, and we sat watching the land approach faster than I would have been comfortable with if I'd been Gina. That woman really knew how to pilot a boat.

❧

Gina didn't leave the pilothouse once we docked at Sayville, so we were all saved having to be polite. I got off and walked Dana to the parking lot.

Things were a little strained, but we were pretty solid when I kissed her goodbye. It's funny how something as simple as a kiss can say so much about a relationship. I'd probably spent a few dozen hours kissing those sensual, warm lips, and I knew them better than any other pair of lips on earth. But just before mine touched hers, she turned her head—not much—just enough to force me to land half on and half off. It felt strange and unsettling to kiss her with less intimacy than I kissed all of my other friends. I certainly wasn't going to try to slip my tongue in when she wasn't on guard, and it hurt me that she'd flinched.

When Renée was around, Dana and I hugged goodbye. We'd never spoken about it, but both of us knew not to appear too friendly in her presence. But Dana had always kissed me on the lips when we were alone. It was never sexual, but it was always comforting. I wasn't sure why she'd changed her pattern today, but I had a feeling it had to do with Gina.

"I'll call you later tonight to let you know I got settled, okay?" She wasn't looking me right in the eye, and that felt odd, too.

"Yeah. Sure. Call anytime."

"Will Gina be at your house?"

Oh, God, was this going to continue to be an issue? "I'm not sure. We don't have plans."

"I just didn't want to, you know, disturb anything."

I smiled, even though it probably looked like indigestion. "If we're fucking, I won't answer, 'kay?"

"Hey!" She held my arm and looked at me, hurt visible in her eyes. "What was that for?"

"Nothing," I said. "This is just uncomfortable. We'll get through it." My smile was closer to normal, but I knew it wouldn't fool Dana.

"Yeah." She nodded. "We will." She hugged me quickly and then got into her car. "I'll call."

"Okay. Say hello to Renée and Maya for me."

"Gotcha. Later."

She closed the door and pulled out before I turned away. As I walked back to the ferry, I saw a lovely woman waiting for me by the dock. Gina's beautiful face brightened when our eyes met, and I felt all of my discomfort about Dana leave my body.

"Want a free ride to Cherry Grove?" She was sitting on a wooden support, and she looked perfectly comfortable perched on the end of the big log.

I put my arm around her waist and leaned against her. "Nothing's free. There's always a price."

"Why don't I come over tonight and we can negotiate." She kissed me then, and even though there wasn't a bit of passion in the gentle touch, it reminded me of what I'd been missing since Dana left me. The comfort of a tender kiss…just because.

"But you'll have already given me the ride. That doesn't put you in a very good negotiating position."

Her arm went around my waist, and she tucked me up against her body like a favorite doll. "You'd be surprised at some of my…positions."

"No, I wouldn't," I said. "Nothing about you surprises me anymore." I looked down at her bag, noting that it wasn't, as Dana said, ostentatious. It was actually tasteful and understated. "I like your bag," I said, twitching my head at the spot where it was lying.

She smiled and picked it up. "It's kinda silly, but I liked it, and I got a great deal."

"Where'd you get it?"

She playfully underlined the word "Milano" that was printed right under "Prada."

"Oh, Milano," I said, using my admittedly awful Italian accent. "Next time you're in Milano, get one for me."

Her eyebrows shot up. "You want a bag like this?"

"Yeah." I looked at hers again. "I'll take black, since you have brown."

Gina's hands went to my waist, and she pushed me up until I was standing. "I'll see what I can do. Let's go. I've got a schedule to keep."

I followed her onboard and got a nod from the old deckhand. We went up to the pilothouse, and Gina let me come in with her. "It's against regulations to have anyone in here, so keep your head down, okay? I'm sure no one will call the Coast Guard on me, but I don't like to ask for trouble."

"Are you sure it's okay? I can sit downstairs."

"I know. But I want you here." She put her hand on my cheek and ran her thumb over my skin. "I like you here."

There was a large, metal box on the floor, and I plopped down on it. My head was even with Gina's thighs, and that was just fine with me.

"You can sit on my chair," she said.

"No. You sit on it. You work too hard."

She smiled and shook her head, but she sat. She powered up the engines and signaled the deckhand through a window. In seconds, we were at cruising speed, and I decided I liked my seat and my companion.

"I thought you might be mad at me," she said. As she always did when she was at the wheel, she was intently scanning the slate gray water.

"I'm not mad at you. Why would I be? I'm a little mad at Dana, though."

She was wearing some seriously dark sunglasses, but I could still see those cute little wrinkles at the corners of her eyes when she smiled. "She's not always so snotty, is she?"

"Of course not. I've never seen her act like that. I still can't imagine why you set her off."

"Joking, right?"

"Huh? No, I'm not joking. What am I missing?"

"Duh!" She sounded like a teenager, but it was endearing.

"Duh what?"

"She doesn't want you to have a girlfriend. It's obvious."

"What? No way! She's married, for God's sake. Legally married. And she and Renée have a baby. She's over me. Hell, she was over me a long, long time before I was over her." I laughed ruefully. "Bitch."

"Bitch might be over you, but she still doesn't want you to have a girlfriend. I'm not saying it makes sense. But that's what it is."

"Maybe she just didn't like you," I said. I ran my fingertip down her bare thigh and smiled when goose bumps bloomed in its wake.

"Maybe. But she also doesn't want you to find a girlfriend. You won't convince me that's not true."

That sentence made my stomach flip. I knew I shouldn't ask, but I did. "Are you…do you…what's your political affiliation?"

"What?"

"You know, Democrat, Republican?"

"Oh." She loosened her shoulders and said, "Kind of a personal question, isn't it?"

"Yeah. But we've been pretty personal. You don't have to answer if you don't want to."

"Really? There isn't some test I have to pass?"

There was, but I felt stupid admitting it. I knew I was closed-minded about politics, but I couldn't sleep with a Republican. I hoped we'd drop it just so I didn't have to stop seeing her. "I shouldn't have asked. Forget it."

"No, no, if you want to know, I'll tell you." I cringed while I waited. "I'm a registered Independent. I vote on issues, not party lines."

Relief flooded me. "Cool. That's cool."

"How about you?"

"Oh. Uhm…I'm a Democrat."

"Always?"

"Yeah, I guess so. I've never voted for a Republican for national office."

"I have," she said thoughtfully. "And I'll do it again as soon as a socially moderate Republican, who isn't up the ass of the Evangelicals, runs." She chuckled for a second. "You seem pretty closed-minded about your politics, professor."

I thought about her comment for a while before I replied. Finally, I said, "I guess I am, in a lot of ways. I'm gonna have to think about that."

"What would you have said if I'd told you I'd voted for Bush twice?"

"I would have wished that you hadn't said that, and then I would have tried to talk myself into not seeing you anymore."

She was quiet for a time. "Would you have been successful?"

"I doubt it." I don't know why I said that, but I knew it was the truth.

Chapter Four

There was a knock on my door at five o'clock. I switched on the porch light and was surprised to see Gina waving at me. I opened the door and said, "Hi. Why so early?"

She walked in and pointed over her shoulder. "Fogged in. I'm usually not very happy to be stranded here, but tonight..."

"Really?" I gazed outside and realized I couldn't even see the trees that lined the path. "Did it come in that fast?"

"Well, to be honest, no." She looked at me with that adorable childlike smile and said, "I shouldn't have come over. There were only two passengers, and I knew I wouldn't be able to get back. But I wanted to see you."

I was extremely pleased by her eagerness, but I couldn't help saying, "Don't drive that big boat if it's not safe."

"I don't have the big ferry. I took the littlest one, but I'm still pretty easy to see. And anybody in a small craft should have had his ass in port an hour ago. I had her at half throttle when I was in open water and cut her down to a crawl when I got near the island. If I hit anybody, he didn't make a noise."

I wrapped my arms around her and squeezed. "You're a bad girl. But I'm glad you're here."

"Me, too. Got anything to eat? I'm starving."

I went into the kitchen, Gina fast on my heels. I opened the cabinet and poked around, looking for something fast. "I don't have much," I admitted. "I don't have any bread, or I'd make you a tuna sandwich."

She reached around me and moved a couple of things. "I could make pasta. Have you eaten?"

"No. I was gonna have a salad, but I don't have much to go around."

"You've got everything I need to make pasta."

"But I don't have any pasta sauce."

She pulled out a box of imported Italian tomatoes and grasped an onion from the counter. "I'm almost there. Got any herbs?"

"Yeah. I have some fresh basil."

"We're home free. Pour me some wine and get hungry."

Gina made me walk into town to get bread, saying it was a requirement. The fog was so thick I had to set my foot down carefully to avoid breaking my neck. The little grocery store usually had a decent selection of bread, but today they only had sliced sandwich bread and uncooked, frozen Italian loaves. I bought the loaves, figuring Gina might hit me with them.

"What are these?" she asked, her face contorted as if she were witnessing a gruesome accident.

I took the package from her and read, "Chef Mario's Italian Loaves. Bake at 375 degrees for twenty minutes, and you'll feel like you're in Rome."

"Rome, New York, maybe. Was this really the best they could do?"

"They said you brought a box of baguettes over this morning, but they were sold out by three o'clock."

She took the frozen loaves from me and playfully tapped the top of my head with them. "Stirati and pane pugliese from Ninth Street Bakery. I'll hurt you if you can't tell the difference between a baguette and a big slice of pane pugliese."

"I know bread," I said, glad that I really did. "And I knew you wouldn't like this. But it was either this or Wonder Bread."

She cradled the bread against her chest. "You did well."

"I live close to Ninth Street Bakery," I said. "I go over there on Saturday mornings sometimes for bread while it's still warm. Mmm-mmm."

"Maybe Manhattan's not that far," she said, giving me a smile that was as close to asking if we could go have sex as any verbal query could have been.

We sat down to dinner at seven o'clock. Gina had made a fabulous sauce by simply halving the onion and simmering it with the tomatoes. She added the basil not long before it was ready, saying she wanted the basil to sing. The bread wasn't great, but it was warm and soft and soaked up butter and sauce, so I was happy. "You are a darned good cook."

She looked at my beaming face and said, "You look like you love to eat."

"I do. Especially when someone cooks for me."

"Did you grow up with home-cooked meals?"

I nodded, since my mouth was full. Pointing at Gina with my fork, I raised my eyebrows.

"Yeah, me, too. My mom cooked every day. Big meals, too. I don't know how she had time to do anything else."

She looked a little wistful. I swallowed and asked, "Is she...dead?"

A nod. "She died in 2000. Barely made the millennium."

"Oh, Gina, I'm sorry to hear that."

"It really sucked. Lung cancer. Less than a year from finding out she had it."

"Fuck," I muttered. "That must have been awful for you and the whole family." I knew she had two or three brothers, but I couldn't recall their names.

"Yeah, of course. My grandmother cooks now, but it's not the same. It just seems like food when I go over there to eat. When my mom cooked, it felt like love."

She started to mist up, and I rose and stood next to her. My eyes were watery, too, and I pressed her head against my chest while I stroked her back. "Poor bunny."

Tilting her head, she looked at me for a moment. "Bunny?"

I shrugged. "My mother always said that when she comforted me. Just a reflex."

She put her arms around me and hugged me. "I like it," she murmured.

We held each other for another minute or so, and then I went back to my seat. "Does your grandmother live with you?"

"She and my grandfather live at the house. I don't live there anymore. I've got my own place now."

"Your mom's parents?"

"Unh-uh. They're both dead. My dad's parents have lived with us since…mmm, I guess since I was about five. They live in a little freestanding apartment my dad and brothers built for them in the backyard. They could live in the house now, but they like their little place. No stairs."

I had this image of a lean-to made out of plywood and tarpaper, but I tried to banish the thought. "What do they do to keep busy?"

"They have a big garden. Not at the house, though."

"What? They have a garden at someone else's house?"

She laughed, her eyes crinkling when she did. "No. There's a big public garden, and they have a couple of plots there. We don't have room at our place."

"Oh." I couldn't think of what to say. Their place was so small that the little tarpaper shack took up the whole yard.

Gina didn't seem to notice my lack of a significant response. "My grandfather's in charge of the garden, and my grandmother's in charge of canning and preserving everything they don't eat during the summer." She smiled, looking so pretty I wanted to kiss her. "It's like a farmer's market in the summer. I keep telling my grandfather he should open a stand out by the street, but he hordes it all. My brothers have to beg to get him to give them sweet corn."

God, where do they live that they can have a farm stand in front of their house? I assume they live in—or is it "on"—Long Island, but it sure doesn't look very bucolic from the train. "We never had a garden. I go to the green market in Tompkins Square, though. It's nice to have fresh vegetables."

"I'll steal some of the good stuff for you when my grandfather's taking a nap," she promised. "I could swipe a bushel of tomatoes, and he wouldn't be able to tell."

"A bushel seems like a lot. How about two?"

She held up two fingers. "Just two tomatoes?" At my nod, Gina got up and walked over to me. My plate was empty, so I didn't mind getting up when she took my hand. Tilting her head, she kissed me and then kissed me again. "I think I could manage two." We stood there at the table, kissing each other for a long time. I loved the way the basil smelled on her breath. It was very fresh smelling and almost sweet. She finally pulled away and patted my belly. "Room for dessert?"

I smiled my sexiest smile and started tugging her towards the bedroom. "Always."

Pulling me to a stop, she said, "No, I really mean it. I need something sweet."

"I'm not sweet?" With another kiss, she assured me that I was. But she headed right back into the kitchen to look for more food. "Do you always eat this much?" I asked, not even trying to be delicate.

"No. But all I had was coffee and half a bagel today. I didn't have time for lunch. It's a long time between 5:00 a.m. and dinner."

"No wonder you're still hungry. You should have told me to buy dessert at the store."

She waved me off. "Don't be a slave to the grocery store. We can find something." She looked thoroughly, but finally had to admit there wasn't much. Holding a box of powered sugar in her hand, she said, "I guess I could just eat a few spoons of this."

"I didn't realize that was powered when I bought it," I admitted. "But I've been using it anyway."

Gina's eyes lit up. "Do you have cooking oil?"

"Sure." I got the olive oil back out.

"No, no, like canola or vegetable or peanut."

"No. I only cook with olive oil."

"Damn." She went to the door and put her shoes back on. "I'll be right back. Don't put that dough away."

Before I could utter a protest, she was gone. Obviously, when Gina wanted something, she was not to be deterred. By the time she got back, I'd cleaned up the kitchen and had dutifully left the thawed dough on the counter. She produced a small can of Crisco and then found a heavy pot she liked. "I hope you have a sweet tooth," she said, "'cause this is gonna be a pain in the ass if I'm the only one who likes this."

"I love dessert," I said, but I had a feeling I didn't like it as much as Gina did.

She heated all of the Crisco in the pan while she cut the thawed bread dough. Her sure hands pulled and stretched the elastic dough, while she nodded to herself in satisfaction. "This stuff is great for this."

"What are you making?"

"My mom called them Italian donuts, but they're also called fried dough or zeppole. All depends on where you're from. These are gonna look funny 'cause they should be round like a tennis ball. But they'll taste good."

"If they're as good as the pasta, I'll…well…I'll let you choose your payment."

Her wolf-like smile made me a little giddy. I stood behind her and held her while she dropped a big piece of the dough in the hot oil. It made a hellacious amount of noise, but soon settled down. Gina turned the piece of dough, making sure it was browning on both sides. After a short while, she pulled it from the oil and placed it on a few paper towels. She poured so much sugar on it that it was nearly white, but when she put it to my lips, I took a tentative bite and nearly swooned. "Fuck me!"

Her eyes were bright as stars. "I know!" She took a big bite and rolled her eyes while she shook like a happy dog. "This is so damned good. Here. You eat this one, and I'll make another."

There was no way I was gonna refuse that offer. When she was finished, we took our prizes into the living room, along with dishtowels to protect the furniture and ourselves. It was hard to finish, since she'd made them the size of textbooks, but I managed. Gina ate carefully, making sure she got a little bit of the crispy edge and then some of the more tender middle. When she finished she wiped her mouth and said, "Now, that was a good dinner."

I wrapped my arms around her and pulled her on top of me. We spent a minute adjusting for our full bellies, and then I kissed her. I licked a tiny bit of sugar from her lips and then kissed her repeatedly. She felt so soft and warm and cuddly lying in my arms that I was perfectly content just to kiss her for the rest of the night. She seemed to enjoy herself as much as I did, and neither of us tried to go further. I was so full and happy that I...

It was hours later when I woke. My arm was sound asleep, and Gina felt as if she weighed seven hundred pounds. Why does sleeping on a sofa look like so much fun in the movies? I nudged my heavy friend, and she woke slowly, finally focusing on me. "Where are we?"

"Living room. Let's go to bed."

She clambered to her feet and grasped my hand, leading me to the darkened room. Yanking off the bedspread, she fell to the bed, taking me with her. With a grunt, she covered us with the spread and then was asleep before I could remind her that we were fully dressed. I let myself fall back to sleep, secretly pleased that we hadn't had sex. It was very nice to know that Gina liked me for more than just sex. Now I knew she liked me for food *and* sex.

❖

I woke to the sound of Gina's voice. I assumed she was on the phone, and I lay in bed for a few moments, waiting for her to hang up. It was raining so hard that the noise prevented me from making out what she was saying, but I hoped she had a day off due to the weather.

A minute later, she walked into the bedroom—now naked, still beautiful. Her hair was mussed, and her eyes were a little squinty, but she looked fabulous to me. "Nice day," she said. Then she jumped onto the bed and grabbed me, rolling around so violently that the sheet came loose, and we were soon twisted in it. "I don't have to go to work!"

I had to catch my breath before I could reply. "Fog?"

"No, just rain. But there's a lot of it. No one will come or go if it's not necessary."

"So, you just...take off?"

She laughed. "No, I don't just take off. I asked my cousin's kid to cover for me. He's gonna start working full-time on Memorial Day weekend, but since he can't do anything fun today, I thought he might like to work."

"Uhm, I hate to remind you of this, but the ferry's here." Gina wrapped her arms around me and rolled me onto her body. We were eye to eye, and for some reason, she stuck her tongue out and licked my face. I sputtered, trying to wipe my nose, but I couldn't get my arms untangled from the mess we'd made. "Blech!"

"Oh, don't be such a baby. You don't mind having my tongue everywhere else."

"I know, but there's something icky about spit."

She rolled me onto my back and then methodically disentangled us. With a bit of the sheet, she gently wiped my face. "There. All better." She put her arm around me and pulled me to her side. "I know the boat is here, smarty-pants. I've never lost track of her."

"How will he get the boat?"

"He'll come over in a smaller boat. No big deal. He knows the ropes. He's been working as a deckhand since he was sixteen."

"Who is this cousin of yours? Is he one of the kids I saw on the boat when the woman in the wheelchair was a passenger?"

"No, you haven't seen Case. He's a nice kid. He's only had his pilot's license for a few months, and he's itching to get to work."

"He wants to do this full-time?" Damn, Gina, shouldn't he be in school?

"Yeah. He's been working at a restaurant near his house. Just a burger shack. He's so sick of it I don't think he'll be able to stand the sight of hamburger for a few years. When he got his union card, he kissed it."

"Did you help him get in?"

"Sure. Italian affirmative action. Also known as nepotism. I bet 75 percent of the people in the union got in through a relative. It's a bitch if you're not hooked up, but it's always been that way. I'm not gonna be the one to stop just when my cousin wants in."

"Case didn't want to go to college?"

"Oh, he went, but he dropped out. I think he was gonna flunk out, anyway. He saved them the trouble of kicking him out." She laughed, clearly thinking it was funny that even the next generation of her family didn't try to improve their lot. I bit my tongue to keep from saying something. If they were happy, it really wasn't my business. It just seemed so odd to me since everyone I knew in high school had gone to college.

"Hey, are we gonna get up? 'Cause I'm gonna need a lot of coffee if we are."

"Let's sleep for another hour. I haven't slept past dawn for over a month."

"It's a deal. Just put your arms around me and snuggle me. There's nothing I like better than to snuggle in bed on a rainy day."

When we got into position, she murmured, "I like it, too. Especially with you." She reached down to touch my hip and said, "You've got clothes on."

"I know."

"Why don't I?"

"I have no idea. You must have stripped in your sleep. You're very talented."

"I sure don't remember doing it. Maybe you stripped me." She grinned at me and tried to lick me again.

I rolled away, just missing getting a wet face. Gina, however, got a mouthful of my hair. While she made a face and pulled a few hairs from her mouth, I took off my clothes and got back into bed. "That'll teach you not to lick."

"Hah." She put her arms around me and hugged me tight. "I predict you'll be begging for a licking by the end of the day."

I tucked my face into the crook of her neck and whispered, "Who's stupid enough to hope you're wrong?"

❖

I could have slept longer, but Gina started kissing my neck while it was still dark out. I shifted enough to give her better access to my throat and opened my eyes just enough to see my clock. "Why's it still dark?" I mumbled. "It's seven o'clock."

"'Cause it's raining and cloudy. Did you forget?"

"Unh-uh. You're still with me. How could I forget?" I snuck my arm under her and rolled her on top of me. She was heavy, but it was surprisingly comfortable to have her weight pinning me to the bed. I looked into her eyes, seeing she was wide-awake and happy. "I like you."

After a gentle kiss, she gazed at me for a few moments. "I like you, too. A lot."

I'm not sure how she did it, but she shifted me while she sat up, and I found myself sprawled across her lap. Playfully, she swatted my bottom and said, "Let's go."

"Go? I thought we'd fool around."

"This is the best part of the day." She helped me to my feet and then hugged me. Her face felt so nice against my bare belly. I tried to push her back into bed, but she was having none of it. "Later, babe. We've got all day."

She got up and suddenly looked unsure of herself. "Is this okay? I didn't even ask if you wanted to spend the day with me."

"Of course, it's okay. It's much better than okay." I put my arms around her waist and soaked up her warmth and the tantalizing softness of her skin. I was seriously in need of a little playtime, but she was just as seriously in need of moving ahead with her day. I didn't get even one tiny vibe of sexual interest from her, so I decided not to press. "What's on your agenda?"

"Breakfast. Then I wanna hear all about what you teach and what you're interested in and what your summer project is. I know we've only been seeing each other a few weeks, but I should know this stuff by now."

I took her hand to lead her to the kitchen. "You're the one who didn't want to date. If we'd had those pre-sex dates, you'd know all sorts of stuff about me."

"Well, if you would have sworn you were good in bed, I might have dated you. You didn't prop yourself up enough."

I swatted her a little harder than she'd swatted me. "My mother wouldn't be happy with my having sex first and dating later. Promise you'll never tell."

"Damn!" She snapped her fingers. "I knew I shouldn't have sent that e-mail."

She squealed when I pinched her. "How are you at making coffee?" I asked. "I need a shower before I can wake up enough to reveal my secrets."

"Go on. Unless you want to shower together."

"I'd love to, but if we get in that shower together, someone's gonna have to do me."

Gina put her hand on my shoulder and said, "If you really want to go back to bed, I will."

"Nah. It's more fun when we're both in the mood. Maybe I'll use my shower massage to clear my mind."

"You're a lot friskier than I thought you'd be," she said, smiling happily at me.

Something about her comment stopped me cold. "If that's a compliment, thanks…I guess. But if you're saying I looked like a tight-ass, I'd like to know why you wanted to see me in the first place."

For the first time since we'd met, she looked like she was hedging. "No, no, I didn't think that. I just thought you were like…not that you were like anyone else, but…I don't know. I just thought you'd be a little reserved. That's it. Reserved."

"And that's why you came over here and basically demanded sex? 'Cause you thought I'd be reserved?" I didn't like the look on her face, and I didn't like the way this whole conversation was making me feel.

"I didn't demand sex!" She seemed truly offended. "But if you were more into dating than sex, I wanted to find out right away. Like I told you, I thought you'd only be here on weekends."

"And you wanted to make sure you had someone lined up for the summer, right?"

"No!" Her lips pursed, and her arms crossed over her chest. "I'm not like that."

"Coulda fooled me."

I could see I'd hurt her, but I didn't expect tears to come to her eyes.

"I'm not like that, Hayden. I'm really not."

I wasn't sure what I'd said, other than recounting the way things had actually been between us. But I didn't want to hurt her, even if she probably deserved to be called on her behavior. "I'm sorry," I said. I pulled her close and stroked her back. "It's none of my business how you are with other women. You've been very sweet with me. That's what counts."

She pulled away and stared directly into my eyes. "I'm not the kind of woman who just picks a girl up and tosses her away if she's not right," she said, her earnestness really touching me.

"Okay," I said. "It's okay. Really. I'm sorry I accused you of that."

She kissed me, her tenderness touching my heart. "I'm not like that," she whispered. "Believe me."

I nodded and gave her a kiss in return. "We're good," I said. "Everything's fine."

Holding me for another few seconds, she gazed into my eyes, obviously trying to see if I was being honest. "Okay. Take your shower, and I'll have your coffee ready when you get back."

I smiled at her and walked away. I couldn't understand why she'd reacted so strongly to what was clearly the truth. She'd told me herself that she was only interested in my ass. How much clearer could a woman be?

I went into the bathroom and started to brush my teeth. Then, it hit me. I walked directly into the kitchen, grasped her shoulder, and turned her around. "One of the deckhands told you what Elaine said about you."

She blinked in surprise, looking as if she was going to tell me I was wrong, but then she nodded. "My nephews have been working on the weekends. Nice kids, but they gossip like old ladies."

I put my hand on her waist and looked into her eyes. "Why'd they tell you what she said? They had to know it would hurt your feelings."

With a soft grunt, she shook her head. "You don't know teenaged boys. It wouldn't occur to them that my feelings would be hurt. They wanted to gang up on you two and trip you when you got off the boat. They had all sorts of schemes dreamed up."

I stared deeply into her beautiful eyes. "But you were just hurt."

"Yeah. I was just hurt."

I hugged her, feeling her pulse beat in her neck. "I'm so sorry. I really am."

"It's okay. Besides, Elaine's the one who said it. The guys still wanted to take you out, but they fingered Elaine."

"Maybe you should have let them. Elaine, that is," I said, smiling at her. "She could use a good dousing."

"You're sharing a house with her," she said, looking at me curiously. "Why live with someone you don't like?"

"Long story. After coffee." I hugged her again and left for the bathroom.

❖

When I emerged from my shower, Gina had one of my T-shirts on and was standing in front of the fireplace, supervising the initial burn of a fireplace log.

"You're good at that," I said.

She flinched and twirled to look at me as if she was afraid I was gonna hit her. Odd. Maybe she doesn't like to have someone come up behind her.

"It's not as easy as it looks," she said, her voice sounding a little strained. "You've gotta bend all the way over to hold that match to the paper. Good thing I got the campfire badge in Girl Scouts."

She handed me a cup of coffee, and I took a sip, pleased that she'd remembered I took a little sugar. "Delicious," I said. After another sip, I added, "Really delicious. You make it better than I do."

Her face began to relax, and she looked much more like herself. "Things always taste better when someone else does it," she said. She sat on the sofa and patted the cushion next to her. I joined her, and we sat quietly for a few minutes, drinking our coffee and watching the log burn. "There's something very calming about a fire, isn't there? Especially one that makes real crackling sounds." She gave me a gentle jab with her shoulder. "How much did that fancy log with the sound effects cost?"

"Too much. I have a fireplace at my apartment, but I refuse to pay for the compressed logs. I don't do it often, but when I build a real fire, I've got my night's entertainment."

Gina put her arm around me and asked, "What do you do when you're at home? Tell me about your life."

"'Kay. It's not exciting, but I'll tell you anyway." I slid out of her grip and put my head on the arm of the sofa and my feet in her lap. "My feet are cold. Will you hold them?"

"Glad to."

She wrapped her warm hands around my feet, and I said, "I spend a lot of time at school. I teach either two or three classes a term, and that takes a lot of time."

"Really? Why?"

I blinked at her, but then realized she wasn't familiar with university schedules. "My classes meet two or three times a week, so that takes up a lot of time. Then I have office hours."

"Office hours?"

"Yeah. Times when I'm in my office so that students can come speak to me."

"Do they?"

"What? Speak to me?" She nodded. "Sure. All the time."

"About what?"

I laughed, thinking of the most common reason. "Usually, they're trying to get me to let them turn something in late or take a quiz over or something like that. Most of them just care about getting a good grade."

"What about the other ones? *Are* there other ones?"

"Uh-huh. Not many, though," I had to admit. "I usually have a small group of kids who want to major in Classics or History. They take up a lot of my time. They want to establish a relationship with me so I'll write them a letter of recommendation for grad school."

Gina smirked at me. "Sounds like a lot of ass-kissing."

I wanted to disagree, but I couldn't think of a reasonable argument. "I guess there's a lot of that in academia, but some of the kids really get into the subjects. It's fun to talk to them."

"What classes do you teach?"

"I have six I'm prepared to teach. They vary from term to term. This term, I taught Elementary Latin, The Greek World from Alexander to Augustus, and The History of the Roman Empire."

"Latin? The language?"

"Yeah. You have to know Greek and Latin to teach the Classics."

"That's so cool! Say something in Latin."

"Uhm…tempus fugit."

She brought one of my feet to her mouth and licked the instep, making me giggle like a child.

"Everybody knows that. I want to see if I can use my Italian to understand Latin."

"You speak Italian?"

"Yep."

"Cool. Will you whisper to me in Italian when we make love?" Did I just say that?

She noticed I'd said love. I could tell she noticed, but she didn't let on. "Sure. But you have to talk back in Latin."

"It's a dead language," I said. "It's a little thin for sex talk." She wiped my foot dry with the hem of the T-shirt. "But I'll try," I added. "Did you learn Italian at home?"

"Nah. I had a little in grade school, and I liked it. So, I took it in high school. After four years, I still wasn't anywhere near fluent. High school courses are so lame."

"That's why people go to college," I said, wiggling my toes at her.

"I decided to go to a language school," she said, ignoring my comment. "No grades. I took classes for two years. I'm damned good now. My accent isn't even bad."

"That's very impressive," I said. "Most people don't have that kind of patience."

"I've got enough patience for the neighborhood if I'm interested in something."

"Tell me about your interest in history."

"That started late for me," she said. "I went to Italy about a year or two after I got out of high school. We had some distant cousins I looked up, and they insisted I stay with them." She smiled broadly. "That was cool. One group lived in Florence, and I stayed with them for two weeks. They didn't take me many places, but they made lots of recommendations. And at night, I'd have dinner with them, and we'd talk about the things I'd seen. My Italian was pretty good then, and it got much better in just two weeks."

"That's fascinating. You're so lucky to have relatives to stay with."

"Yep. I've been back every year. I met some cousins in Bologna and a great-aunt in Palermo. So, now I have to visit all of them or they're hurt. Italians." She made a gesture by holding her flat hand in front of her stomach and moving it up and down while making an aggrieved grimace. "Che barba!"

"You're adorable," I said. "Absolutely adorable."

She acted as if I hadn't complimented her, but she smiled at me. "So, one of my cousins is a teacher at their equivalent to a high school. She got me started on my love affair with Italian history."

I hoped I didn't look as amazed as I was. She traveled extensively, was bilingual, and was a remarkably hard worker. How could she afford to travel on her salary? I guess the union must pay well…or her relatives paid for everything when she was there. If she only had to pay for airfare, I guess that wouldn't be too bad. Oops! It was my turn to talk. "What's your favorite period?" I asked, after forcing myself to recall where we'd left off.

"It's hard to vote against the Renaissance," she said thoughtfully. "But lately, I've been reading about the city-states of the eleventh century."

"You're coming my way," I said. "Better watch it, or you'll be studying the guys wearing sandals."

"Oh, I'm interested in it all. I've worked hardest at getting through some of the classics."

"Who've you read?"

She blew out some air, making a funny noise with her lips. "Let's see…Gibbon, of course."

The Decline and Fall of the Roman Empire. That's not for slouches.

"Edith Hamilton. I liked *The Greek Way* best of her stuff."

Gina wasn't blowing smoke. She was reading college-level books.

"I got through one of Werner Jaeger's books, but it took me a while," she said, chuckling.

"Damn, that's deep stuff."

She looked a little hurt, but continued. "I read Theodor Mommsen's *History of Rome.* That guy could write. And I agree with him that the oligarchy was a bad idea. It's a shame he didn't get to write about the empire. I mean, the republic is damned interesting, but I'd love to hear his thoughts on the empire."

I hoped my mouth wasn't open. Gina was reading things graduate students were plodding through. I was stunned, but realized it was my turn to talk. "When someone writes something so fantastic, something that's still entertaining a hundred or two hundred years after they wrote it, it just makes you wish they'd had a couple of extra decades, doesn't it?"

"Sure does," she said, nodding. "I tried Thomas Tyrwhitt, but couldn't get anywhere. Too hard for me."

"He's too hard for anyone," I laughed. "He doesn't have many fans in Classical circles. You didn't miss a thing."

With a luminous smile, she said, "Thanks. I never know if I'm reading the right stuff. I just go on recommendations I read about on the Internet or with writers another author praises. If everyone agrees that someone's great, I'll try to get through it no matter how long it takes me. But like I said, I'm usually just guessing. I could be reading total crap."

I couldn't contain my feelings any longer. "Gina, I can't begin to tell you how impressed I am with what you've read. You've tackled some remarkably difficult stuff. I'm truly in awe of your having gotten into this with no one leading or guiding you."

She looked pleased, but also a little defiant. "If I wanted to be spoon-fed, I could have gone to college. I like to think for myself."

She was a real solipsist about college, but I didn't think I should try to convince her she was wrong. Besides doubting that I could, I didn't want to come off as the expert. "What are you reading now?"

Her eyes lit up with delight. "A really interesting book by Charles Pellegrino."

"I don't think I've heard of him."

She looked to make sure I was being serious. "You've gotta read this, Hayden. It's called *Ghosts of Vesuvius*."

I hoped it wasn't a historical novel. Those things drive me nuts. They're so simplified that their focus is way too weak, and they never get past being topical. "Tell me about it."

"This guy's cool. He's into physics and forensic anthropology, and he's also a vulcanologist. He's one of those big thinkers. Know what I mean?"

"No, not really."

"Sure you do. He's not limited to one thing. He doesn't stick to one field. I'm just at the part where he's talking about 9/11 and how cataclysmic events like that mold societies. It's really making me think," she said, looking very happy. "I read a paragraph or two and have to stop to think about what he said. That's my favorite kind of book."

"Mine, too," I said, sharing her smile.

"Did you read *Pompeii*?"

I swallowed. I had read it, and it *was* interesting—for historical fiction. I'd had to read it because all of my undergrad Classics students were proud of themselves for reading a book that hadn't been assigned in class. It's rare that a Classics geek saw a book in his field on the best-seller list. "Yeah, I did read it," I said, smiling encouragingly, hoping she moved on.

Didn't work. Gina scowled slightly. "Didn't you like it?"

"No, no, it was good. Very entertaining."

Her eyebrows almost touched. "You say that like an insult."

"Well," I ran my hands through my hair, finding the band I usually kept on my wrist. I pulled my hair into a ponytail, trying to think of how to get myself out of this discussion. "I mean it. It was an entertaining book."

"You don't like to be entertained?" One eyebrow rose.

"Of course, I do." No way out. I had to say it. "I prefer books that focus more on scholarship. He did a good job for a journalist. But it was mostly an entertaining story about things I already knew. He had to simplify things to move the story along."

Gina looked at me as if I were a very odd creature. "I wouldn't read a book like that if I was trying to find out every little detail about Pompeii. But for someone like me—someone who wants to know the big picture—it was great."

I put my hand on her arm and stroked it. "There's nothing wrong with that," I said earnestly. "It's just not my thing. I'm not wild about historical fiction."

She looked a little annoyed, but she shrugged and said, "So, what do you read for fun?"

I made a face. "I hate to admit it, but I like mysteries."

"Mysteries? Like murder mysteries?"

"Uh-huh."

"Interesting. What do you learn from a mystery?"

"Nothing, really. It's just a way to relax."

"Isn't reading a historical novel a way to relax? What's so bad about reading something that gives you a little history while it entertains you?"

"Well, when you put it that way…"

"You've got your head up your ass a little bit, Hayden."

"What? *What?*" She was smirking at me. *Smirking!*

She scooted around so she could look me in the eyes. "You're pretty judgmental about this stuff."

"I'm not judgmental. What stuff?"

Gina took my hand and squeezed it. "Don't get upset. I'm not trying to insult you or anything."

"Well, you are."

"I don't mean to." She looked at me with so much caring in those gorgeous eyes that I couldn't be mad. "I just think you have to loosen up a little and not turn your nose up at things that aren't good enough for you."

"I don't—"

"Yeah, you do. You really do."

My lips were pursed so tightly that they started to get numb. Gina was on the verge of laughing, and that only made me angrier. But then I tried to think of what she'd said, and I had to admit she had a point. A small point, but a point nonetheless.

"Okay," I said. "I wouldn't like it if people looked down on my reading mysteries. I know they don't expand my mind, but after reading journals and academic papers and student essays, I want to put my brain on hold and read about your normal, everyday, gruesome murder."

She leaned over and squished her body onto the sofa so she was lying next to me. "Makes sense. I wouldn't want to read Coast Guard regulations when I got home."

"I'm immersed in history," I said. "I teach it all day, and I have to be discerning about the quality of the things I read. There isn't enough time for all of the important books."

She smiled and snuck in a pinch. "I'll let the 'important books' thing slide. But you've got a point. I don't have to think for my job, so I can make my brain work on my free time."

"Oh, don't say that. You have to think to do your job."

"Not really," she said blithely. "I have to pay attention and be aware and remember stuff and be nice and all that, but I don't have to think much. Once you know what you're doing, it's just repetition."

"Do you…like that?"

"It's fine," she said. "I love the water, and I like being around people. I sit up in the pilot's chair and think about stuff. I get a lot of breaks, and I'm always reading something. So, it works out for me. I'm happy."

"You know, that's all that matters. That's truly all that matters." When I said that, I believed it with all my heart.

⬥

I didn't have nearly enough in my kitchen to satisfy Gina's breakfast requirements, so we went to the café. I'd only been there a couple of times, both times with Gina. It was fairly clear that she had much higher standards than I did in terms of what we put into our bodies. I watched what I ate, but I was mostly concerned with calories. I bought a lot of low-calorie frozen dinners and popped one into the microwave at school or home. They were cheap, easy, and fast—terms that Gina didn't seem to view as positives when it came to food.

When we reached the café, her face lit up, and she went up to a very tall black woman, who wore what most would think was an excessive amount of makeup. Actually, her makeup was applied tastefully and professionally, but it was eight o'clock in the morning on a rainy day on a nearly deserted island, and she and the cook were the only people in the place.

Gina hugged the woman, and I realized just how tall Gina's friend was. She had to be six foot five, and her high heels made her several inches taller. Gina looked like a child next to her, and Gina was around five foot ten.

She snapped me out of my musings when she said, "Hayden, meet my old buddy, Ruby."

I extended my hand, but Ruby laughed and pushed my hand away before wrapping me in a full-body hug. I was a little stunned as I moved back and realized that Ruby was a man. She had a prominent Adam's apple, and her makeup failed to conceal a hint of a shadow from her beard.

"I'm pleased to meet you," I said, shifting my gaze from Ruby to Gina.

"I never thought you were gonna show up," Gina said to her friend. "You're usually here by the beginning of May."

"Girl, I had some *big* plans," she said, laughing. Her voice was smooth and modulated like a woman's, but a little too deep to fool many people. "I hardly know how it happened, but I wound up in Paris."

"Paris?" Gina's eyes widened. "What were you doing there?"

"Oh, this and that. This and that." Ruby patted Gina's shoulder and smiled. She was obviously not going to reveal many details, but Gina didn't seem to mind.

"I'm sure you had a great time," Gina said.

"I always do," Ruby agreed, laughing again. Her laugh was so melodious, so pleasantly infectious, that I found myself liking her immediately.

"We need breakfast," Gina said. "Can you make us something wonderful?"

"Sure can." Ruby put a hand on her hip and studied me for a second. "Are you allergic to anything, honey?"

"No, not that I know of."

"Then sit down. We'll fix you up."

Gina took my hand and led me to a table facing the water. It was a nasty day, blustery and chilly, and the waves were crashing against the building with a frightening force. But I'd gotten used to having all of the stores rest on pilings, and I knew we were safe.

"Ruby's something, isn't she?" Gina asked, grinning at me.

"Sure is. Is she transsexual?"

"No." Gina leaned back in her chair, shaking her head. "She's a man most of the year. But she comes out here every summer to 'get her groove on,' as she calls it. I don't know her real name or what she does the rest of the year, but she's Ruby out here."

"Fascinating," I said, as I leaned in to find out more. But Ruby floated through the café on her heels and delivered a platter of something, along with small plates.

"These look great," Gina said. "Blueberry?"

"That's what you like," Ruby said, bending to kiss Gina's head.

"You're my girl," Gina said, giving her one of her mesmerizing smiles.

"I wish," Ruby said theatrically, before walking away shaking her shapely ass.

"What is this?" I asked, poking some small, golden pillows of dough. "And is she straight or gay?"

"Blinis," Gina said. "Blueberry. My favorite."

I took a bite and found myself smiling involuntarily. "These are fabulous."

"Mmm, sure are." Gina looked as happy as she did when we were having sex, and it dawned on me that eating good food and being sexual were nearly on the same plane for her.

She ate another bite, chewing slowly and studiously. "I don't know how she gets them to be so light. I wish she'd tell me her secrets."

"Is she the cook?"

"Not usually. But she's great. She makes more money as a waitress." She took another quick bite and said, "I'm not sure who she dates. I think she's gay, but she flirts with men and women in exactly the same way. I don't try to figure her out. I just flirt back." She smiled, looking impish.

"You're a good flirt, so you shouldn't waste your talents."

"Am I good?" she asked, looking a little shy.

"Oh, yeah. I think you flirt without even knowing it. I think it's part of your personality."

"I'm just friendly," she said. "I like people."

"You're a lot friendlier than I am. I'm not unfriendly…"

"You're reserved," Gina said. "Maybe even shy."

"No, not shy. But I am pretty reserved. Most of the people in my family are."

"Wait'll you meet mine," she said, laughing. "You'll have to fight to get a sentence in."

Chapter Five

L ate that afternoon, Gina proposed we go into town for lunch.
"Oh, I forgot." I ran into my room and returned with a hundred dollars. "You were lucky," I said, tapping her cheeks with the bills. "Twenty-four and a half percent of Americans have college degrees."

"Fuck!" She took the money from me and said, "I didn't think ten percent did. Good thing Dana called the number."

"She was pissed," I said, even though I knew I shouldn't rat on her. "She hates to lose a bet."

"Who doesn't?" She looked at me as if I were mad.

✦

At around two o'clock, we got on the ferry and went to Sayville—the town on the island where the ferry docked. I met Case, and he did seem like a nice kid. Cute, too. Gina saw someone in front of the dock, and she waved at him. "Hey, George!"

He turned and waved back. "What are you doing on land?"

"I wanna go into town. Will you take us to Main Street?"

"Sure. Hop in."

We got into his van, one of the fleet which took passengers from the Long Island Rail Road to the ferry and back. The smell of cigarette smoke was so strong that I was sure he had three or four packs smoldering somewhere. He wasn't smoking at the moment, but his van didn't know it. Besides the lovely aroma, the van rattled so badly that it was hard to hear. Gina sat in front, and she and George chatted about the upcoming season. It was still raining, but not as hard, and when we got into town, George barely had to have his wipers going. Gina insisted on paying for the ride, but he wouldn't take her money. So, as the van pulled away, she threw ten dollars into the open window, laughing when the van nearly rolled onto the sidewalk as George tried to throw it back. "Gotcha!" Gina crowed. "Come get us in two hours!" Still smiling, she took my hand and said, "Sorry I didn't try to include you in the conversation. But I knew you couldn't hear a damned thing back there."

"Oh, that's all right. Besides, I was trying not to breathe. Talking would have made me lose too much air."

"Do you hate cigarettes?"

"Yeah. Very much. You?"

"I used to smoke," she said, looking sad and wistful. "Everybody I knew did. But I stopped the day I found out about my mom's lung cancer. I got so damned mad at cigarettes I couldn't stand to ever buy another one."

"It's funny how you say that. You were mad at cigarettes and not the tobacco manufacturers?"

"Yeah. I know it's dumb to be mad at inanimate objects, but I hate the little fuckers."

I took her hand and squeezed it. "I'm so sorry about your mom."

She looked down and peered at the sidewalk. "I know. Thanks."

"How do you feel about people who sue the tobacco companies?"

Gina shrugged. "You've gotta be nuts to think cigarettes are good for you. Have you ever smoked?"

"No. Never."

"When you first start, your head hurts, your stomach turns, and you get dizzy. You get this heaviness in your lungs that never leaves. If you smoke a lot, you cough up all sorts of crap every morning. Even if everyone in the world told you cigarettes didn't hurt you, you'd know better. So, it doesn't seem fair to get zillions of dollars for your own stupidity. I smoked 'cause I thought it was cool. That's my stupid fault."

"But the tobacco companies target young people with their ads."

"So? It's not the ads, Hayden; it's that your friends smoke. And your friends smoke because it's cool to do something dangerous. If they didn't kill people, kids wouldn't be interested."

"But they're so addictive. People say it's as hard to stop as it is to quit heroin."

She gave me a slow smile. "I have a feeling you and I don't agree on a lot of things. I think you've got a lot of do-gooder liberal in you."

"And what are you? A do-bad conservative?"

"Nope. I'm more of a libertarian. I want to make my own decisions and suffer the consequences. I might not be the smartest woman in the world, but I'm a hell of a lot smarter than any government I've ever encountered."

I put my arm around her waist and squeezed it hard, making her laugh. "Don't make me think on a rainy day. My head's all fuzzy, and you didn't help me clear it by giving it to me good."

"I promised we'd get to that, and I don't make idle promises." She took my hand and guided me along Main Street, jumping over puddles every few feet. "Do you have anything special in mind for lunch? If the van didn't ruin your appetite, that is."

"No, it certainly did not. And I've never been here except to catch the train, so if you know of any good places, lead away."

"I feel like having a hamburger. Is that okay?"

"Sure. I haven't had one since I've been on the island."

We walked for a while, stopping at a diner that looked like a railroad car, one that proved to be authentic. "This place is adorable," I said. "It looks like it's been here forever."

"I think it has."

We sat at a booth, and a waitress came over and mussed Gina's hair. "Where've you been, gorgeous?"

Gina smiled up at the waitress, a woman who looked like she might have been working at the place since it opened. "I've been working. But I'll have some free time starting next week. My cousin's kid is gonna take over for me in the late afternoon. I'll be able to have dinner again." She looked at me and said, "Betty, this is my friend, Hayden."

"Hi, there, Hayden. You been keeping my girl company?"

"Only when she has free time, which isn't very often."

"Gina's always bass-ackwards," Betty said. "Just when everyone else is gettin' busy, she cuts back."

"I like to go against the tide," Gina said. "I hate to be too predictable."

"You're doing great," I said, thinking of how she'd surprised me more each time I saw her.

"I know what Gina wants," Betty said. "She's *very* predictable when it comes to food. What can I get for you, hon?"

"I'll have what Gina's having," I said. "She has very good taste."

Betty smiled at Gina, and she looked so happy that I could feel my heart swell. The waitress didn't take her eyes off Gina. "You look great, gorgeous. Keep doin' whatever it is you're doin'."

When Betty walked away, Gina looked into my eyes and said, "I guess I'd better keep doin' you, huh?"

Even though we were in a busy diner, and her statement seemed offhanded, there was something utterly serious in her gaze. I reached across the table and covered her hand with mine. "I think Betty's a pretty smart cookie."

I'm sure we didn't sit there staring into each other's eyes for long, but we were still doing it when Betty came back with our food. I started, and the waitress chuckled. "Knock it off, lovebirds. Time to eat." I didn't usually blush, but I made an exception. Betty set down one chocolate malt, one cheeseburger, and one order of chili fries. "I thought I'd save you some money. Gina never eats more than half of her food, and since you're a little skinnier than she is, I figured you wouldn't need much more than she does."

"Good thinking," Gina said, unruffled by Betty's comment. "Maybe we'll have room for dessert."

"Keep dreamin'," Betty said, walking away.

Gina started to divide the burger neatly, glancing at me as she worked, "If you need more, don't be afraid to ask. She just hates for me to spend a dime more than I have to."

"I think it's sweet," I said, and I truly did. I loved the fact that people cared enough for Gina to make sure her salary went a long way. I had no idea how much she made, but given her penchant for European travel, she couldn't have much to squander. Gina took a little bit of onion and slathered mustard on her bun. "That's exactly what I like on my cheeseburger," I said, enormously pleased that we shared a taste in condiments. "And if I'd had to order for myself, I would have picked the same thing."

She grinned broadly. "Do you like mustard on your fries?"

"Only on chili fries," I said. "I like ketchup on regular ones."

"Me, too!" She took her spoon and put a dollop of mustard on the plate of fries. "That's weird, huh? I've never met anyone who likes mustard and onion on her burger."

"Only on a cheeseburger," I said. "I like mayonnaise, onion, and tomato on a hamburger."

She made a face. "That's just weird."

"What do you like on a hamburger?"

"Don't like 'em," she said, taking her first bite. "Only like cheeseburgers. And only cheddar cheese. If you're gonna use that cheese-food crap, I'd rather go hungry."

"Narrow-minded," I sniffed. I took a big drink of the malt and rolled my eyes. "Fantastic."

Gesturing at me with a fry, Gina said, "You still haven't told me about your summer project. Spit it out."

"Oh. Right." I took a bite of my half of the burger, chewing quickly so I could reply. "I've got a contract with the University of Chicago Press to write a book. That's how I could afford a share in such a nice house. My advance paid for my share; now I have to write the damned book."

"You're fucking kidding me!"

She said this a little too loudly, but she was smiling so brightly that the other diners didn't seem to mind. "No, I'm serious."

"You're writing a book? A real book?"

"Yeah. This is my second."

"You're shitting me!"

"No, really," I said, enormously pleased that she was so excited about my writing. "I don't really like teaching all that much. I got into academia so that I could write."

"Really?" She looked completely puzzled. "Why not just write?"

"It's not as easy as that. Especially when you want to write about history. University presses are the best places to have a serious history book published. They don't make much money, but they'll take on an important book even if they don't think it'll make them a big profit. The commercial houses won't do that."

"I don't know shit about publishing," she said, "but I'm so excited about this I could scream."

I smiled back at her. Her expression was so infectious that I remembered how I'd felt the day I learned my dissertation was going to be published. "This book is gonna be a little different for me," I said. "It's for the U of C's Worlds of Desire Series on Sexuality, Gender, and Culture."

"I like all of those things," she said, still beaming.

"I read a book a woman wrote on Sappho's popularity in early modern England. I contacted her editor and made a pitch."

"Cool. What's your book about?"

"It doesn't have a title yet, and I'm still working some things out, but it's basically going to be about whether men in classical Rome self-identified as gay or straight."

"Huh?"

"You know about how men would routinely have sex with young boys, right?"

"Sure. Happened all the time."

"Well, the common belief is that they didn't have any concept of being gay. That this was just a right of passage for boys and a way for men to help train boys to be good little warriors. Men loved women, and they loved having sex with women, but they also routinely had these avuncular relationships with boys."

"Avuncular?"

"Like an uncle."

"Right. Right." She nodded. "The Greeks and the Romans both did that."

"Exactly," I said. "Well, I think that some men had to have had a different view of the whole thing. That they loved boys and just had sex with women to fit in. The women were their beards."

"Oh! Like Hadrian and Antinous."

She looked at me with those big brown eyes, like a child waiting for a compliment. I didn't have to fake my enthusiasm. "That's exactly who

I'm going to focus on." Now *I* was excited enough to squeal. It was unthinkable for me to tell a non-academic my idea and have him or her know what the hell I was talking about.

"Fuckin'-a," she said, smiling contentedly. "That's fantastic."

"It's fantastic to be able to talk about this with you," I said. I was bouncing around in my seat as if I had ants in my pants. "I never get to talk to anyone who really cares about this stuff."

She looked puzzled. "Not your friends at school?"

"No, not really," I admitted. "Everyone has his or her own thing. No one ever seems to be truly interested in what you're doing, and no one is ever, *ever* excited about it."

"That sucks," she said. "What kind of friends do you have?"

"Not very good ones, I'm afraid. Everyone wants his or her little piece of the fiefdom. They might want you to do well, but not as well as they do. It's really bad with the other assistant profs."

"Why? Aren't they like you? I'd think you'd band together."

"No, no, that's not how it works. There are only so many tenured professor jobs in the country, and competition for them is really fierce. I tend to hang out with as many full professors as possible 'cause at least they're settled in a job for as long as they want it. The other assistants would cut your throat and step over your body to get a job."

"And you like this?" she asked, her eyes narrowed.

"No, I hate this. I just want to write, but it's hard to get your work noticed if you're not a professor at a good—actually, great—university. I hope that I get tenure and can produce enough that I don't have to teach more than a grad seminar or two. Schools love to have their professors write well-received books."

She looked down, and I could almost see the shame rising up in her. "I don't know what tenure is," she said softly. She met my eyes. "I mean, I know what it is…kinda. But I don't know what you mean when you say you wanna get it."

I reached out and covered her clasped hands with my own. "It's technical, Gina. There's no reason for you to know something like that."

She looked so relieved my heart ached. "Really?"

I had to say yes, even though it had never occurred to me that every adult didn't understand academic tenure. "Sure. It's a teaching thing."

"Oh." She nodded. "Not a regular thing, huh?"

"I think it's only in academia. The deal is that I was hired into a tenure-track position. If I do well, they'll promote me in a year or two. At that point, I have tenure at NYU. They won't be able to fire me after that unless I do something prohibited in the code of conduct."

"Huh?" She said this so loudly that I saw heads turn. "You're in for life?"

"Yeah. That's about right."

"Shit. How can they afford that?"

"They can't afford too much of it, so they have limited tenure-track positions. Getting one in my specialty was ridiculously hard," I admitted, smiling a little at my accomplishment.

"How many are there?"

"At good schools?"

She nodded.

"There might be one in Classics every three to five years."

"What? Shit, Hayden, that's worse than openings for stevedores! You must be fantastic." She grinned. "I knew that already, of course."

"There are a lot more positions in European history, but spots teaching strictly Classics are like hen's teeth."

"Cool. They're special like you. So, if you can just keep your head down, you're set, huh?"

"No, not yet. I haven't had my tenure review. And when I do, I want to have two books out—my dissertation and the one I'm working on now."

She gave me a very concerned look. "And if you don't?"

"I might still get tenure because my dissertation is published, but I want some cushion."

"You'll make it. You'll be Professor Chandler in no time."

"Oh, I'm a long way from making professor. It usually takes seven years, if you're really moving quickly. My next stop is associate professor."

"Fuck. That's a long time."

"And I only have a rough outline of my book finished. I've got to work like mad to finish my first draft this summer."

"Can I read it as you write it?" She looked like a child waiting to open a present. I didn't like to share my work until it was polished, but I didn't have the heart to say no.

"Of course. You can be my editor."

Gina looked like I'd thrown cold water on her. "Oh, no, I don't know how to do anything like that. I can't write. I just like to read."

"That's what I need," I said, surprising myself. "I need to see how a person who loves history reacts to what I've written. I need an avid reader to give me her honest comments."

"I'll do my best," she said, looking as serious as I'd ever seen her.

"In all likelihood, only students and teachers will read my book, but I want to avoid the pompous language that most academics use. I want this to be accessible to bright people who're discerning about what they read—people like you."

The sun started to peek through the heavy cloud cover, and if I didn't know better, I'd swear that the rays came from Gina's smile.

❖

Two hours after he'd dropped us off, George's green van pulled onto Main Street. He was yelling at Gina before we got the door open. "Will you stop paying me? You've given my kids more free ferry rides than I can count. Now, stop it!"

"Okay," Gina said. "You can chauffer Hayden and me around all summer long."

"You didn't give 'em *that* many rides," he said, laughing so hard he had a coughing attack.

We got out at the dock, and Gina took my hand. It seemed such a natural thing for her to do that I moved closer to her automatically. "I don't even know where you live," I said. "I was thinking about how you got home at night, and I realized I didn't know how far you had to go."

"That's why we're dating," Gina said, giving me a sweet smile. "So you can learn all of that stuff about me. I live right here in Sayville."

"Really? Can you walk?"

She looked down at her feet. "Yep."

"That was lame. Really lame. Can you walk to work?"

"I could, but I don't live very close. It'd take me a half hour to walk, and that's not something I want to do at five in the morning."

"Then why didn't we take your car into town? Not that I didn't enjoy the ride in the smoke-mobile."

"It's bad, isn't it?" She laughed. "I like George enough to overlook it, but it's close." She walked over to the dock and slapped her hand on the seat of a bicycle that was locked to a metal support. "I ride my bike."

The bike was of an indeterminate age, color, and make. The entire frame was covered with transparent blue-tinted inner tubes that Gina had used as a protective covering. Either that or the rubber was holding the thing together. "Nice," I said. "Good thing you've got it locked up."

"Yeah," she nodded, not getting the fact that I was teasing her. "I couldn't get another one this nice, and I don't wanna have to walk home late at night."

Damn, is she dirt poor or does she spend all of her money on things I don't see? I could get her a bike in Manhattan for ten bucks if she isn't picky about its provenance. I tucked my arm around hers, and we walked back to the ferry. "I don't know if I like you riding your bike home in the dark. You don't have a light or anything."

"Aw, you care." She gave me a silly grin and said, "There's no traffic around here, especially when I'm going home. I'm careful."

"Be extra careful, okay? I can't afford to lose my editor."

※

We stopped at the store on the way back to the house and bought a few things to make a salad. Just before we left, I spied the basket of bread and grabbed the last loaf of pane pugliese. "Once burned," I said, smiling at Gina.

We walked home along the beach. The sky had cleared, and the sun peeked out here and there through the vast swath of pearl gray clouds. We held hands, and our snaillike pace reflected the fact that that neither of us was in a hurry to go inside.

"Hey, you told me about what you do at school," she said, "but I still don't know what you do for fun."

"I didn't tell you everything I do at school, either," I said. "But for fun…" I thought for a few moments, finally coming up with a lame response. "I do what I've always done. I read, go to movies, visit museums. Nothing exceptional."

"You've always been a little bookworm?"

"Yeah. Always. That's how I got this pale skin. My mother made me take vitamins so I wouldn't get rickets. She did everything she could to get me interested in sports or playing an instrument or anything to get me out of the library, but I'm a natural-born bookworm."

"Not me," she said. "I was outside until my father called me in at night."

"Your father, huh? It's usually the mother who has that task."

She was looking out at the ocean, so I wasn't sure of her expression, but she said, "My mom called the first ten times, but when my dad called, I ran like the devil. You didn't wanna be on his bad side."

I was going to ask what she meant by that, but she interrupted with another question. "Tell me the other things you do at school. It's important to me to know what you do."

"Oh. Okay. Well, I'm on all sorts of committees and panels, and I have to be a student advisor for a bunch of underclassmen. I have a long day. I'm usually at school from eight until four or five."

She smiled indulgently. "Most people work from eight until five. That's not really like pulling a double shift at the steel mill."

I looked at her for a second and realized how lovely it was to talk to someone who didn't think teaching was the equivalent of scaling Everest while wearing flip-flops. I squeezed her arm tightly and rested my head on her shoulder. "You're good for me," I said. "My co-workers act as if they have the weight of the world on their shoulders, and it's easy to fall into that mindset. Sometimes, I feel so damned put upon when a kid shows up at my office right when I'm getting ready to leave."

Gina looked out at the sky, obviously thinking. After a while, she said, "Really sounds like you don't like teaching."

I gave her comment the time I thought it deserved. "I think I'd like it better if I was supposed to like it, you know?"

"No. No clue."

"Well, most of my peers are trying to get ahead. They want to do their research and write journal articles and books. The common belief is that teaching keeps you from doing what you really love. And when you're teaching an elementary history course, that's kinda true."

"Huh." We walked in silence for a while. "If you had the job you wanted, like being a professor, do you think you'd like it more?"

"Hard to say. I guess I would, in a way. Most professors teach the advanced subjects. You know, graduate-level courses. They get to teach the people who're really into the topic. But they must not love it too much, since some of my professors were the worst teachers I've ever had." I laughed, but then realized it wasn't funny. "That's kinda sad, isn't it?"

"Uh-huh." She looked at me briefly, and then her attention settled on the sea again. "Maybe you'd be happier if you did what you enjoyed now, instead of banking on something that won't happen for three or four or five years. There's no guarantee you'll ever get there, ya know. Sure would seem like a waste to wish away the years and then get blown up in a building."

Her tone was so sad that I had a feeling I knew what she was hinting at. "Were you…affected by 9/11?"

"Yeah." She nodded slightly. "I drove a boat from the Battery to Jersey City all that winter. Public transportation was so fucked up that the company moved as many boats as they could downtown."

"I was still in New Hampshire then. I bet it was awful around here."

"Yeah. I was down there about a week after it happened. The dust and the smoke were still so thick your eyes and throat burned. I coughed up gunk every night."

"How did it affect you…mentally?"

"It was scary. For a while, everyone thought they were gonna keep picking off buildings, one by one. Nobody knew how powerful Al-Qaeda was. But people really acted different, too. We were all nicer to each other for a while."

"I read about that," I said. "Seems like things are back to normal now."

She smiled. "Yeah. We're all flipping each other off in traffic again and honking at old ladies to get out of the crosswalks." We walked a little farther, and she said, "I used to think about the people who died. I wondered how many of them would have been doing what they were doing if they knew they would die on a beautiful day in September. I'm sure a lot of them had jobs they hated." She shrugged and suddenly seemed chilled. "I thought about that a lot. It made me reassess how I was living my life."

"What did you discover?"

"That I was happy with my job, but unhappy at home. I tried to fix things, but I couldn't. I broke up with my girlfriend about a year later." She nodded. "Yeah, it was winter, probably January in '03."

"Wow." I stopped abruptly. I don't know why, but I'd never thought of Gina with a girlfriend. I knew she'd had sex partners—probably a lot of them—but I'd never considered that she'd been partnered. "What made you decide to break up?"

"I wasn't getting what I needed from Lacey. My mom had died about a year before 9/11, and Lacey was tired of me being down in the dumps about it. She didn't get it, you know?"

Her eyes were filled with sadness, and I had a feeling that some of it was about her mom and some was about her relationship. "Were you together long?"

"Yeah. Kinda long. Five years."

"Were you in love with her?"

"Of course!" Gina looked annoyed with me. "We'd still be together if I hadn't felt like she deserted me when I needed her."

"Do you mind talking about her? I don't, you know, wanna make you uncomfortable."

We were nearly at my house, and without a word, she took the groceries and ran to the deck that spanned the ocean side of the place. After depositing them, she trotted back to me and walked alongside me for a minute before she said, "I'll talk about her."

She seemed a little distant, so I put my arm around her waist and held onto her until she didn't seem like she wanted to squirm out of my hold.

"You don't have to," I said. "I'm only interested in learning more about you. I don't want to bring up things that make you unhappy."

She nodded, and I could see that she understood. "It's cool. I haven't talked about her in a long time. It just feels odd."

"I mean it. Don't feel like you have to for my benefit."

"It's okay. She was important, so you have to know about her to know more about me."

I smiled up at her. "I want to know a lot more about you."

"Then I'll talk." She took in a deep breath and gazed out at the sea. "Lacey was my first real girlfriend. The one I made my family come to terms with."

"Oh. That's almost always hard."

"Yeah. It was, but they got used to her. She was a lot like us, you know? She was from the Island. Catholic, Italian, all the important things." She smiled at me, and I pinched her waist. "Both sets of parents had to make some adjustments, but they did. Her dad never really liked me, but we still went to her house for dinner and holidays. And she came to my house, too. My family...well, my mom was nicer to her than hers was to me, but that was cool."

"Really? You didn't mind?"

She looked at me, obviously thinking. "No, not much. She was what was important. Not her family."

"That's very mature. I don't think I'd be cool about that."

"You never know how you'll feel about things. In my case, Lacey was just what I wanted. She was beautiful, calm, funny, liked most of the things I liked, and very sexy." Gina smiled her sexy smile, and I could see in her eyes how attracted she'd been to Lacey.

"Sounds like you were a good pair."

"We were. We had a nice, stable relationship. She had a good job, and she was home most days by the time I got home. I'd cook, and she'd tell me about stuff." Gina gave me a slight smile. "She liked to talk more than I do."

I bumped her with my hip. "You talk a lot about things you like. You're just not a small talker."

"True. Lacey was. She'd sit there and drink a glass of wine while she entertained me with tiny little things about her day. It was always…comforting." She nodded thoughtfully. "Yeah. It was comforting."

"But it didn't last."

"No. She was very supportive when my mom was sick and real good for months after she died. But then, I guess she got tired of it."

"Of you or of your grief?"

"Same thing," Gina said. Her face had grown cold, and her expression was stone like. "She wanted me to get over it. But I couldn't. So, I broke up with her."

"Just like that?" As soon as I'd said it, I knew I'd shown my amazement too obviously. But I was amazed. Why would you break up with a long-time lover for letting you down in one area?

"Yeah. Just like that." She shrugged my arm off and moved away from me.

I reached for her, grasping the fabric of her jacket. "I didn't mean for that to sound as if I was judging you."

"Weren't you?" Her eyes seemed black and hard.

"I wasn't trying to. I was just surprised. You sound like you really loved her."

"I did," she said, icily.

"I guess I'm surprised that you didn't hang in there and try to make her understand what you needed. You don't seem like the kind of woman to give up easily."

Her body grew less rigid, and I could tell she wasn't as angry as she'd been just a minute before. "I don't usually. But it'd been a hard year. Real hard. Like I said, she was great for a few months, but then she'd come home and kinda sigh if I looked down. After a while, I didn't feel like we were sharing the pain. It was mine, and she was sick of it."

"Aw, Gina, that must have been awful for you."

Her lips were firmly pressed together, and she looked as if she might cry. "I tried like hell to get over how I felt, but I couldn't, and having Lacey not seem to understand just made it worse."

"Had she ever lost anyone?"

She thought for a moment and then said, "No, all of her grandparents were still alive. Probably still are." She gave me a half-smile. "She had some great genes. Her mother looked about thirty. Lacey's probably gonna see a hundred and ten."

"It's hard for some people to understand grief if they've never lost anyone."

"Yeah, I know, but it was more than that. She didn't seem to want to work to meet me in the middle. I decided that if I couldn't trust Lacey when I really needed her, I'd never be able to trust her." She put her hands in her pockets, and we walked in silence for a while. "I might be more patient now. Sometimes, I think I should have hung in there and given her more of a chance. But I was too hurt."

"Did you try therapy?"

Her head snapped back as if she'd been slapped. "I wasn't nuts!"

I grasped her arm and hugged it to myself. "I didn't mean anything of the sort. But a lot of couples get through hard times by going into therapy."

"Not me," she said, leaving no room for argument.

"I can understand," I said. "I really can." I took her hand and was pleased that she didn't pull back. "It takes a lot of trust to love someone. If you don't feel that trust, it can be hard to stay."

"Yeah. That was it. Not enough trust."

"Do you ever see her?" For some reason, I hoped she didn't.

"No. I mean, I've seen her at different places. We kinda hang in the same circles. But I haven't spoken to her in about two…two and a half years. For about six months, she tried to get me to come back, but I just couldn't…or wouldn't. I still don't know which." She let out a breath and stood tall. "She's with someone now. They're living in the apartment that Lacey and I had."

"Is that when you got your own place?"

"No. I went to Italy for a long time after we broke up. Stayed until I had to come back for the spring season. That's when I decided I couldn't live with my father anymore. Once you've left the house, you can never go back."

"Did he want you to stay at home?"

She gave me one of her frequent looks. It was the one that wondered if I was kidding and, if not, what was wrong with me. "Of course. He's my father. He's still not happy that I have my own place. It was one thing to move in with Lacey, but living alone showed that I didn't want to live with him. "

"Ouch. That must have hurt."

"It did. But I learned that I can't make my family happy at my expense. It'd be different if he needed me, but he just wants me there because it feels familiar. But I'm never gonna be able to take my mom's place. I keep hoping that he'll start dating, but that hasn't happened yet."

"Mmm. My dad hasn't dated either. It's been fourteen years."

"Maybe they can hang out," she said, smiling at me with that crooked grin.

"Does your dad like to play strategy games on the Internet?"

"No. He doesn't have a computer at home, and he isn't crazy about the one at his office."

"Then they wouldn't have a thing in common."

<hr />

We hadn't been in the house for ten minutes when my sister called. Damn! She always called when I didn't have time to listen to her. Okay, it's possible that I'll never have enough time to listen to all of her complaints. "Hi, Karen," I said, hoping I didn't sound annoyed.

"I wanted to see when you'd be here this weekend."

"This weekend?"

"Hayden!" I knew I was in trouble when it sounded like my name had six y's.

"Oh, Roger's party. I...uhm...I'm not sure I can make it."

"You have to. You absolutely have to."

"Why? You can represent both of us."

"I can't," she said, her stoic, martyr-like sigh dragging on. "It would hurt Dad too much."

"Huh? How would he even know you went?"

"It's in the papers, Hayden," she said, as though our father read the society pages of the *Philadelphia Enquirer*.

"And you told him."

Now she sounded pissed. "I knew he'd see it in the paper, and I thought he should hear it from me."

"What did he say?" I asked, knowing that he had probably just shrugged his shoulders.

"He acted like he wasn't hurt, but I know him better than that."

"Oh, Karen," I said, before I could stop myself. "He wasn't hurt. He doesn't care. He doesn't care about anything. Go to the damned party and leave Dad alone."

"Hayden!" she snapped. "Don't even think about telling me what Dad needs. I'm the one who's here for him."

Gina was right next to me, not looking at me, but tenderly stroking my back, which was coiled with tension. "Fine," I said, sighing. "What do you want me to do?"

"I want you to go to the party. Mom won't like it if neither of us shows up. Besides, Roger's in your line of work, and you can meet some important people."

"But it's an all-day trip for me. It'll take me five hours to get there, and I don't want to stay overnight."

"I know it's asking a *tremendous* amount from you, but I can't do everything around here. We have two parents, and they each need us this weekend."

Something caught my eye, and I turned to see a note Gina had written. "I can drive you," it said. Uh-oh. Now I had to take Gina. There was no way to turn down a ride after making such a big deal about getting there.

"Okay," I said to Karen. "I'll call Mom and tell her I'll be there."

"You have to stop and see Dad," she said. "But don't let him know you went to Roger's party."

"No deal," I said. "I'm going to bring a date, and I'm not going to tell Dad we got all dressed up and drove to Philly just to drop by and say hi."

"A date? You're dating someone?"

"Yes," I said, smiling at Gina's innocent expression. "I'm dating someone very special."

After we'd made what were probably going to be our very ill-fated plans, I started to make dinner. Gina was in my room, going through the two boxes of books I'd brought to help with my own book. She called out questions every few minutes, but then she fell quiet, and I didn't hear a peep out of her for twenty minutes.

She made me jump when she put her hands on my hips. I'd had the water running and hadn't heard her come into the kitchen. "Hi," she said. Her hands slid around my waist, and she held me loosely.

"Hi. You scared me. I didn't hear you coming."

"I'm pretty quiet. Like a cat."

I glanced at her and said, "You are a little cat-like. Very surefooted, quiet, a little picky."

"Picky?"

"Hey, who had to walk to the store to get bread the other night? You're very particular about what you eat."

"Why wouldn't I be?"

One hand left my waist and delicately pulled my hair from my neck. Then I felt her mouth touch my skin. It felt positively divine to have her warm, moist lips touching me so gently. Her lips moved over my neck as if they were gliding—barely touching, but smoothly progressing.

Her breath was warm as well, and she was so close to me that I could hear as well as feel her breathing. Her breasts rose and fell against my back, and I had to put my hands on the counter to steady myself.

I'd been wanting her since I'd opened my eyes that morning and hadn't, despite my threat, availed myself of the shower massage. It couldn't hold a candle to Gina, and there was something fiendishly satisfying about denying myself, especially when I knew I'd get to have her eventually. Her kisses reminded me of how much I wanted her and how inconsequential dinner seemed.

I sighed and rolled my head back and forth, making sure she kissed every part of my always sensitive neck. She chuckled at my antics, but didn't stop slathering me with her tender touch.

Unaware that I'd moved, I felt her press her hips against my ass. Realizing that she was responding to me, I tried to clear my head enough to get a grasp on what my body was doing.

I was holding on to the counter, my fingers grasping the stainless steel sink, while I pushed against Gina, swaying my hips into her pelvis. I was moaning just enough to be heard, and she increased the force, but not the pace, of her kisses. Arching my back, I reached behind her and threaded my fingers into her hair while she sucked and bit my sensitized skin. We moved against each other like twined cobras, our sensual dance driving our desire.

Panting, she palmed my breast and then compressed it, just like she'd done the first night. I pressed my ass hard against her, shivering when she squeezed me roughly. Her hand slid down between my legs, and she pressed her fingers right onto my clit, making me purr. She alternated pressure from one finger to the next, playing me like a keyboard.

It sounds funny, but I like to have her touch me with my clothes on. She's rougher and more aggressive, which turns me on more than I ever would have imagined. She purposefully ran a finger along the seam of my pants, pressing hard. It felt so damned good that I found myself thrusting against her hand, begging her to fuck me through my clothes.

Unable to resist for another moment, I twisted in her embrace, and we began to kiss. My head was swirling in the dizzying haze of lust that Gina made me feel every time she made love to me. My only desire was to consume her. To take her into my body in ways I didn't even understand. But it was a need that overwhelmed me.

As usual, Gina sensed my loss of control. She grasped me by my waistband and hefted me onto the counter. *Ah…* Wrapping my legs around her made everything feel just fine. I could move my hips just enough to create a nice amount of friction against my cunt, and holding her so tightly satisfied that indescribable urge to *have* her.

Now she kissed me hard while holding me just as fiercely. Things were getting out of control—fast—and I had a feeling I was going to lose my khakis and panties and find myself bare-assed on the kitchen counter. I didn't mind a bit, even though I knew the counter was cold.

But instead of stripping me, Gina's touch grew lighter and slower. She gently but clearly turned my thermostat down until I wasn't thrusting against her like a common strumpet.

I was panting for air, and she was hot and clammy. She leaned against me and rested her head against mine. Her brow was damp, and she struggled to breathe.

"If you've changed your mind, I'll strangle you," I gasped.

"No," she said, chuckling softly. "I haven't changed my mind. I just want to slow down a little. Make it last."

"Let's hurry up and then do it again," I suggested, subtly pressing her hand against the seam of my pants and growling.

She lifted her head and gazed into my eyes. Then she straightened my hair and drew her thumb across the bead of sweat at my hairline. "Let's slow down and pay attention."

"Huh? Every nerve I have is paying attention."

Tenderly stroking my cheek, she kissed my forehead again and again. "I want to pay attention up here." She touched my temple. "Not just with our bodies."

I looked into her eyes and knew that I'd agree to anything she wanted. Anything at all.

❖

Gina's arm was around me as we walked into my bedroom. She was only partially holding me up. No, I didn't have any patience at all when I was turned on, but it had only recently been brought to my attention how much I liked sex. Don't get me wrong. I'd always *liked* it, but with Gina, it was a need. A need that didn't seem to have an end. And when she got me hot, as she could so easily do, I lost all sense of perspective. I acted like a mass of twitching nerve endings with no off switch.

That's why I agreed with her idea of slowing down and being a little more deliberate. If fast, hard sex was fun, slow, hard sex should be fantastic!

I was standing in front of Gina, dreaming about the moment she'd toss me to the bed and we'd catch fire, when she put her hands on my hips and pulled me close. For at least a minute, she merely looked at me while running her fingers through my hair. It was a delightful head massage, and I slowly noticed how sensitized my scalp was. All of my nerves seemed to pay attention to her touch, and I found myself swaying under her gentle stroking.

Our eyes never parted, and my desire for her grew, but I didn't feel it in my groin. This time, I felt it in my heart. I closed my eyes, the emotion of the moment suddenly too powerful for me. Her hands left my head, and I felt her breath on my cheek. Then her arms begin to slide around me. Her lips touched mine as her arms encircled me, holding me tenderly.

We kissed gently, softly. Her lips were so incredibly soft and welcoming that I nearly forgot about my pulsing clit. Almost. Amazingly, Gina's kisses eventually led me to focus my attention on nothing but her mouth. And what a lovely mouth she had. I heard her sigh as she continued to kiss me, and I could deeply feel the connection that had grown between us in the past few weeks. I knew her hands and her face and her body. I'd touched every part of her, and she'd touched me—body and soul. That realization nearly made me cry, and I pulled away from her mouth and buried my face in her shoulder while holding her tightly.

We rocked together, slowly swaying to some beat that we both seemed to feel. Then she lifted my chin, and she kissed me again, pausing to look into my eyes after each delicate kiss. We were fully clothed, but I felt completely naked, laid bare to her. My defenses were destroyed. I gave her full access to everything I had, and I could see that she was entirely open to me.

Her fingers started to work the buttons of my shirt, and when she'd removed it, she stood still and looked at me encouragingly. I copied her, taking her shirt off and letting my hands wander across her shoulders, her chest, her breasts.

We undressed each other carefully, not in a mad rush as usual. And somehow, it was so much more intimate to have her looking at me shyly, standing there in her bra and panties, even though I'd seen her naked many times.

When the last of our garments fell to the floor, Gina pulled the covers back, and we got into bed. For a few moments, we knelt facing each other, kissing and being kissed. Then we lay down and made love. There were no other words for what we did that night. We made love.

Chapter Six

I was lying in her arms, listening to her heart beat slowly and steadily. It was hard—very hard to stay awake—but I was trying to think. I was clearly falling in love with Gina, and given how she'd treated me tonight, she was falling for me, too. But this wasn't supposed to happen. It couldn't happen. Not for me, anyway. I had too many things going on. Okay, I had one thing going on—my career.

I knew Gina wouldn't understand. I could barely explain it and not think I was a total asshole. But I *wasn't* an asshole. I really wasn't. I just understood how my life was and how it would be in the future. I've worked since I was six years old to succeed at my career. My whole life has been learning and taking the right classes and going to the right schools and finding the right mentors to get me where I was. And I couldn't think of stopping until I'd gotten to where all of my work would lead me. I might never make it to Harvard or Yale or Princeton, but I would make full professor. And I'd make it at a damned good school.

Gina's warm body shifted, and I could feel the muscles in her chest where my hand rested. She was so absolutely beautiful in every way, but she would never fit in. She'd never *want* to fit in as the spouse of an academician.

I hadn't known her long, but I knew she would never be a top-notch ass-kisser. And if an assistant professor could have only one skill, she'd better make sure it was ass-kissing. And having a spouse who wouldn't at least try to impress the members of the department and the deans and the provosts and the innumerable other wonks at a university would be a career killer.

But even if she wanted to be my spouse and go to all of the stupid events I had to attend, we still had logistical problems. I supposed she could move to the city and I could support her, but I couldn't imagine her letting me. And having my lover two hours away by train wasn't something I could live with. Maybe she could get a job in the city, but what could she do? I guessed she could drive—I mean, pilot—a ferry, but she sure seemed to hate Manhattan.

I knew that I had to talk to Gina about all of this, but I couldn't do it right then. What we'd shared was too precious to ruin. I just wanted to let her hold me until we fell asleep. Maybe I'd think of some alternative in the morning. Maybe there was a middle ground where we could both get what we needed.

She shifted again and wrapped her arms around me. With a smooth hip thrust, I was on top of her. "Thought you'd fallen asleep," I said. Then I kissed her on the tip of the nose.

"Gotta go home."

"What?"

"I've gotta go home. Case can probably handle it, but I'd feel better if I was there when he put the boat to bed. I hate to throw too much responsibility on him until I'm sure he's ready."

"Oh, Gina, do you really have to go?"

She could see how disappointed I was, and her smile was filled with empathy. "I don't want to. But yeah, I have to."

I rolled off and lay on my side, watching her get up and glide into the bathroom. She *was* like a cat. Like a big, beautiful Abyssinian—all bones and muscle and motion. I've always loved cats. But I've never had one.

On Friday afternoon, I got on the ferry, feeling a little odd as the only person relatively dressed up. I hadn't brought much with me to the island, and to be honest, I didn't own much in the way of dressy clothes. I didn't need them for work, and I didn't go many places that required me to make a statement.

Gina had grilled me about the party: who would be there, what everyone would wear, what we'd eat, who she should and shouldn't interact with, even who she should tip. She asked more questions than a freshman who was pulling an "F" would ask a week before the final exam.

I was a bit worried that she didn't have anything dressy, but she laughed rather lustily when I expressed my concern. That puzzled me, but as was often the case, I couldn't get any more info out of her. She wasn't secretive, but she didn't just throw information at me. I got the impression that she didn't answer questions she found silly. And for some reason, many of my questions seemed to strike her as silly.

She was waiting for me at the dock. At least, I was fairly sure that the gorgeous creature standing there was Gina. I was blinking in surprise when she extended her hand to lead me off the boat. I knew she was pretty, but this was ridiculous!

"I don't have words for how wonderful you look," I said, suddenly feeling as if my outfit were only appropriate for a dogfight.

"You look lovely," she said, kissing me on the cheek.

"You smell fantastic," I said, still a little dazed.

"Thanks."

She took my hand and led me to a car...or maybe a truck. It was certainly odd-looking and impossible to miss. It was yellow—very yellow. As we came nearer, I saw the logo of the ferry company on the rear...whatever you call the back of a truck, if it was a truck. Gina opened the passenger door, and I slid in. She closed the door and walked around the back, giving me enough time to decide it was a truck. There were only two seats, and whatever was behind me had to be for cargo. Gina got in and smiled at me, nearly making me forget to ask about our ride.

"Does this belong to the ferry company?" I asked, trying to resist my desire to go to her apartment and chew the clothes off her.

"Yeah. It's one of the trucks."

I giggled. "I wasn't sure it *was* a truck. I've never seen anything like it."

"There aren't many of them," she said. "But it's a Chevy. Do you like it?"

"Sure. It's awfully bright, but I'm pretty conservative when it comes to color." I scooted around a little on the black, leather seat. "It's certainly comfortable."

"Yeah, it is. Runs like a bat out of hell, too," she said, grinning wickedly. "Wanna see?"

"No!" I put my hand on her arm. "I don't want you to get into trouble."

She pulled away from the parking area, giving me the smile she often used when she was trying not to laugh at me. "I won't get into trouble."

"Gina, we're not on Fire Island. This is a real city."

"Not really. Sayville is a hamlet of Islip."

"Islip? I've never heard of it."

"Well, you're in it…kinda," she said, smiling that "I wanna laugh at you" smile again.

"I don't want the Islip police to haul you away when you look so wonderful."

"There aren't any Islip police," she said. "Suffolk County police at this end of the county. The east enders have police in their towns. They always have to be special." She wrinkled up her adorable nose, making me laugh.

"I never know what in the hell you're talking about," I said. "Good thing I'm not gonna be tested."

"Speaking of tests, will I pass tonight?"

"Pass…oh, you mean with the Penn crowd?"

She nodded, looking a little unsure of herself.

"God, yes. You'll look better than any woman there."

Her eyes grew wide. "Then I should go change. I don't wanna stand out."

"Gina," I said, lightly rubbing her arm. "You can't help standing out. You're so pretty every man or partially bisexual woman will be drooling over you."

"I'm being serious, Hayden," she said, looking decidedly so. "I want to fit in."

"Well…" I looked her over, doing my best to give her an objective assessment. "Here's the problem. Women in academia aren't known for fashion."

"But I'm not wearing anything very fashionable," she said, sounding defensive. "I made sure to wear something ordinary."

I looked up and down her lovely body, shaking my head. "The problem isn't the clothes, Gina; it's the person in them. You don't look ordinary in anything."

She gave me a reluctant smile, but didn't let go. "Should I change?"

"No, no, really. You're wearing a simple dress. What would you change into?"

"I don't know. I could wear slacks like you."

"No, you look wonderful. And your dress couldn't be simpler. It's that you look so elegant in it. And everything…matches."

Now her smile was warm and full. "It's supposed to."

"Yeah, I know, but my mom has a nice, black purse that she carries whenever she goes out. She doesn't buy a new purse to match new clothes. Wouldn't occur to her."

"Oh." She looked a little discomfited, but then she nodded. "I can understand not wanting to spend a lot of money on clothes and things. I just like to shop."

"That makes one of us." I put my hand on her thigh, slipping under the hem of the simple, brown shift that perfectly matched her brown eyes. "What's this?" I asked, investigating with my fingers.

"Stockings," she said, slapping my hand away. "We've got a long drive ahead of us. If your hand goes much higher…"

"But I think you might have on some very sexy underwear. I can't ignore such evidence."

"You're gonna have to. But you can do whatever you want when we get home."

"Let's get there, have a drink, kiss everyone we need to kiss, shake a few hands, and then ditch."

"Sounds good to me. But you're the only person I need to kiss."

Damn, how did I get such a sweet woman to look at me like that?

❖

As we sat in traffic, I spent much of my time just staring at Gina. She'd obviously gone to a lot of trouble to look good, and I hoped she hadn't had to buy too many things just for this event. Her earrings were clear, round, pink stones—probably crystal or sapphire. They looked fantastic against her dark skin, and I began to reassess my dislike of all things pink. The chunky bracelet of large, alternating pink and chocolate beads looked nice, too. I snuck another look at her shoes, noting they were also chocolate, but they had a small, pink leather stripe around the top. I guess where you put your foot in is the top. Why does everything about Gina make me feel as if I have a small vocabulary?

I put my hand on her neck, gently touching her hair, which was swept up in some style I couldn't name, but definitely liked. It made her neck look so kissable.

"Nope," she said, very businesslike. She took my hand and put it on her knee. "That's all I'm giving you. You're gonna have to wait to play with anything else."

"Damn, you're tough."

"Only when I have to be," she said, smiling the smile that melted my heart.

❖

We parked at my mother's house just to avoid having to find a spot on campus. Gina got out and twisted her body a little, obviously trying to loosen up from the long drive. "This is it?" she asked, squinting a little as she gazed at the place.

"Yeah. She and Roger have lived here for about eight years."

"Wow. It looks big. And old."

"Yeah, it is. Would you like to see it?"

"Sure." She perked up noticeably. "I love houses."

"Well, I'm sure they're at the event, and I don't have a key, but I'll take you on a tour afterwards if you want."

She gave me a funny look. "You don't have a key to your mom's house?"

"No. She's never offered, and I've never had a reason to need one." I took her hand, and we started to walk. "Is that odd?"

"It would be in my family. We're all up in each other's business," she said, chuckling.

"We like to keep our distance."

She squeezed my hand. "You probably get fewer colds that way."

❖

The event was being held at the University Club, a place I'd only been to once or twice when Roger took my mother and me to lunch there. But I'd been hanging around Penn since I was old enough to sneak into a library. I knew the place backwards and forwards, and this seemed to impress Gina.

"You're like a little walking map. Are you sure you didn't go to school here?" She took a long look around as we walked, looking at the summer flowers just starting to bloom. "Why didn't you go here?"

"I didn't even apply here. I wanted to get away from home, I guess."

"I can understand that. I wanted to get away once I was out of high school."

"That's pretty common. I think it's good to have to make decisions on your own. Being away at school helps force you to do that."

"So does going to work," she said, giving me a wink.

That comment made me ask her a question I'd been dreading, but still thought was wise to ask. "Just about everyone you meet will ask what you do for a living." I paused, watching her face fail to react in any way. "Is that okay?"

She nodded. "I expected that. I have an answer. You don't have to worry that I'll embarrass you."

I stopped and reached for her, searching her eyes while I held her. "Don't be ridiculous. I just wanted to warn you in case anyone acted strangely when you tell them you actually work for a living."

Her body was pliant, and she was giving me a faint smile. "No problem. I'm cool."

I nodded to the attendant who opened the door for us to the Inn at Penn, which housed the University Club. I grasped Gina's hand, hoping she could maintain her cool with what I knew would be a bunch of stuffy academics.

❖

The Harrison Room, which was the largest space for private events and also held the daily luncheon buffet, was decked out as merrily as a lunchroom can be. I was disappointed that the university hadn't paid to use one of the hotel's special event rooms, but I knew every departmental budget was tight when it came to entertaining, so I tried to be happy they'd had the party at all.

I stood near the entrance to the room, trying not to look as nervous as I was. Strangely, Gina seemed cool and confident, which made no sense at all. This was my milieu, while she was still shaky on the difference between a university and a college. After scanning the room, I spotted Roger, his head a bit higher than the professor-types who surrounded him. My mother was off to his left, looking politely bored by another fellow, who was gesticulating with what had to be an empty pipe since smoking wasn't allowed in the building.

Gina squeezed my hand and said, "There's your mom."

Startled, I looked at her. "How'd you know?"

"Black purse," she said, chuckling softly. My mother was wearing what was probably a new cream-colored suit with a slightly darker shell under the jacket. Her shoes matched her suit rather well, but as predicted, she carried a black purse that I now realized didn't match at all.

"Really?" I searched her eyes and detected a little glint she got when she teased me.

"No, Hayden. She looks just like you."

"Oh. Right. I guess she does." I looked at my mother in a way I rarely did. She was a pleasant-looking woman, but she definitely looked her age or maybe even older. I realized that part of it was her clothing. My mom wasn't sixty yet, but she looked just the same as some of the wives of the retired faculty members I recognized—people who had to be in their eighties.

Her haircut was annoyingly similar to mine, as was her hair color. But hers had begun to gray, and she'd recently taken to dying it herself, keeping the same uninspired color we shared. I cast a quick look at Gina and saw a chasm between her style and mine, and I wished we hadn't come at all. But my mother caught my eye just as I was planning our escape, and I walked over to her, Gina at my side.

"Here's my daughter," she said to the man with whom she was talking. "Hayden, this is Professor Geddes, one of Roger's mentors."

"Nice to meet you," I said, extending my hand. His skin was as white as parchment, his hand soft as a baby's.

"NYU, eh?" he said loudly. "History?"

"Uhm, yes, I'm in the history department, but I teach Classics."

"They don't have a Classics department."

"I know," I said, trying to smile. "Mom, Professor Geddes, this is my friend, Gina Scognamiglio."

"Scone-ya what?" the charming old professor demanded.

"Scognamiglio," Gina said, taking the old man's hand and leaning over so she was right in his line of sight. "It's Italian."

He rocked back on his heels after her image filled his rheumy eyes, and he smiled goofily. "Lovely name. Lovely. Lovely."

I had a feeling he wasn't talking about her name, but I was pleased he was distracted. I hugged my mother and smoothly guided her away from the professor. "How's it going?" I asked, knowing she hated to be the focus of attention.

"Good. I'm so glad you came, honey. You aren't going to leave your friend with that old coot, are you?"

I snuck a quick glance at Gina, seeing that an elderly woman was approaching, probably the professor's wife. "She'll be over as soon as someone claims him."

My mother laughed. "He's tried to cheat on his wife for the last thirty years, but no one will have him."

"Hard to imagine why not," I said, laughing. Gina strode over to us, standing by my side.

"It's good to meet you," Gina said, and I realized I hadn't introduced my mother properly.

"I'm sorry I did such a poor job of introducing you two, but the professor distracted me. Gina, this is my mom, Carol Wright."

"Call me Carol," my mom said.

"Call me Gina." They shook, and I could almost see my mother wondering who this lovely creature was.

"Do you teach at NYU?" my mother asked.

"No, I'm not in academia. Hayden and I met on Fire Island. Just a few weeks ago."

"Oh, how nice. I've never been there. Is it nice?"

"It's wonderful," Gina said, smiling that smile that neither man nor beast could resist. "It's much nicer now that Hayden's there, of course. She's improved the island significantly."

My mom and I both laughed at Gina's obvious exaggeration. "As Gina said, we've only known each other a few weeks, but I'd have been commuting from there if I'd known that's where Gina was hiding." What? Who was that? I never talked like that!

I could tell Gina and I puzzled my mom, but she was too polished to show it. "Let's go tear Roger away. He's going to be delighted you were able to come."

"I wouldn't have missed this," I said, lying just a little. "Receiving a lifetime achievement award from the Society for American Archaeologists is a major coup." I didn't know beans about the Society for American Archaeologists, but my mother didn't need to know that.

✦

After the reception, Gina and I walked back to my mother's house. "Which one of us is in academia?" I asked, holding her arm tightly to my body.

"That's you," she said, nudging me with her shoulder.

"No one would have believed it, except for the fact that you look 300 percent better than anyone else. Most archaeologists don't spend a lot of time on their appearance."

"I noticed," she said, giggling. "There was more dandruff on more old, blue blazers than I could believe. Do they make those guys wear blazers? Is it some kinda uniform?"

"Kinda," I said. "It's part of the preppy uniform. It's not cool to look like you spend money on clothes or jewelry or cars or things like that. Everything should be kinda shabby, but of good quality. There's a certain penurious quality to my clan."

"So, you try to look like you have money by not spending it, huh?"

"Yeah. That's about right."

"Whew. You'd never fit into my family. We believe if you've got it, shove it in everyone's face."

⟡

Gina seemed remarkably comfortable around my mother and Roger. Roger had taken us on a lengthy tour of some of the treasures he'd acquired through the years. I'd seen all of his things, but he loved his field so much that I didn't mind hearing about the digs he'd led in the Sichuan province and the discoveries he'd made. I ruminated that he'd probably been a good teacher, but I knew he rarely saw the inside of a classroom anymore.

We sat in the stuffy living room on the furniture I knew was at least fifty years old, discussing the evening. "I thought it went spectacularly well," Roger said. I noticed his blueblood, slightly nasal delivery, wondering why it had never sounded so odd to me.

"It was a lovely party," Gina said. She sipped brandy from a delicate, cut-crystal glass that glittered in the low lamplight. "I've never been to Philadelphia, so this entire day has been a revelation for me."

"Never?" Roger asked, cocking his head. "You've never seen Constitution Hall or the Liberty Bell?"

"No, and I don't think we'll get a chance to do that unless they're open all night."

"Why don't you two stay over?" my mother asked. "I hate to think of you driving all that way."

"It's not that late," Gina said. She looked at her watch, and I noted the band was a nice, dark brown that matched her outfit. "We can be home by one o'clock if we leave now."

"Are you sure?" Roger asked. "We have plenty of rooms upstairs."

"I need to be home in the morning," Gina said. "Hayden?"

"I need to go, too. I've got to work on my book."

Roger stood and took my hand, helping me to my feet. "We're proud of you, Hayden," he said, his delivery stentorian. "It's quite an accomplishment for someone your age to have her second book underway."

"Thanks," I said, smiling at him.

My mom stood and hugged me and then shook Gina's hand. "Thank you so much for coming, girls. It meant a lot to both of us that you went to such great lengths to attend."

"It was my pleasure," Gina said. "I'd like to come again and see some of the sights."

"You're always welcome," my mom said.

Roger shook Gina's hand and gave me one of his stilted hugs. They walked us to the front door and said goodbye once again. We walked to the truck hand in hand. Gina let me in, politely closing the door once I was seated. She got in and grinned at me. "How'd I do?"

"Gina Scognamiglio, if I didn't know better, I would have guessed you spent all of your spare time chatting with boring, old archaeology professors. You have remarkable social graces."

"Nah," she said, looking very pleased with herself. "I'm just a good bullshitter. I bent Ruby's ear for a couple of hours during my breaks this week. She worked at a college for a while, and she knows all about 'em. She gave me lots of tips."

I stared at her, charmed. "You did research?"

"Sure. I didn't want to embarrass you."

"Gina," I said, gazing at her beautiful profile, "I could never be embarrassed by you." I meant that with every bit of my soul. I really did.

❖

As predicted, we reached Sayville just after midnight. "Wanna wait for the ferry or stay here?"

"Do these seats recline any further?" I asked, teasingly.

"You could stay at my place if you want."

Something about the way she said that seemed tentative. "Do you have to work in the morning?"

"Yeah."

"Then you go home, and I'll take the ferry. I don't want you to have to get up even earlier to rush back here."

She leaned over and kissed me, smelling of a sensual perfume and aged brandy. "I thought you wanted to see my underwear."

"Oh, I do. But I like you enough to wait until tomorrow."

"You mean later today."

"Right." I kissed her, lingering for a long while, trying to get more of her scent imprinted on my memory. "As soon as possible later today." I put my hand on her thigh and let it slip under her hem. My questing fingers found stockings and the undoubtedly mouthwatering garter belt that held them up. "Not fair," I moaned. "I love a sexy woman in sexy underwear."

"You can change your mind and come to my place," she taunted.

I leaned back and looked at her. She looked like she'd love a good roll in the hay, but her eyes didn't sparkle like they usually did. She had to work in just four and a half hours, and I couldn't abuse the poor woman that badly. "I can't do that to you," I said. "I've got to leave some energy in you so you can come over the minute you get off work. I've got a thousand things I want to do to you to thank you for everything you did for me today."

"Just one thing is plenty," she whispered. She leaned over so close our lips brushed. "Just kiss me."

❁

I've gotta be honest. Tonight went so incredibly well that a normal woman would assume that she'd jumped a big hurdle. But no one ever accused me of being overly normal. The fact that Gina can dress beautifully and avoid questions like a politician is great. But that's not life. She can't avoid questions forever, and neither can I. I wish I could say that it doesn't matter that Gina didn't go to college. I wish I could say it doesn't matter that she has a blue-collar job. But it does. Damn it, it does. It makes me sick to admit that I feel that way, but it's not going to do any good to lie to myself.

I've been fixated on the differences in our backgrounds, but there's another thing that could be just as big a threat to our staying together. This has been in the back of my head every since our not-so-nice meeting, but I keep putting it aside. Since she's starting to get under my skin deeper than a tick, it's time to think about her temper. I've never been with a person who has such a short fuse. And I'm not just talking about lovers. I don't have a friend or a relative who has a bad temper. And

Gina's is bad. Sometimes, I feel myself tensing up when she gets that look in her eye, and I can't be with someone who frightens me.

Maybe there's a way we can work things out. I mean, it's possible, right? People have gotten over bigger differences. But I haven't. I'm drawn to people who are like me in terms of personality and background. I've always chosen the path of least resistance, and I'm not sure I have the guts to change.

I got up early on Sunday morning. Not as early as poor Gina had to, but I felt I needed to make an effort after keeping her out so late. When the second ferry of the day pulled in, I was waiting for her with a large cup of coffee and a muffin. She gave me such a lovely smile when I reached the pilothouse that I was a little sorry I hadn't gotten up for the first ferry.

"For me?" she asked, tilting her head in the slightly shy way she had.

"All for you. Me, coffee, and a muffin."

She flipped the metal bar up and tugged me into the space by my sleeve. After a long kiss, she whispered, "You're sweeter than any muffin ever made."

"Aw." I kissed her back, rubbing my body against hers. The boat was empty, and the return-trip passengers wouldn't be let on for a few minutes. "Got time for a quickie?"

She smiled and took a sip of the coffee. "No, but I've got time for a slowie when Case comes on duty."

"Slowies are better." I put my arms around her and hugged her, holding on when she took another drink of her coffee. "I can hear you swallow," I said into her fleece jacket.

"Let's sit down and hug."

She sat on one of the benches right behind the pilothouse, and I sat on her lap. After wrapping an arm around her neck, I rested my head on her shoulder. "This is nice."

"It is. Mind if I eat? I'll try not to drop crumbs into your hair."

"I don't mind if you do. I haven't taken a shower yet."

"I had fun last night."

I moved my head so I could see a portion of her face. "Really?"

"Yeah. Kinda. I mean, I wouldn't want to go to things like that all of the time, but it was nice to know it wasn't..." She trailed off and didn't pick up the thread.

"Wasn't what?"

She was quiet for a few moments and then said, "I was worried people would pick me out as a fraud."

"You're not a fraud. You're a beautiful, intelligent, sophisticated woman, and that's just how you appeared last night."

She didn't say a word in reply. I heard her take another sip of coffee and a bite of her muffin. "I wish I could have met your sister."

"Really?"

"Yeah. Why wasn't she at the party?"

"Hard to tell. She's not very interested in being close to Roger. I think she feels it's being disloyal to our father."

"Yuck."

"Yeah. Plus, Larry, her husband, is out of town, as usual. She doesn't like to go to things without him."

"What's going on there? Is he trying to get out of the marriage?"

That made me sit up straight. I looked at her curiously. "Why do you say that?"

"You said he traveled all of the time. You don't do that if you're really in love."

"Sure you do. A lot of people have to travel for their jobs."

"Right. And I bet most of them wind up getting divorced. It's not good for a marriage. I wouldn't put up with it."

I slipped off her lap so I could look into her eyes. "But what if it's how the person makes his living? He's a salesman, Gina. He has to see people to sell to them."

She shrugged. "He should find a new job."

Oh, she irritated me when she made pronouncements like that! "What if you were with someone who didn't like that you drove a ferry?"

Her expression didn't change a bit. "If it was gonna hurt a relationship I cared about, I'd quit." She touched my cheek, gently stroking it. "You can't have everything, Hayden. It's nice if you can have the job you want and live where you want and have the lover you want. But if I had to choose, I'd always pick the lover first. Always," she said, her big, brown eyes bright with certainty.

God, when she looked at me like that I wanted to crawl back onto her lap and never let her go. No one has ever put me first. No one. Of course, I've never put anyone else first. Maybe both people have to be selfless to have a good relationship. Perhaps I'll write a book on that. I'm sure that's a brand-new discovery.

Chapter Seven

W ell, the time has come. Dana delivered the goods. After at least a year of dropping hints and doing God-knows-what behind the scenes, she finally got me an interview with the Dean of the Department of the Classics at Harvard. Dana made it sound like this was just a perfunctory interview—that the job was mine. But that didn't make sense to me. In any way. Harvard's Classics program is one of the best, if not *the* best, in the country. You don't hand out jobs in a department like that just because an associate professor of history vouches for you.

Obviously, I have to take the interview. You don't turn down an opportunity like this. But what do I tell Gina?

I have to be brutally honest about this, even though it sounds like I'm full of myself. Gina has a job; I have a career. And I've always made choices that served my career. Okay, if I'm gonna be honest, that's not *entirely* true. Even though my career has always been paramount, I would have taught at a second-tier college if I thought Dana had really wanted me to join her in Boston. But I knew in my heart she was done with me once she got the offer at Harvard. She barely considered Columbia, and that wouldn't have been the case if she'd really loved me. We both wanted Princeton, Harvard, or Yale, but Columbia isn't very far down the ladder. It wouldn't have hurt her career one bit to stay in New York. But she never even made a halfhearted offer to do so. She just said that I could find something—eventually—in Boston. Not the most glowing profession of love.

Maybe Gina and I would grow so close that I'd be willing to make the sacrifice that Dana hadn't been willing to make for me. It just didn't seem kind to tell her I wanted to leave New York. That she was, in effect, on probation. That if she made me love her with all of my heart, I might put her before my job. How do you say that to a woman? How do you admit that to yourself?

❖

I was so proud of myself. I'd decided to tell Gina the truth. The whole truth. I just couldn't make up an involved lie that would let me go to Boston for the interview. But that damned Dana arranged for me to have lunch with the dean in New York. He's going to a conference, which I was going to attend anyway. I've already told Gina about it, so technically, I don't have to lie. But it is lying, isn't it? Of course, it is. I have a feeling I'm going to regret this, but I'm going to go to the lunch without telling her. I honestly think it's kinder to find out what's going on with Harvard before I make her start worrying about it. And that's the real truth. I'm not willing to torture her if I don't have to.

❖

I came back to the island on a late train. I'd spent the entire ride— almost two hours—talking to Dana on the phone. It turns out she was right. The interview was fairly perfunctory. But not in a good way. Harvard is like the prettiest girl at a party. She can flirt with every guy, tease each of them, promise nothing, and then demand something ridiculous, like a fifty-mile ride home, and every guy reaches for his car keys.

Harvard wants me to give them a fifty-mile ride home, and for my trouble, they might—if the mood strikes them and the stars are properly aligned in the heavens—reward me with an assistant professorship. Yes, you heard me properly. If I swab the decks for a year or two, they might give me the same job I now have at NYU.

Why didn't I tell them to shove it? Because they're the prettiest girl. No one tells the pretty girl to shove it. They all line up, hoping she chooses them. I hate to admit it, but I'm tempted to swab those decks.

Dana insists that this is common practice at Harvard. That many people have to get in through a side door. But I really prefer to enter through the front, thank you, just the way she did.

The dean, a nice enough guy named Ernst Schonnenberg, wants me to show up in September and teach elementary Latin and Greek, my least favorite subjects, to freshmen, my least favorite students. I'd be a lecturer. A lecturer. That's what post-docs or all-but-dissertation candidates are before they're made assistant professors. That's what I was four years ago.

The enticement is that a living relic, Mathilde Bronner, is finally going emeritus in a year. I'd step in as an assistant prof—a tenure-track assistant prof—and allow someone to fill Dr. Bronner's shoes as the top dog in the Classical history program. So, I'd be where I wanted to be in the first place, but it will have taken me five years to get there. The question is whether it's better to start over at the place I want or stay where I am. I'll probably make associate in a year at NYU. Another two or three years, and I'll make full professor if I don't screw up. Or I might choose to go to a smaller, although still glorious, college as a full prof after I make associate. Then I might be able to go into Harvard or Yale or Princeton through the front—my favorite—door.

No matter what I do, it's a crapshoot. Remarkably few students major in the Classics, and once you have a degree in the subject, you're left with little to do but teach or write. Microsoft doesn't seem to need many people with a thorough knowledge of Ancient Greek.

The train's just about to reach Sayville, so I have to put on my happy face for Gina. I missed the little dickens, even though I was only gone one night. I'm still not sure what I'm going to tell her about today, but I hope I make the right choice.

❖

The doors of the train swept open, the whooshing sound always taking me by surprise. I stepped onto the platform to find a smiling sea captain waiting for me. She looked divine. It was a warm night, the first really warm one of the summer, and she was dressed for it. She wore seersucker shorts and a crisp, white blouse that showed at least two inches of her fabulously tanned tummy. Every man in front of me did a double take when he walked by, and I felt several sets of eyes on us when Gina took me in her arms and kissed me soundly. This is one place where I always go in through the front door. I love it.

❖

We'd been at my house less than five minutes when I coughed up a portion of the truth. "I had an interesting lunch," I said, trying to sound casual.

"Yeah? Tell me about it." Gina was making me a whiskey sour, my new favorite summer drink. The blender whirred for a few seconds, and then she poured two drinks and motioned for me to open the slider to the front deck. We don't sit out here very often, but we should change our habits. It's a lovely place to watch the moon glinting off the sea.

We toasted, and I took a sip, relishing the cold, tangy, mossy flavor of the whiskey. I started in on my story again. "I had lunch with the dean of the Department of the Classics at Harvard."

"Wow," she said, nodding. "Sounds like a VIP."

"Indeed." I smiled, taking another sip. This was going well.

"How'd that happen? Was it a conference thing?"

"Uhm, no, not really. He'd heard about my new book, and he wanted to talk about my approach." This was all remarkably true. He even seemed a little disappointed that Harvard hadn't picked it up.

"Cool," she said, her beautiful dark eyes glinting in the moonlight. "Did you have fun?"

Fun. Gina's so good for me. I don't know another soul who'd ask that question. Everyone would ask about what the lunch did for me or what I found out or if Harvard had a tenure-track available for an associate entomologist. But Gina asked normal questions. Like a normal person. "I wouldn't say it was fun," I admitted. "He's pretty stuffy. But he was interested in me and in my book. That was kinda fun." Hey! I'd revealed a lot!

"Who wouldn't be?" she asked, letting her soulful eyes drift up and down my body. "I sure am." She put her drink on the deck and leaned forward to kiss me. I kissed her back, then she kissed me, and then the real fun of the day began.

✦

Okay. It's over. It only took two days for me to tell Harvard officially that their offer of next-to-nothing wasn't good enough. The dean honestly sounded shocked. Like you'd have to be crazy to give up a real job just to take a flier on a job with Harvard—even though in a year, you might wind up with no job at all.

I admit I was torn, even though it was a terrible offer. And if I hadn't been with Gina, I would have taken it. Call me stupid, but I would have taken it. But Gina's worth too much to me to move to Boston in the hopes of getting a job in a year. It's too early in our relationship for me to think I could move away and still make things work. Not to mention her clear feelings about long-distance relationships.

I've already decided I'm not going to tell Gina about the entire experience. It's off the table, so there's really nothing to tell. But Dana…Dana's another issue.

Once again making a decision that will probably bite me, I'm not going to tell Dana the whole truth, either. I'm going to tell her the essential truth, which is that I wasn't offered a position. Being a lecturer for a year is no position. It's just not. Dana doesn't need to know the details. Harvard didn't make me an offer to join the faculty, and that's the truth…pretty much.

✦

The long Memorial Day weekend was coming up, and Gina had already told me she had to work all three days. But the silver lining was that on Tuesday, she would start her summer shift. She'd be off by four every day, and that would give us some quality time to see where this thing could, or would, go. After playfully begging her to spend every evening with me, she gallantly agreed. We were going to have a lot of time, and I was determined to find out if what I felt was love. I hoped it was because I'd never felt so good in my entire life.

✦

The Memorial Day weekend started off with a thud. A cold front blew in on Thursday night and brought rain and fog and wind. Lorna, one of my housemates, didn't even make the trip, deciding to stay in New York rather than sit around waiting for the weather to clear.

But Elaine and Sheila arrived on Friday afternoon, wet and a little grouchy. Elaine was grouchier than Sheila, and I had a feeling that Sheila was mainly grouchy from listening to Elaine moan about the weather.

I didn't know Sheila well. At least, not as well as I knew Elaine and Lorna, since the latter were both in my department. Sheila was in the psych department, and most of our encounters had been at the ad hoc get-togethers that the gay and lesbian faculty occasionally had. But I liked what I'd learned about her. For one thing, she still taught freshmen, even though she was a tenured professor. That was rare. And she was one of the faculty advisors for the Queer Union—the gay / lesbian / bisexual / transgender student association. Something that must take up a lot of her time and probably give her more than her share of headaches.

I tried to get some work done, but it was hard to concentrate when there were other people in the house. It had taken me over a week to get used to the quiet of Fire Island, and now a pair of soft-spoken women reading in the living room seemed loud. Or maybe it wasn't them at all. Maybe I missed seeing Gina.

Monday morning surprised all of us. Overnight, the temperature rose, the sky cleared, and the wind calmed, leaving us with crystal-clear blue skies. Everyone's mood lifted, and we decided to go for a long walk.

"What's your preference, Hayden?" Sheila asked. "Found anyplace you like?"

"To be honest, I haven't explored much," I said. "I've been working."

"Then let's go over to The Pines. We can walk along the ocean and see the sights."

"I took the ferry from there one day, but I didn't look around. That's where the guys go, right?"

"Pretty much," she said. "Some guys like Cherry Grove, and some women like The Pines, but it's mostly young guys looking to party. But don't worry. We'll walk by a lot of women on the way." Sheila's button nose wrinkled in a very cute way, and I could see why everyone said she still had her pick of women to choose from, even though she was on the far side of sixty.

We left via the door on the ocean side of the house, and I was so stunned I almost gasped. Every other nice day had brought out a small group of determined sunbathers. Most looked like they were dedicated to their craft, having earned their leathery skin over a period of many years.

But today, a whole new crowd had moved in. Women from twenty to seventy now dotted the beach as far as the eye could see. There were men, too, but they were a decided minority. Volleyball nets had been set up. Women were throwing Frisbees, playing Hacky Sack, and throwing footballs around. Some had babies in playpens or on big blankets. A few small kids ran around screaming, but it was mostly a lesbian adult playground.

And many of those adults were topless. And a few more daring souls were bottomless. I'd always said I hated nude beaches because all of the wrong people took the dare. That wasn't the case on Cherry Grove. From what I could see, all of the *right* people were topless. "Hot damn!" I muttered, earning an elbow from Sheila.

"What'd I tell ya?" she asked, laughing.

"They're gonna get sunburned," Elaine said, scowling.

What had I been smoking when I decided to sleep with her? She'd find a hair in the caviar at the world's best brunch. "They probably have sunblock on," I said. "And if they don't, I'll go down the beach with aloe later."

Sheila laughed and said, "I'll be your assistant, Hayden. We'll be Florence Nightendykes."

"Let's get to The Pines, so we can get back here and get to work," I agreed.

It was a long walk, but the sand was firm, and the tide was low. It was fascinating to watch the crowd change as we traveled. The women-to-men ratio was four to one by our house, and it dropped little by little until it reversed near The Pines.

"These guys don't look like they need sunblock," I said. "How'd they get so tan?"

"They look like circuit boys to me," Elaine said. "They probably just travel from one White Party to the next, working on their bodies and finding new men to pay for them."

Sheila and I looked at each other, but I said it first. "Why can't women get jobs like that?"

She slapped my back and said, "You probably could, Hayden. Put your bikini bottom on and stroll up and down for a while. You'll have a sugar mama by the end of the day."

I was a little embarrassed by her comment, but I shrugged it off. I knew she didn't mean a thing by it, but Elaine was eleven years my senior and spent a lot more time on her appearance than I did. I could see her mouth set in that "I'm pissed" look I'd learned to flee from.

During the short time we'd been together, she often chided me about not caring more about my looks. She spent a lot of money having her hair cut and highlighted, and she was always having some special skin treatment performed. I could tell it irked her that Sheila hadn't included her in the category of sugar-mama bait, but it certainly wasn't my fault. I was just younger, at the moment. In a few years, I'd be her age. It seemed silly to me to put too much stock in such transient things. You could grow more interesting and become a nicer person with time, but your youth only diminished, no matter how much money you spent attempting to halt the process.

"Is anyone ready for lunch?" I asked. "I'll run ahead and put our names in somewhere."

"I could eat," Elaine said. "See if we can get into the place right on the dock."

"Will do." I took off, glad to have a few minutes alone. I would have preferred to have had Elaine stay in the city, but Sheila was nice, and I was glad she'd come. The restaurant Elaine wanted was, of course, packed to the gills. But I got our name put in and a promise that it wouldn't be more than an hour.

When my companions arrived, I gave them the bad news. "Let's look for someplace else," Elaine said. Dutifully, Sheila and I followed her through the small town. Every place was swamped, and we finally decided that it made more sense to wait than to walk all the way back to the house for lunch.

I perched on one of the big timber dock supports, listening to Elaine and Sheila argue about some new policies the administration might implement concerning admissions. As with most things about the university that didn't affect me directly, I paid scant attention. Assistant professors were truly at the bottom of the food chain, and since no one ever asked me to vote, I tried to ignore the rampant political fights.

My attention was so lacking that I didn't hear her the first time Sheila said, "Hayden, some great-looking woman is trying to get your attention."

The sentence hit my brain when Elaine said, "Hayden, that's your ferry driver."

My head turned so quickly I almost fell off my post. It was indeed Gina, driving a small boat that bore stuck-on letters declaring it was the "Water Taxi." She looked right at me and waved, a beautiful smile on her lovely face.

But I didn't wave back. I stared at her, unsure of how to react. I didn't want Elaine to torture me about her, and I wasn't ready to admit how close we'd become. And what in the hell was she doing driving such a little boat? She wasn't supposed to be down here at all.

"Hayden, do you know her?" Elaine's voice, sounding altogether too gleeful, grated overhead.

All of these thoughts and sounds cascaded into and bounced around my brain while I stared at her. Gina's brain obviously processed information quicker than mine did because by the time I raised my hand, she had turned away. A few people got into her boat, and she turned it so quickly and so loudly that everyone on the dock turned to look.

"Well, do you?" Elaine said again, still giddy.

"Yes, of course, I do," I said. "She's the ferry driver." I got up and added, "I'll check on our table."

Even though I'd sounded relatively calm, I was stricken with terror. I knew Gina well enough by now to know that she could take a lot of things, but being ignored wasn't one of them.

I ran into the bathroom and dialed her cell phone. I got her voicemail and left a message. "Gina. It's me. I'm sorry I didn't say hi just a few minutes ago. But I didn't recognize you at first. That was a strange little boat you were in, and it caught me by surprise. The sun was in my eyes, too. It wasn't until one of the women I was with told me you were waving that I realized it was you. Call me back, okay?"

I knew she always had her cell phone on, and I knew she got great reception on the water. But I tried to stay calm and hoped things didn't get out of control. My hands were shaking, so I went to the bar and bought a beer. I drank half of it in seconds and then left the crowd to go back to the restroom. Voicemail again. This was not good. Very not good. She was purposely ignoring me, which meant she was angry. Very angry.

I paced up and down the long, narrow bathroom, chugged the rest of my beer, and paced some more. One more call to her cell phone made things clear when I heard her new message: "Leave a message or call my home." Her voice was cold and clipped, and I could almost see the look she'd give me if I were there.

What I'd done finally hit me, and I went into a stall and cried. Cried because I was stupid and weak and inferior to her in every way. She was a good, openhearted woman who deserved someone better than me. But it hurt like hell to acknowledge that. It hurt all the more because I knew I'd ruined something that could have been very, very special.

By the time I went back outside, I had a fresh beer. "Where have you been?" Elaine asked. "I went in to look for you."

I held up the beer. "Chatting with the bartender."

"Really, Hayden," she sniffed. "Who's next? The waiter?"

"If she's cute," I said, trying to be flip even though I felt dead inside. I'd let Elaine get to me. I'd let someone I didn't like or respect make me betray a woman who'd never, ever do the same to me.

<hr />

We arrived home at three o'clock, and I immediately called Gina again. "Look, I know I dissed you, but I can explain. It really did confuse me to see you in that little boat. Really. Come on, Gina. Give me a chance. Please, I'm begging you."

After waiting for half an hour, I acknowledged she wasn't going to call. I put on my swimsuit, grabbed another beer, and headed down to the beach. The water was cold, too cold to think about going in. But I sat right at the edge of the tide, letting the icy water hit me with every dying wave. I was shivering, from both the cold water and my growing certainty that Gina would probably never speak to me, much less forgive me.

My beer was empty, and I was using the bottle to play a mournful non-melodic tune. I got the best sound out of it when I put an ounce or two of seawater in it, and I was determined to sit there playing my instrument until I could stand to be around people again. I had the feeling that might be awhile.

Sheila plunked down next to me and handed me another beer. I gratefully accepted it and sucked a few ounces down. The sun had warmed my back to the point where I was no longer shivering, and the beer felt cold and soothing.

"Wanna talk about it?" Sheila asked.

"Talk about what?"

"The ferry driver, crying in the bathroom at the restaurant, looking like you've lost your best friend…or anything else you have in mind."

I looked at Sheila for a minute and then started to cry again. "I fucked up," I whimpered. "I fucked up bad."

❖

I felt a little better after talking to Sheila. Not a lot, but a little was better than nothing. She agreed that I had to talk to Gina, and she guessed, after hearing my description of the woman, that it would not be easy. I screwed around the rest of the day, mostly lying on my bed, trying to think of how to approach her. I wasn't up for dinner, and I was thankful when Elaine and Sheila went into town to meet up with some other friends.

They still weren't home when I went to catch the last ferry to Sayville. I assumed Gina wasn't driving, but I still shook noticeably just from looking up at the pilothouse. I didn't know why the beer hadn't calmed my nerves, or perhaps it had. Maybe I'd be worse if not for the medicinal properties of beer.

Two young men were working the main deck, and one of them looked familiar, but I wasn't sure if he was the same kid I'd seen during the famous wheelchair caper.

We arrived in Sayville right on time, and I got off the boat like a Christian going into the Coliseum when it was topped off with lions. But Gina wasn't on the dock, either. Case came bounding off the ferry, and he looked nervous when I caught his eye. Before I could ask, Gina rode up on her bike. Case stood there, frozen like Lot's wife, while Gina brushed in front of him and jogged up the stairs to check that he'd closed down properly. He and the other kids started laying the excess rope out in neat, flat curls on the deck. By the time Gina came back, they were standing, nearly at attention, waiting to be dismissed.

"Good job," she said, and before she enunciated the "b," they were race-walking for the parking lot.

She brushed by me when I tried to stand in her path, and then she picked up her bike and threw her leg over the crossbar.

It must not have been my day for logical thinking because I jumped in front of her right as she started to pedal. The wheel went between my quickly spread legs, but the handlebars caught me right under my ribcage. I let out an "oof" and felt my feet leave the ground before being deposited on my butt, quickly followed by my head banging onto the wooden deck.

I heard the bike drop to the ground while I tried to blink the stars from my eyes. "Are you all right?" Gina was holding me still, pinning my shoulders to the ground.

My head was throbbing like a bitch, but my thoughts were clear. "Yeah. Just a bump."

"Did you black out?"

"No. No. Just bumped it." I reached back to touch the spot, amazed to feel it had already begun to swell. "Fuck."

Her firm, gentle hand glossed over the back of my head, making me wince again when she touched it. "You're gonna have a bad knot. You'd better get some ice on it." She sat on her haunches and looked me in the eyes. "Are you sure you didn't black out?"

"I'm sure."

"Can you get up?" She held out a hand and helped me to my feet.

I stood there and felt the pain radiating from my tailbone and my head.

"Sure you're all right?"

I looked at her and nodded. In another blink, she was on her bike again and started to pedal away. This time, I wisely grabbed her shirt, making her wheel skid when she kept pedaling. "The least you can do is stay here a second. Jesus! You practically gave me a concussion."

"I'm not the one who stood in front of a moving vehicle." I didn't realize that soft brown eyes could look that hard.

"You've got to hear me out, Gina."

"I don't *have* to do anything." She pried my hand from her shirt and started to ride again.

This time, I grabbed the bike seat and then moved around until I was straddling the front wheel again. I was getting mad, something that was so rare for me I hardly felt like myself. "You can't just ignore me."

"The fuck I can't!" She tried to back up, but I held on to the handlebars and the wheel.

"Fine. Fucking keep it."

She got off and started to walk, but I grabbed her again as the bike fell. I had gained strength from somewhere, perhaps my anger. Amazingly, I spun her around. "I don't want your stupid bike. I want you to hear me out. I deserve that."

Stepping close, she grabbed my shoulders and spat, "You deserve nothing! I had your number the first time I saw you. You and Elaine are two of a kind, and you both deserved to be taken down a notch. If she'd been on the island that first night, I would have picked her."

"What? *What?*" I shook her so hard I would have hurt a smaller woman.

"You heard me." She leaned close and spoke clearly. "I never would have approached either one of you. Ev...er. I wouldn't have given you a second look." She sucked in a breath, and her eyes grew even more fiery. "Check that. I wouldn't have given you a *first* look. I was trying to humiliate you. I was sure you'd chicken out, but you took me up on it, and I had to go along. The last—the very last—thing I wanted to do was fuck you that first night."

I'd never hit a person in my life. But I hit her. Hard. As hard as I could. She'd hurt me as surely as if she'd stabbed me. And I had to—had to—hurt her back. My hand stung where I slapped her, particularly where my ring struck something hard. Feeling her head snap back from my slap brought me back into some form of sanity, and I immediately reached for her.

Slowly, she turned towards me, her hair hanging in her eyes. It took her a second to collect herself, but as soon as she did, she spat at me. A fine spray of her blood hit my face and my chest, making tiny red speckles, which turned my stomach violently.

"Fuck! Oh, fuck!" I tried to reach for her again, but she pushed me hard enough to send me stumbling backwards trying to keep my balance. She used the opportunity to yank her bike up and get astride it. As she pedaled away, she spit again, leaving a bright red stain on the weather-beaten gray planks.

I stood on the dock for what seemed like seconds, but had to have been longer. Case sheepishly approached and asked, "Are you all right?"

I nodded, too upset to reply.

"Shit." He stared at the ground. "I knew she was pissed, but I didn't know it was at you. I never would have let you get on the boat."

"Did she say anything?"

"To me?" He looked surprised. "No, Gina would never tell anybody anything personal. I just knew to stay out of her way."

"I guess I haven't learned the rules," I said, trying as hard as I could not to cry.

"You need to go back to the Grove?"

I turned around and looked at *my* little island, golden lights blinking in the distance. "Yeah. Can you give me a ride?"

"I wish I could. But she'd kill me if I took a boat without permission." He scrunched up his eyes in thought and then said, "I know. You can come home with me. My mom won't care."

Case looked quite proud of himself, but I shook my head. "I don't want you to get involved. Besides, I think your mom might mind your bringing a thirty-year-old homeless woman home with you."

"Not if I told her what happened. She knows how bad Gina's temper is."

"I appreciate it. I really do. But I'd better think of something else. Is there a motel around here?"

"Yeah. They're probably all sold out, though. Memorial Day."

"Oh. Right." I stood there for a few moments, trying to stop my mind from thinking about Gina spitting her blood on me. "What about the train?"

He looked at his watch. "We time the last ferry so that people can make the one o'clock train. It'll be close, but we might make it." He started to run, calling out, "I'll get the car. Meet you on the street."

By the time I'd dashed to the street, he was already there, his engine revving. "Hold on," he said before I was fully in the car. We took off like a rocket and, in fewer than five minutes, were pulling into the LIRR parking lot. "It's coming," he said when the bright light on the engine scanned across the tracks. "Buy your ticket on the train."

"Thanks a million," I said and then ran up the stairs to the platform.

I jumped on just as the conductor called, "Board," and the pneumatic doors slid shut. I went into the car to my right, where two other passengers were sound asleep. The conductor approached me a few minutes later and asked, "Stop?"

"Uhm…Penn Station," I said, having to use all of my brainpower to recall my station.

"Change at Babylon." He looked at me and said, "Are you all right? Do you need a doctor?"

"I'm fine," I said. I took fifteen dollars out and held my hand out for my change.

He placed a couple of dollars in my hand and looked at me again, very seriously this time. "I can have the police meet you at Penn Station to take a report. You don't have to let people beat on you."

"I…I beat on someone else," I admitted. "This isn't my blood."

With a weary sigh, he walked away. I slunk down in the seat, feeling sick to my stomach and a deep sense of shame, which was new to me. I'd never acted as I had tonight, and I'd never had someone think I was a battered woman. Looking down, I saw Gina's blood again and felt bile in my throat. I ran for the bathroom and vomited, hitting the toilet and my shoes. When the room stopped spinning, I made a valiant attempt to clean the floor while trying not to vomit again. Then I yanked off the shirt, stuck it into the tiny sink, and worked on cleaning it until I had to get off and change trains.

We had to wait about ten minutes, and for the first time in my life, I was the most battered and slovenly looking person on a public conveyance in New York. No matter where I'd gone, there had always been someone dirtier or drunker or crazier than me. But tonight, I won the prize. No one would stand next to me on the platform, unsure of what to think about the otherwise normal-looking woman wearing the shirt she'd obviously just washed in the sink. There was a little blood on my shorts, some puke on my shoes, and the lovely odor of too much beer and sweat and stomach acid floating around me. I'm sure I wouldn't have stood next to me either, but it still stung.

At Penn Station, two cabdrivers asked me, unkindly, to exit their cabs. The third guy didn't seem to mind, perhaps because he smelled worse than I did.

I got to my apartment at around three o'clock in the morning. I didn't know the night doorman very well, so I hoped he'd just nod when I walked by. But things weren't going my way. I tried to turn my face to the wall and scamper right by him, but he woke from his catnap when the elevator dinged. "Hey! Wait! Where are you going?"

I stopped and faced him. "Hayden Chandler," I said. "I live here."

"Apartment 5B?" he asked, studying me.

"Yeah. I got caught in the rain."

His eyes were wide, but he just nodded slowly. I knew my neighbor, Mrs. Nordstrome, who hung out in the lobby most evenings, would hear the whole story, but I didn't give a fuck.

I entered my apartment and felt the rush of the familiar scents and sounds. I shucked my shoes and shorts, used the bathroom, and then opened my sofa bed and fell onto it. I don't know how long I was awake, but I'd guess it was less than a minute. Amazing what half a dozen beers, a brawl, and having your heart broken can do for your sleep.

Chapter Eight

I'm not sure what time I woke on Tuesday, but it was late. My cell phone was ringing, and I found it to see that Elaine was calling. I didn't answer, but took the opportunity to pee. I turned off the phone and then went back to bed after closing the curtains. That damned sun was annoying when a woman was trying to get some rest.

❖

I got up some time later, stumbled into the bathroom, relieved myself, and then shuffled into the kitchen to search for something—anything—to eat. I'd cleaned out all of the open packages of food before I'd left for the island, but Dana had succumbed to a sweet-tooth attack and had purchased a box of vanilla crème cookies. I'd hoped for something a little more substantial, but I had nothing. No eggs, no cereal, not even a box of crackers. So, I stood at the counter and shoved cookies into my mouth, chewing just enough to be able to swallow. I don't think I'd ever eaten solely to stop hunger pangs, but that's what I was doing. I didn't even taste the cookies. They could have been made of molasses or mint, and I wouldn't have noticed the difference.

When I thought I'd consumed enough to feel better, I walked back into my room and thought briefly about my options. My shared house was empty, and I wanted to go back. But I knew Gina was driving the ferry, and there was no way in hell I could see her. Since Case had taken over the evening shift, I decided I'd go back at night. Judging from the sun, that left me with a few hours to kill.

I looked at the TV and then at my stereo. It was almost like looking at an iron or a scale. I couldn't figure out why I'd want to use either of them. I had a wall full of books, but they created no resonance, either. The only think that looked familiar was my bed. As if being called, I walked to it and fell onto the mattress face first. As my mind shut down, my last thought was "This must be what depression feels like."

The phone rang, and it took me a minute to recognize it for what it was. The odd, chirping ring indicated that someone from the lobby was calling. Reaching across the arm of the sofa, I slapped my hand around until I knocked it off the cradle. Closing the curtains hadn't been a good idea, since my house was now so dark I couldn't find the receiver. But I caught the cord and pulled until the reluctant receiver was finally in my hand. "H'lo?"

"Hayden?"

"Yeah."

"It's Ralph. You okay?"

Ralph. Ralph. Oh, my doorman. "Yeah, I'm fine. Fine."

"You have a visitor."

"What? Who?"

I could hear him ask, "What was your name again?"

"Just say it's Gina."

Oh, fuck.

"It's Gina," he replied.

I didn't want to get Ralph involved, but I didn't want to see her. Ever. Ralph was a nice guy and a great doorman, but he was a huge gossip. If I didn't let her up, he'd tell everyone in the building about it.

"Hayden? Are you sure you're all right? I didn't even know you were back in town. Do you want your mail?"

Fuck. "Yeah. I…uhm…I've been under the weather. Just came home to get some rest. Send Gina up."

"I'll send the mail up with her, okay?"

"Sure. Thanks, Ralph."

"Can I get you something? I'm gonna take my break soon. I can go to the bodega."

"Thanks, Ralph, but I'm fine. Thanks for holding my mail."

"No problem. I hope you're better soon."

"Thanks. So do I."

By the time I hung up, she was knocking at the door. I desperately wanted to comb my hair or wash my face, but she was knocking loudly, and if I didn't answer, Mrs. Nordstrome would be peeking out of her door, asking what all the trouble was. I flipped the lock and pulled on the door, but it didn't open. Then I flipped the lock the other way, realizing I hadn't even locked the door when I came home.

Gina walked in and actually gasped when she saw me. My closet was just opposite the door, and I looked in the full-length mirror. I nearly gasped, and I was looking at myself. I was still wearing the shirt I'd had on the night before. It was a little worse for wear, especially after having been washed in the sink on the train. My cotton panties were sagging and drooped in the back. I hadn't showered, and my hair was beyond description. "C'mon in." I turned and went back to my sofa bed. I felt safer there, and I could at least cover myself with the sheet.

Gina put down the shopping bag of mail and stood in the kitchen for a moment, looking unsure of herself. She started to walk into the room and then stopped at the doorway. "Do you want me to leave?"

"Yes." I rolled onto my side and pulled the sheet up to my chin. I hoped I'd close my eyes and she'd disappear. Forever.

Of course, she didn't. I heard a muffled whine and then sobs. Big, heavy, pain-filled sobs. I looked at her and watched her stumble into the room and sit in one of my chairs. "I'm so fucking sorry," she whimpered. "I didn't have any idea. I didn't think you'd even care."

I couldn't manage any feeling. I just looked at her, almost as if I were watching a movie. "Why are you here?"

"Because I couldn't find you. Your cell phone is off."

"Oh." I rolled onto my back and stared at the ceiling. "Why did you want to find me? Shouldn't you have moved on to Elaine by now?" I didn't feel the antipathy that my words related. I felt nothing…truly nothing.

She stood up and walked over to me. Her face was flushed, and she was still crying. "I didn't…I was just…I tried to hurt you like you'd hurt me."

"Good job." I turned away from her, just wishing she would leave so I could go back to sleep.

I felt the mattress compress when she sat down. "Hayden, please, please let me talk to you."

"Who's stopping you?" I reached for an extra pillow and hugged it to my chest.

"Can I open a window? It's stifling in here."

"Whatever." I guess it was a little hot. I hadn't bothered to open the windows when I got home on Tuesday morning, but now that Gina mentioned it, I realized that the sheets were wet with sweat. She opened one set of curtains and cranked open the window. The breeze felt good and helped move some of the stagnant air around.

Her body moved the mattress again, and I wondered how long she'd torture me. I just wanted to be left alone. Why she couldn't see that was beyond me.

"I've never been so sorry for anything I've done," she said. I noted how rough her voice was and then recalled that she'd been crying. "I've been mean, and I've said awful things when I'm angry, but I've never, ever been crueler to anyone than I was to you. I'm so fucking sorry."

"S'all right. Can you push the button on the knob when you leave?" I was sure I'd be able to sleep a little better with the window open. I waited, but she was still on the bed. "I said it's all right. You can go now." What did she want from me? I said I forgave her. Then I heard her crying again. Jesus! What was with all the Sturm und Drang?

I rolled over and looked at her. She held her face with both of her hands, like a little girl who didn't want anyone to see her cry. There was something so Gina about the gesture that I felt something. I wasn't sure what, but I definitely felt something. Then I realized that I hadn't felt anything since I'd returned home. Huh. That was odd. There was a little more life in my voice when I said, "It's all right, Gina. It's no big deal. Go on home now."

"I can't," she said. Or I think that's what she said. It was hard to hear her when she was crying so hard and had her hands over her face.

"Why not?"

Her hands dropped, and she looked at me. I could feel her eyes scrolling up and down my body. They were red-rimmed, and her lids were swollen and so intense they nearly gave off heat. "Look at yourself! I can't leave you like this."

"You don't look go great in the morning, either. I'll be fine when I get up and take a shower. Bye-bye." Back onto my side I went, hoping for the sweet sound of the door closing. But I got a hand on my hip instead.

"It's seven o'clock at night. Wednesday night."

Really? Wednesday? What happened to Tuesday? "So? Is it a crime to go to bed early?" Okay, I'd been in bed for a while. But I was obviously tired. Couldn't she see that?

"You're wearing the clothes you had on Monday night," she said. I'd never realized how grating and harsh her voice was. It sounded like fingernails on a chalkboard. If only she'd shut up! I didn't even mind if she stayed for a while. I just needed a little more sleep. "You obviously haven't gotten out of bed since then. Jesus, Hayden, this place smells like a dirty gym."

"I wasn't expecting company. If I can just get a good night's sleep, I'll be fine."

Gina put her hands on my shoulder and hip and forcibly turned me towards her. My head was suddenly being held in one of her hands, while the fingers of the other one pulled open my right eye. "Did you take something? Sleeping pills? Anything?" She was so agitated she was sweating. That wouldn't help the smell. Now that she'd brought it up, I had to admit the place was a little rank. The fresh air just made the stale air smell worse. Maybe I should have her close the window when she leaves.

She shook me, and I remembered there was a question hanging. "No, I didn't take anything. I don't have anything to take."

Placing me back onto the mattress, I heard her go into my bathroom. The creak of the old, metal medicine cabinet indicated she was looking through my things. She had a lot of cheek; I had to give her that. She came back into the room with the bathroom wastepaper basket. She'd picked up the one from the kitchen as well and was going through them, looking for I had no idea what. Satisfied, she stood over me and asked, "Are you sure you didn't take any drugs?"

This was getting old. "I don't have any now. I didn't have any before. I've never had any. Happy?"

"No. I'm not happy," she said, starting to cry again.

"Damn it, Gina. Can't you have your meltdown somewhere else? I'm so damned tired I can't see straight."

For a moment, she just looked at me. I don't know why she looked as if she was watching her favorite pet die, but I didn't really care. "Okay. Go to sleep. We'll talk when you wake up."

I was too tired to roll my eyes, so I closed them. I'm not sure how long I slept, but I woke up when it was dark outside. Gina was lying on the floor. She'd put the cushion of my chair under her head for a firm pillow. The trashcan was next to her, and it was filled with dozens of tissues. I had to pee, but I sat on the edge of the bed for a moment, watching her sleep.

I hadn't noticed it before, but her lip was noticeably swollen. Damn, why did I hit her? I'm not a hitter.

I focused on her face, thinking of how pretty she was when she slept. How she looked so peaceful...serene, really. She seemed so innocent and sweet. I thought of how she'd started to hold me when we slept, keeping me close to her no matter how many times I turned over. Whenever I woke, she was holding me in some way. With her hand on my back or her arm around my waist. Sometimes cradling my head against her shoulder. Always trying to touch me, to reassure me that she was there. Her touch made me feel more loved than I'd ever felt.

I'm not sure how I got from the bed to the floor, but before I knew it, I had her shirt in my hands and was shaking her as hard as I could. "How could you do that? How could you ruin what we had?" I was screaming, screaming so loudly that Mrs. Nordstrome would probably call the night doorman or the police. But I didn't care. This bitch had destroyed the best thing that had happened to me in years, and I had to knock some sense into her.

Gina didn't fight back. She sat up a little and took me in her arms, holding me so tightly that I couldn't grab her anymore. "I'm sorry," she said, crying again. "I'm so sorry, baby. Please, forgive me. Please."

I struggled in her grip, but her years of heavy lifting had made her much stronger. Still, I twisted and fought, until I started to cry as well, and all of the fight went out of me. She held me tighter, letting me cry against the fabric of her shirt. Gina shed so many tears that my hair was wet, and I finally had to find a tissue or blow my nose on her shirt. She could see that I wasn't going to grab her again, so she let me get up and go to the pantry for more tissues. By the time the box was open and I was blowing my nose, she was right there like a faithful puppy.

"Why don't you take a shower? I'll go get you something to eat."

"What time is it?"

She checked her watch. "Three o'clock. I figure some of those stores that keep making so damned much noise must be open."

I made an attempt at a smile and got off a decent one. "The deli on the corner's always open. Would you get me a bagel?"

"Sure." She moved to the door and then said, "Are you sure you're okay to be in the shower alone?"

"Yeah. Go on. Take my keys. They're…" I looked on the counter where I usually threw them, but they were missing. "Somewhere."

"You had the front door unlocked for two days. Another fifteen minutes shouldn't hurt." She opened the door and closed it quietly. I stood there for a moment and then got into the shower, surprised that Gina would know I was going to feel woozy. I turned down the temperature and held on to both walls until I started to get my equilibrium. Then I was able to wash my hair and scrub away two days of sweat.

I'd just started to blow my hair dry when Gina returned. I heard her bustling around in the kitchen, and when I left the bath, I saw that she'd filled two vases with spring flowers. The windows were wide open, and the sheets were stripped from my sofa bed, which was now a sofa again. "It's kinda nice to have a store that close," she said. "It wasn't the cleanest place I've ever seen, but the guy behind the counter was nice."

"That's Mahmood," I said. "His cat kills most of the rats."

She glanced at me to see if I was kidding. I could tell she wasn't sure when she waited for me to take a bite of my bagel before she touched hers.

"I got you a fried egg with cheddar cheese," she said, even though I'd already taken a bite. "Some orange juice, too."

"What've you got?"

"Same thing, but cream cheese." She took a bite, and I knew she was trying to ignore thoughts of the vermin that she hoped were in Sphinx's belly. This probably wasn't the time to tell her that Sphinx didn't like cockroaches. She also had a cup of coffee that was definitely not good. Mahmood made coffee in the Egyptian way, which, as near as I could tell, meant throwing finely ground coffee into boiling water. It was the chewiest coffee in town.

"Little early for coffee," I commented.

"I've gotta go soon." She checked her watch again. "First ferry leaves at six."

"Oh. I thought Case might take over for you."

"No. He worked last night. I don't have the nerve to call him this early. Besides, my cousin would kill me."

It was easier between us now that we'd both released some emotion. Being topical was surprisingly comfortable, but I was about to venture into deeper waters. "So, we're cool? I can ride the ferry again?"

She dropped her bagel, and it hit the plate so hard it rolled off and landed on the floor. "I...I don't want it just to be okay," she said. "I want to try again." Her lip quivered. "Don't you?"

"Gina, you told me that you never would have dated a woman who looked like me. You admitted you fucked me just to keep up a ruse. You might think I'm ugly, but I'm surprised you think I'm stupid, too."

She scrambled to pick up her breakfast, looking at me while she did it. It wasn't easy, but she was doing a surprisingly good job. "Hayden, everything I said was true. But I was being stupid." She got up and sat next to me on the sofa. "I've always been attracted to Italian girls. That's my type. I like a lot of dark hair and dark eyes and tan skin. But that's just my preference."

"So, you now love dirty-blonde, blue-eyed women who look like they live in a library."

"No, that's not true." She placed her hand on my thigh, and I felt its warmth through my thin robe. "I love the way *you* look. I think you're very, very beautiful, and if I haven't told you that, then I'm an idiot."

"You haven't," I said, looking down at my bagel.

Her hand closed a little. "I truly think you're lovely," she said. "I just don't see how a person looks once I get to know them. I forget that I should stop and look at a woman and tell her what I see."

I didn't look at her as I asked, "What do you see?" But I could tell she was thinking hard in order to say the absolute perfect thing.

"I see a woman with beautiful, thick, sandy-colored hair that probably used to be white blonde when she was little."

"It was," I agreed.

"I see fantastic cream-colored skin that hasn't been ravaged by the sun." She took my hand and pushed the sleeve of my robe up. "Not even a freckle. Perfect, pure, soft skin…just like a baby's." Her fingers skimmed across my eyelid. "No wrinkles. No crow's feet from staring at glare all day."

"Just books."

"Clear blue eyes, like the Mediterranean at dawn. Such beautiful eyes," she whispered. Her lips were close to my face, and I could feel her breath on my cheek. "The softest, sweetest lips I've ever kissed."

With a sidelong glance, I turned just enough to face her. She kissed me—a tender, almost worshipful kiss that made my heart beat faster when I felt her lips trembling.

"I don't want this to be over," she said. "I'll do anything to explain, to show you that what I said isn't what it sounded like."

"How is that possible, Gina?"

"I said I never would have asked you for a date, and that's true, but it's only because you weren't my type. Being with you has made me see that it was childish to approach only women who looked a certain way. It's not that I didn't think you were pretty. I swear that."

I looked into her eyes and felt confident that she was being honest. But that wasn't the worst of what she'd said. "What about the fact that you came to my house to scare me? You said you didn't want to have sex with me. Was that because I was so pretty?"

She closed her eyes, and I knew she was having a hard time looking at the pain in mine. "No. I didn't want to have sex because I was really angry with you. I'm not attracted to people I'm angry with. I thought you were a snotty bitch, and I wanted to put a scare into you. That's the truth."

"You wanted to scare me by having sex with me? What kind of tactic is that?"

She audibly blew out a breath. "It's a stupid tactic. I thought you were uptight and full of yourself. I wanted to make you see that you weren't better than I was. That I could have you begging for sex from a blue-collar ferry worker."

"So, you were gonna fuck me to show me I was no better than you." I squinted, somehow thinking I'd be able to understand her better if I looked at her through slits.

"Yeah." She shrugged her shoulders helplessly. "I didn't say it was smart. It's just what I came up with."

"So, that's why you wouldn't even take my clothes off or touch my skin," I said, getting angrier by the minute. "That's why you jerked off rather than letting me touch you."

"Yes." She nodded, her head hanging in shame. "I was angry and didn't want to be intimate."

Something didn't make sense. Something big. "So, why did you go to bed with me after you came?"

Her lips slowly moved into that adorably beautiful smile that I'd come to need as much as sleep or food. "Believe me, Hayden, I had no intention of getting turned on. I was very, very pissed off. I just wanted to embarrass you and leave. But watching your body and feeling you get so excited turned me on. A lot. I thought I could just take care of myself and take off, but you looked at me, and I felt myself falling into those fantastic eyes." She shrugged. "It didn't even occur to me to say no."

"So, once we were having sex, you decided you liked me?"

"Yeah. That's true. But I also thought that I'd been wrong about you. I felt badly for tricking you."

Hmm…how do I tactfully tell her that she's using "badly" wrong? Maybe this isn't the best time. I'll work it in if we see each other after today. "So, the first time we had sex was a game, but by the second, you were honestly choosing me for sex?"

Her eyes shifted, and she looked away. She was clearly hiding something or…

"I've never picked anyone up like that. I've never had sex with someone I didn't know well. I was kinda freaking out about jumping into bed with a stranger. I knew you thought that's the kind of woman I was, but that's not me! That's why I got upset the time you teased me about having picked you up."

"You…really? That's the real reason?"

She looked at me with such sincerity that she could have told me she was a Venutian and I would have believed her. "You're the fourth person I've had sex with. I don't have sex just for something to do. It means something to me."

I took her hand and felt the clamminess. She was so endearingly embarrassed. "Me, too. You're the fourth person I've had sex with."

"Are you serious? You'd only been with three people, and you let me come to your house?"

"Yep. I tried to get you to slow down, but when I saw it was right then or never…I chose right then."

She leaned back and gave me a stunned stare.

"I'm being honest," I said. "I had sex with a woman in college, but that was just a coming-out fling. Then with Dana, then with…Elaine. I swore I'd never have sex again before I'd do it with someone I didn't care for." She blinked, clearly stunned. I wasn't sure which part of my sentence surprised her so much. There were many options.

"But why?"

"I still don't know," I said. "Maybe because you're so pretty." I ran my fingertips along her cheek and felt her swallow when I touched her neck. "Maybe it was fate."

"I think it was fate," she said, her expression very serious. "I believe in fate. I really do. And I don't think we should screw with it. I believe we can make this work. Please, please let me try." She'd taken my hand and was squeezing it while she stared into my eyes. How could I say no?

"But I haven't apologized for ignoring you on Monday. That's what started all of this."

"Forget about it. I don't even wanna know. Sheila found me on Tuesday morning and told me you didn't come home that night. I've been trying to track you down ever since. All that matters is that I've found you and that you're all right." She took me in her arms and rocked me gently. "That's all I care about." She nuzzled against my neck for a few minutes, and I could feel her tears on my cheek. "I was so worried about you."

"How did you find me?"

"I hired a detective," she said. "I told him you worked at NYU, and I gave him your cell phone number. He found you in fifteen minutes."

"That's not very long," I said. "Kinda creepy."

"Yeah, it is. I was gonna hire a sky-writer next."

She didn't look like she was kidding. I put my arms around her and held her for a minute. "We've got some things to work out," I said. "It's going to take me a while to trust you not to hurt me again. You frighten me when you get angry. That's a big deal."

Gina kissed me again, and I could feel the relief pouring from her body into mine. "I'll change," she promised. "I *will* change."

<hr />

Gina promised she was awake enough to drive all the way to Sayville. Amazingly, I was still tired, so after I finished both of our bagels, I lay on the couch, afraid that the lure of the bed would be my undoing.

After a comparatively short nap and another quick shower, I got dressed, went through my mail, and went to the train station. Two hours later, I was in Sayville, waiting at the dock for Gina. We both got on for the outbound trip, this time with Gina as a passenger since Case was there, too. We didn't talk much, but she held my hand while looking out the window. The window was open a little, and her hair was blown straight back from the breeze.

She had such beautiful, classically Roman features. She could have been the model for a frieze or a statue three thousand years old. How did I not guess she was Italian? I've been looking at women who look so similar to her for my entire professional career. Huh. Maybe that's why she appeals to me so much. It's not just that she's beautiful. Her looks touch something deep inside me. Some spark of recognition of the ancients. The kind of beauty that made a man pick up a chisel and hammer and express his desire through a block of marble. I'd sculpt her if I could. I'd show her strength and her courage and her frailty and her vulnerability. It all comes together to make her who she is.

But that vulnerability is what makes her lash out at me when I do something that hits her in an unguarded place. We have to figure out a way to get past that. I don't know how many times I can forgive her for hurting me, and I'm not sure she can stop. But I hope to God she can because I want to be sitting next to her, holding her hand while I look at that fantastic face, for a very, very long time.

When we got to the house, we were both feeling ill at ease. She kept walking to the glass doors, looking out at the ocean. Finally, I went up to her and pressed my cheek against her back. Gingerly, I put my arms around her and felt her begin to relax. "Let's go out on the deck," I said.

It was a pretty nice afternoon. The sun was hidden behind a bank of clouds, as it usually was at that time of day, but it was fairly warm and dry. I settled myself on the railing after ignoring Gina's raised eyebrow of warning. She stood in front of me and held me tighter than she needed to. But it was a very nice way to get comfortable with her again. We didn't say a word to each other for a very long time; we just held each other. Unconsciously, our breathing synced up, and we let some of the barriers fall.

It was almost dusk when she put her hands on my waist and lifted me from the railing. Without a word, she took my hand and led me to the fireplace. She opened the flue and lit one of the logs Elaine had purchased and written her name on. Good for Gina. As soon as she was sure the log was going to burn, she turned to me and lovingly started to undress me. Soon her clothes were lying next to mine on the floor. Then she took me in her arms and started to kiss me with so much feeling I honestly thought I might faint. Somehow, we wound up on the rug, the dry heat from the fire warming our feet while the cool, moist air blew in through the open door.

She made love to me like a woman possessed. Her hands, her lips, her mouth seemed to be everywhere at once. I'd never known her to be so intense, so intent on touching every part of me, especially my heart.

Lying together afterward, she said the first words to leave her lips since we got on the ferry. "I'm gonna have to go soon. Can I see you on Monday?"

I looked at my clock and saw that it was only half past eight. "So soon?"

"Yeah. I didn't get much sleep the last few nights. I'm running on fumes. Besides, I don't have a way to get to Sayville if I miss the last ferry."

"I understand. Come over any time you want. I got hold of Elaine and Lorna and Sheila today and told them that I had a girlfriend."

She gave me a surprised, but pleased, smile. "I'd ask how that went, but I don't wanna know."

"Lorna's fine, and Sheila's nice. You'll like her."

"I like her already. She cares about you." A thought must have struck her because Gina cocked her head in question. "Can you work when they're here?"

"No, not really. Why?"

"'Cause you've lost a few days work. Why don't you come to my place for the weekend? I'll be working most of the time, but it'd be wonderful to come home to you."

"Really? Do you have a place where I can work? Like a table or something?"

"Yeah," she said, smiling inscrutably. "I could find a little spot for you."

"Okay. Should I come tomorrow night?"

She rolled to her knees, got up, and held her hand out to me. "Come now. I need to sleep with you."

"All right. That'd be nice for me, too." I put my arms around her and squeezed her. "I've missed you so much."

"If it's half as much as I've missed you…" She trailed off, shook her head, and then went into the bathroom to get ready to leave.

❖

We were back in Sayville by nine, and after walking a few feet, Gina came to an abrupt halt and stared at me. "I rode my bike."

"And…?" I looked at her for a second and then caught her drift. "I guess I'll walk."

"Shit!" She walked over to her bike and unlocked it. "I'd leave it here, but someone would steal it."

I doubted that anyone would steal a bike covered in spare tires, but maybe Sayville was the hub of a big bike-theft ring. Gina walked the bike over to me and said, "I just wasn't thinking clearly. Sorry I screwed up."

"Do you have a car?" My mental picture of Gina getting around town was astride her bike, but I realized that it would be tough to get around Long Island without a car.

She nodded, a slight frown on her face. "Yeah. A truck. Remember? We went to Philadelphia. Are you sure you didn't jostle your brain?"

"I don't think I did, but I did lose a day. It was weird." We walked a little bit, and then what she said registered. "The truck we drove in is yours? I thought it belonged to the ferry company."

"It does."

I looked at her, seeing the concern in her eyes. "I'm fine, Gina. I just don't know what's yours and what you borrow."

"Well, the company actually owns everything, but I don't think of it as borrowing. It's mine, too."

"Whatever," I said, thinking that NYU would can my ass if I took one of the vans and drove it to Philadelphia. "You looked kinda butch in that truck. I liked it."

"Butch? Really?" We walked in silence for a few minutes, since I had to concentrate to adjust to the darkness and the lack of sidewalks. "Do you think I'm butch?"

"No, not really. You're no nonsense, and you can be aggressive—"

"Assertive," she corrected. "I'm assertive."

Laughing, I agreed, "Especially in bed."

"I'll freely admit to being a top," she said, laughing as well. "But I don't see myself as very butch. I think people assume I am because of my job, but…well, your opinion matters more than mine."

"What about me? How do you see me?"

She looked me over, as if assessing me for the first time. "I've usually gone out with girly-girls, and you're not like them. You don't have your nails done or spend a lot of time on your hair or makeup." I must have been frowning because she added, "You look nice—really nice. But you don't bring out six different outfits for me to choose from before you can be ready for dinner."

"We've never gone out for a real dinner," I said. "You might be surprised."

"Now that I'm off work early, we're gonna have some real dates. You can surprise me all you want."

"I didn't bring anything nice with me," I said. "I don't know how pleasant the surprise will be."

"You look nice in everything I've seen." The moonlight was the only illumination at that point in our walk, and it made her eyes glimmer with satisfaction. I don't know how the woman did it, but she could make me feel like an ugly hag and a lovely woman all in the same day.

"Thanks." I tried to hold her hand, but she needed both of them to steady her bike on the banked road.

"Hey, ya wanna try riding the rest of the way? We're not even halfway there."

"Okay, but where will you be?"

"I'll be driving," she said, her teeth shining in the soft light. "You'll be riding."

"On your shoulders or the crossbar?"

"You're a funny girl," she said. "C'mon, I haven't done this since I was a kid. It'll be fun."

I gave her a playful shove. "For you." But I was game to try something new, so I stood still and waited for instructions.

"I love people who aren't afraid to look silly," she said. She dipped the bike towards me, and I sat on the crossbar. "Now...hmm...I guess you have to put your arms around me."

"No! Not that!" I giggled while I awkwardly encircled her neck with my arms. She was bent over and really had to struggle to get the bike vertical, but she did it. She was halfway on the bike seat and still had one foot on the ground.

"Now, you might want to slide a little more of your weight over," she said. "Then you won't be sitting on your tailbone."

"That's scary," I said, but I scooted back a little bit.

"Here goes." She started to pedal, and the bike wobbled more than I liked at first, but within three or four strokes, we were gliding along pretty nicely.

I moved one of my arms around her back, making me strain less to hold on. That let Gina sit up straighter, too, and she was able to pedal faster. "You've done this before," I said.

"Not for twenty years. But it feels good, doesn't it?"

"It does," I had to admit. "Maybe we should go around town like this."

"Okay, but you have to drive once in a while so I don't look too butch."

I didn't reply, but it was obvious that she didn't like the thought of appearing too butch. I wasn't sure why that was, but I knew I'd get it out of her eventually.

In just a few minutes, Gina slowed and then gently stopped the bike. She dipped it again and I got off. We'd stayed fairly close to the water, but just before we stopped, she turned down a short street. Now we were right along the ocean. "You live this close to the ocean?" I asked, stunned.

"The Great South Bay, really. I've gotta teach you some nautical terms. Your house faces the ocean."

"Good enough!"

She laughed and led me along a sidewalk until we reached a moderately sized, ultramodern house. It was shaped like a box, but the roof tilted down to a forty-five degree angle in the front. The entire façade was glass, and a gauzy drape across the vertical glass wall obscured the interior. "This...this is your house?"

"Uh-huh." She was the epitome of casualness. "Will you hold my bike while I get the mail?"

She walked up two steps to the landing, retrieved her mail, and opened her door. I picked up the bike to bring it inside and realized it weighed less than any bike I'd ever held. I followed her in and nearly dropped the bike. Gina lived in a showroom. A showroom for an ultramodern furniture store. I would have been less surprised if she'd lived in an igloo.

"Let me take the bike," she said, lifting it from my weak hands. "I shouldn't be so fussy about it, but I had it made in Turin. I rode it all over Italy, but it's overkill for Sayville."

"Uh-huh." I knew she was speaking, but I didn't hear a word. Gina's home was absolutely stunning. The slanted roof presented a view of the night sky, and I saw more stars than I'd seen since I left New Hampshire four years earlier. The main floor housed a living-dining space and had a kitchen that ran along the entire width of the house. A waist-high glass wall skirted the kitchen, making the whole floor seem like one large space.

A second-story loft bore a matching glass wall, and I noticed the open spiral staircase to the loft behind the entry door.

Even though the design of the house was fantastic, the décor was what really made one gasp. The whole floor was decorated in shades of pink and gray. I'd never been a big fan of pink, but the pastel pink, shag area rug in front of a low, gray flannel sofa and matching chairs was surprisingly calming and serene. Lipstick-pink pillows, which looked as if they were made of cashmere, rested on the sofa, and smaller, furry pink pillows were placed on the chairs.

A collection of low, dove gray cabinets lined the wall that fronted the water, and I assumed Gina's TV and stereo were housed within.

A slate gray steel dining table was located behind the sofa, surrounded by six chairs covered in velvet so pale it barely read pink, but pink it was. The chairs looked soft enough to curl up on and take a nap, and it struck me that the focus of the entire room was texture.

I looked at Gina, who was patiently waiting for me to react. She was smirking and said, "Not what you expected?"

"Are you a descendent of Victor Emmanuel?" The male descendants of the deposed king of Italy were permanently barred from living in Italy after World War II, but I hadn't considered they might be in Long Island.

"No. I'm a descendent of Vincenzo Scognamiglio, though." She looked downright smug.

"Is he the CEO of Fiat or Bulgari?"

"No, not even close. But he started a nice little ferry company." Her hands were linked behind her back, and she was swaying back and forth like a happy child.

"Your family *owns* the ferry?"

"No." She shook her head. "*I* own the ferry. My family owns the ferry company."

"Huh?"

"Can we move away from the front door?"

I flinched, not having noticed that I hadn't moved an inch. The front door was still open, since I was blocking it. "Shit, I'm sorry. Bugs are coming in." I walked into the living room and sank into one of the chairs. "Fuck!" I reached behind my back to grasp the little pillow. "What is this covered with? It feels like…" I rubbed the pillow on my face, delighting in the short, slick fur.

"Faux sealskin," she said. "I can't bear to kill a seal just to sit on it, but I love the feel. Besides," she said, laughing, "real seals don't have pink fur." I stared at her so long that she finally said, "What? You're looking at me like I'm a ghost."

"I'm…I…I thought you just piloted a ferry during the summer. I assumed you lived like a pauper and spent all of your money on travel." I looked around. "You don't live like a pauper."

"I told you the union paid well." She sat on the sofa and transformed into a woman made to live in a sensually luxurious, modern home. My whole perception of her started to change, and it felt odd…discomfiting even.

"Can I have a drink? I'm struggling."

She gave me an understanding pat on the leg when she got up. "Sure. What would you like?"

"What do you have?"

"You tell me what you want. I probably have it."

"Alcohol," I said. "I want alcohol."

She laughed and walked over to one of the gray cabinets. Lightly pressing on the edge of the doors caused them both to open, revealing a very well-stocked bar. "Name your poison."

"What are you having?"

"I usually have a grappa in the evening."

"That's like brandy, right?"

"Same concept. They're both high in alcohol and usually served after a meal. But they aren't really the same."

"I'll have some grappa. I like that high alcohol thing."

She bent over and took out two bottles. One was thin and tall and clear and the other was shorter and a deep amber. Another cabinet yielded two glasses—one tall and thin with a slight curve to the lip, the other shorter and rounder with a more distinctive curve. "I hope you don't mind, but I'm going to pour you a little Port. If you haven't had grappa before, you probably won't like it."

"I'm tough," I said, showing a half-smile when she handed me my glass.

She touched her glass to mine, and they made a melodic tinkle. "To tough girls."

She sat down and took a sip of her drink, looking over the rim of her glass while I tasted mine. "This is fantastic," I said. "This *is* like brandy, right?"

"Yeah. It has more of the original wine flavor than brandy. I know you like wine, so I thought you might like to keep the flavor while turning up the alcohol."

"Let me taste yours." I got up and took her glass, tipping it to my lips. I've never had grain alcohol, but I can't imagine it tasting worse. "You like that?" I must have looked like a baby tasting Brussels sprouts for the first time.

"Yes, but it's an acquired taste. My great-aunt in Italy drinks it, and it's all she ever offered me after dinner. She doesn't have a TV or anything, so I'd drink some grappa for entertainment." She laughed. "Two glasses of grappa, and I can entertain myself for hours."

"I'd be happy to watch you drink it," I said. "But I'm sticking with Port." I sat down and raised my glass to her. "My new favorite drink for when I'm trying to figure out what my girlfriend's story is."

Smiling that sexy, endearing, childlike smile, she asked, "Am I really your girlfriend? Even after all I've done?"

I got up and sat next to her on the stunningly comfortable sofa. "Do you want to be?"

"Yes." She licked her lips and almost broke my heart with the soulful expression she gave me. "More than anything."

I opened my arms, and she fell into them, snuggling against me like a puppy seeking her mother's heat. We held each other for a long time, slowly getting used to being intimate again. Finally, I asked, "Will you tell me about your family?"

She sat up and straightened her hair. "It's pretty simple," she said. "My grandfather started a small ferry business, my father made it a big ferry business, and my brothers and I have made it into five divisions. We're each president of our own company, but while my father is alive, he's the CEO."

I hoped to God I wasn't wrong, but I had to get this clear. "You don't have four brothers."

"No. Just two. But each of them runs two divisions. I just have one."

"'Cause you're a girl?" I batted my eyes at her, knowing that couldn't be the reason.

"Nah. I didn't wanna work as hard as they do. They make a lot more money than I do, but they work three times the hours."

I couldn't figure out why you'd need more money than Gina obviously had, but to each his own. "So, you don't have to work *on* the ferry if you don't want to?"

"I could stay in the office, but I like to pilot. Plus, it saves me from having to hire another person. I make a good salary, but I have a pretty tight margin. It'd cost me seventy or eighty thousand to hire someone part-time. Saving that keeps me in the black."

"Eighty thousand! For a part-timer?"

"Told ya we had a good union," she said, smiling that devilish smile. "That's including benefits, which are a load."

"Still…" I looked around. "You know how to make eighty thousand go a long way."

Gina laughed so hard her grappa almost flew from her glass. "I don't take a pilot's salary. I pilot to save the salary. But I take a nice draw as president."

I blew out a long stream of air. "It's gonna take me a little while to get used to this."

Gina looked at me for a moment. "You seem almost unhappy. Does it bother you that I'm not poor?"

"You're a long way from not poor," I scoffed.

"Yeah, yeah, that's true. But I probably don't have as much money as you think. My dad gave us all money to build our homes. He and my mom started putting money away for each of us a long time ago. It was partially for tax reasons, but he also did it because he'd had to really struggle to afford a nice home, and he didn't want us to have to do that."

"This is definitely a nice place," I said, looking around. "A very nice place."

"I know that. And it did cost a lot. But it's pretty small. Only two thousand square feet. And my cousin's husband was the contractor. I got a sweet deal. My brothers have *big* houses. Big, showy houses."

I wasn't certain, but I think I detected a note of distaste when she talked about their homes. Given that she still hadn't mentioned their names, I was getting the impression that the family wasn't super close. "Well, your house isn't big, but it's very well put together."

"Thanks. I love design. I'm probably gonna turn this one over pretty soon. I had more fun designing and decorating this house than I ever would have imagined."

"You did this yourself?" I was stunned. Truly stunned.

"I didn't draw the plans or anything, but all of the ideas were mine. I've been into home design since I was twenty. I'm really into it," she said, smiling. "You still haven't answered my question, you know. Does it bother you that I have some money?"

"No, no, why would anyone mind dating someone with money?" I knew I was scowling, but couldn't seem to erase it. "It's just...it changes my image of you. Like you have this secret life."

"I wasn't trying to be secretive," she said, jumping in quickly. "I just don't feel comfortable telling people I own the ferry. I mean, you've never really asked me any questions about my job. I would have told you all about it if you'd asked."

Scratching my head, I said, "I didn't know I should ask. You told me about having to work since you were in diapers. I thought you were poor."

Looking at me with a very confused expression, Gina said, "Oh! I didn't say I *had* to work. I said I worked. We got a very small allowance, so I worked at my dad's office for extra money. He wanted to teach us to be industrious."

"Still…" I drank some more of my Port, swirling it around in my mouth while I thought. "It just changes my image of you. Like finding out you have an ex-husband and three kids. It's not bad. It's just not what I thought was…you." I looked at her for a second. "Does that make any sense?"

"I guess. But you know everything important. Does it bother you that I'm more like you? I mean, *you* grew up around a lot of dough *and* a lot of class."

"That doesn't make you more like me. *We* didn't have a lot of money."

"Hayden, I saw where your mom lives. Give me a break."

"No!" I said this louder than I had to. But she had me all wrong. "My mom and Roger have money. But we didn't have money when I was growing up. High school teachers don't make a lot of money, you know. I was one of the scholarship kids in high school. Me and the smart kids from the inner city who did well on the entrance exam."

"What? How can that be?"

"It just is. You didn't ask," I said, giving her a well-deserved glare.

"But you went to all of those schools. Ruby told me how much schools like that cost."

"I got academic scholarships. I never had to pay a dime of tuition." I must have looked as proud of myself as I really was because Gina beamed at me.

"I admire that so much more than thinking you had it handed to you. And even though I had the ferry handed to me, I've worked on it from the time I was about twelve. I never had a summer off. To this day."

I took another drink, letting the liquor warm me from the inside out. "I guess getting to know someone is all about adjusting your expectations and beliefs. We just have to roll with the punches."

"Fewer punches, okay? You almost loosened a tooth."

"Oh, God." I put my drink on the gray steel table by my chair. My head dropped into my hands. "I will never be able to explain that. Or apologize enough."

"It's okay." Gina got up and knelt beside me. She hugged me tightly and then said, "We've had a tough week. Let's go to bed." She stood and picked up both of our glasses. "Follow me."

I did. We ascended the stairs after she touched a switch, and the lights in the living room dimmed and then went out. Another touch made the upstairs lights power up.

I'd climbed a few spiral staircases, but never a modern one. This one looked like it was made of stainless steel, but I guessed it was aluminum. It was sleek and shiny and very minimalist. A little like Gina.

There were two bedrooms upstairs, but one served as a den. We bypassed that one and went into her bedroom. It was just as modern as the living room, but the color palette had changed to warm off-whites and pale blues. It was also more restful than I would have guessed. Gina's low platform bed had an angled headboard with pale blue cushions, and I could imagine sitting in bed reading for hours.

She obviously did what I imagined doing, since the floor on one side of the bed was a repository for a neatly piled stack of hardbound books. One book was open and lying on its face on the floating nightstand. It was mine. We locked eyes, and she said, "I had to search for it. Amazon had the paperback, but I had to have the cloth."

I reached for her, and we held each other for a while. "You make me feel so, so special."

"I wasn't going to tell you I found it until I'd finished," she said. "I had no idea you'd come over before I could tell you how much I love it."

I've never been more tempted to tell a woman I loved her. But it had been too hard a week, too long a day. And I didn't want it to seem like I loved her just because she'd gone to the trouble to hunt down my dissertation. So, I kissed her instead.

❖

We got into bed and moved around for a minute or two, trying to accustom our bodies to a new and much more luxurious bed. "I'll never go back to my sofa bed," I sighed.

"That's fine with me." Gina was on her side, looking at me with that intense look she sometimes gave me. The one that always made me a little uncomfortable. I loved having her look at me with all of her attention, but this look was so focused that I could almost hear her thoughts.

I put my hand on the small of her back and pulled her closer while I scooted in her direction. When we were chest-to-chest, I ran my fingers through her hair until her eyes lost some of their fire. "You look so tired," I said.

"I am. Long day. Long week." Holding her close, I rocked her a little, and she began to relax. I could feel her muscles soften, and she molded her body to mine. It felt wonderful to hold her, to feel the soft, smooth body that just hours ago I'd been sure I'd never hold again.

I tried to lie still and let her fall into the deep sleep that usually claimed her within moments, but I was anxious—far too anxious—to relax. Having slept about forty of the past forty-eight hours might also have contributed to my hyper-alert status.

Even though she was tired, Gina was, as always, sensitive to my signals. She was on such a thin edge of wakefulness it was comical, but she slurred out, "You 'kay?"

"Shh," I whispered while patting her back. "Go to sleep now."

She didn't open her eyes, but she smiled that adorably sweet, childlike smile that always made my heart swell. "Make love?" She'd learned that a good orgasm at bedtime knocked me out like ether.

"No need. You go to sleep. I'm just a little wired. Don't worry."

Her voice grew more alert. "Wanna read or watch TV? There's one in the armoire." She pointed over her shoulder to her nightstand. "Remote's in there. Won't bother me at all."

I almost refused, but I knew she wouldn't be able to sleep well if I was agitated. "I'll read," I said. I turned on the tiny halogen spotlight on my side of the bed and walked around to hers.

"My bookcases are in the den. Take anything."

"I can find something here," I said, looking at the books on the floor. I heard her sigh and shift while I looked, and I knew she'd be asleep by the time I got back. I picked a beautiful book full of photographs of the Ligurian region in Italy. It was in Italian, but that didn't deter me. I started to tiptoe out of the room, sure that the thick gray carpet would allow me to leave undetected.

But Gina obviously didn't use sound to track me. Her breathing pattern changed, and she asked, "Where ya goin'?"

"I don't want to keep you awake."

"You'll keep me awake if you leave. Get back here." She patted the bed. "Come on."

I started to walk back to her, asking, "Are you sure? I could go downstairs and sneak back in when I'm tired."

"'M sure." She rolled onto her back and looked at me. "I missed you so much. I really need to feel you next to me."

"Me, too," I said, realizing the truth of the statement as I said it. I hadn't been looking forward to being downstairs all alone. "Sure I won't keep you awake?"

"Uh-huh." She waited until I was settled comfortably against the perfectly angled headboard to move her pillow next to my hip. She wrapped herself around my leg, and she kissed my thigh. "This is good. And don't forget your drink. That'll help you relax. G'night."

I let the book rest on my lap and started to touch her hair and her face. Even after all of the turmoil and strife we'd been through in the last few days, I felt nothing for her but tenderness and love. I'd never been as hurt as I'd been just a day earlier, but at that moment, I would have given my life for her. She was sound asleep in moments, not making a sound. Her chest moved in a slow rhythm against my leg, and I felt an almost irresistible urge to scoot down and kiss her until she had to leave for work. But I did resist it. We'd put each other through the wringer since Monday, and I let my need burn in my heart while touching the barely noticeable waves in her dark, thick hair. Taking my glass, I took another sip of the rich, warm Port, thinking only of the enigmatic woman who'd introduced me to such a delightful taste.

✦

Once again, I slept through Gina's shower. She touched me just enough to wake me and then settled onto the bed next to me. "Gotta go. Call me when you get up, and I'll direct you around the kitchen."

"I think I can figure it out," I said, yawning loudly. "It's the place with the stove, right?"

"Right." She bent and kissed me gently. "Sleep tight."

I rolled over and pulled the covers up, feeling perfectly content and happy. "Love you," I murmured.

"Love you, too," she said after a beat, her voice strangely raspy.

I kept my eyes closed, but I'd woken myself up with that little slip of the tongue. I'd known that I was falling in love with her, but I didn't think I'd just toss off a comment to tell her so. But there was something appealingly natural about the spontaneity and her emotion-filled response. I wanted to call her back, to look into her eyes and tell her the truth—that I *was* in love and that I'd do anything to make this work. But I knew she'd be late for work, and knowing Gina, that wasn't something she could stomach. So, I lay in her bed, daydreaming about her and her home and the life we could fashion—together.

Chapter Nine

I got up pretty close to my normal time. By seven thirty, I'd showered
in the tremendously cool shower stall, allowing the four showerheads
to relax every muscle. I called her as soon as I got downstairs. "Where are
you?" I asked.

"Ah…forty degrees, thirty-eight minutes north, seventy-three degrees,
sixteen minutes west."

"English, please."

"Just left of Cherry Grove. You're up bright and early. Feel okay?"

"Feel great. That's some shower you've got."

"I haven't had a girlfriend," she said, chuckling. "Gotta have some way
to get the kinks out of my back."

"I think you're a spendthrift, young lady."

"No, I'm not. I just like creature comforts."

I reached the kitchen just as she said this. "And gadgets," I added.
"Lots of gadgets. How in the hell am I supposed to make coffee?"

"The easiest way is to take my truck and go into town," she said,
laughing. "But I can walk you through it if you wanna be wild."

"They launched the space shuttle with fewer machines."

"It's not that bad. Just three machines."

"For a cup of coffee? Are you nuts?"

"Unh-uh. I'm particular. I don't like coffee much, so I never bought a
regular coffee pot. I'm an espresso girl."

I looked at the three machines, neatly lined up like stainless-steel
weapons of minimal destruction on her stainless-steel counter. The
kitchen itself was so clean and bright that it was a little overwhelming

before I'd had my coffee. Lots of chrome, glass, granite, and steel, all glinting in the bright under-counter light. "Can I make tea?"

"Sure. You just have to go to town to buy some. I hate the stuff."

I blew a raspberry at her. "You've left me in quite a fix, lady. I have to get a degree in engineering to make coffee, and I'm supposed to be working."

"Make you a deal," she said. "Go outside and get the paper, and by the time you've finished the front section, your troubles will be over."

"No, don't come home. I don't wanna screw up your day."

"I've got forty-five minutes," she said. "If I stay here, I'll just wind up loading the cargo ferry. You're giving me an excuse to get outta work."

"Oh, all right," I said. "But only if you're sure."

"Flip the toggle switch on the right side of the biggest machine," she said. "Did a red light come on?"

"Yep."

"Be there in…twenty," she said and then hung up.

Just for my own edification, I set the timer on the oven—something I could figure out without a course in electrical circuitry. I wasn't even surprised when the buzzer went off just as Gina was closing the front door. "Bring a notebook," she said as she glided into the kitchen.

I ran in after her and threw my arms around her waist. "I don't wanna learn how," I said. "I want you to come home and make coffee for me. Then I can get some hugs when I'm awake."

"No time for hugs," she said, laughing hard enough that I could feel her stomach muscles twitch. "Pay attention. You might want some later."

I still held on to her, but I looked around her shoulder.

"You take this portafilter," she said, "and hold it under the grinder. It's set for espresso, so all you have to do is fill it." She touched a switch, and the machine purred as finely ground coffee filled the thing she held in her hand. "Then you put it under this tamping machine." She put the thing in another thing and pulled a lever. There was an audible click, and the coffee was now perfectly level and looked as hard as a rock. "Latte? Cappuccino? Americano? Espresso?"

"Espresso," I said. "A double."

"Tough girl," she said. She put the thing in the last machine and seated it. Then she flipped another switch after she'd placed a lovely espresso cup on a crosshatched metal grate. The caramel-colored liquid poured out in a steady stream. "Done."

She handed me the cup, and I sniffed the hot, rich-smelling espresso. I took a tiny taste and nearly swooned. "It's God...in a cup."

"Might as well have one myself," she said. "I could use a little liquid God."

She repeated the process, and I had to acknowledge that even though it was a bit of a pain in the ass, it was worth it. "I guess if I had to factor in how long it would take to drive to a good coffee house, this is almost a time saver," I said. "But having my Mr. Coffee make it while I'm waking up isn't bad, either."

"Pagan." She touched my cup with hers and then took two sips and set her cup on the counter. "Will you clean the kitchen, honey?" she asked, giggling. "I'm late for work." Gina held me in a surprisingly firm embrace and kissed me with so much verve that I wondered how many espressos she'd had already. "The fridge is full," she said. "You're on your own." She started for the door and then said, "Call me again if you want to watch TV or listen to music." Shrugging, with an adolescent-looking grin, she said, "They're not easy, either."

With a little wave, she was gone, and I missed her before she got on her bike.

※

I don't know how I did it, since, as a historian, I'm naturally curious, but I didn't snoop while Gina was gone. I was tempted. God, was I tempted. But that seemed like a betrayal of her trust, and I thought I'd done enough of that for one week.

I got more work done than I'd thought I would, especially after going into the backyard and finding a lap pool and a decadently comfortable chaise longue. But the cool, clear day was perfect for sitting under the pale pink umbrella and working on my detailed outline.

My work had engrossed me so much that I didn't hear her come in. I also didn't hear her strip off all of her clothes. Nor hear her tiptoe outside.

But her racing dive into the pool caught my attention enough to make me scream, which delighted her to no end. "A burglar could have wiped me out!" she said, after surfacing to spit water into the air. "Strip and get in here with me."

What had I been doing wrong all these years that this was the first time a gorgeous woman had given me that instruction? I complied in a rush, throwing my shirt and shorts on the ground and running towards her. "It's shallow!" she cried, just in time to make me tuck my legs up and absorb the blow with my feet.

I jumped up and shook my head. "I know it's shallow," I said. "But I forgot."

Gina moved behind me and tucked an arm under my breasts. She pushed off and kicked so that we floated on our backs, the warm afternoon sun shining in our eyes. "Nice?"

"Nice," I agreed. "Very, very nice."

"Hey, Gina?" I said, after we'd floated and played and kissed for a while.

"Yeah?"

"What do you call a person who loads cargo on a ship?"

She stopped kicking her way down the pool and stood up. "Trick question?"

"No, I'm serious."

"That's a longshoreman," she said, giving me a funny look. "Why?"

"Are you a longshoreman?"

A big smile lit her face. "Uhm…kinda. Why?"

"I just wondered why you would have had to load cargo this morning if you hadn't come home to make espresso for me. And how are you kinda a longshoreman?"

"Oh!" She laughed and jogged over. With her arms around me, she pulled me onto her chest and lay back again. "You don't like to ask direct questions, do you?"

"Sure I do. I'm a researcher." My chin was in the water, and it was hard to keep my head back far enough to avoid sucking in a mouthful. "But I like to tease you, too."

She put me back onto my feet. "I like it when you tease me." After a gentle kiss, she splashed some water right into my face. I spit it right back at her, and she laughed and hugged me. "I own a few boats. Different boats for different purposes."

"You didn't mention that, buddy. Holdin' out on me?"

"No." She smiled that adorable half-smile. "I forgot."

"That's a big thing to forget. Anything else? A high-rise office tower? A cattle ranch in Texas?"

"No, I think that's it." She held up a few fingers. "Just six things. Oh. And the water taxis. Just nine things. And I'm in the Longshoreman's union, but I wouldn't say I was a longshoreman. Pilots are more like a branch of the union."

"Okay," I said. "For holding out on me, you have to tell me a secret. Something you hate for people to know."

"People in general?"

I shrugged. "Whatever. Personal or public."

She put her hands on the deck and pushed until she could put a knee on the tile and get out. There were no towels around, but she didn't seem to care. "I'll tell you something big," she said. "Real big."

I got out of the pool and stood near her, but she backed up, just out of reach. "I'm extremely…extremely…ticklish."

"Really?" I squinted at her. "I've touched every place on your body. You giggle when I tickle you behind your knees, but…"

Gina shook her head. "I'm a little ticklish everywhere. But it's off the charts from ear to ear."

"Ear to ear?"

"Yep. From behind one ear, across the back of my neck just under my hairline, over to my other ear." She looked at me and tilted her head down. "It's bad—real bad."

I slowly walked over to her, taking small, sure steps, my eyes locked on her. "How bad?" My voice was low, and she looked like she was deciding whether to run or kiss me.

"Bad as it gets," she said.

Standing so close that my nipples rested just under the swell of her breasts, I asked, "Are you afraid I'll use this information to hurt you?"

Her head nodded quickly, and she shifted her weight from foot to foot.

"You look like you have ants in your pants," I said and then ran my hand over her ass cheeks. "But you're not wearing pants."

"Nervous."

She looked so adorably childlike that I felt like a kid, too. As fearful as she looked, there was a glint in her eyes. Almost a taunt. I was sure there were many secrets she could have told me, and the fact that she told me this one, while staying within reach, made me give her a little test. I raised my hand, and she flinched. When my hand got closer to her neck, she tensed up and crossed her arms over her breasts. I gently touched the lobe of an ear, a place I'd kissed and licked and sucked many times. But now that I knew the secret, she started to squeal and squatted down a little, making herself into as small a target as possible. She could have darted away or held my hands. We both knew she was stronger than I was, but she didn't even attempt to press her advantage. She just stood there—or quivered there—waiting for me to tickle her. That was the only thing that made sense.

So, I tickled her. Gently at first, then more aggressively as she started to shake and whimper. I was having a ball, and her nipples showed me she liked it, too.

The funny thing is that she didn't tell me to stop. She wriggled and giggled and squirmed, and she panted and gasped to catch her breath, but she didn't try to get away, and she didn't complain.

I kept up the assault, making her squeal so loudly that she was nearly screaming. My nipples were hard, too, and my clit felt like it'd been pinched. I could tell it was getting to be too much when she writhed almost out of reach. She jumped up and down and then moaned, "Gonna pee!" She ran as fast as she could, scampering into the kitchen, her adorable butt jiggling.

I trotted after her and saw that she had run into the half-bath by the entry door. The door was open, and I waved at her. "Hi, there."

"You took advantage of me," she huffed, clearly joking.

"I think you liked it as much as I did." Wiggling my eyebrows, I asked, "Does somebody get hot when she's tickled?"

"A little." She finished up and came out, taking my hand. "Just a little." Slapping her butt, I let her lead me upstairs. "Shower?" I asked.

"Uh-huh. I hate chlorine on my skin."

We got into the shower together, and I realized why she'd splurged on such a nice one. It was roomy enough for two, and one of the showerheads was hitting somewhere nice all of the time. We hugged, then kissed, and then kissed some more. Gina soaped up her hands and washed me all over, spending a little extra time on some of those nice places. I did the same for her, delighting in the feel of her body shivering when I washed between her legs. Someone was ready for fun, and I was ready, willing, and able to give it to her.

⁂

We decided to go out to dinner, so I took out the extra clothes I'd stashed in my backpack, thinking I should have done so when I'd removed my laptop. I didn't think I looked awful, but once Gina came downstairs, I changed my mind.

She was wearing shorts and a sleeveless sweater. That doesn't sound like much. But her clothes fit her so well and were so neatly pressed and chosen to compliment her skin tone that it took me a second to even be able to compliment her. "You look fantastic."

"Thanks." She smiled that sexy smile that showed she knew just how good she looked. "We're gonna have to get dressed up and go out soon."

"I don't have anything nice, remember?"

"Then we'll go into the city to get some of your things. I can handle it. I got there yesterday, right?"

"I don't have much in the city, either." I knew I looked embarrassed, but I couldn't help it. "I've never spent much time on how I look."

She put her hands on my hips and gazed at me for a few seconds. "You don't have to. You're naturally beautiful."

That was a load of crap. Gina was naturally beautiful, but she obviously spent time and attention on how she looked. She had a very good haircut, and her clothes were always perfect—even to load cargo. It wasn't that she dressed in designer clothes. She just chose things that made her look her absolute best. And I didn't. I went to The Gap or Old Navy and bought things without even trying them on. If my pants were a little big or a little small, I barely noticed.

Elaine busted my chops for wearing lavender and pale green and tan shirts, since they made my pale skin look even paler. But I liked those colors and didn't pay any attention to her. Elaine also chided me for pulling my hair back in a band most of the time. But it was so much easier to do that. In fact, I'd done it tonight. I can make my hair look pretty good if I blow it dry and use a curling iron on the ends. But I was in a hurry, so I just pulled it back. Now I wished I'd taken the time.

It had happened in a flash. After thirty years, I noticed how slapdash I was about my appearance. After being with Gina for just a few weeks, I wanted to change. I wanted to look nice for her. I cared about how she saw me. "Will you go shopping with me sometime?"

"Huh? You wanna go shopping?"

"Yeah. With you."

She shrugged and nodded. "Sure. I'll go anywhere you want."

"Right now, I want dinner. I'm starved."

❖

We walked out the front door, and I started to turn left. I hadn't seen her car yet, but I assumed it was in the garage next to the pool. But Gina took my hand and led me towards the path that ran along the water. "Are we walking?"

"No. It'd take…days," she said, after thinking for a bit.

"Where are we going?"

"Montauk. Ever been there?"

"I don't think so. Is it on Long Island?"

"Barely. Montauk Point is the last stop before…Europe, I guess."

"Gina," I said, pulling on her arm. "You're fucking with me."

Laughing, she agreed. "You're fun to fuck with. But I'm being honest. We're going to Montauk because they have the best lobster rolls. You *do* like lobster rolls, don't you?"

"Lobster rolls? Like cinnamon rolls?"

"Yep. Just like cinnamon rolls. I can tell you're an aficionado."

"You can make me one. Now, how are we going?"

"The fast way. By boat."

"A boat? We're going by boat?"

"It's faster," she said. "A lot faster."

"Cool. One of those little taxi things you have?"

"Unh-uh. That's a business asset. I don't use business assets for personal use."

"You used your truck for me."

"Yeah, but that's my personal vehicle, too. I account for business and personal use. I don't do that with the boats. They're all business."

We turned off the path and walked up to a locked gate by a dock. "You have your own boat?"

Giving me a big smile, she said, "Why would that surprise you? I've got six ferries, a cargo ship, and three water taxis. Don't you see the theme?"

Right before I was able to pinch her, we stopped at a low-slung, bright yellow boat. Gina unsnapped a black cover that covered the passenger area. "How cute!" I gushed. There was a small checkerboard design around the top of the boat that made it look like a very low-slung cab.

"Be nice to me and I might name it after you," she said.

I walked to the end of the dock and saw that it was named, "Taxi! Taxi!" "Cute. Very cute. I'm glad it's not named after some other woman."

"I sold Lacey," she said. "Not just because of the name, of course. I'm sentimental, but I'm not stupid."

"Well, I'm glad you sold Lacey." I saw the look in her eyes that came over her whenever she talked about her ex-lover. "But I'm sorry you and she broke up. I know what it's like."

Gina took my hand and tugged me into a hug. "I'm not sorry tonight. Tonight, I'm very glad I'm with you."

✦

She hadn't been kidding about the speed thing. And I was glad I'd put my hair back. If I hadn't, the wind might have pulled all of it off. Taxi!

Taxi! wasn't huge, but the engine must have run from the front all the way to the back. We started out slowly and carefully, but once we hit open water, the boat accelerated at a speed that could have snapped my neck if not for the nicely padded headrests. "You don't mind going fast, do you?" Gina yelled.

"No! I like it!"

"Good girl!" She hit the throttle again, and we started to fly. I'd been on boats, and I'd been on some that had seemed fast, but I'd never been on a boat like this. I was a little frightened because it seemed as if we might hit a big wave and crash into a million pieces, but having Gina at the wheel allowed me to relax more than I would have with anyone else in the world. Still, with the wind noise and the butterflies in my stomach, I didn't speak the whole way to Montauk.

Gina didn't seem to want or need to talk. She looked very relaxed. Much more relaxed than she did when she was piloting the ferry. She steered with one hand, the other arm resting casually on the edge of the boat. I wanted to ask her what everything was called, but I thought I'd wait until we were stationary for that.

It took nearly an hour to reach Montauk, but it sure didn't seem like it. Once I'd gotten used to the speed, I could relax, too. And it really was relaxing. Amazingly relaxing given that we were hurtling across the ocean like a jet. I was a little disappointed when Gina slowed down and said, "Keep your eyes out for a parking space."

Since I never knew if she was kidding, I scanned the docks we passed, looking for…what, I wasn't really sure. But she slowed even more and pulled into a slip without a pause.

"You didn't really need me to look, did you?"

"Unh-uh. I just like to see if you'll do what I tell you." She smiled at me so lovingly that my heart nearly stopped. Leaning over some controls that separated us, she kissed me. "You usually do. I like that."

"I'm your slave," I said, making use of the closeness to kiss her back.

"Ha! You're no one's slave, Hayden. You're just obedient when you don't know any better."

She had me there, so I didn't argue. After buttoning up the cover, we held hands and walked to a restaurant that was close to the dock. "I've been coming here since I was a baby," she said. "This is one of my dad's favorite places. He might even be here tonight."

I was pleased that she'd take me to a family favorite, but I hoped her father wasn't in attendance. I wanted to be alone with her tonight. I still missed her. "It's cute," I said when we walked inside.

She looked around, seemingly for the first time. "I guess it is. I come here so often, it barely registers." Gina touched my bare arm. "Are you warm enough to sit outside?"

"Yeah, I think so. It's a nice night."

We walked through the place, Gina giving a quick wave to a couple of waitresses whose eye she caught. The patio was packed, but she went over to a young man, put her arm around his shoulders, and jostled him a bit. He hugged her, and she turned to me and called me over. "Hayden, this is Randy. He's gonna hook us up."

"Hi, Randy," I said. "Looks a little busy tonight."

"It's busy from Memorial Day until Labor Day," he said. "But we've always got room for Gina."

Sure enough, the next table went to us, despite the grumbling I heard from a few couples who had clearly been there for a while. I looked around and saw one man who was still staring at us, clearly perturbed. "Should we cut in front of people like that?"

"Like what?" She was totally oblivious.

"We just walked in and cut in front of all of those people."

"So?" She shrugged. "You go to a place for forty years, you get better treatment." She looked at the man who was now speaking to Randy, looking like he was giving the young man a piece of his mind. "When that guy comes here twenty times a year, he can cut in line."

I fidgeted in my seat. "Makes me a little uncomfortable," I said. "I don't like to make people mad."

With a frown, she said, "We can go inside if you want."

"No, no, then you'll be mad."

"Uhm…" She nodded. "I think the problem is that you don't get the difference between tourists and locals."

"Probably not."

"The locals are here all year. We come here in December and February, when the tourists are back in New York. A place like this can't survive on three months of profit, even though they're packed to the rafters. They need their base, and that's the locals. So, in return for coming here all year...and for coming here for many years...and for spending about twenty dollars in gas to get here..." She smiled, showing her teeth. "I get a table."

"I guess that makes sense," I said. I looked over my shoulder and saw the angry guy and his girlfriend leave. "But it's not good for business to make customers mad."

"Fuck him," she said, dismissively. "You can't make everybody happy. Besides, he'll be back. Every place out here is crowded. Every place lets good customers in first. Like I said, he can remedy his problem by driving out here in December and getting to know everyone."

"Okay," I said. "I see your point. They do that at all of the clubs in New York, too. Maybe that's why I don't like it," I added. "I'm always the one who doesn't get in."

"How often do you go?" Gina asked.

"Almost never."

"I rest my case."

The waitress came over, and Gina accepted a hug. "Sheryl, this is Hayden. She's never had a lobster roll."

"You from thuh islan'?"

Wow. Thank God Gina's accent wasn't that thick. "No. Philadelphia."

"Gina's muthuh and huh fathuh brung huh heeyah when she wuz a baby," she said. "Like twenty yeeahz."

"A little more than that," Gina said. "But thanks. Can we have some oysters, too, Sheryl?"

"Shuah. Malpeque?"

"Got Peconics?"

"Shuah."

"Six of each," Gina said.

"'Kay. Beeyah?"

"Yeah. I'll have one. Hayden?"

"Uhm, sure." I hoped I was ordering a beer, but I wasn't certain.

"Yoonglin' okay?" Gina asked.

Now I really wasn't sure. "Fine." It sounded like I was getting something Chinese, but I couldn't imagine what.

Sheryl left, and Gina reached across the table and took both of my hands. The sun had just disappeared, and the sky glowed pink and lilac. "You look fantastic in the sunset."

"Mmm, so do you. It makes your skin look like…I'm not sure what, but whatever it is, it's pretty."

"Thanks."

"You know, I have no idea how old you are. We keep forgetting some pretty important questions."

She smiled, looking so relaxed and happy that I wished I could stop time and just stare at her for hours. "Those little things don't mean much to me."

"Come to think of it, they don't mean that much to me, either. I guess that's why I've never asked. But I'm asking now. How old are you?"

"Twenty-seven."

My eyes popped. "You're younger than me?"

She chuckled. "The sun ages a person's skin, but you don't have to be rude."

"No, no! I just…you seem so much more mature."

"Ha." Her grin faded. "That's a laugh. I'm like a toddler having a temper tantrum. I'm surprised you didn't think I was three."

"You're not like that very often, Gina. Not often at all."

She looked down and smiled at the picture of our hands interlaced. "You don't mind me holding your hands, do you?"

I blinked in surprise, puzzled that she'd even ask. "No, of course not. Why would I?"

She looked thoughtful and then said, "Sometimes, you seem like you think you have to behave. You know…to not do things that make people notice you."

"Oh. Right." I considered her comment and said, "I'm getting better about that, but I still have some issues." I turned my hands over and held hers, giving them a squeeze. "This is probably a good time to try to explain to you what happened on Monday."

It wouldn't have taken an expert in body language to tell she didn't want to talk about it. I still held her hands, but she leaned back and looked as if she'd smelled something rancid. "Do we have to?"

"Yeah. Might as well do it now." A busboy came over with two beers, and I saw that he was delivering Pennsylvania's own Yuengling, not something Chinese. That accent of hers can really play havoc with my comprehension. I took a sip, nodded my approval, and said, "I acted like I did on Monday because of my need to fit in. To make people think I'm one of the crowd."

"Which crowd?"

"That depends. On Monday, I was worried about what Elaine would think if she knew I was dating you."

Her face clouded over, and she set her beer down on the table harder than she'd needed to. "Thanks."

I squeezed her hand hard. "Hear me out before you get mad, okay? I really don't want you to get mad."

She nodded quickly, looking like she was willing to do anything to stay calm.

"This is about me, not you."

Looking at me curiously, she took another drink and leaned back. "Go on."

"It might not seem like it, but this isn't that different from your not wanting to approach me for a date."

"It most certainly..." She stopped, and it looked as though she were literally biting her tongue.

"Just be patient," I said gently. She looked like she was suppressing a deeply felt need to argue, but she didn't. She did take her hands back though, which hurt me a little bit. "You said you never would have approached me because I wasn't your type. Well, you're not my type, either. And I don't just mean from a looks perspective."

"You mean from a wop perspective," she said, her expression dark and simmering with anger.

"Hey, you might have a thing about being Italian, but I don't."

"I don't have a *thing* about being Italian," she said. "Nobody minds dating some businesswoman from Milan or Rome. Wops are people like me—working-class people with bad accents and statues of the Virgin Mary in the front yard."

I wasn't sure whom she was talking about, but it clearly wasn't herself. I spent a minute thinking about what I wanted to say, trying to make sure I didn't offend her. "Gina, I still wouldn't know you were Italian if you hadn't said something. It's just not obvious, honey."

Her eyes widened at my calling her "honey," and I wondered how it'd come out of my mouth so easily.

While she was distracted, I continued. "It wouldn't have mattered if you were a park ranger on the island, a waitress, a gardener, or a bookkeeper. It also wouldn't have made any difference if you were French or Hungarian or Finnish. What mattered was that you weren't one of us. You have a job where you *do* something."

She looked annoyed. Very annoyed. But she didn't raise her voice. "What does that mean?"

Sheryl brought our oysters, and Gina nodded at her when she set them down. The waitress paused for a second, saw that things were tense, and left quickly.

I waited to see if Gina was going to start eating, but she was still staring at me, so I answered. "It means that you're not in the professional class. It's a stupid, ridiculous class thing, and I'm embarrassed that I let it influence me."

"That's the same thing I was talking about," she said, steaming, but under control. "My father wears a big gold crucifix around his neck, and he yells and cusses and drives a big, showy Cadillac. We're low-class wops."

"It's not about money or ethnicity. It's just not." I could see I wasn't making a dent. "Look. Dana comes from the inner city of Baltimore. Her parents both work for the city at pretty low-level clerical jobs. She's black. But she fits in perfectly because of her degrees and because of her job. I'm not defending myself, Gina, because it's just as ridiculous to discriminate based on profession as anything else. But it's not your ethnicity, and it's not your family. My crowd pushes out people who don't make their livings with their big brains."

I could see her start to relax, so I thought I had a chance of convincing her I was a different kind of asshole than she thought I was. "Then why did Elaine make fun of me that first day?" A look of incredible hurt flashed across her lovely features, and just seeing it made me want to cry. "She said not to cross me or I'd have you whacked."

That was it! Damn, I knew it was obnoxious, but I hadn't even paid enough attention to Elaine to recall what she'd said that day. "I have no idea. It barely registered, other than to irritate me."

"Everybody thinks I'm mobbed up 'cause of the boats."

"What? I certainly don't. Why on earth would I?"

She looked at me as if I was slow. "Everyone knows the mob used to control the waterways. But they don't control us. We're legit."

"Gina," I soothed. "I'd never heard that. The thought had never crossed my mind. You come across very differently than you think you do."

"I do not. I know what people think. I've heard it my whole life."

Boy, this wasn't easy. "You've heard things from people you grew up with, people who must have preconceived ideas that I don't have. I swear, Gina, I've never, ever considered whether your family was in the Mafia."

"We're not," she said again. "My grandfather took a bullet because he wouldn't let them put the squeeze on him." Her pretty chin was jutting out, and I could see how proud she was of his bravery.

I took her hand again and looked into her eyes. "Here's the total truth. I've never dated anyone from outside of academia. My whole world has been connected to schools and universities. I'm a degree snob, and I deserve your censure for that. But I'm not anti-Italian, and I don't think you're in the Mafia, and I don't care whether you or your family has money. I'm flawed, Gina. But I recognize that, and I'll try never to let what other people think influence me in that way again."

She met my eyes and brought my hand to her lips, where she kissed it. "Let's put this to bed, okay? I was a mean asshole on Monday. You were…I don't know what to call you," she said, smiling a little. "Neither one of us should be proud of ourselves for the way we acted that day. But it's gonna make me nuts to try to analyze every little thing. Let's start over and try to forget that Monday ever happened."

"Okay," I said. "I can if you can."

She picked up an oyster, freed it from its muscle, and put the shell to my lips. "Bottoms up." Gina smiled when I chewed and swallowed. "I woulda made you wait in the boat if you'd turned your nose up at a Peconic. There are some things I can't ignore."

✦

After eating what had to be the best lobster rolls on the planet, even though I had no others with which to compare them, we walked back to the boat. Quickly and efficiently, Gina got her ready to go, and she backed out of our parking spot without a hitch. She was in a fantastic mood, our talk having taken down the last barrier we'd built up over our fight. Once we were in open water, she didn't gun the engine as she'd done on the outbound trip. This time, she drove at a moderate speed that allowed us to speak without shouting.

I reached over and snuck my hand under Gina's sweater, giving her a little tickle. "Trying to save gas?"

"No, not at all." She put her arm around me and pulled me over until she could kiss the top of my head. "I want to enjoy being out on the water with you. Two of my favorite things."

"This is nice. I've always loved the water, but I've never been out at night. It's pretty cool."

"It is. That's also why I'm not going fast. There aren't many people out at night, but damned if you don't find 'em when you're really movin'."

"I think you're just careful."

"Maybe. About some things." She glanced at me, and I saw her teeth shining in the moonlight. "Wanna drive?"

"Drive? Me?"

"Sure. It's not hard. Tell ya what. You sit on my lap and steer; I'll do the rest." She cut the throttle, and we slowed to a stop.

I was already moving when I said, "I think this is just a ruse to paw me."

"Like I need a ruse." She laughed as she grabbed handfuls of my more intimate parts.

It wasn't easy trying to fit into a small space while being mauled, but I managed. Gina had moved the seat back, giving me room to settle between her legs. "This is pretty nice," I said. "We should drive like this all of the time."

She placed a couple of wet, sloppy kisses on my neck and then dutifully wiped me dry. "I don't know why I like to slobber on you," she said. "But I sure do."

"Probably because I told you it weirds me out." I turned my head so she could lick my cheek. "See?"

"Must be it." She hugged me tightly, nuzzling her face against my back. "You're fun to play with."

I leaned back, squishing her against the seat. "So are you." I let her breathe again when she blindly stuck her hand up the leg of my shorts and started fishing for something to pinch. "Let's go before somebody hits us," I said. "I was freaked out by *Titanic*."

"Not many icebergs out here," Gina said. "Now, be careful with the wheel. Turn her a lot more gently than you would a car. A little correction goes a long way."

"Okay. Just don't drive too fast." I was nervous, but it was hard to be too anxious with Gina right behind me. Her arms were around my waist, and I knew she could take the wheel in a moment if she needed to.

"I won't. I'm careful, remember? Ready?"

"Uh-huh."

"My part's pretty easy." She reached around me and slowly moved the throttle just enough so that we were moving. "Let me know when you're comfortable, and I'll give you a little more power."

"How fast were we going on the way out? It felt like we were flying."

"I had her up to about sixty."

"Miles an hour?"

"Yeah. What else?"

"I don't know. I thought you had some kinda nautical terms you use."

"We do. But nobody understands knots. I simplified it for you."

I looked down at the controls and saw there was a regular speedometer. "Then why does this little thing say we're going fifteen miles per hour?"

"Oh. I guess they simplified it for both of us." She squeezed me tight and laughed. "Just tryin' to show off."

"You don't have to," I said. "You're spectacular without adding a thing."

✦

An hour later, we'd finished putting the boat to bed. "That was so much fun!" I squealed. "Can I drive again?"

"Any time you want. As long as you sit on my lap."

I took Gina's hand as we headed back to her house. "You don't drive a very hard bargain, captain. Your lap is one of the nicest places I've ever been."

She put her arm around me, tucking me close to her body. "You called me honey."

"Huh?"

"Tonight. You called me honey."

"Oh." I glanced up at her and saw how contented she looked. "I didn't think about it in advance. You just seem like my honey."

Gina pulled me to a stop. Deftly, she removed the band around my hair and slid her fingers through it. She'd learned that running her hands through my hair was a surefire way to relax me. And turn me on. Not always in that order. "You seem like my honey, too." She kissed me, teasing my lips open with her tongue. I was no longer relaxed. We kissed for a long time, holding each other in the warm, still night. "Let's go, honey," she finally said, taking my hand to lead me home.

✦

For the first time, we were a little shy around each other as we got ready for bed. There was no question that we were going to have sex. I could see the fire in her eyes, and I was squirming with desire. She came to bed wearing a sexy, tight, chocolate-colored tank top, and she looked a little tentative, like she was waiting for me to make the first move.

Now that I'd gotten to know her better, I realized that Gina wasn't very butch at all. Truth be told, she was quite a few notches higher on the

177

femme scale than I was. But she was definitely a top. She'd taken charge of our lovemaking that first night and hadn't relinquished that position since. But now…now she seemed almost passive. She lay on her side and gazed at me—not touching, just giving me a warm, loving smile.

"You're so pretty," I said. I touched her cheek, stroking the soft skin with the back of my hand. "You have the prettiest eyes and the loveliest smile I think I've ever seen."

"I was just thinking the same thing about you. I never knew how much I loved blue eyes until I saw yours."

"No one will ever mistake us for sisters," I said, scooting closer to her. I tugged her top up, exposing her chest, and then snuggled up so our breasts touched and compressed into each other. "Look at the contrast in our skin."

She did, while running her hand along my hip. Then she reached down and pulled my leg over hers. Ah, she was starting to take over now. Just how I liked it. "I can see your veins," she said, tracing them through the nearly translucent skin on my breast.

"I can only see one on you." I let my finger wander over the one vein her dark skin revealed. It circled her nipple, which began to harden as I touched it gently.

Gina pushed on my hip to put me on my back. Her eyes had taken on that glow they had when she was feeling sexy and confident. "I love to look at your body." Her hand glided over me, and my nipples stiffened before she'd even reached them. She took one between her fingers and pinched it. "I love how responsive you are. Just a touch, and you have goose bumps." Where she'd touched me, my arm was covered with the tiny bumps, illustrating her point. "I love how fair you are, how delicate and fine your skin is. It's almost alabaster in some places…like here." She gently touched my breast, making it sway under her hand. "You're so beautiful, Hayden. Your body could have been crafted by Ghiberti, Verrocchio, Donatello…"

She was *so* full of crap. But there was a slight chance that she was delusional enough to believe what she was saying, so I didn't try to dissuade her. Besides, her accent was so incredibly sexy when she named the Italian artists that I could feel myself getting wet. I put my hand on her hip and then slowly brought it up her body, creating my own wave of goose bumps on her tanned skin. "The things you do to me," I murmured.

Gina's face was right over mine, smiling at me in that lovely, sexy way. "What do I do to you?"

"You make me melt," I said. "I feel totally limp when you touch me and kiss me. Like I could sink into the mattress and never move again."

"It doesn't seem like that when you're moving *with* me," she whispered into my ear. "When your legs are wrapped around me and you're thrusting against me like you can't get enough."

"That comes later," I said, smiling up at her. "First, I feel limp and languid and lethargic. Like I could lie here for hours and let you touch me. But then...then I start to need you. And once I need you...God knows what comes over me."

She laughed softly and kissed me. "You do come alive," she said. "You're so passive at first. You lie there and only move enough for me to reach new spots. But then you get going, and it's all I can do to keep up with you."

"You do pretty well. You're always right there when and where I need you."

Gina kissed me again, and I felt her nipples touch mine. They were so firm they barely felt like flesh. "Know what?" she asked, lying next to me.

"What?"

"I've never enjoyed sex more than I have with you. You make me feel so...I don't know," she said. "Open, I guess. You make me open up and let you in."

I pulled her leg over my hip, loving the way her neatly trimmed curls tickled my belly. "I was just thinking that," I said. "No one's ever reached the part of me that you do. I've never, ever reacted like I do with you. You set me on fire, Gina. From the first night."

She smiled at me in the soft light, her eyes like warm pools of topaz and amber. "Is that just luck?"

"No," I said, confidently. "It's more than luck. I think it means something. Something special."

"What?" she asked innocently, even though I knew she was just trying to make me say it first.

But for some reason, I couldn't. Maybe it was still too soon after our fight. Maybe I was still worried about her ability to control her temper. Whatever the reason, I couldn't do it. So, I tried to say something that would make up for my reticence. "I think fate is guiding us."

"Fate?"

"Yes. Fate. And I think we have to let her take us wherever she wants to."

Her arms were around me before I'd finished speaking, kissing me with so much emotion that I could hardly take it all in. Then Gina pulled back for just a moment. "I know where I want to go, Hayden."

"I do, too. But I'm not going to interfere with fate. We'll know when we're there." I pulled her down, and we kissed and kissed and kissed. No one could kiss better than Gina. I wasn't sure of many things, but I was sure of that. She made me feel so sexy and lovable and desirable. And no one had ever done that with just a kiss.

I was panting when she paused, hovering above me with so much love in her eyes.

I felt a burst of energy, and I rolled her onto her back. I felt so full of love for her that I wanted to gobble her up. "You are so damned loveable!" I pulled her top off and kissed her body, starting at her neck and working my way down until I reached her waist. She was especially ticklish on the side of her waist, and I couldn't resist teasing her with my tongue in that most sensitive spot.

"No!" She rolled away, grabbing one of my hands in the process. "Don't!"

We wrestled like cubs, rolling around in the big bed, tearing the covers from their moorings. She was stronger than I was, but not by a lot. And since she was more ticklish, it was almost a standoff. We finally collapsed, panting and giggling. I was spent, and she surprised me by sliding her arms under my head and knees, holding me like a big sack of potatoes. My arms were trapped, so my tickling tactic was lost to me.

"I don't give up," she said, licking me from my chin to my forehead.

"Blech!" I shivered. "Stop it!"

"Such a baby." She wiped my face with her cheek, doing a fairly good job, given her lack of supplies. Then she looked into my eyes, and I could see a dozen emotions pass across her face. "Do you think we'll get there?"

"I do," I said, gazing into the depths of her lovely eyes. "We've got our work cut out for us, though. It's not gonna be easy building a relationship."

"Why?" She smiled at me. "You'll quit your job and be my wife. We'll travel to Italy in the winter, and you'll hang out at the beach all summer. Who wouldn't like that?"

"You make a good case," I said, kissing her nose—the only thing I could reach, given my position. "Or you could live with me in Manhattan as soon as the summer season is over. We could go to Italy over my winter break and spend the spring and summer here."

"Ask a hundred people and see how many choose option two," she said, grinning like a wolf.

"Ask a hundred people what they'd rather do: make love to you or talk. See how many choose option two." I had her there. Number two wouldn't get a single vote. "We've got all summer to figure things out. All we have to do now is let fate carry us. Things will fall into place. I'm sure of it."

"You sure you're sure?" she asked. "'Cause I'll lick you again if you're not."

"I'm sure!" I squealed. "I'm sure!"

"Okay." She released me and settled me along her body. "I'd rather make love than talk, too. Most people talk too damn much."

"I just have one thing to say," I said, smiling at her, feeling the love that I had for her infusing itself into my bones. "I promise we'll work things out. I promise."

"If I can't hook you by the end of the summer, I don't deserve you." She grinned at me and added, "I deserve you."

Chapter Ten

I stayed the whole weekend, and by Sunday night, I had no desire to go back to my house. But wearing the same clothes for three days had grown old. Gina and I were floating in the pool, and I said, "How about a little spin in your boat?"

She paddled over to me. "Does someone need a lobster roll?"

Laughing, I said, "Now that you mention it ..."

"They're good, aren't they?"

"They're much better than good, Gina. But I need some more clothes and some of my books."

She stood up and stared at me for a second. "Are you gonna stay here this week?"

A flash of panic hit me. "Don't you...?"

"Of course, I want you to!" She jumped up and down, her beautiful breasts jiggling. "I just didn't think you'd want to."

"I do. I'm able to work really well here. I miss the beach a little bit, but your house is so nice and calming and tranquil. I love it here."

"You don't have to miss the beach," she said. "Let's go right now." She was out of the water before I could react. "We'll go over in my boat and hang out until sunset. Then we'll zoom up to Montauk for dinner and head home."

"It sounds so easy," I said.

"It is." She put her hand out to pull me from the pool. "Put your suit on, and we'll go."

"Suit? Why do I need a suit?" I blinked at her, trying to look innocent.

She slapped my rump hard enough to leave a handprint. "Because I don't want to have to chase women away all afternoon. It'll be hard enough running 'em off when you're wearing a suit. There's just no way I could turn 'em all back if you were naked."

"I thought the Irish were full of blarney. Italians must be, too."

"No way. Italians tell the truth. Nothing but the truth."

❧

I decided that living in Sayville and having a very fast boat was the perfect way to summer on Fire Island. The ferry wasn't a bad way to go, but you had to abide by the schedule and crowd onto it on busy weekends. Hopping into our little taxi was positively decadent in comparison. We were at the dock in ten minutes, and it would have taken even less time if we hadn't had to backtrack a little to go through the cut of the barrier islands to reach open water.

It was about five o'clock in the evening when we reached my house. There were a few butterflies in my stomach, but I was calmer than I thought I'd be. Elaine liked to stay on the island until late Sunday night, so I knew we'd probably run into her. But not only wasn't I angry with Elaine anymore, I honestly didn't care what she thought about me. I wasn't sure why I'd had this epiphany so quickly, but it seemed perfectly natural. Having Gina hold my hand as we walked down the paths to my house made everything but her seem inconsequential.

We entered the house, met by delightful silence. "Let's go to the beach for a while and then pack up," Gina said. "I wanna see you in your suit."

"I think I have a pretty good one," I said. "My sister went shopping with me."

Gina laughed, shaking her head at me. She followed me into my bedroom and asked, "What is it with you and shopping? Do you really hate it?"

"Kinda," I said. "It seems like a waste of time when I can just order things from Eddie Bauer or L.L. Bean or The Gap. I can almost always wear an eight in pants, so I'm not hard to fit. Seems easier to do it online."

"I'm sure it is," she said, watching me undress with a certain spark in her gaze. "But not all eights are created equal."

"Close enough," I said.

She didn't reply, just shrugged her shoulders. "If that works for you, go with it. You look great to me."

"I wanna look greater," I said. "Every lover I've had has tried to get me to dress better. I think you're just too polite to tell me how you really feel."

Her eyes widened. "Hayden, don't put thoughts in my head. I wouldn't change a thing about you. But if you want me to go shopping with you sometime, I'm in."

Now naked, I went to her and kissed her. She tasted so good, and her body was so soft and pliable where it touched mine. She responded quickly, and soon her hands were roaming over my body. "Fuck the beach," she murmured as she guided me to my bed.

"Mmm…fuck me," I growled. "Fuck *me*, Gina."

❖

Gina knew how to follow instructions. By the time she'd fucked me senseless, it was after six, and the sun was sinking behind a big bank of clouds on the horizon. It was too late to lie on the beach, but I was the last one to complain. I'd rather have Gina's talented tongue tickling all of my tender spots than some sticky old sand any day. She looked pretty happy, too, lying next to me with one foot planted on the bed and the other stretched out along my leg. Her face was relaxed, and a small, contented smile barely creased her lips. "Happy?" I asked, knowing the question was rhetorical.

"Yeah, I'd say I'm happy. How about you?" Her foot dropped, and she turned onto her side, propping her head up with her hand.

"Blissful." I took her hand and kissed it. "One of my favorite memories of childhood is going swimming on a hot, humid day and then going home and taking a nap. I'd have a fan on, blowing air over my body, and I felt so relaxed and happy. I'd be stark naked, lying on top of the covers on my little bed, the fan moving back and forth over me. And I'd feel like every day would be summer." I turned on my side and saw her eyes fixed on me, taking in every word. I kissed her gently. "I feel like that today. Like every day with you will be warm and sunny and…"

"Endless," she said, her eyes brimming with tears. "I could lie here listening to you talk for the rest of my life." She wrapped an arm around my waist and pulled me close. "I want to know every thing about you. Everything."

"Me, too," I whispered. "I'm interested in every part of you. All the things that make you you."

She drew away and looked at me for a few seconds. I could see something in her eyes, but I wasn't sure exactly what it was. Whatever it was, I didn't like it.

"I have to tell you something," she said. Her body had tensed, and now mine was tense, too. She looked so serious and...almost afraid.

"What, honey? What is it?"

My calling her honey brought a flash of a smile to her face, but it only lasted a second. "I haven't told you the whole truth about something."

"What?" She didn't answer immediately. "*What?*"

"I said I didn't go to college because I didn't want to."

This was a strange path in our conversation, but she obviously needed to go here. "Yeah?"

"That's not the whole truth." She bit her lip and then blinked a few times. "I barely got through high school. I didn't take the SATs because I knew I'd get a terrible score, and I didn't want to have to tell people my score for my whole life."

My heart slowed to its usual pace. I stroked her hip and said, "What difference does it make? Many people aren't serious about high school. A lot of very bright people aren't turned on by school."

She shook her head, and I could see that she was frustrated. I just wasn't sure with whom she was frustrated. "That's not it," she said. "I couldn't do well in school." She broke eye contact and added, "I have a learning disability."

"You do?"

"Yeah."

I touched her chin, moving her head so I could see into her eyes. "Wanna tell me about it? You don't have to if you don't want to, but I'm interested."

"I'll tell you," she said, pushing her chin down again. "They thought I was lazy for a long time."

I pulled her closer and threaded my fingers through her hair. "What idiot would think you were lazy?"

Her eyes met mine for just a second. "My dad. My teachers."

"Not your mom?"

"No," she shook her head. "My mom knew I was trying. I guess she thought I was dumb, but she never said so."

"Oh, Gina." I hugged her close. "What did *you* think, baby?"

"I thought I was dumb 'cause I knew I wasn't lazy. My brothers thought I was dumb. The kids in my class laughed at me when I had to stand up and answer questions."

"You don't think that now, do you? Because you're one of the brightest people I know."

She smirked and grunted. "Sure I am."

"You are." I sat up and stared at her. "You're very quick, and you have more intellectual curiosity than most of my colleagues. I don't just like being with you because you're gorgeous, you know. I love your brain." Leaning over, I kissed her head and then petted it. "You have a beautiful brain."

"I do all right," she admitted begrudgingly. "Given my limitations. But I have a hard time taking tests, and I get stuck if I have to answer when I'm not prepared."

"I never—I mean never—would have guessed," I said. "When did they finally figure out you were having trouble?"

"I think I was in fourth or fifth grade," she said. Her eyes narrowed, and she said, "It was fifth. Mrs. Longhorn. She talked to my mom and said she thought my trouble was writing and thinking at the same time. They sent me to some kinda specialist, and he said I had dysgraphia."

"Do you have trouble with all writing?"

"No. Not really. I'm lucky because I can write what I want to say if I think about it and go over it a couple of times before writing it down."

"But it takes you longer?"

"Right. A lot longer than normal people. I'm good with math. I could do my own accounting if I wanted to. But it takes me forever to write a business letter. I knew I'd never be able to get through college without having all kinds of special stuff."

"What helps? Did they make special arrangements for you in school?"

She made a face. "Yeah. It helped, but it made me stick out like a sore thumb. I couldn't take notes in class, so I had to record my classes and listen to 'em again at night. My mom would sit with me and write down the important stuff. And they gave me extra time for tests. Sometimes, they gave me oral tests, and that was so much easier. But it was a fucking struggle every goddamned day. The day I graduated from high school was the happiest day of my life."

"And you had to go to school twice," I said. "Once is bad enough. Having to listen to those boring classes twice must have been horrible."

"Yeah, it was. I should have been home schooled, but my dad never really believed there was anything wrong with my brain. He stopped harassing me, but I think he always suspected that I was sandbagging."

I didn't say a word. I didn't have a good feel for how Gina felt about her father, and I was not going to say what I was thinking until I was certain. Some people get touchy when you say you want to strangle their father with your bare hands.

❖

I'm not sure how it happened, but we found ourselves making love again. It didn't usually make me hot to think of Gina having trouble of any kind, but she seemed so relieved once we'd finished talking that she started whipping me into a frenzy. A very good frenzy. We were laughing and tickling each other and squealing as we lay in bed. Then Gina chased me into the bathroom where we giggled through a shower.

The sun was nearly ready to set when we left my room and found Elaine, Sheila, Lorna, and two men I didn't recognize sitting on our balcony. "Time to meet the roomies," I said.

"Gosh, I'm excited."

"Come on," I said, tugging the reluctant woman along. The sliding doors were open, and I announced our presence. "Hi, everyone."

"Hayden!" Sheila got up and hugged me. I liked Sheila.

Lorna was sitting right in front of me and reached back to pat me. "Hey, kiddo."

The men looked at us with polite interest, and Elaine looked at us with impolite interest. "Hayden, introduce us to your friend."

"This is Gina Scognamiglio," I said. "She drives the ferry from Sayville. You might have seen her around." I was going to say she owned the company, but she hadn't told me right away, and I didn't want to say more than she usually did. "Oh, and I'm Hayden Chandler." I shook the hands of the men and tried to look interested when Elaine tried to make them sound like Socrates and Aristotle. It turns out they were friends of hers from Columbia, but I wasn't in the mood to talk about academia. I wanted to get into a fast boat with a fast woman and go eat some lobster.

"Hayden's an associate professor of history and the Classics," Elaine said.

"I'm just an assistant," I said. I didn't need Elaine to boost my credentials.

"You'll have your tenure committee in no time," she said. That's one thing about Elaine. She never cuts you down in public. She waits until you're alone to do that.

"Maybe. Maybe not. Well, we're going up to Montauk for dinner. See y'all later."

"Won't that take hours?" Sheila asked. "Traffic's horrible on Sunday night."

"Not in a fast little boat," Gina said. I could tell by the way she was smiling that she liked Sheila, too. She had barely looked at anyone else.

"That sounds like fun."

"We'll have to plan a little outing," I said. I would have invited Sheila to go along with us, but there was no way to do that in even a marginally polite way and ignore the others.

"Are you coming back here?" Lorna asked. "I'm not going back until the morning."

Gina put her arm around me and said, "No, she's coming home with me."

"Really?" Elaine looked at Gina for a second and then back at me. "You paid a lot of money for this share not to use it. I hate to have you waste your investment."

I snuggled up against my girlfriend and looked into her eyes. "I'd have paid every dime I have to meet Gina."

"And you could have done that with a fourteen-dollar ticket," Gina said, smiling only at me.

❖

After dinner, I got to drive again. I was more confident this time, so I allowed Gina to give the boat a little more throttle. It was a rush—a real rush—to make the boat fly across the waves. I wasn't going half as fast as Gina had the first time we'd gone out, but I'd get there.

I'd stuffed one suitcase full of clothes and another with books. Gina had carried the heavy one, but even the light one sapped my strength. Luckily, her house was much closer to the dock than mine was, and I wasn't even out of breath when we arrived home. *Home?* Yes, home. I was already thinking of this as my home. Well, not really my home, but more so than the rental. The rental felt like a rental. This felt like a home, and since Gina was here, it felt like my home.

❖

I was bored and wasting time. Some days I can write. Some days I can't. And forcing myself to sit in front of the computer never makes a difference. I've never been the kind of woman who can work productively just because she's under a deadline, and I'm not gonna start now. I can only produce when I'm in the right creative mood.

So, I closed up my computer and walked down to the ferry. Gina was right. It was a little far to walk as early as she had to leave. But a nice June afternoon proved the perfect time to take a stroll along the bay. I couldn't walk right along the water, since people owned the land to the water's edge, but I was close enough to smell it and catch a salt-tinged breeze between houses. It took me about forty minutes, and I was singing to myself the whole way. Everything seemed so bright and clean and perfect.

I haven't decided if I'm gonna tell her this, but I keep singing a song from *Carousel*. Even though it's called, "When I Marry Mr. Snow," parts of it remind me of her. Especially the lines about "bold and daring, young seafaring, darling Mr. Snow."

The character who sings the song says that Mr. Snow stinks of fish so badly that the first time he kissed her she fainted. But now that she loves him, her heart's in her nose, and fish is her favorite perfume.

That's how I feel about her. I've grown to love that adorable little accent she has, even though I thought my students who spoke that way sounded grating and course. With Gina, I love to hear it come out, even though it's obvious she tries to hide it. If she's tired or angry, she sounds like the waitress from the restaurant in Montauk, which, if she were in the right mood, she would pronounce "Mawntawk."

How can you resist a woman who says Mawntawk or muthuh? I'm sure my muthuh won't be able to understand her if she lapses into her Long Islandese, but that's my muthuh's problem. I wouldn't change one bit of Gina's phonics.

Knowing that I'm going to see her has lifted my mood. Actually, it's soaring. The Cherry Grove ferry was sitting at the dock, meaning Gina was nearby. I went into the little office in the building, which also housed a bar and grill, and saw her sitting at a desk with her feet up on the wood.

Her face lit up in a massive grin, and I realized I would have walked to Manhattan to see that face. She put a finger up, indicating she'd be a minute, and I nodded to the woman at the other desk. She was middle-aged and not particularly pleasant looking or acting. She gave me a look that questioned my invasion of her space, so I turned away and looked at Gina, knowing she was happy to see me.

I don't know to whom she was talking, but she sounded mildly irritated. "Yeah, I do know how long we've been doing business together. That's why I can't understand why you tried to sneak this load of crap by me."

She drummed her fingers on the desk, looking bored. "Sure, you can call my dad. Go right ahead. You can call anybody you want. But I wouldn't." She smirked at me and rolled her eyes. "No, I'm not threatening you. I'm telling you that I'm the owner of the company, and if you don't like the way I run it, you're wasting your time complaining to my fathuh."

I was sitting close, so I put my hand on her bare knee and gave it a squeeze. She grinned at me, made her hand like a gun, and pulled the trigger at the phone. "Let me say this as clearly as I can. You're a supplier. The fact that you've supplied my company for sixty years doesn't mean shit to me. If you're not the best company today, you're wasting my time. My granfathuh might have done business with you guys, but he'd kick my ass for sticking with you if you weren't the best. Now, deliver another load by tomorrow, or this is our last conversation. G'bye." She placed the phone in the cradle delicately and then stretched in her chair, saying, "Hey, Marge, will you see if you can line up another reliable supplier to replace Magliozzi Brothers? I'm not sure we'll need 'em, but I wanna be ready."

The woman looked at her as if she'd been hit. "You can't switch! We've been with them forever!"

"So? I haven't been happy with them for two years. The sap they have running the place isn't up to it. He's trying to cut corners, but he's not gonna use me to beef up his bottom line."

Marge looked as if she wanted to argue, but she snuck another look at me, pursed her lips, and went back to typing at her computer. Gina didn't say another word, but she stood and put her hand on my shoulder. "Wanna take a look around?"

"Yeah, I thought it was about time I saw the empire."

She squeezed my shoulder and said, "Marge, this is Hayden. Hayden, Marge."

"Hi," I said. Marge still didn't look happy to make my acquaintance, so I didn't even offer my hand.

"Hello," she said and then looked back at her computer.

Gina led me out and whispered, "She doesn't like for me to have girlfriends."

I stopped. "What?"

"You heard me." She guided me away from the building. "She was my father's secretary, and she thinks she's related or something. She's always telling me what I can or can't do. And she won't admit it, but she doesn't like that I'm a lesbian."

Knowing Gina, I was stunned at this piece of information. "Then why do you have her working for you?"

"Eh, I don't care if she's bossy and opinionated. She's good at what she does, and she never makes stupid mistakes."

"Hmm, I don't think…no, I know I wouldn't like that."

"She doesn't bother me much. I can count on her, and that means a lot."

Ah, being able to count on someone is clearly more important to her than most other things. This is critical, Hayden. How many times have you seen the evidence?

We walked over to the ticket booth, and I noted the very attractive, very young, very blonde woman standing in it, getting ready to let people board. "I thought you didn't like blondes," I teased, pinching Gina's waist.

"I told you I changed my mind," she said innocently. "But you can thank my nephew for her. She's his girlfriend."

"Ooh, he's got good taste."

"She's all right. But she's not very bright. I can see her using her fingers to figure out how much change to give people."

I giggled. "Really?"

"Really. And given that the fare is twelve dollars for a round trip and almost everybody gives her a twenty, by now she really ought to have figured out that she owes most people eight dollars."

"Oh, that's pretty bad."

"Yeah, but my nephew's no rocket scientist either."

I pinched her again. "That's not nice."

"He's nice looking. And he's a nice kid. But I'd be lying if I said he was smart. He lucked into a family where he can make a good living even if he isn't, so it won't hurt him much."

"Is he your brother's son?"

"Yeah. How else could he be my nephew?"

"Right." I blushed, feeling stupid.

"My brother's not too bright, either. But he doesn't know it." She chuckled, and a rather demonic grin settled on her lips. "Come on. I'll introduce you." We walked past the booth, causing a little grumbling from the passengers who were lined up, waiting to board. But the ones who saw Gina's official shirt were happy to see her since they knew that her going to the boat meant they were ready to load.

We walked down the dock and climbed aboard. "Christopher! Dominick! Come on down."

Two young men scampered down the stairs like a couple of well-trained black Labradors. They were physically similar with black, wavy hair, very dark eyes, and olive-toned skin. With their broad shoulders and trim waists, they looked like competitive swimmers. "This is Hayden, guys."

I didn't know which was Christopher and which was Dominick, but they looked even more alike when their mouths dropped open simultaneously. I could only assume that Case had told them about our fight on the dock.

One of the boys had longer hair, and he reached up and pushed his long curls from his eyes. "Hi," he said. He stuck his hand out, and I shook it. "I'm Chris."

"Nice to meet you, Chris." The other kid mimicked Chris, and we shook hands. Now that I looked at him carefully, he did appear to be a little younger. "Are you two brothers?"

"Yeah," Chris said, smiling uncertainly and adding no information. It was clear the Scognamiglio's didn't waste many words.

"It's nice to meet you both," I said, just to avoid an extended silence.

"Back to work," Gina said, and both young men ran back upstairs. She turned and smiled at me. "I love being the boss."

I bumped her with my hip and winked. "I know."

She glanced away, always a little shy about her assertiveness. She looked at me through the hair that had fallen forward, partially obscuring her eyes. "Wanna go for a ride?"

"Sure. I can't get a thing done today."

She grinned at me, and I had to stop myself from wrapping my arms around her and kissing her. "Let's go."

It took a few minutes for the passengers to get on, and I checked Gina's watch as we pulled out. Right on time, as I expected. She didn't speak until we left the channel, but I was content to watch her. She looked so smart and self-assured. So in command. Damn, I love that in a woman.

"Tell me about your empire here," I said, sweeping my hand towards the dock.

"Nothing too big," she said. "I told you about the boats."

"What about the building? Do you own that?"

"Oh, sure. It's not much. I really should replace that half-assed tin roof over the ticket booth, but it's not leaking. Hard to get motivated."

"What about the bar?"

"I own the space and the fixtures, but I lease it out. My father ran the bar, but I didn't want the liability. It's easier to collect rent."

"Really?" I was a little puzzled. "Is it a lot of work?"

She shrugged, her favorite—and one of her cutest—gestures. "Yes and no. It's more of a pain in the ass than hard work. It's only open in the summer, and there's no one here until a half hour before the ferry. So, it's not busy most of the time. But I'd have to hire and watch at least four bartenders. I don't have the patience to run a cash business like a bar."

"What does cash have to do with it? Doesn't that make it easier?"

"Yeah. But it also makes it easier for the bartender to have…profit sharing." She grinned at me and made my heart beat a little faster, just because of the radiance of her smile.

"Oh. I guess it would be easy to cheat."

"Yeah, and that's a problem. But it's also easy for a bartender to cheat you by being too generous. You know, making his friends' drinks extra stiff, giving drinks on the house, stuff like that. I don't like to be a nursemaid. I'd rather make less money and know I was getting every dime." She grinned again. "I hate to be cheated. I'd rather make five hundred dollars from a tenant than a thousand on my own if I suspected my staff was cheating me."

More vital evidence on the philosophy of Ms. Scognamiglio. Make a note, Hayden. You *will* be called on in the future to remember these points!

❖

The next Friday afternoon, we were lying on a beach blanket on the fluffy sand directly in front of my rental house. It had taken us a little while to get from my house to the beach, since we each had to admire the other's swimsuit. Gina's was remarkably revealing, a fact that I was demonstrably in favor of.

Once again, I noted that her choice highlighted all of the best parts of her body and minimized the less perfect ones. There really weren't many less-than-perfect parts on Gina, but she was a little thick around the middle. It wasn't fat; she just didn't have much of a waist. But she still managed a nice, womanly curve—mostly because of her shapely ass.

Her dark orange bikini bottoms started right at the curve, making my eyes focus on the curve, rather than her boyish waist. I have no idea how long it took her to find a suit in a color that made her skin look so fantastic, while also forcing my eye to dart between her luscious breasts and delightful ass, but it was worth it.

Gina brought a bag filled with toys and a little rake, and she'd used it to groom our spot with determination and precision. I was covered with sunblock, and she kept poking me with a finger to make sure I wasn't getting pink. She was really fond of my pale skin, and even though I assured her I could tan a little bit, she protected me like an infant.

We'd each had a beer and had been in the water for a bracing swim. Now we were both sleepy and warm, with the bright sun baking us into a semi-stupor. Gina seemed to have a little more energy than I did because she managed to get her arms around me and start kissing me. I didn't have a problem with that. I liked taking a late-afternoon nap after sex, and we usually had sex after she started kissing me with lascivious intent. And she was seriously lascivious today.

I was on my back, and she hovered over me, teasing me with her fantastically talented tongue. My hands roamed over her back, and if the closure had been on the back, her top would have been off by now. But her beauties were protected by the front-closure orange top, which perfectly displayed their magnificence.

I was nearly lost to all outside sensation when a shadow blocked the sun. My eyes opened slowly and tracked the source. Oh, boy! It was Elaine!

"Mind if I join you?"

I had to hand it to her. The girl had balls. Big ones. Not many people raised in polite society would have the nerve to stand over a couple on the verge of devouring each other and casually ask if she could join them. Gina lifted her head, and I nearly laughed at the zoned-out look in her eyes. "Huh?" she asked.

"I just got here and saw you two and wondered if I might join you?"

Hmm, Elaine was in her "nice" persona. The one that convinced me to sleep with her. What was up with that?

Gina's gaze sharpened, and she pushed herself into a sitting position. The sun was in her eyes, and she raised her hand to shield them. "Join us?"

Elaine dropped her towel and sat. "Not join you *that* way," she said, laughing. "I just haven't had a chance to get to know you, Gina."

Gina's hand dropped, and she glared at Elaine. "Why do you want to?"

Not many people were so direct with Elaine. Most people at NYU were a little intimidated by her. Gina wasn't, nor would she ever be, intimidated by Professor Newman.

The professor's mouth opened a bit, and I could see her trying to decide how to play this. She was a pretty calculating woman, and she didn't often speak without considering her options. "Why wouldn't I want to?" she asked, ignoring the gruff tone Gina had used. "You and Hayden are getting close. I'll probably be seeing a lot of you. I'd like to get to know you a little better."

Gina shot me a look. "Did you tell her that I heard her on the ferry that first day?"

I shook my head, stunned at how direct Gina was being. This woman didn't fool around!

Elaine had lost a little color, and she looked a bit nonplussed. Before she could say a word, Gina said, "My nephews are my deckhands on the weekends. They heard you tell Hayden to be careful with me or I'd have her killed."

"I...I..."

This was kinda fun. I'd never seen Elaine get a dressing-down.

"So, don't act like you wanna be my friend," Gina said. "I'm sure you wouldn't wanna get on my bad side."

"Oh, damn! I have no memory of saying anything about you. But I'm very sorry if I did."

Now Gina looked a little nonplussed. I think she'd expected Elaine to deny it or shrug it off. Having her apologize was...surprising. I still couldn't figure out what she wanted.

"You did," Gina said, her tone a little softer.

"That's inexcusable," Elaine said. "I can only blame my comment on my smart mouth. Sometimes, I say things just to get a laugh. I don't mean them, Gina. I just...I just don't think sometimes."

Gina still wasn't smiling, but I could see and feel her body lose some of its tension. "I don't think mob jokes are very funny," she said.

"They're not," Elaine agreed. "My mother is Italian, and her side of the family makes comments like that all of the time. It's harmless, but I forget how something like that would sound to a stranger."

"It's not harmless," Gina said, her eyes dark. "A few thousand people in this country are in the Mafia, but that's how the rest of us are identified. It makes me sick to go to a pizza place and have the logo be a mobster with a machine gun. Everybody thinks an Italian with money is dirty."

"Everybody doesn't think that," I said. I touched Gina's arm, but she pulled it away.

"I don't think that," Elaine said. "My family jokes about being Italian the same way lesbians joke about being on lesbian time when they're late or moving in together on the first date."

"Big difference between being late and whacking someone," Gina said. "It's not funny, and being Italian is no excuse."

"Gina," Elaine said, gazing directly into those dark eyes, "I'm sorry. That's all I can say. There's no excuse for my being so rude. None."

With a tiny shake of her head, Gina muttered, "'Kay. Let's drop it."

"Okay." Elaine looked at our empty beer bottles and said, "Can I get both of you a refill?"

"Yeah," Gina said, and I nodded.

Elaine took our empties and started for the house. "What's she want?" Gina asked, staring at Elaine's retreating form.

"I don't know." I watched her walk away. "She's acting like she did right before she asked me out."

"Good," Gina said, her brow furrowed in concentration. "I've been wondering what made you go out with a bitch like that, but I didn't know how to ask."

Ouch! "She has a nice side," I said, a trifle defensively. "But I don't think that's the real Elaine. I think the real Elaine is a self-involved snot."

"I don't trust her." She looked at me. "Is her mother really Italian?"

"Search me. I don't know a thing about her background. Well, that's not true. I know she's from Michigan, but that's about it."

Gina gave me a look that I didn't particularly like. I wasn't sure what was behind those brown eyes, but it didn't seem like approval. "You were really into each other, weren't ya?"

I was just about due to get my period, and I can be a little snappish when I have PMS. "I'm really into *you*, Gina. That's all that you have a right to comment on." I stood up and said, "I'm going to cool off." Without waiting for a reply, I jogged down to the surf and tried not to scream when I waded in. It was damned cold, but if I moved briskly, it only took about two minutes to catch my breath.

The sea was pretty calm, and I felt like working off some of my pique, so I swam about fifty yards, turned, and came back. I did that a couple more times and then headed in. To my surprise, Gina and Elaine seemed to be getting along. I sat down, and Gina took a towel, wiped me dry, and then sat close to warm me up.

"Hayden, did you know how many times Gina's been to Italy?"

"A lot," I said. "Probably twelve or thirteen times."

"Thirteen," Gina said, smiling at me.

"Tell her how many times you've been," Elaine said.

Gina nudged me. "Let me guess. I'd bet you've been to Greece more than Italy."

"No," I said, giving Elaine a look that I hoped would kill. "Same number. Zero."

Elaine laughed, saying, "Have you ever heard of an ancient history scholar who's never been to either Greece or Italy? I'm still surprised that Hayden got her Ph.D. without doing some research on site."

"What's up with that?" Gina asked.

"She's afraid to fly," Elaine declared, saving me the time and effort of answering for myself.

"Really, baby?" Thankfully, Gina didn't laugh at me. She looked genuinely concerned.

"Yeah. I've been planning on taking the QEII or the Queen Mary II over to England and then taking a train or a boat to Greece."

Always understanding, Elaine said, "Take a Valium like everyone else does, Hayden. It's much more dangerous to swim alone in the Atlantic than it is to fly."

"Fear and logic have nothing to do with each other," I said. "A mouse won't hurt you, but I bet you'd scream if I tossed one on your lap."

She shivered, and I smiled, having made my point.

"Maybe you'd be able to fly if we went together," Gina said. "I'd love for you to go with me this winter."

"We'll see," I said. I wouldn't fly if Jesus was holding my hand, but I wasn't going to make a big deal out of it. Not with Elaine sitting there gloating.

"If not, I'll take the boat with you," Gina said. "It'll be fun."

"Do you two have any idea how much a transatlantic crossing is?"

"No," Gina said, "but if Hayden wants to take a boat, we'll take a boat."

"You'd better have five or six thousand dollars lying around," Elaine said, snickering.

"I can manage," Gina said, her voice dropping a little as she gave Elaine that inscrutable smile that attracted me from the first.

"Well, Hayden can't," Elaine declared, laughing. "She can barely pay for her co-op."

Gina's eyebrow twitched, but she didn't look at me. "We can both manage," she said. She took my hand and pulled me close, giving me a kiss on my salty head. "The bigger problem will be taking time off at the same time."

"Especially if she changes jobs," Elaine said.

Gina's hold tightened, but she didn't respond. I decided I'd have to say something, so I piped up. "That's not likely. I would have heard by now if anyone else wanted me."

"You never know," Elaine said. "One of the reasons I invited Rich and Hans over last week was so you could meet them. Rich has some very good contacts in the European history department at Yale."

"You could have said something," I snapped, instantly angry. "If you want me to meet someone, I'm always a phone call away."

"I was trying to do you a favor," she said. "But I'm sure you didn't impress him by not even sitting down to chat."

I could feel my temperature start to rise. Even when she started out being nice, Elaine had a way of reverting to her natural state of disapproving schoolmarm. "I didn't know who he was," I said. "I assumed you were talking to some friends."

"Well," she said, making a dismissive gesture with her hand, "once we all heard you…in your room…it would have been uncomfortable. It was probably best that you left."

"Great," I muttered. "That's great."

"One more reason to stay with me," Gina said. "No unexpected visitors."

"If she'd known she was going to be at your apartment so often, Hayden wouldn't have had to spend all of her book advance on this rental," Elaine said. Damn, I was glad I'd confided in her. This way I wouldn't even have to talk to Gina; I could have Elaine do it.

"My place isn't as big," Gina said, that sly smile on her face, "but it's quiet. Hayden needs a place to write, so as long as she can do that, where she does it isn't that important." One of these days, I was gonna get a word in edgewise. I hadn't had two women discussing me without my involvement since my last parent-teacher conference in high school.

"People save all year to be on Fire Island," Elaine said. "I hate to have her…where *do* you live?"

"Sayville," Gina said. "Right across the sound."

"Well, Sayville isn't Cherry Grove."

"No, it's not," Gina agreed. "It's quieter, and there are fewer distractions."

I got up and headed for the water. It didn't seem necessary to excuse myself since I wasn't being included in the discussion. I had almost hit the water when I felt someone grasp my hand. "Go for a walk?" Gina asked.

"I don't wanna break up your talk with Elaine. You might not have settled on who was gonna feed me tonight."

She made a face and said, "Don't be silly. We weren't excluding you."

"The hell you say! Every time I opened my mouth, one of you was deciding what was best for me."

"Fine," she said. She dropped my hand and started to walk down the beach.

I followed behind her and caught up in a few paces. "What's bugging you?"

"Besides not knowing you were looking for another job? In another state?" She turned and glared at me. "Nothin'. Fuckin' nothin'."

"Don't be dramatic," I said, struggling to keep up. "I have some feelers out. That's all there is to it. School starts in late August, and it's already June. I'm not going anywhere."

"But you were tryin' to. And Elaine knows all about it."

"Gina!" I was sick of running to keep up with her. Everyone within a hundred yards heard me, but it got her to stop. She walked back to me and stared insolently. "Elaine knows because last year, when I was trying to decide what to do, I asked for her advice. She's got a lot of friends at a lot of schools, and she gave me some people to contact."

"Why didn't you tell me?"

She was steaming mad, and people around us were staring, but I was too mad to care. "Because...it's complicated."

"You've said I'm smart. I should be able to understand something complicated." Her eyes were smoldering, and I started to feel tense. "What if you get an offer? Then what?"

Her hands were clenched, and she looked like she wanted to shake me. "I am not...*not*...going to have a fight out here with a hundred people watching us. You can either calm down right now or go home."

"You want me to go home? Fine. I'll fuckin' go home!"

She turned and headed for the house. But I grabbed her arm before she got too far. "You're being an idiot! Quit running away from me when you're angry."

"You're the one who told me to go home."

"I meant," I said, taking in a calming breath, "that we'd go to your house together and finish talking about this."

She put her hands over her face and stood there for a moment. I could see her chest heaving and wasn't sure if she was trying to control her temper or crying. Exhaling heavily, she dropped her hands and said, "I'm sorry. Let's go for a walk. I won't yell anymore."

We started for the shore, and after a few minutes of silence, she said, "I swear I'm workin' on my temper. I get mad too damn fast."

"I know," I said. I took her hand and held it tightly. "It's hard to change, honey. I know you're trying."

She gave me a sideways glance. "Does it bother you?"

"Yes. I've never been with anyone who gets very angry. And even though I can get a little wild myself, it takes me a long time to get there."

"I hate that I do it 'cause it's what my dad did, and I hated it."

I snuck my arm around her bare waist, pleased when she moved closer to me. "I do some things my parents do, and I hate it, too. Maybe we can break each other of bad habits."

"Maybe." She grinned at me. "Don't count on it, though. I've been trying to control my temper my whole life and haven't gotten very far."

"I've had two therapists," I admitted. "I'm still doing the same old shit."

"I'd never tell my secrets to a therapist," she said. "No way. Never."

"At least you're open-minded," I said, grinning at her when her head snapped in my direction. "I'm kidding, baby. Besides, you seem pretty well adjusted to me."

"What do you know?" she asked, laughing. "You've been to two shrinks."

I pulled her to a stop and slipped my arms around her, holding her loosely. "Give me a kiss. A nice one."

She was very obedient when she wanted to be. We stood at the edge of the surf, kissing contentedly for a few minutes. This might have drawn stares anywhere else, but Cherry Grove was definitely a "public display of affection" kind of place.

We started to walk before we got too frisky. "I'm gonna tell you about my looking into a new job as long as you promise not to get mad."

She looked at me for a long time and then nodded. "Deal," she said, tersely.

<hr />

Gina was darned upset that I hadn't told her about my desire to change jobs, especially since I admitted I'd intentionally decided not to tell her about it once I realized we were getting serious. But she eventually accepted my explanation that telling her might have made her feel as if she were on probation. She wasn't angry, and she didn't yell, but I knew it hurt her.

By the time we got back to the house, we were fine, and I was completely relaxed. We went in to find that Sheila and Lorna were there as well. "Thanks for bringing our things in," I said to Elaine.

"Happy to," she said. I could tell by the way she was eyeing us that she was looking for signs of discord, but if so, she was disappointed.

To my surprise, Gina said, "We're going out to dinner. Anyone wanna come with us?"

"Where are you going?" Lorna asked.

"Ocean Beach," Gina said, which was news to me.

"Is that on Fire Island?" Lorna inquired.

"Yeah. It's the big town. You haven't been there?"

We all admitted we'd never heard of it. Gina decided we all needed to see a few places where the locals gathered, so we all went to get dressed.

"Do you really want to take them?" I asked when we were in my room.

"It's June," she said. "I wanna be able to come to the beach and have a place to shower and change. I'm gonna make those pointy-headed dames like me if it kills 'em."

<hr />

We went to a spot called Matthew's that Gina said was just a few years younger than she was. It wasn't fancy, but it had its own dock, which came in handy when you had to park. No one had said much when Gina led us to Taxi! Taxi!, but Elaine caught me as soon as we reached Ocean Beach. "Whose boat is that?"

"Gina's."

"You mean the ferry company's," she decreed, deciding on her own version of the truth. "They'll fire her if they catch her driving it."

"She has permission," I said, getting a certain pleasure out of fucking with her. "The owner's a real softy."

❖

By the end of our evening, Shcila was playfully flirting with Gina, and Lorna looked like she wouldn't mind taking her for a spin, either. I couldn't tell what Elaine thought, but Gina had been her most charming, which was pretty darned charming. I caught Elaine looking at Gina nearly every time I cast a glance her way. It was clear that Gina had her baffled, and I liked watching her try to figure her out. I began to see that Gina got pleasure out of revealing tiny things about herself, but only as needed. By the end of the night, the women had learned that Gina spoke fluent Italian and that she hadn't been to college. But I'd learned things about my co-workers that I'd never thought to ask. Gina could have been a darned good district attorney, but I decided she was probably happier on her boat.

After dropping the girls off, we headed home. As usual, Gina wanted me to sit on her lap to drive. I was glad she hadn't asked me to do it when my roommates were with us. I liked that it was our little secret.

She kissed my neck and said something that I couldn't hear over the engine. "What?" I asked.

"I said that I'm really glad you're not going to move to another school, but I hate to think of you staying here if it's not what you want."

"NYU's a good school," I said, turning my head so she could hear me. "I wouldn't mind being there my whole career."

"I want you to be happy," she emphasized, her voice rife with earnestness. "But I'd be going nuts if you were interviewing at other places. I'm really glad you'll be here this year. I might be able to be more open-minded by next year."

"Don't worry about it, Gina. Please don't. We'll work things out together. That's the important thing. Working together."

"Sounds nice," she said, kissing my neck with tiny, love-filled kisses.

By the time we got home, Gina was so tired that I didn't even try to entice her into having sex. I kissed her and let her wrap me in her arms, only briefly thinking of how I'd kill Elaine for disturbing our perfectly wonderful afternoon.

Chapter Eleven

When Gina got home the next day, I was on the phone with my sister. Gina kissed my cheek. Then she stripped off her clothes and took my hand to lead me outside. She kissed me again and then asked, "Are you on hold?"

"Uh-huh," I said to my sister.

"Who are you on hold with?" Gina asked.

I mouthed "my sister," but she didn't understand. So, I went into the house, wrote a note, and then went out and handed it to her. She nodded, kissed my cheek again, and dove into the pool. Gina did laps while I murmured sounds of agreement with an occasional "Of course. Anyone would feel that way."

After she'd finished her laps, Gina motioned for me to join her in the pool. I knew that was trouble, so I took off my shorts and panties and sat on the deck. Gina played with my feet, rubbed my calves, and turned around so I could run my toes down her back while she giggled. "I know, Karen," I finally said, "and I'll do anything I can to help. I just don't know what I *can* do."

Gina stilled, listening to me talk, her eyes trained on me. I listened for a few more minutes and then began trying to extract myself from the one-way conversation. It took a few more minutes, but I finally freed myself. I dropped the phone on the grass and took off my shirt and bra. "Free!" I said and then slid into the water, submerging myself.

Gina pulled me up and kissed me properly. "Problems?"

"No. The usual."

She stood in front of me for a second and then said, "I don't know what the usual is."

"Oh." I looked at her, realizing that she knew almost nothing about my family. "Sometimes, I think you know everything about me. Like we've known each other forever."

"We will," she said, wrapping me in a hug and smiling that adorably sweet smile.

"But I've got to catch you up a little bit."

"That'd be nice."

"Mind if I float? I think better when I'm floating."

"Be my guest." She held my feet so I didn't go anywhere while I lay on my back and made some fluttering motions with my hands.

"Karen lives fairly close to our dad. He's depressed. Has been since…well, as long as I remember."

"Your whole life?"

"Yeah. Definitely. He should be on medication, but he won't go to therapy, and he won't even talk to a doctor about it."

"Sounds like me," she said.

Her voice was muffled, since my ears were underwater, but I could hear her just fine. "I'd have a doctor come to the house if you were as depressed as my father is," I said, surprised I'd responded so quickly and decisively.

She didn't ask the obvious question, but she did raise a questioning eyebrow.

"It's different when you're the kid," I said. "He's my dad, not my partner. I can't order him around like I would you."

She tickled my insteps, and I could see that she was disappointed that I didn't react as much as she would have.

"It's true," I said. "I can only suggest things. Karen can't stop at that, though. She thinks that taking her kids over there three or four times a week and making him dinner are going to make him better."

"Not gonna, huh?"

"Hell, no. My mom made him dinner every day of the week, and he had two children around that he largely ignored. He's not a bad guy; he's just barely there."

"Does this run in his family?"

"No, I don't think so. But he's an only child, and his parents were dead by the time I was born, so I don't have much to go by. My mom says it's how he came back from Vietnam."

"Ooh, my dad served, too. He lucked out, though. He was in the Navy on a supply ship in the South China Sea. It was no picnic, but he didn't have to be in hand-to-hand combat or anything like the guys in the Army and Marines did." She touched me very gently, while looking in my eyes. "Was it bad for your father?"

"Yeah. At least, my mom said it was. He won't talk about it. But the most life I've seen out of him was when Kerry ran for president. He'd sit and yell at the television when those swift boat jerks started airing those commercials."

"My dad thinks Kerry's the same as Jane Fonda." She grinned at me. "Guess family get-togethers are gonna be fun, huh?"

"Ah, yeah. A real ball. My brother-in-law is a Republican. My sister doesn't seem to have strong feelings one way or the other. But my dad's not a big political guy. He only woke up when Kerry ran. He'd be just as supportive of anyone who fought and then protested. Of course, most of those guys wound up being Democrats."

"Probably," she agreed. "My dad volunteered, and he thinks people who protested are traitors. He can still get worked-up about it."

"Well, my dad didn't protest. He was too depressed." I gave her a smile, but I knew it was a sad-looking one. "Guess that's one benefit of his depression."

"There aren't any benefits," she said. "Not for him and not for you." She held me tenderly, rocking me for a few moments. "It must have been like growing up without a dad."

"It was, in some ways. He spent most of his time in the basement, working on God knows what. My mom divorced him when he got a computer and discovered the Internet. He'd barely stop playing games to eat dinner."

"Was he drafted?"

"Uh-huh. He'd just finished his requirements for his Ph.D. in chemistry, but he hadn't finished his dissertation. My mom says he was working hard, but whatever he was trying to prove wasn't working. The dissertation committee assumed that anyone who was dawdling was trying to get out of being drafted, so they invalidated his student deferment."

"Fuck!" Gina breathed. "That must have been a kick in the teeth."

"Yep. And my mom was pregnant. He was drafted just a few months later."

"So...did he get to finish his Ph.D.? A lot of what you said is Greek to me, but I think I got the gist of it."

"Nope. He wouldn't go back, even though he could have finished and gotten a good job. My grandfather pulled some strings and got him a job at the prep school where he works."

"Why'd he have to pull strings? None of my teachers had a Ph.D."

"'Cause he didn't really want the job. He didn't wanna work at all. My grandfather had to assure them he'd snap out of his funk...but he didn't."

"Your dad's father?"

"Unh-uh. My mom's."

"Why'd your grandfather have pull?"

"The usual. Money, power, prestige." I smiled. "The things that have always made things happen."

"Ooh, I knew you had some money somewhere," she said, grinning at me. "You've got that 'old money' look."

"Old money once removed. My mom didn't get much when my grandfather died. He left her his house, but that was about it."

"A house is a nice gift," she said. "Is that where she lives now?"

"Yeah. It is a nice house, but he had money to burn. He left most of it to charity. My mom and her sister got all of his personal effects, and they each got a house. Everything else went to museums and things like that. I'll take you on a tour of the family monuments the next time you go to Philly with me."

"Any time."

"I don't look forward to it. It's always tense."

"It's like that at my house a lot of the time, too," Gina admitted. "I guess that just happens with parents."

"Maybe."

"So, your mom has rich relatives, huh?"

"Yeah, she has some. She doesn't see them very often, though. Just at funerals and an occasional wedding."

"Really?" Her brow was furrowed. "Did they cut her off?"

"Hmm, not that so much as I guess they didn't have a lot in common when she married my dad. They didn't go to the same country club or the same benefits or parties. I don't think they dislike her; they just don't quite know what to make of someone who married below her status."

Gina flopped onto her back and started to kick the length of the pool. On her second lap, she stopped and said, "It's been kinda the same for me."

"What do you mean? What was your status?"

Gina smiled a sad, almost wistful smile. "I went the other way. My friends stopped calling me when I started to go to Italy and take language classes. They didn't get it."

"Oh, baby." I stroked her cheek and looked into her eyes. "Is that true?"

"Pretty much, yeah. I hung out with the slacker-party crowd. I didn't do well in school, so that's kinda the group I ended up with. I was never into partying as much as they were, but they were still my friends. But we've drifted apart. I see 'em a couple of times a year now. We usually have a big party at the end of the summer and another one around Christmas. That's it." She shrugged her shoulders, looking rather helpless.

"You don't have any close friends? No one you tell your secrets to?"

She touched the tip of my nose. "Just you. I'm kind of a loner," she admitted. "I can entertain myself just fine."

"Me, too," I said, smiling back at her. "I have Dana, and we're very close, but I only see her a few times a year. I like being able to go home, take my clothes off, and entertain myself. It's fine with me if I don't leave my apartment all weekend."

She put her arms around me and pulled me along behind her while she kicked furiously. "That's a little weird. You need some sunshine, baby."

"Sitting in my apartment gave me the skin color you like," I said. "There are benefits to isolation."

"I don't mind being alone, but I've talked more in the last month than I have in the last year," Gina said, grinning at me. "I like it."

"And I've been with you more than I've been with anyone since Dana," I said. "I like it, too."

"Let's keep doing it," she said.

"Done. Done. Done."

⬥

The following Sunday evening was cool and rainy. We'd spent the whole day reading and snacking—a perfect day in my book. Gina got up from the sofa, where we'd been entwined most of the day. She stretched, looked around aimlessly, and said, "I've gotta go to my dad's to pick some stuff up. Wanna go with me?"

I sat up. "Do you want me to?"

"I'd always rather have you with me, so yeah."

"Hmm," I said, looking her over. "You seem a little tentative."

She sat on the arm of the sofa and put her hand on my shoulder. "I'm not tentative. But I don't know if you're interested in meeting him."

"Honey, I told you I'm interested in every part of you. Your dad's a big part. If you're ready for me to meet him, I want to go with you."

She smiled, but there was a tinge of sadness or ennui about her smile. "Okay. Let's go."

I stood and ran my hands down my wrinkled khakis. "Shouldn't I change?"

"Nah. He wouldn't appreciate the effort."

Hmm. That didn't sound very promising. It's been weeks now, and I still don't have a good read on how she feels about her family. Maybe I'll get a clue tonight.

⬥

We got into her truck, and I rolled the window down a little bit. The engine purrs in such a deep, throaty way that it turns me on just the tiniest bit. I've become such a sex fiend that I hardly recognize myself. Who would have thought a car engine could be an aphrodisiac? But with Gina, many, many things reminded me of sex. I sure hoped meeting her father went well 'cause I was ready to get busy.

"Where are we heading?" I asked.

"Bayshore."

"One more place I've never been. I assume it's on Long Island."

Gina smiled at me. "Everything is."

"Are we going north?"

"West. He lives a little farther west than I do. Not too far. Maybe ten miles."

"Does he live in the house you grew up in?"

"Kinda." She was staring at the road with the same concentration she used when she piloted the ferry. "I was about ten when we moved to the big house."

I giggled. "I guess I should disabuse myself of the notion that your grandparents live in a little shack your father built out of salvaged wood, huh?"

Even though I could tell she didn't like to, she took her eyes off the road. "Why on earth do you have those ideas about me?"

"Because I thought you just drove a ferry."

"Hayden," she said, shaking her head. "I don't know how much you make, but I'd be surprised if you made a whole hell of a lot more than a full-time pilot. You've got funny ideas about people who work for a living."

I studied the side of her face. She had that smug grin settled comfortably on her lips, and I had yet to knock it off. But that didn't stop me from trying. "I make about eighty thousand."

She glanced at me. "Is that your base salary?"

"Uhm...that's my only salary."

Her dark eyebrows shot up. "No overtime?"

I couldn't help but laugh. "No, Gina. No overtime. That's my salary for two semesters' work. I get more if I teach summer school."

"Shit," she mumbled. "I had no idea."

Ha! I finally got her! "How much does a pilot make?"

We were near a stop light, and she waited until we'd come to a complete stop to answer. "It depends on what union you're in and what your duties are. But a full-time pilot who worked a regular schedule on one of my brothers' boats would probably make around a hundred and twenty-five thousand dollars."

"You're shitting me!"

"No." She looked completely serious and a little…sad. "I can't believe you've gone to so much school and they pay you so little. Damn." She shook her head. "That just doesn't seem fair."

"Case makes more than I do?"

"Oh, yeah," she said, nodding her head with a certain amount of regret. "How old is he?"

"Nineteen. Sucks, doesn't it?"

"Goddamn it! I can't believe that! He's barely out of high school."

"I know. But that's why it's hard to get into the union." She smiled at me, her expression holding some sympathy. "I told you we got paid well."

"I thought you meant twenty-five dollars an hour or something."

"Who could afford a house on that?"

"That's why I live in a studio in a shaky neighborhood. I don't live in a tiny space because I like to touch both walls when I sit on my sofa."

She looked at me and shrugged. "You need a better union, honey."

❖

We were getting close to Gina's family home. I knew this because she pointed to a dark, tree-filled park and said, "The first time I kissed a girl was on that golf course."

"Really?" I stared at the place, not sure what I was looking for. "Were you serious about kissing her or just playing?"

"Serious. All of the kids in the neighborhood used to climb the fence and fool around over there."

"How old were you?"

Her face scrunched up, and I could see her figuring out the time. "About fifteen, I think."

"Wow! You started early. You know, you've never told me about your first time."

"You've never told me about yours."

"We'll have to swap stories."

"Eh...I'd rather not. Not that I have anything to hide. I just don't think it's smart to talk about the past." She caught my gaze. "Is that okay?"

"Yeah. It is." I thought of the smart remark she'd made about my sleeping with Elaine, and I saw the brilliance of her reticence. Besides, I didn't want to know the gory details about her and Lacey. I could see from her expression whenever she talked about her that Lacey had really had her number.

Gina turned into a driveway lined with those really tall bushes that look like green columns. I have no idea what they're called, but they make a nice, tall hedge. There were lights at the base of each bush, casting a small pool of light that made the drive seem like it went on for years. We pulled up in front of a house that could only be described as palatial. Well, I'm sure someone could come up with another word, but palatial was apt. It looked like a traditional seaside cottage, but on steroids. It was two stories tall, and it looked like there might be more buildings in the back, since I saw just a hint of gray shingling back there.

"Some house," I managed.

"Yeah. It's not what my dad wanted, but they have some kinda approval process before you can build here."

"What did he want?"

"Something bigger," she said, getting out of the truck.

Gina walked around to my side and held my hand as I exited. "I don't wanna stay long, okay?"

"Fine with me."

We walked up to the front door, and to my surprise, Gina opened the door and walked in. "Dad?" she called.

"In here," a hearty, masculine voice replied.

Gina dropped my hand as we walked through a large, formally furnished living room and then past an impressive dining room, the twelve-person table set as though guests were expected for dinner. The next doorway opened to a very large den, and a flat-screen television the size of a cab caught and held my eye. It took me a second to tear my gaze from the Mets game and find a beefy man sitting in a recliner.

Walking over to him, Gina bent and kissed his cheek. "Hi. I came by to get that stuff for the accountant. I brought my friend Hayden."

The man turned and looked in my direction, but he didn't get up. "Hey," he said without much enthusiasm.

"Hi." I stood there awkwardly, waiting for an introduction. But one was not forthcoming.

Gina looked at the TV, asking, "Mets up?"

"Nah."

She watched for a few seconds and then said, "Where's the stuff?"

"My desk."

"I'll go get it. Hayden, have a seat. I'll be right back."

If looks could kill, Gina would have a severe wound. But she didn't seem to notice, and she took off before I could offer or demand to go with her. I walked around a big table that held a big lamp, a big bowl of pretzels, and a sweating beer. The beer was normal sized and looked good. I wondered if there was a bottle of Port around to help me stop shaking.

It wasn't that Mr. Scognamiglio was particularly imposing—even though he was. He looked big and ornery. I know that's a rash assessment, but he honestly looked like he wanted to pick a fight with anyone in reach. His hair was thick, black, and curly, with just a little gray on the sides. Dark, unlined skin was made darker by the stubble on his chin and cheeks. He had a prominent brow and bushy eyebrows, and even though I knew all men had a certain amount of estrogen, he looked a little deficient.

Gina must take after her mother 'cause this guy looked like he was wearing a hair shirt. He had on an undershirt, which allowed me visual access to his shoulders, which were broad and as furry as a chimp's.

I sat down on a sofa that rested at a right angle to Mr. Scognamiglio. He didn't make eye contact or conversation, and for a change, I decided not to make the effort if he didn't. My usual reaction in situations like this is to babble, but the guy wouldn't even spare a look in my direction. Given that I knew he wasn't particularly sweet when it came to Gina, he could kiss my ass.

After what seemed like a very long time, he said, "Where you know Gina from?"

It barely seemed like a question, but I answered anyway. "Fire Island. I'm renting a place for the summer."

"Where you live?"

"New York…City," I added, just to be clear.

"What a hellhole," he grunted.

I don't know what came over me. "It's the hellhole I call home," I said. I never gave a smart answer to a lover's parent. What's going on?

He looked in my direction, but once his dark eyes settled on me, I wished he were ignoring me again. "You seen Gina's house?"

"Yes. It's lovely."

"Ha!" He took a long draught of his beer and set it back down. "Only to somebody that lives in an apartment. You do, right?"

"Uhm…right. I live in a studio apartment."

"Lemme tell ya, that's no house Gina has. She wasted my money on that cracker box, and if her mother hadn't put Gina's name on the account where we kept the money, she never woulda gotten a dime from me." He scratched his chest, and I saw the large, gold crucifix that Gina had once referred to slip out of his undershirt. His hands were the size of catcher's mitts, and I shuddered to think of those big things holding me. Thank God Gina's a girl!

I knew it wasn't politic, but I had to defend my girlfriend. "I love Gina's house. It's one of the loveliest I've ever been in."

He picked up his beer bottle and waved it around. "*This* is a house. Nick and Tony have houses. Gina has some twinky little box. I could put her house in my garage."

"But it's all she needs," I said. "Why have room that you don't need?"

"You don't know nothin' about real estate." Well, at least he didn't make snap judgments. "Big sells. Especially on the water. Nobody wants a two-bedroom waterfront house these days. She'll never unload it."

"Maybe there's another person who'll love it as much as she does."

He was about to reply when Gina walked back into the room. "I looked everywhere and could only find the stuff on two of the boats. Do you have it in a folder or something?"

He stood up, sighing dramatically as he did. Brushing past Gina, he went to find the "stuff" in question. Gina sat by me. "Want a drink?"

"No, thanks. You said you wanted to get going. Is that still true?"

She yawned, stretching her arms out. "Yeah. Wanna see the rest of the house?"

"If you want to show it to me."

Standing, she held her hand out. I took it and got up, and she led me to a wall of windows at the back of the den. Opening one, we walked outside, where we were hit with a gust of salty air, and I heard water slapping against something I assumed was a dock. "I knew you were close, but I didn't realize you were this close to the ocean."

"Yeah. We always have been. I don't know what I'd do if I had to live inland."

There was a long, low building close to the seawall. "Is that where your grandparents live?"

"Yeah." She scanned the place quickly. "Looks like they're out or in bed."

"I can meet them another time." I took her hand and kissed it. "Everything okay?"

"Sure." She was staring out at the sea, and I could see storm clouds in her eyes.

"Okay. Just checking."

She turned and gave me a lopsided smile filled with sadness. "It's always hard to be here. Makes me miss my mom. Doesn't seem like home without her here."

Damn, that hadn't occurred to me. I assumed she'd be offended by her father's staggering lack of manners. "Let's get going, then."

We walked back inside, but not before I noted the two-story garage that probably could have held Gina's house.

Mr. Scognamiglio had piled some papers on the table next to his chair. "That's them," he said, nodding in their direction.

Gina picked them up and leafed through them, her dark eyes intent. "All the boats here?"

"Yeah."

"Okay. Thanks." She bent and kissed his rough-looking cheek again. "See ya."

"Yeah. See ya around." He looked at me briefly, and I nodded.

"Good to meet you."

"Same here."

With that, we walked back through the house, exiting into the cool, wet night.

Gina didn't say anything for a long time, so I finally said, "Thanks for taking me, honey."

She looked at me with a tender gaze. "Thanks for going. Made it easier for me."

"Any time." I put my hand on her leg and felt a little misty. I wish I could have met her mother since she's obviously the one person Gina related to. I had a feeling I'd only learn about the parts of Gina I wanted to erase by spending time with the imposing Mr. Scognamiglio.

⁜

A few days later, I was sitting outside, lying on my belly, when Gina came home.

"Hey! Don't even think of burning that pretty skin."

I pushed myself up onto my elbows and beamed at her. "My girlfriend has some great sunblock she got in Italy. It's too cool to even sell in the U.S."

She squatted down next to me and kissed me gently. Her warm, callused hand ran up and down my bare thighs. "Are you sure you're covered?"

"Yeah. I couldn't reach the small of my back, so I put on this tank top. But every other spot is slathered."

She started to play with my hair, pulling a bunch of strands up and comparing them to others. "Your hair's getting blonde."

"It's starting to. That's one of the reasons I like to lie in the sun. It'll bleach out a lot this summer."

"Looks good," she said, thoughtfully gazing at various locks. "Really good."

"It's driving me nuts," I said. "I've gotta get a haircut."

She looked like she was going to speak, but then didn't. I waited for a few seconds, but she wasn't going to say what was on her mind.

"Is there someplace cheap around here?" I asked. "Like a Quick Cuts or something?"

I'm sure she was hiding a look of distaste, but she didn't otherwise comment. I could see her think for a second. Then she said, "I'm about due. Go with me."

I pushed myself up and sat on the chaise. "How much?"

"My treat."

"Gina…"

She sat next to me and took my hand. "I'd like to go with you. It'll be fun. We can have a beauty day."

"I can pay for my own haircuts, even on my meager salary."

"I know you can. But I'd like to treat. Besides, you need to spend your money on buying something nice to wear."

"Okay, where are we going?"

"My cousin Case's mom, Linda, and her husband Norm are having their twenty-fifth wedding anniversary party next Saturday night. I wanna take you and show you off."

"You do?" I don't know why I was shocked, but I was.

She smiled at me, and I could feel my stomach do a flip. I don't know why it still did that every time she gave me that luminous smile, but I wasn't in a hurry for it to stop.

"Yeah. Definitely. The whole crowd'll be there, and it'll be better than having to go meet each of 'em. Much better to do 'em all in one whack."

"Okay," I said, my nervousness already showing. "But only if you help me pick out something to wear."

"It's a deal." She leaned over and kissed me. Then I kissed her back. Then I wasn't wearing my tank top anymore. Then she had my bikini bottoms off and my legs dangling over her shoulders. Dinner was served very late that evening.

❖

That Friday, Gina and I walked to a shop off Main Street for our haircuts. It was just about a mile, a distance I covered several times a day in the city. But just a few weeks of sitting on my butt had obviously had an effect on my stamina. Luckily, I hadn't gained weight despite my inertia. Having Gina cook helped me in that regard. She cooked in the traditional Mediterranean fashion, with big salads and generous helpings of lightly cooked vegetables that complimented small portions of fish or chicken. She didn't skimp on using oil or butter; she just used a moderate hand. As we walked, I vowed to take a break every day and go for a long walk. Where could I go? I know! I could go to the dock to have lunch with Gina! Damn, I don't know if she thinks about me all day, but I'd be rich if I had a dollar for every time I thought of her.

"Here we are," she said, snapping me out of my musings. I turned and gave the place a long look. It certainly looked nice enough, but I would have never gone to a place like this in the city. For one thing, it would probably cost $150 for a cut at a chic place like this. For another, I don't feel comfortable being in a place where everyone is so focused on how they look. Sure, I want to look nice for Gina, but the women in places like this seem to spend most of their time looking good. I can't relate. But Gina obviously didn't have any such qualms, since she opened the door and greeted a very trendy-looking woman with kisses to both cheeks. Well!

"Hayden, this is Gabrielle." She put her arm around me and pulled me close. "We're going to a party next Saturday, and Hayden's gonna be under the microscope. Everybody in the family's gonna be there, and she's never met most of 'em."

Gabrielle regarded me as most stylists do. She barely looked me in the eyes—just put her hands in and on my hair, forcing it to perform some dance that only stylists understood. "Do you have anything in mind?" she asked, still looking at and touching and twisting my hair.

"I just wanted a trim."

Gabrielle shot Gina a quick look and then narrowed her brow. "What will that let you do?"

"Do?"

She dropped her hands and finally made eye contact. "If I just trim it, you won't be able to wear it up. That *is* why you've been letting it grow, isn't it?"

"No," I said, beginning to get irritated, "it's been this length for years. I just need a trim."

Wordlessly, she guided me into a chair and stood behind me. Addressing Gina more than me, she said, "This isn't a good length for you." Gently, she drew her finger across my jaw line. "Your face is a little thin, and this length makes it look longer than it is. You've got a good jaw, delicate but defined. If we took about this much off..." She gathered my hair in her hands and lifted it to mid-ear. "It would show off your bone structure."

"But my hair's so lifeless," I said. "It'll just hang there."

"No, it's not. It's just too long. And too dry. You need a nice glaze."

I turned and looked at Gina, who was nodding thoughtfully.

"What's a glaze?" I asked.

"A deep conditioner," Gabrielle said. "I could give you a glaze with some color in it, and your hair will look fantastic. Shiny and bouncy and fresh."

"Oh, I've never wanted to color it. I don't want peroxide on—"

"Semi-permanent," she said, as though I knew what that meant. "It'll wash out in a month. It won't hurt your hair; it'll help it. It's a conditioner."

I looked at Gina's reflection in the mirror. I tried not to, but I couldn't help making a face. "I hate change," I said, pouting a little.

She moved behind me and put her hands on my shoulders. Gabrielle disappeared, and Gina leaned over and spoke into my ear. "You don't have to do anything you don't want to do. If you want a little trim, Gabrielle will do it."

"What do you want?" I asked, trying to guess what she really wanted via her sometimes hard-to-read eyes.

"I let Gabrielle do what she wants. She's a professional, and I only hire professionals that I trust."

"Do you think I'd look better with my hair shorter?"

Gina surprised me by kissing my ear. "It's not possible for you to look better. The scale only goes to ten."

I was grinning like a dolt when Gabrielle returned bearing a little cup and saucer. "Espresso," she said, handing it to Gina. "What would you like, Hayden?"

"Whatever you think I should have," I said, surrendering my control to a stranger and my taciturn lover.

❖

Gina didn't make over my new look as much as I thought she would. Clearly, she liked it. She complimented Gabrielle on her advice and told me that I looked lovely. But I expected her to fawn a bit, to tell me she loved the change. God knows *I* did. Immodestly, I thought I looked as good as I'd looked in my adult life. But not having Gina adulate my cut took some of the sheen off the experience.

We walked to the diner she'd taken me to a few weeks earlier, and our waitress from that day was on duty. She waved and then did a double take. Rushing over to us, she looked at me and said, "You don't look like the same girl!" She circled me slowly, tsking and clucking. "My gawd. A haircut can change your whole face."

When I looked back at Gina, she had a very contented look on her face. She didn't say a thing, but her grin didn't dim during the whole meal.

That night Gina was in bed when I walked out of the bathroom. I was leaning over the bedside lamp to switch it off when she said, "Don't move for a second."

"Okay." I didn't know why, but I dutifully remained bent over.

Her dark eyes raked over me, studying my face and my hair. The intensity of those dark orbs held me in sway, and I barely noticed that my back was getting stiff. "Kiss me," she said, rolling onto her back and closing her eyes.

I switched off the light, and she opened her eyes and said, "No, no, leave the light on." Going along with her whim, I turned it on and sat on the edge of the bed. Bracing my weight on my forearms, I leaned over and kissed her gently. Her beautiful eyes opened, and she gazed at me for the longest time, holding me still without saying a word. She lifted her hands and tenderly ran them through my hair. Then she let her fingers glide along my features. "You're so beautiful, Hayden. So remarkably beautiful." She smiled—that half-smile that made me want to eat her alive. "I don't know why a thousand other women hadn't swept you off your feet before I got there, but I'm so glad they didn't."

I kissed her again and then again, licking her tender lips as if they were made of candy.

Then she wrapped her arms around my waist and tumbled me onto the bed, where she showed me that she loved every part of me. You know, I kinda forgot that she hadn't made a big deal about my haircut. As a matter of fact, it was nice that she hadn't. If she'd kept telling me how nice I looked, I probably would have felt as if she'd been itching to change me, and that would have made my suspicious little mind assume she didn't think I was attractive before. I wonder if she knew that. Oh, who the fuck cares? I'm happier when I stop analyzing and just experience how it feels to lie in her arms.

❖

I'm not sure how I wound up in this dress, but here I am, looking at myself in an ocean blue, silk sheath that makes me look—yes, I'll say it—it makes me look hot. Damned hot. The makeup Gina had applied for me didn't hurt the look, either. I had no idea I could look so much better with just five minutes of fussing, but I swear that's all the time she spent.

I'll admit to being uncomfortable, but I've never gotten dressed up like this. Hell, I don't think I've worn a dress in...I can't even remember how long it's been. High school graduation? Maybe. That's the last time my mother was able to mold me to her wishes.

It's not like that with Gina. When we went shopping, she analyzed the dresses I tried on as a designer would. And she was brutal! She must have told me to take at least ten dresses off before I zipped them. But when she liked something, she simply told me why. She never made a big deal out of it; she just said that a particular dress made me look taller or more elegant or brought out the color in my eyes. Then she'd double-check the fit and nod her head. After we found three dresses that fit properly and we both liked, she dropped out of the game. No matter how much I begged, she would not tell me which one I should buy. I must confess that I wasn't as diplomatic as she was. As soon as she put on the outfit she finally bought, I began taking all of the other things out of the dressing room. There was no way I'd let her buy anything different. But she gamely played along and bought it without a moment's hesitation. That's one more thing I like about her. She doesn't mind my bossing her around. That's a very good trait in a woman.

"Fix my straps?"

Damn! I almost jumped out of my skin. She's so quiet! "Sure, as soon as my heart starts beating again. Could you be just a little bit noisier? You make cats sound like hippos."

"Sorry," she said, flashing me the grin that indicated she had no intention of doing what I'd asked.

I made sure her straps were straight and then put my hands on her hips to turn her around. "It's not possible for a woman to look any better than you do right now," I said, meaning every word. She wore a simple, cream-colored camisole and a short skirt in the same shiny, slinky fabric. That might not sound like much, but when you add the flash of her bare, tanned tummy, which showed when she walked, and the delicious cleavage that the bra she'd chosen revealed, believe me, you would have run me down to get at her.

I was a little surprised that she'd agreed to buy the outfit. It was awfully sexy, and no one in my family would go to an anniversary celebration in a revealing top, but Gina hadn't voiced any discomfort about my choices, so I wasn't going to mention it.

She went to her dresser and took out a tiny bottle of perfume, removed the stopper and ran it between her breasts, and behind each ear lobe. "Wanna smell like me?" she asked.

"No. I don't want my nose to get used to the scent. Then it won't smell as good on you."

"Good point." She put the perfume away and held out her hand. "Ready?"

"I guess I am."

Gina picked up a small purse that coordinated perfectly with her shoes, and I realized I didn't have a thing to carry other than my backpack. "Do you have a purse I can use? It looks stupid not to have one, doesn't it?"

She shrugged. "Sure, I can lend you one, but you don't have to carry one if you don't want to. I've got my wallet and my car keys. That's all we need."

"Really?"

"Hayden," she said, putting her hands on my hips. "You don't have to follow any rules you don't want to follow. I like to get dressed up. That's the only reason I do it. If I didn't want to, I wouldn't. So, if you want to carry a purse, I've got one for you. If you don't, don't."

I smiled at her and kissed her tenderly. "I don't."

"Good. Besides, you're gonna need both hands to keep all of the guys in the family off you. You look fantastic."

It must have been the combination of her smile and the sincerity in her eyes, but I believed her. As a matter of fact, for one of the first times in my life, I agreed with her. I looked fantastic. Weird.

✦

I needn't have worried about Gina looking out of place. Her family and friends were a bit—okay, a lot—more casual than mine. I saw a lot of big cars, a lot of big jewelry, a lot of big breasts—some real and some purchased—and a lot of big hair. Big, big hair. Hair that I didn't know existed north of Texas.

I'd been introduced to about thirty people and had yet to meet anyone from her immediate family. But I'd gotten to hear that beautiful Long Island accent at full throttle.

When my family has an event, we all speak rather softly and kiss each other on the cheek, not actually trying to make skin contact. Gina's family greeted each other boisterously, enthusiastically, and physically. I was clutched to bosoms, squeezed like a melon, and had my cheeks pinched by more than one short, rotund, ancient woman. Gina dragged me away from a gentleman who seemed intent on taking me home with him and steered me towards the bar.

"Uncle Nico wasn't being too grabby, was he?"

"Uhm…" I grimaced, not wanting to cause any trouble, but not wanting to lie.

"Lacey used to run when she'd see him coming. She swore he was trying to hump her leg."

I burst out laughing. "Doesn't it bother you that your uncle is so…forward?"

"Oh, he's not my real uncle. He's just a family friend. He's one of my grandfather's buddies. My grandfather probably squeezes all the young girls when he goes to things with Nico's family, too." She laughed, obviously not bothered by such things. "If you don't like being pawed, I'll keep you away from the usual suspects."

"No, that's fine. I guess I'm just not used to it." Who wants to be pawed? We have dirty old men in our family, but they're discreet about it. Uncle Nico's wife was standing right there when he had his hand on my ass and grabbed a handful!

Gina put her hand on my shoulder and then let it slip up to caress the side of my neck. I don't know why, but that calms me as quickly as a big hug. She looked deeply into my eyes and said, "You don't have to get used to anything. If you don't wanna be touched, you won't."

Damn, she knew just what to say. "I…don't like being touched by people I don't know. It's just—" She put her finger to my lips to cut me off.

"No explanations needed. If you're uncomfortable, that's all that matters."

I turned my head to kiss her palm. "You're a very good girlfriend."

The corner of her mouth turned up, and her eyes became playful again. "I'm learning. You're teaching me a lot."

That was a major load of crap, but I was more than willing to go along with her sophistry. "Buy me a drink?"

"Open bar, baby," she said, leering a little. "I can get you drunk for free. What'll you have?"

"Surprise me." I turned my back to the bar and watched the guests mingle. The crowd was massive, much bigger than I'd anticipated. I thought it would just be family and a few friends, but the bin Ladens didn't have this many family members.

I briefly thought of the time Gina had classified herself as being a wop, talking about gold chains and statues of the Virgin Mary on lawns. Now I know what she meant. She wasn't like that—at all—but her friends and family were clearly prone to exuberance in their dress, their manner, and their speech. I was working out how she fit into this mélange of excess when she leaned over and said, "Here comes my brother."

I looked to my left and saw a mildly attractive, slightly paunchy man approach. He was smiling, but there was an insincerity to his smile that made me stiffen. "Hi," she said.

"What's goin' on?" the man asked.

"Nothin'." She put her hand on my back and said, "This is Hayden Chandler. Hayden, this is my brother Anthony."

He blinked, but stuck his hand out. "Hi. How you doin'?"

"I'm fine," I said, unsure of where to go with this conversation. It was pretty clear he hadn't heard of me, so I felt uncomfortable saying that Gina had spoken of him, especially since she hadn't except in the most general way. "Nice party."

"Yeah. It's good." He turned and ordered a couple of drinks, and Gina handed me mine. I took a sip and nodded my approval, pleased with what tasted like vodka, orange juice, and cranberry juice.

Anthony leaned on the bar, waiting for his drinks to be delivered. "So, how do you know Gina?"

"We met on Fire Island."

"Oh." He nodded, looking as if he wanted to say something else. But he didn't. He took the drinks the bartender handed him, gave us that odd smile again, and said, "Gotta go. See ya around."

"Nice to meet you," I said to his back as he threaded through the crowd.

Gina's smirk didn't tell me much, but I could see she wasn't entirely comfortable. "Let's head outside. The music's a little loud."

That was an understatement, so I gratefully followed her onto the veranda of the country club. I had to give the family props for choosing a nice place. It was over-the-top opulent, the room was big and lavishly decorated, and there were plenty of French doors leading to an elevated stone veranda overlooking the golf course. Gina pulled out two chairs for us, and we set our drinks on the small table between them.

We both sat down and didn't speak for a few minutes, letting the noise behind us fade a bit, as we looked out on the verdant, undulating landscape.

"Havin' fun?" she finally asked.

"Sure. It's a nice party. I've got my eyes on that tower of oysters in the corner."

"You hungry? I'll go get something."

"No rush. It's nice to be out here alone with you." I took her hand, noting it was a little stiff. "How about you? Are you having fun?"

Her shoulders moved a bit, and she made a familiar expression. Even though it was familiar, I wasn't entirely sure what it meant. Her lips pursed, and one of her eyebrows rose, and that was it. Sometimes, she held her hands palms-up in front of herself when she used the expression, but she had her drink in her hand at the moment, so I didn't receive the usual flourish. Given the situations in which she'd used the gesture, I'd come to assume it meant, "Can't complain," although it might have meant, "Not particularly." I'd have to continue my study.

"Your brother seemed nice." Yeah, I know that was a lame thing to say, but what were my choices? "Is he the eldest?"

"No, Nick is. Anthony is ten years older than I am, and Nick is twelve."

"Really? You've never mentioned there was such a big age gap."

She took a drink, nodding. "Yeah. I was the little surprise. My mom always wanted a girl, but I think my dad was happy with two kids."

She said this with such ease that it didn't have the sting it should have had.

"I'm gonna go get some oysters for you." She smiled at me and made my muscles go weak. "You look hungry."

I took her hand before she could rise and brought it to my mouth. "I am. For you." Teasingly, I sucked her index finger into my mouth and laved it with my tongue. "Let's not stay out too late. I have to show you how good you look tonight."

"We can leave now," she said, smiling so lovingly that I almost got up and ran for the car.

"We can't leave until I meet your family, honey."

Her eyes met mine, and I could see that she had a clear desire to take off right then. I was about to tell her we could leave immediately if she wanted to, when a rather harsh woman's voice said, "There's the baby of the family! Where've you been, Gina? I've been looking all over for you!"

Suddenly, Gina wore the smile her brother had pasted on his face. What in the hell was up with the fake smile? Gina stood up, and I turned to see her wrap her arms around a small, flinty-looking woman. "I was just trying to get away from the loud music, Grandma."

"Loud! My gawd, have you evah heard anythin' so loud? I told Linda to tell them to turn it down or she's not payin'. And did ya see the outfit on that little hoah that Case brought? She looks like she's chargin' by the owah."

Oh, boy! This is gonna be fun!

"Grandma," Gina said, moving to direct the woman's attention to me, "this is Hayden Chandler. Hayden, this is my grandmother, Rosalie."

"It's nice to meet you," I said.

Rosalie looked as if she'd been sucking on a lemon, but she managed to reply, "Yeah. Nice. How you know Gina?"

"We met on Fire Island this spring."

"Oh." She turned back to Gina and said, "You aren't lettin' those boys take the boat out alone, are you?"

"No, of course not. Case is the only one with a pilot's license."

"And you let him?" Rosalie could've made a living etching glass with her voice, but I thought it prudent not to mention that.

"Yes, Grandma," Gina said patiently. "He's fully certified, and he's logged hundreds of hours with me sitting right beside him. He knows what he's doing."

"So, why does he have that hoah with him? He's pro'bly gonna knock her up, just like his fathuh did with his muthuh."

"I haven't met his girlfriend," Gina said, staying remarkably calm. "But he knows how to pilot the boat, and that's what I care about."

"He's gonna get that girl knocked up, and then he's gonna havtah quit school."

"He's finished with school, Grandma. He graduated last year."

The older woman paused for a second and then asked, "Who's in school?"

"All of Nick and Anthony's kids."

"Oh. Well, Chris's girlfriend looks like she could be working 3rd Avenue in Bay Shore."

Gina looked annoyed, but she kept her tone calm. "Lindsay's a nice girl. She's working the ticket window for me this summer."

"And 3rd Avenue at night," the old woman sneered. God, I hope Gina was adopted.

Obviously deciding to switch subjects, Gina asked, "Is Grampa around?"

Rosalie made a vague gesture with her hand. "Yeah. He's somewhere. I'd better go check on him. He gets drunk in ten minutes now that he's on that new heart pill." With that, she turned and left, saying goodbye to neither Gina nor me.

Gina shrugged, clearly a little embarrassed. "My mom's side of the family is…uhm…easier to take."

"Are they here?"

"Unh-uh. Wanna leave?"

"Only if you do, honey." I stood close to her and hugged her chastely. "I think we should check out all of the slutty girls before we go."

She laughed and kissed my forehead. "I'll go get you some oysters. No sense in leaving when they've got good food."

"Any chance they have lobster rolls?"

She winked at me. "No, but I'll take you to Montauk tomorrow night. You're due." I watched the lovely fabric glide over her legs and stared at her hips swaying as she walked away. Nothing was sexier than seeing just a sliver of bare skin when those hips slid up and down. Whew! I'm glad we came out to the veranda 'cause my pulse is racing!

❖

Gina was right. It would've been dumb to leave and miss the great food they had at the buffet. It must have cost a fortune, but I made sure they got their money's worth for my portion. After eating enough clams, oysters, and shrimp for four people, we went to look for the rest of the family. Gina honestly seemed willing to leave without my meeting her grandfather and her other brother, but that seemed silly. I wasn't planning on getting this dressed up for quite a while, and I decided it was best to let them see me at the height of my charms.

We went back inside, and Gina headed towards a large group of people. I saw her nephews, Chris and Dominick, in the crowd, as well as Anthony, the brother I'd met earlier. They'd pushed several small tables together, and Gina's father was sitting right in the middle, obviously regarded as the head of the family. Even if I hadn't met him, I would have known he was her dad and not only because she had his nose and his chin. He also looked at her with the same sense of familiarity and incomprehension that I often got from my mother.

"Hi, Dad," she said, walking right to him.

"Well, well, well," he replied, drawing it out. "People keep telling me you're here, but you couldn't of proved it by me."

"I'm here," she said, not rising to the bait. "You remember Hayden."

"Nice to see you again, Mr. Scognamiglio," I said, pleased that my pronunciation had gotten so much better.

His face darkened, and he snapped. "That's not my name."

My eyes widened, and I wasn't sure how to reply. But Gina rescued me. "I changed my name after I graduated from high school. I thought I'd told you that."

"No, no, you didn't," I said, trying to smile.

"*Our* name is Scoggins," her father said. "But it wasn't good enough for Gina. Not Italian enough."

Oh, boy. I think we should have left after the oysters.

"I used to be a Scognamiglio," the elderly man seated next to Gina's father said.

"This is my grampa," Gina said, with a little more warmth in her voice. "Vincenzo Scognamiglio."

He waved her off. "I haven't been called that since I wore high-button shoes. I've been Vincent Scoggins since the Depression. What's your name, honey?"

"Hayden," I said.

"Hayden? Sounds like a man's name."

"It can be. But it's a family name. My mother was a Hayden."

"Huh. Well, your name doesn't sound as pretty as you are." He wiggled his bushy eyebrows at Gina. "She's a nice lookin' girl."

"I know," she said evenly.

We were still standing, and it didn't appear that we'd be sitting down. Gina looked as if she wanted to make introductions and hightail it outta there. I was more than happy to accommodate her at that point.

"What do you do, honey?" Vincent asked.

"I teach."

"Where?"

"The city." I'd learned that Long Islanders generally referred to Manhattan as the city, and I wanted to blend in.

"You live there?"

"Yes. I live in Greenwich Village." Technically, I lived in the East Village, but people out here didn't seem to get the distinction.

"I grew up on Bowery, just north of where it crosses Broome."

"Really? I live in Alphabet City. Avenue D and East 4th."

He looked flummoxed. "A cute girl like you? When I was a kid, that was a good place to dump a body."

"It's a little better now. But you could probably still get away with dumping a body or two."

He laughed, and I could see some of Gina in his smile and twinkling eyes. So far, he was the winner of the whole bunch, and he looked like he wanted me to sit on his lap so he could grope me. "You teach in one of those piece o'shit schools in the city?"

Charming. Simply charming. "No, I teach at NYU."

Both Scogna…Scoggins men looked at me. The younger asked, "The college?"

"Yeah. I teach history."

Gina's father reached around and grasped a younger man by the shoulder. He was obviously Gina's brother, and he looked more like her than anyone else at the table. "Nick! Hear that? This girl's a teacher at college."

The younger man stared at me. "Really? Why you hang out wit' Gina? Dad had to pay off her teachers just to get her outta high school."

I nearly slugged him. I didn't even care if I'd ruin the nose that looked so lovely on Gina. "I've never been overly impressed by the correlation between academic success and intelligence. Especially when one has to deal with a learning disability." I knew my face was red, but I wasn't ready to stop. "Gina's one of the brightest people I know, and I'm surrounded by people with degrees from every good school in the country."

Nick's stupid smile faded a little, but he wasn't ready to concede. Gina's hand was on my back, but she didn't seem to mind that I was dressing down her brother, so I continued to glare at him.

Her father took over. "She can't be too smart if she's happy with the Fire Island route. There's no money there. And who'd close down a moneymaker like a bar? That was just ignorant."

Gina started to speak, but I got the first word in, and she shut up. "Maybe she doesn't think money's the most important thing in the world. If she knows what's important to her and willing to do what she has to do to achieve her goals, that sounds pretty damned smart to me. And she's clearly not ignorant. She told me exactly why she didn't want to run the bar, and she didn't seem unaware or uninformed."

"She's lazy. Always has been," he said dismissively. "She wants to take long vacations and act like she's an Italian. She's never been happy to be just another dago from the island."

Gina's grandfather interrupted. "Aw, leave her alone, Vin. She's just a girl. And she's done damn good for a girl. She don't cause no trouble."

Wow! He was quite the defender!

"She takes the scraps the boys give her," her father said. "That's weak."

"I'm happy," Gina said, not looking or sounding upset. "I make a good salary, and I have a good life. Why kill myself?"

Her grandfather put his hand out, and she took it. "She's a real Italian," he said fondly. "She's happy with a good bottle of wine and a basket of melons. She's like my father, God bless." He ostentatiously made the sign of the cross, and Gina's father did the same, albeit with less élan.

I noted that Vincent didn't have a Long Island accent. Being born in Italy and raised in the city gave him a unique and rather pleasant accent. I still chose him as my favorite, even though he looked at my tits more than my face.

"Your father was murdered over a boat that didn't cost him a hundred dollars," Gina's dad said. "How smart was that?"

"He might not've been smart, but he had guts," Vincent said. "And you never knew him, so don't act like you did. He always told me, 'Those who make themselves sheep will be eaten by the wolf.'"

"He might not have made himself a sheep, but the wolves got him anyway, didn't they?" Gina's dad looked very self-satisfied. Have I mentioned I wasn't yet crazy about him?

Vincent put his hand to his chest, turned his fingers towards the floor, and acted as if he was brushing something away. I'd seen Gina make the same gesture, but I'd never thought to ask what it meant. From the context and the expression on his face, Vincent was telling his son the conversation was over.

I must have been correct because the older man got up and steadied himself for a moment before saying, "Gina, take me to the bar."

Rosalie snapped, "Don't you dare, Gina! He's had enough."

Vincent's fingers scraped the area under his chin, making it pretty clear that he wasn't listening to her advice. Gina and I directed Vincent to the bar, where he smiled at her and cuffed her on the cheek. "Your old man's a pain in the ass sometimes, isn't he?"

Gina smiled at him and shrugged. "He's the same."

"Screw him," he said. "He's lucky to have you. Promise me that you don't let him get to you."

She made an "X" with her index fingers and said, "Giuro."

"That's my girl." He signaled the waiter and said, "Seltzer with a lime." When the waiter walked away, he said, "I like to make your grandma think I'm drinking."

"You're not?" Gina asked.

"Fuckin' heart pills make me sick when I drink. Doctors just wanna take an old man's fun away. Thank Jesus I can still go to the track."

Gina wrapped her arm around him and kissed his cheek. "I love you, Grampa."

He gently pushed her away. "Enough! If I let you kiss me, all the girls will want to." He moved in my direction. "Won't they?" His eyes lit up like Gina's did when she was teasing me. I couldn't resist and placed a kiss on both of his slightly stubbly cheeks. "See?" he said, beaming a smile at my girlfriend.

"I think we're gonna take off," Gina said. "I've got to get up by five."

"Lazy, huh?" the old man chuckled. "Everybody in the company should be so lazy." He kissed her cheek and squeezed her shoulder. "Be strong."

"I will."

"It was nice to meet you, Mr. Scoggins," I said.

"I forgot your name already, honey, but I'll remember how pretty you are."

"Thanks." What the hell. There are worse ways to be remembered. "I hope to see you again."

"Come for tomatoes," he said as we left.

We made our way through the people gathered around the dessert table and escaped to the relative quiet of the massive hallway. "Thank God that's over," Gina sighed. "I always want to go to family parties, but I almost always wish I hadn't."

I took her hand and squeezed it. "What about tonight?"

"Eh, tonight wasn't too bad. Sorry I didn't introduce you to most of my relatives, but they'll be there the next time."

"Okay," I said, deciding to wait for a better time to dig a little more dirt from the fertile Scognamiglio fields.

Chapter Twelve

As soon as Gina got home from work the next day, she lay down on the chaise in the sun and fell asleep. It was rare for her to take a nap, but we had been out a little late, and I'd kept her up for a long time, kissing every part of her I could get my mouth on.

I don't know why, but I fell in love just a little bit more with her last night. Maybe it was because I got more of a sense of what she'd had to overcome to get what she wanted out of life. Or maybe it was because I saw how resilient she was when her family treated her like shit. She was so goodhearted. Most people would have told their father to fuck off and stormed out of there. But Gina let him bitch and let it slide right off her. That's admirable in my book. Anyone can get into a fight, but most people can't let people ride them and not have it ruin their evening.

But I wonder why she loses her temper so quickly with me? If she detects even the slightest bit of deceit or disrespect—ka-boom! How does that jibe with letting her family bust her chops? I don't think it does, but that's sure what happens.

"Hi," a sleepy voice said, stirring me from my thoughts.

"Hi." I got up from the table and sat on the edge of her lounge chair. "Feel better?"

"Yeah. A little nap was just the thing I needed."

"You hungry?"

"Starving. Want that lobster roll I promised?"

"Yeah, unless you don't wanna drive that far."

"Mmm...I know another place that's almost as good. We could get there in half the time."

"Sounds good. But I still get to drive."

✦

We went to a place in Ocean Beach—a little shack that didn't even have chairs. So, we ordered our lobster rolls and a couple of beers and walked to the beach.

It seemed as if Gina knew this beach like I knew the research library at NYU. She guided me up the beach about a hundred feet and indicated that I should have a seat. I noted that the wind was in exactly the right spot to blow the hair out of my eyes. I knew she'd picked that spot on purpose. Damn, she's cool!

I had questions about Gina's family—lots of them—but I didn't want to interrogate her. So, I tried to be a little subtle. "So," I said, "you seem tired today. Did last night take a lot out of you?"

"Not really," Gina said. "It wears on me after a while having to get up so early."

I didn't buy that for a minute. Gina got up early every day. And we hadn't stayed out very late last night. But I could see either she didn't realize last night had sapped her strength or she didn't want to talk about it.

I was going to have to be more direct. "How did you and your brothers decide on who got which ferry route?" That was pretty direct.

She cocked her head in question at my query from out of left field, but she answered immediately. "My brothers had been on my dad for years to get him to let them run a line independently. We didn't all work together very well, and we'd sort of taken to our own little fiefdoms, but nothing was formally set in place. Not long before my twenty-fifth birthday, my father said he was ready to let us separate the ferry lines."

"Do you think he waited until he thought you were old enough?"

"I do." Gina seemed to contemplate that for a minute, and she showed a faint smile. "I should thank him for that. My brothers would have eaten me alive if my father had given in to them when they first started begging."

"Why?" I asked, stunned at this revelation. My sister had her faults, but she always watches my back.

Gina held up her hands. "That's just how they are."

"They'd take advantage of you?"

Gina chuckled lightly. "They take advantage of anyone and everyone. They're very competitive. Brutal, really."

"How did you protect yourself?"

Gina gave me a sidelong glance, and for the first time, I'd have to say she looked foxy, wily even. "I was finally smart enough to trick them by letting them believe their preconceived notions about me."

"And those are?"

"That I'm dumb and lazy. Their favorite kind of victim."

"Gina! Why would you let them think that?"

"It was the easiest way to get what I wanted."

"You voluntarily let them take advantage of you?"

"They thought so." She chuckled rather evilly. "Just shows how stupid they are."

"Tell me how letting them believe that helped you."

"It's simple, really. I suggested we choose in birth order. That made Nick happy and pissed Anthony off. So, Anthony said it was only fair if we drew straws."

"Did that piss Nick off?"

"Oh, yeah." Gina laughed.

"Making both of your brothers mad helped you somehow?"

"Yeah. My father decided to let us choose straws. He thought that was most fair. I drew the long straw, so I got to pick first."

"Ah. So, you got to choose the one you wanted."

"No. Too easy. I said I thought it was only fair to pick in birth order, so I waived my pick to let Nick go first."

"But…"

Gina put her hand on me, still grinning slyly. "Hold on. Nick is the more powerful of the two. He's also the meaner. Doing that let him think I respected him and his place in the family."

"But you don't?"

"Fuck, no!" She laughed heartily. "He's dumber than Anthony, and that takes some doing."

"So, why did you do it? This makes no sense."

"Sure it does. I'm dealing with a couple of snakes, Hayden. It's best to let them think what they want, while still getting what you need. Nick took the biggest ferry, and then Anthony demanded he get to go second. My father wanted me to fight him for it, but I meekly gave in."

My mouth was obviously open because Gina tenderly closed it.

"Anthony took the second biggest, as I knew he would. The revenue for Fire Island is just a little less than the lines that were left, so it didn't seem completely out of whack when I chose it. I said I wanted to stay close to home, and they all bought it."

"So, what happened to the other two lines?"

"My father said that since I wanted to give away first choice, I had to give away fourth choice, too. Nick took one of the little ones, and Anthony got the other." She looked pleased with herself, but I was still lagging behind.

"So, each one of them got two companies, and you got one. But it's the one you wanted, so you're happy, right?"

"Yeah. I only wanted one. But I couldn't admit that in front of my father. He might have kicked me in the butt and given me nothing. Acting like I respected my brother gave me some small measure of stature, but he still thought he was punishing me by letting the boys pick again and shutting me out."

"Wow. Is that why he thinks you're lazy?"

"No. He thinks I'm lazy because I haven't tried to stab my brothers in the back or try to buy another line from a competitor. He isn't capable of understanding that I'm happy with one small line. Plus, I've got all of the school stuff as evidence that I don't work hard."

"Damn, Gina, doesn't it…doesn't it hurt to know you don't have his respect?" I hated to say it, but it was a question begging to be asked.

"I lost his respect by the time I was in fifth grade. When you disappoint my father, he never gets over it. I knew it was gone forever. Since then…" She smiled, her pretty teeth gleaming, "I'm free. I don't argue, I don't get mad, and I don't let my feelings get hurt. I accept him for who he is, and I thank him for giving me a way of life I love."

I was stunned. Simply stunned. "You're not bitter?"

"Nah. He's not the supportive type. I wish he was, but he's not." She shrugged. "I got over it. We're fine now. I see my family when I want to, and I leave when they bug me. I've got it a hell of a lot better than most people."

Damn, I hated to admit this, but I think I wasted a lot of time and money on therapy. Gina figured out everything I learned from three therapists and did it without paying a cent.

❖

Saturday was so lovely that I went over to Cherry Grove to lie in the sun. Gina tried to hold on to me so I couldn't get off the ferry, but she relented and promised to come over as soon as she was through for the day.

I went to my house and saw bags and suitcases lying all over the place, so I knew it was a full house. I was more than a little miffed to find that someone had taken over my room, but I decided it wasn't worth an argument. I'd made it pretty clear that I preferred living at Gina's, and my roommates had obviously taken me at my word.

Good old Elaine was sitting on the beach right in front of our house. I decided to be friendly, so I stopped by on my way to a quiet place. "Hi," I said,

"Hayden." She looked around, probably trying to determine if I was alone. "Join me."

I had work to do, but I wasn't in a huge rush. I sat down and got settled.

"Are you alone today?"

"Just until Gina's off work. Why?"

Elaine looked…I'm not even sure what word I would use. Interested? Fascinated? Maybe intrigued. But there was no doubt that she had something on her mind. "What's the story with Gina? Are you going to keep this up all summer?"

"A lot longer than summer," I said.

"You plan on seeing her once school starts?"

"I do. Neither of us thinks this is a summer fling. She's an incredible woman, Elaine, and even though you haven't seen her best side, it's there."

"What's so special about her?"

"That's very difficult to answer. I'm better at describing things that happened in the distant past. I'm not always best at putting words to my current feelings."

Elaine looked thoughtful, pensively staring out at the ocean for a few minutes. I didn't have anything to say, and I wasn't interested in starting another thread to this conversation, so I let her think.

"I can't figure out who she is," Elaine said. "When I first saw her on the ferry, she looked...like a tough Long Island girl. She looked like she was trying to make a statement. She honestly reminded me of my cousin in New Jersey."

"I didn't know you had family in New Jersey. I thought you were from Michigan."

"I am. But I told you my mother is Italian. She was born in Secaucus, and her brother still lives there. I have a cousin a little older than I am who acts like he should be in a Mafia movie."

"Is he a criminal?"

Elaine laughed. "He works for the post office. But he adopts this persona in which he comes across as a tough guy. I don't, in any way, understand his need to do this, but it's something I've seen fairly frequently, especially in the New York area. It's like there's some cachet of being viewed as a possible hoodlum. Have you ever been to the San Gennaro Festival in Little Italy?"

"No. I've never heard of it."

"You should go this year. I think it's in September. It used to be a carnival with a religious theme, but now it's a place to buy Mafia CDs and T-shirts and license plates that say "Fuggedaboudit" and things like that."

"Sounds like fun," I said. "One can never have too many Mafia CDs."

Chuckling, Elaine said, "I wasn't suggesting you'd buy much. But it's a nice place to do an anthropological study on people like my cousin. When I first saw Gina, I thought she was like him. But after seeing her in a social situation with Lorna and Sheila, she doesn't seem like that at all. She seems bright. I felt sorry for her because she's obviously of a class that didn't allow her to have many opportunities. It must be hard for someone like her who's intelligent, but didn't get the guidance she needed to improve herself."

I didn't, in any way, need to explain Gina to Elaine. But I didn't want her to have such a patently false impression of my girlfriend. "Gina has a lot of opportunities, Elaine. Her family is quite well-off, and she alone owns the Fire Island ferry company."

"What?"

"It's true. She has money, and she could have gone to college except for one major thing. She has a learning disability that makes it hard for her to summarize things in writing. Her teachers didn't discover it until she was almost through grade school, and by then, she'd learned to hate school. Once you've been turned off so thoroughly by school, it's hard to get back into it."

"Damn, that's awful."

"Yeah. It was hard for her. So, she could be better educated, but education wouldn't make her any brighter. She's clearly my equal intellectually, and she surpasses me in almost every practical way. I'm just glad that she does something she loves and has time to do the things that mean a lot to her. I don't know if that would have been true if she'd gone to college and felt she had to do something in the professional world."

"You can't be serious," Elaine said.

"About which part?"

She flapped her hands in frustration. "Any of it! Why would the owner of the company be driving the ferry?"

Smugly, I said, "She's the pilot, not the driver. And she does it because she likes it and it saves her having to pay another pilot. I've learned that Gina does what she wants to do after thinking it through thoroughly. So, if she says it makes sense for her to pilot, I believe her."

"I don't think I've ever been more surprised."

"I hate to admit this, but I was surprised, too. I've learned a lot this summer, and one of the most important things I've learned is that I have my head up my ass when it comes to judging people by their academic accomplishments. There's a reason they say we're in an ivory tower, Elaine."

Elaine no longer looked surprised. Now she looked suspicious. "You're not planning on abandoning your career to be a deckhand, are you Hayden?"

"No, that's not where my interest lies. I still want to become a professor and write books. Gina and I just have to figure out a way to be together while both doing what we love."

Regarding me suspiciously, Elaine said, "I can't see you spending two hours on the LIRR every morning."

"I can't see that either, but we'll figure something out. I have more flexibility than she has since she can't bring the Fire Island ferry to Manhattan."

"It's not a surprise to me that you hooked up with someone out here, but Gina would have been the last person I would have picked for you. I know I don't have the right to speak about her as if I know her, but she seems of two worlds."

Now I was intrigued. "What do you mean?"

"It's like I was referring to earlier. There's part of her that seems—I hate to use a generalization—but there's part of her that seems like a low-class Long Island girl. You know the stereotype: harsh accents, gaudy jewelry, long fingernails, loud fights, and lots of 'proshute' and 'mozzarell.'"

"I hate to admit my stupidity, but I wasn't aware of that stereotype. That's why I was surprised when we went to a family party recently and I saw the very people you're speaking of. Gina seems like she's from a different world than most of those people, but she's also part of them. I've been confused about it ever since I went to that party."

"One of my little fields of interest is doing some research on the people you're talking about. There isn't a lot written about it, probably because it would be nearly impossible to get funding to do research. But I'm interested."

"Why the interest? Because your mother is Italian?"

"No, more because of my cousin. His behavior and the mien he creates seem common, and I wonder if people consciously adopt it or if it's part of their upbringing. It wasn't part of my cousin's upbringing, so I know he adopted it."

"So, his parents didn't act like they were members of the Mafia?"

"God, no! My maternal grandparents distanced themselves from those stereotypes as much as they possibly could. They realized that education is the key to success in the United States. They'd only graduated from high school, but they were determined that their children would be college graduates. My uncle didn't finish, and he wound up working in a factory in New Jersey. But my mother got her degree, and even though she's proud of her Italian heritage, she doesn't fly a red, white, and green flag from the front porch, if you know what I mean."

"I'm not sure that I do," Hayden said. "Are you equating pride in your heritage with this subculture of Mafia homage?"

"No, of course not. It seems to me that most of the Italian immigrants who came to this country during the big wave of emigration came from Sicily. There's nothing wrong with Sicily, but it's been a poor region for hundreds, if not thousands, of years. People in the north of Italy still try every few years to come up with a secession plan to separate the north from the south."

"I had no idea."

"Most of the immigrants didn't come because things were going well for them in Italy. They were the poorest of the poor, and it was either scrape together the money to emigrate or possibly starve to death. Many of the immigrants were illiterate, the vast majority of them were under-schooled, and almost all were poor. Like any group, some wanted to stay rooted in the past, just in a new country. Many others, probably the majority, tried to adopt American ways and values and be a success. My mother's family was like that. But somehow, my cousin seems to have reverted to the group that acts as if they're still have one foot in Sicily and one foot in the United States. They insist on using that bastardized Sicilian dialect to pronounce the few Italian words they know."

"Is that what you are referring to by 'proshute'? I heard people saying that at the party we went to. I know that's not how Gina says it, and she speaks Italian beautifully."

"Most people who act like my cousin don't speak Italian. They've never been to Italy; they don't seem to have any interest in going to Italy. It seems that they've created this small, Sicilian underclass and revel in the fact that they're an underclass."

"I hate to admit this, but I heard Gina's father referring to the family as a bunch of dumb wops. I was amazed."

"I'm not a sociologist, so I'm not the right person to come up with the definitive study on this. But there's definitely been an upsurge in Italian Americans reveling in their lack of education and lack of sophistication. Maybe it started with the Godfather movies. Maybe it's been there ever since the first Sicilians emigrated. But there's a big difference between people of Italian dissent like my mother and perhaps like Gina's father."

"Fascinating," I said. "Sometimes, Gina seems like she's caught in the middle. Like she expects people to think she's dumb and a member of the Mafia and classless. But she's nothing of the sort. She's elegant and tasteful and refined, and even though she's very fond of Italy, she doesn't seem boastful about it. I'm certain that she would never fly the red, white, and green flag. For one thing, it would clash hideously with her décor." For some reason, I found the mere thought of that very humorous, but I'm sure Elaine didn't realize why it was so funny to me. Of course, she hadn't seen Gina's pink house.

❖

When Gina came home today, she spent her usual few moments going through her mail. I watched her out of the corner of my eye waiting to see what she did with what looked to me like an invitation. I saw her pause and heft the envelope in her hand for a few moments, but then toss it aside. Trying to sound casual, I asked, "Anything interesting?"

She waited a few moments to reply. "I don't know if it's interesting, but it's something, since I don't want to open it."

"What is it, honey?"

"It's from Lacey. It's probably an invitation to the party she and her friends always have." Gina picked up the envelope again, tossing it in the air and letting it fall to the table. "Funny. They usually have a party around Labor Day. I wonder why it's early?"

I wanted to grab the envelope, rip it open, and find out what the fuck it was, but I behaved. "You seem funny about it. Like you're afraid to open it."

Gina nodded slowly. "I don't know why, but I am a little afraid. I haven't heard from her in so long…"

"Didn't Lacey invite you last year?"

"No, she didn't. It makes me a little antsy to hear from her now. My mind is racing trying to figure out why she's contacting me."

I walked over to Gina and stood by her. I rested my head on her shoulder, and as usual, she loosely wrapped her arms around my waist. We hugged for a few minutes. We did this several times a day. I don't recall when it started, but if she didn't hug me a few times a day, my day wasn't complete. As was often the case, I could feel the tension drain from her body. I have to admit I was more than a little proud of my ability to calm Gina down. As soon as her body felt loose and pliable in my arms, Gina reached around me and picked up the envelope. I heard the paper tear, and then I heard and felt her take in a deep breath. "Yeah. They're having their party. I just can't figure out why they invited me."

"There is an easy way to find out, honey."

"Yeah, I could call Lacey, but I don't really want to."

"I thought maybe we could go to the party, and you could figure it out that way."

"What?"

"I'd kinda like to meet your friends. Is that weird?"

"No, not at all. It's just that I'm not sure they're my friends."

"All of them? Or just Lacey?"

Gina released me and went to the refrigerator. She poured herself a glass of water and leaned up against the counter while she slowly sipped from the glass. I'd learned not to rush her when she was thinking, but it was darned hard. Sometimes, I wanted to light a fire under her to make her think faster. She drained the glass and placed it on the counter. "All of them, but in particular Lacey."

"How long have you known these women?"

"Pretty long. More than half of them were my friends before I knew Lacey. But I think I told you that some of them started treating me funny when I started going to Italy and learning Italian and changed my name. Most of the people I hung out with in high school were slackers, and I think they thought I was trying to upstage them or be better than them or…I don't know what the fuck they were thinking to be honest."

"Didn't Lacey go to Italy with you?"

Gina made a cute face, the one where she stuck her lower lip out and half closed her eyes. "No. She never wanted to. She only got two weeks of vacation, and she liked to take it as three- and four-day weekends throughout the year. Besides, she thought my interest in Italy was pretty weird."

"I can see why this has you puzzled," I said. "You and Lacey have been broken up for a few years, and you don't see your old friends anymore. It does seem funny that they'd choose now to invite you to a party."

Gina walked over to the counter and picked up the invitation. She held the corner of it to her temple and tapped a few times. "Would you like to go with me?"

My heart flew to my throat, but I gathered my courage and said, "Yes."

❧

It's not always a good idea to gather your courage. Sometimes, it's best to let it lie in disorderly little bundles. Gina just walked downstairs, all dressed for the party. I don't know why this had to be the one day of the summer where we aren't getting any of that cool, wet air off the Atlantic. No, today is hot and sticky, with not a cloud in the sky.

Gina dressed appropriately, as always. Besides being in fine form for a beach party, she'd fit right in as a model at Victoria's Secret. I love seeing her tanned skin exposed, but it didn't occur to me that Lacey would once again be laying eyes on that little piece of Paradise. It's not a surprise that I'm unenthusiastic about this development, since I'm far from secure about my hold on Gina. Although I have no reason to be insecure, I've never let reality stop my neuroses.

Gina hasn't spoken much about the party, so I've decided to let my insecurities run wild. Why is Lacey interested in being in contact with Gina at this point? I can't answer that question, and I won't be able to until we meet, if then. I've been gnawing on that issue for quite a few days. But the reason I'm all atwitter today isn't Lacey; it's Gina. Ah-ha! Yes, Gina. Why is Gina interested in being friends with Lacey again? That is the big question, and it's driving me ape shit.

I believe I've covered every variation of paranoia known to the human race. Most of my musings are too insane to even be written down. I hate to have tangible proof of my warped mind. There's one where the scenario is only slightly insane, and that's the one that worries me. I'm worried that Gina is looking ahead to the future and figuring we'll part at the end of the summer. Should that happen, why not see what old Lacey's up to? It's not a bad idea to have a backup plan. God knows I've been trying to have one and have only been thwarted by my undesirability as a Classics professor.

If Gina is trying to plan ahead, I certainly can't fault her. But I also don't have to like it. I'm going to do my best to assume the best— that Gina got an invitation from some old friends and she wanted to see them once again. Sometimes, a cigar is just a smoke. I wonder if Freud really said that.

❖

Not many women would complain about being on a beautiful beach on a beautiful day with a beautiful woman. I've decided I'm not going to be one of them. I'm going to enjoy myself today. Yep, I'm going to have fun. But before I start having fun, I think I'm going to have a couple of drinks to calm my shaking hands. It's hot today, but it's not so hot that my hands should be as wet as they are. Thank God this group looks like they know how to throw a good party. I see at least three massive, plastic trash barrels filled with beer and wine. Gina said we each have to contribute twenty-five dollars for the food and drink, so we may as well get our money's worth.

❖

My fears have, I'm happy to say, been groundless. The women Gina has introduced me to are all nice and friendly. Most of them remind me of how Gina would probably be if she didn't have such a thirst for new experiences and improving her mind. In short, they seem like a nice bunch of friends. I have, however, noticed that the women she's spoken to are the ones who look like they planned on going to a beach party. They're wearing their swimsuits or shorts and T-shirts and flip-flops. But there's another clique, and they look like they're trying to be noticed.

Gina looks like she's one of them, to be honest. It's clear she spent some time in front of the mirror before she left the house. Her hair is up in a casual-looking twist, but I watched her style it, and it took more than simply putting a band around it. And her white tank top and Madras plaid shorts fit as if they were made for her, even though I know they weren't. She looks classier than the women she's introduced me to, but she's not. They went to the same high school, the same church—It never dawned on me that Gina would have belonged to a church, but she assures me that all Italians have a home parish. I'll have to check on that later—and seem to talk in a lingua franca about which I'm clueless.

But this other group, made up of the snobby-looking ones, seems as if they're from a higher social class. Once again, I can't quite figure out where Gina fits in. But the fact that we seem to be avoiding one group gives me a clue.

I haven't had the pleasure of meeting Lacey yet. Gina assures me she's always the last to arrive. She'd better hurry up, or she's not going to get any food. People have been playing volleyball and swimming for hours, and this looks like a hungry group.

I noticed a little fluttering among the snotty girls, and even if I'd had no idea what Lacey looked like, I would have picked her out. All Gina had told me was that Lacey was beautiful, dark-haired, and had dark eyes. This woman, traveling alone, had all three of those attributes and many more.

There was no doubt in my mind that Gina was an uncommonly beautiful woman. There was also no doubt in my mind that Lacey was substantially prettier than Gina. I wonder how that feels? It must be odd for a woman to know how pretty she is and then have her partner be even better looking. Somehow, that gives Gina some extra points in my book. I like the fact that she didn't look for a woman she could always outshine. Hey! Maybe that's what she's doing now!

Okay, Hayden. Put your head on straight. She and Lacey have been broken up for four years, and if she'd wanted her back, I assume she could have gotten her. Gina said that Lacey tried to get back with her numerous times, and Gina obviously refused. Don't let your paranoia and your jealousy ruin what has been a very nice day.

There were at least fifty women spread out on the beach, and Gina didn't rush to say hello to Lacey. Instead, she squeezed my hand and said, "Are you as hungry as I am?"

"I don't know. Are you hungry enough to go into the water and try to catch fish with your bare hands?"

Gina laughed and kissed my hand. "You've never been fishing if you think you can catch them with your bare hands. Suckers are hard enough to catch with the right equipment. Come on, let's go eat before these chicks clean us out."

❖

Not all the women at the barbeque were Italian. Either that, or Italians could cook a mean slab of ribs. I was gnawing on a bone like a hungry dog when Lacey approached, catching me sucking on my fingers. Luckily, she got to see my face spackled with bright red, sticky barbecue sauce. The ribs were damned good, but I don't know if they were good enough to have Gina's friends and former lover catch me looking like a street urchin. It must have been bad because when Gina turned to introduce me, she chuckled and took her napkin and wiped my face thoroughly. Thank God that wasn't embarrassing.

Lacey was perfectly charming, and she didn't jump into Gina's arms or slather her with kisses or in any way act as though she laid claim to her. Gina seemed her usual self, and that reassured me. "Hayden, this is Lacey Cha-cho. Lacey, Hayden Chandler."

I was going to have to ask Gina how to spell Lacey's name, since I'm pretty sure no one outside of a Latin-Chinese gang was named Cha-cho.

"Nice to meet you," we said in near unison. She smiled, and I had just a moment of longing to take her in my arms and kiss her. Hey! Don't be so quick to judge. You weren't there.

Lacey didn't seem to have the same urge, or if she did, she concealed it well. She was polite and friendly, but she didn't seem very interested in me. She didn't, in any way, seem rude. She just gave me the usual quick hello that you give to people you meet at a party. If Lacey was jealous, you sure couldn't have proved that by me. Actually, her demeanor reassured me because she not only seemed uninterested in me, she didn't seem overly interested in Gina, either.

"It's been a long time, hasn't it?"

Gina nodded. "Yeah, it has. You'd think we'd run into each other more often."

"We would if you worked normal hours. Are you still working fourteen-hour days?"

"No," Gina smiled while shaking her head. "I'm down to 10 hour days now. You remember my cousin Case?" Lacy nodded briefly. "He got his pilot's license this year, and he's working the late shift."

"Shit. He was just a kid last time I saw him."

"He still is. He's only been out of high school for a year, but I trust him." Gina laughed again, her eyes crinkling up from the effort. "I trust him more than my lunkhead nephews."

Lacey's eyes grew wide. "Don't tell me those idiots have their pilots' licenses, too!"

"No, they both want to get their licenses, but I'm not sure either of them can pass the test. They're both working for me this summer, though. Chris's girlfriend is working for me, too. Nice girl, but s-l-o-w. My grandma says she looks like a hookah," Gina said, imitating her grandmother perfectly.

Lacey's head rolled back, and she laughed heartily. Hard to believe, but she was even prettier when she laughed. If there was a just God, Lacey had a hairy back or uncontrollable flatulence or body odor to rival a frightened skunk.

"Your grandma must be feeling good to be up to her old tricks. I don't think I ever heard her say a nice word about anyone."

Smiling, Gina said, "Give her time. She's only eighty."

It seemed like an unconscious action, but Lacey reached out and grasped a few stray strands of Gina's hair, tugging on them gently. "Your hair looks great. I guess I was wrong when I told you not to cut it."

"I can do more things with it at this length. When it was longer, I had to either pull it back or do something fairly dressy with it. Now I can wear it up and not look like I'm going to the prom."

"Well, it looks great. I'm really glad you guys could come," she said, looking at both of us.

"I'm glad we came, too," Gina said. "It's been too long."

"Yeah, it has." Someone must've caught Lacey's eye because she gave us a quick wave and walked away.

"That wasn't too bad, was it?"

"No, she seems nice."

"Oh, yeah, Lacey's a really great woman. I don't go out with women who aren't nice."

"She doesn't have a hairy ass or six toes does she?"

Gina laughed, but it was clear she was bemused. "That's the strangest question you've ever asked me. Where did that even come from?"

"Women that pretty should have something seriously wrong with them. It's just not fair if they don't. So, I was imagining she had a butt so furry that the dogs laughed at her."

Putting her arm around me, Gina gave me a hearty squeeze. "You're something else, Hayden Chandler. I'm not sure what you are, but whatever it is, I like it a lot."

❖

For the next couple of hours, I kept my eye on Lacey…surreptitiously, of course. I didn't want Gina to know that I was mesmerized by her ex-girlfriend. Gina had told me Lacey had a new partner, but if she had one, she wasn't in attendance today. No, to me, Lacey looked entirely single.

Gina didn't want to go swimming, but it was such a hot day that I went in several times. Just before dusk, I took another swim with a few of Gina's friends. We played around in the water for quite a while. At hearing a shrill whistle, I looked up to see Gina pointing in the direction of one of the paths to town. I took that to mean she had to go the bathroom. Gina was not the kind of girl who would squat in the bushes. She was very earthy in many ways, but I couldn't imagine her risking wrinkling, much less staining, her shorts.

We stayed in the water for a while, emerging when it was getting too dark to see anything that might be in the water. Gina's friends had rented a motel room for the weekend, and they invited me to go with them to shower. I didn't want to be gone that long, so I refused. The evening wind was picking up a little bit, and even though it was still warm, I was a little cool. So, I stretched my towel out next to a short wall built of cases of beer. The little wall stopped the wind from hitting me, and I lay in the dying sun luxuriating in the feel of its warmth.

I'm not sure if I fell asleep, but voices relatively near me caught my attention. I couldn't see who was speaking because they were sitting on the other side of my little wall, near the bonfire that someone had built. But they must have been close because I could hear them very well. They both had strong Long Island accents, but one woman sounded particularly nasal. Hers was the first voice.

"She didn't tell me to ask, but I'm gonna tell Lacey that Gina has to be single."

"Yeah, she has to be. Maybe that girl's her cousin or something. There's no way Gina's dating her."

"No way—ever! Gina could get anybody on the island. There's no way she'd choose that girl."

"Maybe things are slow this summer. Maybe she's the best Gina could find."

"You don't go from a ten to a four no matter how slow things are. Besides, Gina doesn't have to date a girl from Fire Island, and I know a dozen women on the island who'd cut off a tit to go out with her."

"There's only one thing wrong with Gina, and I'd put up with her bad moods any day. Besides, she seems happier now. She's probably over feeling shitty about her mom. That's the only thing that kept her away from Lacey."

"I guess when you look like Gina, you can demand perfection. I've gotta put up with a seven who cheats on me." She laughed ruefully.

"Mine doesn't cheat on me, but she probably would if she could lose fifty pounds. Lucky for me, she's too lazy to do that."

"I knew Lacey would never be happy with Jenny. She was a nice girl, but she was no Gina."

"There aren't a lot of Gina's around. If there were, I'd have one!"

I think it was windy enough that neither of the women could hear me cry. At least, I hope it was. I'm not entirely sure why I cried. I suppose it never feels good to be called a four on a scale of ten, but to have your lover's friends think you're a dog smarts. I wonder what number they would have given me before my haircut. I look 100 percent better than I did before, but I'm not sure if that made me a three or zero. Either way, I feel like a zero.

It was dark enough that I was sure no one could tell I'd been crying. I walked around the periphery of the group, trying to find my girlfriend, but she was nowhere to be seen. Regrettably, I also noted that Lacey was absent. The women I'd been swimming with came back, and I asked them if they'd seen Gina. One of them helpfully volunteered that Gina and Lacey were sitting on a bench down by the next lifeguard station. I thanked her, went to get a beer, and took a walk in the opposite direction.

I didn't walk very far, mostly because I wanted to be there when Gina got back. I knew my paranoia was making me think crazy things, but that didn't stop me from thinking them. I hated to admit it, but it was very easy to make me feel like the unattractive little girl that I was. I guess I should say "had been." But sometimes, I still felt like that little girl. Pale skin, pale hair, a school uniform that never fit properly, sturdy leather shoes to correct a turned-in foot. Damn, even now that sounds ugly. But it was more than looks that made me feel like an outcast. I got to go to the best schools, but not because of fitting in socially. The Haydens were well known in Philadelphia, and by the time I was in middle school, the other girls knew that I had the name, but we didn't have the money to fit in. I'm still not sure if I became a bookworm because I didn't have friends or if I didn't have friends because I was a bookworm. Either way, it was painful being left out during those formative years. I wish I could just let that be in the past, but it's pretty easy to make me feel like that again.

I found myself back at the party, so I had another beer. I found the women I'd been swimming with, and they wanted to do some shots of Jägermeister. So, partially to fit in and partially to distract myself, I played along. I don't know if I've mentioned this, but I don't have a particularly high tolerance for alcohol. I'm not sure how many shots we did, but I kept drinking beer to get the taste out of my mouth. After a while, I had to lie down or fall down. Gina's friends found my towel, and I lay down to take a little nap.

Chapter Thirteen

N ear as I can tell, I'm alive.

I'm in Gina's bed, but I have no idea how I got here. Her shiny bathroom wastebasket is next to the bed, and there's a plastic trash bag lining it. That is not a good sign. Gina's always prepared, but she wouldn't have put the basket there if I hadn't given her very good evidence that I needed it.

I turned away and felt paper crinkle under me when I did. I'm sure the sound was very soft, but my brain was very confused and registered it as equivalent to a 767 taking off over my head. It took a while, but I was finally able to pull the paper out from under my shoulder and see it was a note. Oh, great. I love to get a note after getting so drunk I'm almost an amnesiac. I'm sure it's to tell me how sophisticated I seemed while being drug by my feet to the car.

I was finally able to focus and read the note Gina left me. It was nicer than one particular note she'd left in the past, but I wasn't really able to read much into it. Maybe that's because I destroyed half of my brain cells last night. I never went through one of those periods in college where you go out to a bar and binge drink until you forget your name. Why am I starting that when I'm thirty years old?

I'm going to answer that rhetorical question. Yes, I know it's a sign of trouble when you ask yourself rhetorical questions and answer them, but I think it's clear I'm in trouble. I'm acting like a college kid because that's how I feel. I feel young and unsure and frightened. This relationship with Gina means so much to me that I feel like the ground is shifting under us. Well, maybe not us, but definitely me.

Her note just said that she hoped I felt all right today and that she'd like to come home and make coffee for me. Most people wouldn't try to read a lot into that, but I'm not most people. I keep thinking that she would've been more lighthearted or that she'd even poke fun at me if things were good between us. But I don't know how things are between us because I was so stinking drunk that I don't have many memories of the evening once she left with Lacey.

Most adults wouldn't lose their minds when their girlfriend spent a little time with an ex-lover at a party. Gina could have had Lacey before she met me. I've never seen her express any regret that Lacey is not in her life anymore. So, why can't I act like an adult? Why can't I believe that I'm the woman Gina wants? I know it's improbable, especially after seeing Lacey, but Gina's obviously lost some of her vision over the years, and she finds me attractive. Why should I try to disabuse her of that crazy notion?

I should act like a big girl and call her. But I feel so stupid—so incredibly stupid. I just don't want to face her. So, I'm going to skip the caffeine, take a couple of Tylenol, and hide in bed, hoping that as the day goes on, she'll see the humor of the situation rather than the stupidity.

❖

I got up and moped around the house for a couple of hours, watching home improvement shows on TV and thumbing through some of Gina's magazines. But I couldn't make myself do anything productive, and I couldn't get up the guts to call her. So, I stayed close to the bedroom and ran for the bed the second I heard her key hit the door. I'm not sure if I fooled her since it's still so hard for me to read her sometimes. She looked a little tentative and a little annoyed with me when she came into the bedroom.

"How are you feeling?" she asked. She didn't give me my usual hug. She sat at the foot of the bed, looking at me intently.

"About like I should. If you didn't feel like crap after acting like an idiot, what would stop us from doing it on a daily basis?"

She gave me a brief smile and nodded. "Anything I can do to help?"

I'm not sure what set me off. Maybe it was the distance I could feel between us. Maybe it was that I still felt awful from the night before.

Whatever the combination of factors, I started crying like a child. Gina hesitated for just a moment. Then she got up, came over to me, sat down next to me, and held me in her arms. I cried for a long time, feeling absolutely bereft.

"What's wrong? Tell me why you're so sad?"

"I'm not sure," I sobbed. "I just feel horrible."

"Does your tummy hurt? Do you have a headache?"

"Yes, but that's not it. I just feel like such an idiot. Like I made a fool out of myself and made you look foolish for being with me."

"Oh. Yeah, I can see you might feel that way."

That was not the right answer in a very big way. I cried harder, cried so hard my stomach muscles hurt.

"Baby, baby, come on. Tell me what's going on in your head."

"It's what I just told you. I'm ashamed of myself. And you're not acting like you usually do. You act like you're mad at me."

She sighed, taking far too long to respond to my comment. But she finally did, saying, "I'm not sure how I feel about last night. I'm certain you didn't make me look foolish for being with you. But I have to be honest. You didn't show your best side."

"If that was my best side, I'd have it removed." That brought a smile to her lips.

"But if you had your best side removed, you know what you'd be left with."

Having her tease me a little bit helped me stop crying. "Maybe my bad side is really my good side."

Gina leaned over and kissed my head. "I like all of your sides. It just takes me a while to adjust to seeing a new one."

"What did you see last night? I was absent for a lot of it."

She shifted and rested against the headboard. Then she kicked off her shoes, put her feet up on the bed, and held me a little more loosely. "I'm not entirely sure what I saw. You had kind of a...transformation while I was gone. So, I'm not sure if you were jealous or angry or feeling insecure or just crazy drunk."

"That's about it. Some of those things were sequential; some were concurrent."

"Why don't you just tell me what happened, honey? I'll fill you in on the things that happened after you...blacked out?"

"One thing I'd like to clear up is that I've never blacked out before, if that's what I did. I don't like to get drunk. It's never been my thing. And I hope last night taught me that it's no fun for me or the people around me."

"That's good to know. I was going to talk to you about that."

"You don't need to. I'm going to figure out another way to deal with my feelings. Alcohol really doesn't work well for me. So, here's the story. I was swimming with your friends, and I saw the signal that you were going to the bathroom. At least, that's what I thought I saw."

"That's pretty much true. I had to go, and someone told me that some of the women had rented a room. So, Lacey and I walked down to the motel right by the dock."

"Why didn't you go to my house?"

"Because I don't have a key, I wasn't sure who was home, and I didn't want to call you out of the water since you looked like you were having fun. It didn't seem like a big deal to me. I needed to pee, and Lacey had a bathroom."

"Okay, you're right. You shouldn't have to jump through hoops to pee in a bathroom that I approve of. So, while you were gone, I got out of the water and lay down behind those cases of beer so I could take a little nap in the sun and not have the wind hit me. A couple of women sat on the other side of the boxes and started talking about you. You and Lacey."

I could feel Gina's body stiffen. Her voice was sharp when she asked, "What about me and Lacey?"

"The gist of the conversation was that you and I couldn't possibly be dating because I was too ugly for you—" Thank God Gina's body tensed up even more. I could feel the anger pulsing through her.

"What in the holy fuck! Who were they? Describe them to me." She was sitting up rigidly, staring at me with every bit of her attention.

I stroked her arms, feeling the firm muscles. "I can't, honey. I didn't get up, so they didn't know I was there. They just talked about how pretty you were and how pretty Lacey was. They seemed to think that Lacy wanted you back and that you'd be stupid not to go back to her. The bottom line was that you were a great catch, Lacey was a great catch, and I was a dog."

"Goddamn, that pisses me off! Why would anybody be that rude?" She slid off the bed and went over to a low cabinet. I thought she was going to kick it, but she blew out a breath, shook her arms for a minute, and then perched on the edge of the piece. "I just…I don't understand saying something like that about a woman. Especially someone they don't know. I mean, I've said mean things about people, but it's always because I'm mad at somebody or they hurt me. I can't for the life of me figure out why you'd sit down and assess how pretty each person was and who they should be with based on their looks." She shook her head again. "That's just…ignorant."

I was kinda hoping she would say that only an ignorant person would think I was a dog, but it was nice to have her affirm my belief that she was too mature to cut people down for no reason at all. "Yeah, it is ignorant. But that's what they said, and it hurt me. A lot."

"Well, hell yeah, it hurt you. It was ridiculously hurtful."

"So, I looked for you, and one of your friends from that bar said you were with Lacey." I took in a breath, but Gina didn't comment in the space I left for her. "After the dog comments, I was feeling insecure and down. Your friends were doing shots…"

She slapped both hands over her face. "Oh, no. Hayden, those girls can drink for days!"

"Yeah, I think I figured that out. I didn't want to admit what a wuss I was, so I tried to keep up. I couldn't."

"Damn." She looked so angry, but I could tell she wasn't angry with me.

"Then what?"

"That's where I lose my ability to recount the evening in a linear fashion. It's all a blur until I woke up with a few hundred pounds of pressure in my head."

"You didn't miss anything good."

"What did I miss? If it wasn't good, it had to be bad."

She looked as if she wanted to change the subject, but she carried on. "You were out cold, but I didn't want to leave you there until you sobered up. So, Lacey and I kinda dragged you to the dock."

"I was talking, wasn't I?" I asked, dreading the truth.

"Yeah."

"Come on, Gina. Tell me what I said."

"It's not important. You were just rambling on about my being a ten and your being a four. Lacey and I didn't even know what you were talking about."

"There's more," I said, certain there was. She was avoiding eye contact, something she never did.

"Not much. Nothing important." She walked back to the bed. "What is important," she said, sitting by me, "is to set you straight on something." She held my face in both of her hands and stared into my bloodshot eyes. "What those women said was bullshit. You're a beautiful woman, Hayden. Sometimes, you don't seem to think so, but I sure do."

Blushing, I looked down at the bed. "You tell me that, Gina, and I believe you think so. But only a dunce would think I was prettier than Lacey. She's...wow." I shook my head. "She's mouthwateringly pretty."

She chuckled. "Yeah, she is. And she takes good care of herself. She's gonna look great for another thirty years."

"I know I don't have the best self-image, but it's really hard to compete with someone who looks like Angelina Jolie's pretty sister."

"She doesn't look anything like Angelina Jolie," she scoffed. "She's a lot better looking than her."

"My point! A good-looking woman would look plain next to Lacey."

"Damn it, Hayden, you are a good-looking woman! And there is no competition. I'm over Lacey. I'm into you. Very into you."

"It just freaked me out when you were with her for so long. I got insecure." I rested my head against her and mumbled, "Sorry."

She held me for a few minutes, stroking my back while I nuzzled against her. "Do you want to know how I feel about Lacey and about you?"

I almost gurgled a "Yes."

"This is unedited, honey. But if I let you listen to it, you'll know—really know—how I feel about things. I had no intention of letting you hear this, but I'm willing to risk it to convince you, once and for all, that I care for you."

"Uhm...what are you talking about? Listen to what?"

She got up and went to her bedside table, withdrawing a microcassette recorder from the drawer. "I record my thoughts on this. It's like a journal, but I can express myself better when I speak. I talked for a long time last night, and some of it might be...I'm not sure...pissed or confused or something. I haven't listened to it again, so some of it might hurt you."

"It's okay," I said, reaching for the device. "I want to hear how you really feel. I need to hear it, Gina."

"All right." She sat down on the bed and draped an arm around my shoulders. "Here goes." She turned on the tape player, and we both listened raptly.

I think I'm going to have to have a talk with Hayden about drinking. I understand needing a drink once in a while, but it seems like she drinks to excess when she's nervous or worried or feeling insecure. That's not a good habit to get into, and I'd hate to see her get into trouble because of it.

It's been a couple of months, but she constantly does things that surprise me. Like tonight. I was surprised and not in a good way. I just don't understand what goes through her mind when she says things like she said tonight.

I grabbed Gina's hand, switching the recorder off. "Tell me what I said," I begged.

But she wouldn't budge. "I told you, Hayden. You didn't say anything worth repeating. You didn't say anything that hurt me or made me feel any differently about you. Now drop it. It's over." She'd never spoken so forcefully to me, but for some reason, I didn't mind. I knew I'd fixate on this if I thought I could get her to talk. But when she was so unyielding, it made me let go. I settled back against her and didn't say a word as she hit the play button again.

I don't mean any disrespect to Hayden, but from a purely impartial perspective, anyone could see that Lacey is a gorgeous woman. When I used to see those lists of the world's most beautiful people in magazines, I'd laugh, thinking how stupid their choices were. Some of the people they said were beautiful were downright goofy looking. I've decided that you don't have to be really gorgeous to be on TV or in the movies. It's more of a personality thing. There are lots of beautiful people who have average, run-of-the-mill jobs. Lacey is one of them. She has a natural beauty that can actually take your breath away. And it sure as hell doesn't hurt that she has a big heart. She's a damn nice woman. I saw that again tonight. I probably was stupid to break up with her. I guess I was just immature at the time, and I hadn't learned that there are times in every relationship where your partner doesn't support you like you need to be supported.

I have no idea what my expression was, but it was enough to make Gina hit the stop button. "This is part of what I thought would hurt you, baby, but just hold on. It gets better." Before I could say a word, she turned it on again.

I'm not going to make that mistake with Hayden. I know she's insecure about some things, and I'm going to try my best to reassure her. This is just a minor issue, but I have a feeling it's going to last for a long time. But we'll get through it, just like we'll get through the other things that come up.

Now I know what expression I wore. It was a big, silly smile. Gina leaned over and kissed me, very gently. Her lips were so close to mine that I could feel their heat. "I told you it gets better," she whispered. "I don't want to be with Lacey. It's over between us and has been for years. I want you." As I kissed her, I heard her voice coming from the recorder again. Damn, I thought she was finished!

After talking to Lacey for a while tonight, I realized what it is about Hayden that I love so much. Lacey and I got along very well, and we were very comfortable together. We came from the same background, and we had the same types of families. She was awesome in bed, and we never lost the spark we had. But Lacey was complacent. She was complacent about herself, and she was complacent about me. She thought I had a wonderful job, and she didn't understand why I wasn't happy with just her, my job, and our friends. She never understood why I wanted to read instead of watch TV. She didn't understand why I spent so much time learning Italian. And she never had even a glimmer of understanding about my love of history. Lacey lived in the present, and she had no interest in the past.

But Hayden…Hayden gets me. She wants more for me; she wants more from me. She wants more from herself. She has goals, and she's very intent on reaching them. But her goals aren't about money and power. She's trying to get into a position that will let her do the things that really fill her soul. I can't express how much I respect her for that. Hayden's the first person I've ever met who thinks I can be more than I already am. She's the first person who's ever seen my potential. She's the first person who's ever made me feel like I'm smart. When I'm with her, I see the future, and it's damned bright.

I didn't care if this tape went on for another hour. I had to wrap my arms around my wonderful girlfriend and kiss her. But she's a persistent woman, and after just a few minutes of kissing, she pulled away and turned on her recorder again.

My poor little lamb is lying next to me, either asleep or unconscious. I have no idea how much she drank, but it must've been a load. She's gonna have a terrible hangover in the morning, and I'm not going to be here. I'll leave her a note to call me when she wakes up so I can come and make her some espresso.

I'm having a hard time sleeping because I've got so many things going through my head. I'm leafing through this photography book I have on Sicily, but I keep thinking of Hayden.

Lacey is like going around the corner when you're driving along the Amalfi Coast. You're hit in the face with a view so lovely that you can barely comprehend it. But after a few hours, you become used to it. It takes something unique to catch your eye again. It's very easy to get jaded when physical beauty is the main attraction. It's not like that with Hayden. Hayden reminds me of being in Sicily. You're riding your bike up a road. It's dusty, dry, almost monochromatic. It's just a road like any other road. You're lulled into complacency until you turn a corner and catch just a glimpse of the sea. It's fifteen different colors of blue, and each one of them is a jewel. That's what it's like when Hayden smiles at me. I can't imagine ever being complacent about her beauty. It's not as showy as Lacey's, but it's so much deeper. Damn, I don't remember the last time I started to cry while I was dictating, but that's what Hayden does to me. I just hope she loves me like I love her.

She finally turned it off, and the room was dead silent for a few seconds. Gina didn't look at me. She just sat there, looking down at her hands. I touched her face with my hand, feeling the trail of a few tears. I'd never had so many urges ripping through my body. I wanted to talk—to tell her how I felt about her. I wanted to hold her—to show her what her words did to me. And I wanted to make love to her—to shower her with kisses until I was too exhausted to purse my lips. But I couldn't do it all, so I went with the most urgent need. I looked into her beautiful brown eyes and said, "I love you, Gina. I love you with all of my heart."

"Kiss me," she murmured, the heat in her eyes burning my soul.

I kissed her. I kissed her and kissed her and kissed her. And after we finished making love—and naming it for what it was—we fell asleep, neither of us waking until the next morning. The alarm made both of us sit up like we'd been slapped. We stared at each other for a few seconds and then started to laugh. "It's dawn!" I said.

"How the hell did that happen?"

"Being in love must make you sleepy." I jumped out of bed, full of energy. "I know it's not approved by the Coast Guard," I said, going into the bathroom to turn on the shower, "but I'm gonna sit right next to you today. I can't bear the thought of having you leave."

She smiled so brightly that the dawn was overshadowed by her luminance. "I was just going to ask if you'd go with me. I'll go make a couple of double espressos."

"And food," I called to her back. "Any kind of food. All I had yesterday was you!"

❖

We drove to the ferry together. It might have been the first time Gina had ever had her vehicle in the lot because both of her nephews came out to stare at her, open-mouthed.

She tossed her keys to the taller one—Chris, I think—and said, "Make yourself useful. There's a cover for it behind the seat. Put it on so the saltwater doesn't hurt the paint."

"Okay," he said and then pushed his brother towards the truck.

Gina stood and watched for a moment. Then she took my hand and led me into the office. Her secretary, Marge, looked happy to see me again. At least, I convinced myself that her scowl and clicking of her tongue meant happiness. We were running a little late in Gina time, which meant we had ten minutes before we had to board the first passengers. "There were only about five people out there," Gina said thoughtfully. "I think we can get away with taking the smallest ferry."

"There might be a crowd waiting to get back," Marge said. "Lots of those people come back on Monday morning."

"I know," Gina said, her voice uninflected. She picked up the phone and dialed and then waited a second, finally saying, "Hey, Ruby. Gina. How's the crowd for the return trip?" She nodded. "Just like I thought. Hayden and I have ten minutes at 6:17. Any chance you could have two orders of blinis ready for us?" She smiled sweetly, and her eyes fluttered a couple of times. Ruby must have been teasing or flirting with her. "Yeah, it is nice. See you in a few." She turned to me and said, "Ruby says there are about ten people there. That might double, but I doubt it'll triple. So, we'll take the smallest boat."

Marge let out an unhappy grunt, but Gina acted as if she didn't hear her. She went to a pegboard and picked up a big set of keys attached to a floating fob. "Be back in an hour." She took my hand, and we walked to the boat together. The people who'd been leaning against the building or sitting on the bench came to attention when they saw Gina. Just like I always did.

❖

I hadn't been on this boat. It was small, but it could still seat about twenty-five people on the main deck. There were benches on the top deck, too, but it was windy and foggy, so only the most hung over would sit up there. This one was named "La ragazza dell'isola," and Gina saw me gazing at the name.

"The Island Girl," she said. "She's my little girl."

"She does look like a girl. Especially compared to the big boys."

"Oh, they're all girls. I wanted to name this one "La bambina dell'isola," but I thought people might feel funny getting onto a boat called the baby."

"So, ragazza means girl, huh?"

"Yep."

"Am I your ragazza amica?"

"No. Italian doesn't have a great word for girlfriend. You'd usually just use ragazza."

"Huh. So, I'm your girl. Not bad. I kinda like it."

She put her arm around me and hugged me to her side, ignoring the stunned looks she was getting from Dominick and Christopher. "You're definitely my girl."

❖

There wasn't much room for me on the Island Girl, but I was never going to complain about being too close to Gina. She had on a pair of very short khakis, and I kept snaking my hand up the leg, snapping the elastic on her panties. She giggled and slapped my hand away when we were at the dock, but as soon as we started to move, she acted as if she didn't know I was touching her. I decided to behave, since I knew Gina took safety very, very seriously.

We were steaming across the bay when she said, "Want to know what I learned from talking to Lacey for so long?"

"Uhm…sure." My heart started beating faster, even though I reminded myself that Gina had, in essence, pledged her heart to me.

"She was, as I suspected, trying to see if I was single."

"Uh-oh," I said. "I don't want to have to ruin such a pretty face, but if I have to…" I punched my open fist, trying to look menacing.

She smiled, but she didn't take her eyes from the water. "Yeah, I can see you clocking her. You're just the type."

"I assume you told her you were otherwise engaged."

"No, I told her I was in love." She grinned, and I could see the little wrinkles at the corners of her eyes peek out from her sunglasses.

"Gina! You told Lacey before you told me!"

"I've been ready to tell you for a month. Not my fault you didn't act like you wanted to commit."

I grunted my displeasure. I hated it when she was right about something so important. "Still…"

"I wish I'd told you first. I should have had more guts. But I was worried that you were still keeping your options open."

"Yeah, you're lucky you got me when you did. Girls like you are a dime a dozen."

"It's not that, and you know it. I've just been worried that you were trying to get out of New York."

I didn't want to get into that mess, so I answered flippantly. "You're stuck with me, baby. So, what did Lacey say to your announcement?"

"She wasn't surprised. She said she assumed you were important to me since I brought you to the party."

"But she wasn't happy."

"Well, no. She said she'd thought about what had gone wrong between us, and she was willing to do anything it took to make it work. I felt bad for her."

"Ooh…that is hard. Well, it's never happened to me, but I can assume it's hard. I'll have to ask Dana."

She gave me a wry grin, but didn't comment further.

"Is that all you learned from Lacey?"

"Nope. That's the least of it. What I really learned made me so damned sad I cried my eyes out."

"Oh, honey, what happened?" I started unconsciously stroking her leg.

"It was weird 'cause I couldn't tell Lacey why I was so upset. But while we were talking, I realized that Lacey hadn't really abandoned me after my mom died. I abandoned her."

"What? How could you have had that wrong?"

"Easy. We did drift apart, and it seemed to me that she was the one pulling away. But when I really look at it, I was the one. I went to Italy for three months after my mom died. I took language classes two nights a week. I didn't want to go out much. I gave her less and less and then got mad when it felt like she was pulling away. I really made things hard for her, Hayden."

"Damn, that does sound difficult. Why do you think you pulled away?"

"Because I wasn't being fulfilled. After my mom died, and again after 9/11, I realized how little time we have. I wanted to do more, learn more, experience more…but Lacey was very happy with things as they were. When I saw she didn't want to follow me, I took off on my own." She snuck a glance at me. "I don't ever want to fall into that trap with you. If we start having different goals or desires, we've got to talk about them. It just isn't fair to pull away, especially when your lover has no idea why you're creating distance."

"But would things have been different between you and Lacey if you'd talked about it?"

"Probably not. She might have tried to do the things I liked, but it's just not who she is. But it would have been nice if I'd owned up to my own need to move on. It's really unfair of me to have been blaming her all of this time. She didn't do anything wrong."

"Did you tell her that?"

"Yeah." Her chin started to quiver, and I wished I could get up from my little seat and hold her. But I knew she wouldn't like that. So, I just leaned against her leg and patted her as we bounced across the Great South Bay.

Chapter Fourteen

I don't know where the summer's gone. Besides being dedicated to Gina, of course. Anyway, it's half over, and I wish I could figure out a way to stop the clock and spend every day just like this.

As soon as Gina got home from work, I wrestled her clothes off, and we played in the pool for over an hour. I've never felt as young as I do when we're playing together. She's managed to bring out the child I'd abandoned twenty years ago—all too soon, I'm now learning. She's shown me that you can be a sophisticated adult and a goofy child at the same time. Or at least sequentially.

Now we're squished together on the deck, lying on the cushions from the chairs. We're going to have sex. There's no question. The issue is who's going to make the first move. Gina's tired; I see how slowly her eyes are blinking. But she's turned on, too. Every time I touch a part of her body, she moves and shifts in the sexiest way you can imagine. She's such a sexy thing!

I scrape my fingernails along the broad expanse of her shoulders, smiling when I see the goose bumps form. "Where'd you get these great shoulders, Scognamiglio?"

"Genes," she said, lazily. "And work."

"I wish I had some muscles. I guess I'll have to pick different parents and get a different job next time around."

She turned her head and assessed me for a minute. Touching my flabby upper arms, she said, "You do *have* muscles, honey. You just haven't done the work to make 'em show. But you look wonderful just like you are. Don't give it another thought."

As always, I had to give it another thought. "What do you mean? You said it's genes and your job."

"Yeah, it is. But you can define your muscles through exercise. They have gyms in the city, don't they?"

"Yes, smart butt, they do. But I hate gyms. I've never heard of anything sillier than spending your time acting as if you're doing something that uses a muscle."

"I've never been to one. But I'm sure I wouldn't like it. Luckily, you can build up your muscles doing something fun if you want to."

I pushed her onto her back and sat astride her hips, one of my favorite positions. "Like what?"

"Oh, like bike riding and kayaking. Stuff like that."

"Don't have either," I said, sticking my tongue out.

"Well, aren't you the lucky girl? I've got both, and you're welcome to either."

"But you ride your bike to work."

"Got another," she said. "You may use it at will. And you'd have a set of biceps that would make the other teachers jealous if you used my kayak every day."

"Where is this mysterious boat? I've never seen it."

"Out at the dock. There's a bunch of them at the end of the pier. Mine's the—"

"Yellow one," I said, wrinkling my nose.

She touched the tip of my nose. "Correct. Do you know how to paddle?"

"Kinda. I've done it on the Schuylkill."

"Is that an ocean?"

"No, bunny. It's a river."

"Then you need instruction. Interested?"

"Sure. There's just one little thing I've gotta take care of."

"What's that?"

"I've gotta get these legs separated," I said, doing just that. "Then I've gotta give your adorable little clit a long, slow workout." I slipped between her legs and started to nuzzle her, biting and sucking on her ridiculously soft inner thighs.

Gina slid her hands into my hair and started guiding me, making the cutest sounds a woman's ever heard. Yep. There's no question in my mind. If you haven't heard my Gina purring and growling, you haven't lived.

By the time Gina and I had finished thoroughly cleaning each other with our tongues and had a bite to eat, it was nearly dusk. The rush of nightfall didn't deter Gina, however, and she led me down to the dock for our first kayak lesson. She was, as I thought she'd be, a very good, patient teacher. Even though I'd paddled a kayak before, I had only been in touring kayaks. I quickly learned that an ocean kayak was a very different animal. For one thing, I had to sit on top of the kayak rather than sitting inside. But with Gina sitting on the dock, instructing me on paddling technique and giving me dozens upon dozens of different directions and suggestions, I was doing pretty well.

By the time it was too dark to work, I felt confident enough to go out on the kayak on my own. But Gina would have none of that. "It's too dangerous to even consider going out alone at this point. We'll need to go out a few times with me in the boat so I can keep an eye on you."

I laughed at her concern. "It's very sweet how you look after me, honey, but I can take care of myself."

I knew I was wasting my breath as she shook her head slowly from side to side. "The ocean isn't like a lake or a river. You can get in trouble very quickly. We don't have much of a protected area here, and some people come by way too quickly in their powerboats. You have to be good at turning your kayak back over after it flips—and it will flip—and you have to be able to get back on it. It's not as easy as it looks."

With most people, I would've put up a fight. I truly hate to be told what to do. I particularly hate it when I'm pretty confident that I already know what to do. But I wasn't like that with Gina. For one thing, she didn't have to be right all the time. She only asserted herself when she was sure she was right. And as I said, that wasn't all of the time. As a matter of fact, she gave me my head most of the time. That was a very nice trait to have in a lover. So, when Gina did assert herself, I took her seriously.

Over the next two weeks, we spent hours working on my kayaking skills. And I'm not ashamed to say that Gina was 100 percent correct. If she hadn't so patiently worked with me, I probably would've been at the bottom of the Great South Bay by now. My arms hurt like hell, but I felt like I knew what I was doing. She had a very nice pulley system that let me lower the kayak into the water effortlessly. All I had to do was pick up her paddle and walk down to the dock. I spent anywhere from an hour to two hours kayaking around the area every day. Some days, I went before I started working. Other days, I went at the end of the day, and sometimes, I took two breaks—midmorning and midafternoon.

I surprised myself at how much work I got done, especially since I walked down to Gina's office nearly every day to have lunch with her. She'd gotten into the habit of making generous portions of dinner, and I took our leftovers down to the ferry just to have a few extra minutes with her.

When I worked at my apartment in the city or at one of the libraries at NYU, I found my mind wandering frequently. But even though I gave myself two or three generous breaks every day, I got more done at Gina's than I ever did at home. Maybe it was because I scheduled my breaks and had so few interruptions in her quiet home, or maybe, just maybe, it was because I was so damned happy.

✦

I've decided that I hate August. I know that sounds harsh, especially since August has never done anything to me, but the first of August signals the start of the last month Gina and I have together before I have to start teaching again.

We haven't even given much thought or discussion to what we're going to do when school starts. I think both of us are consciously ignoring it, acting as if we've got all the time in the world to figure out what we're going to do. But my powers of denial are failing me. We have to make some decisions, and not one of the options I can think of is ideal for both of us. One of the few downsides of being in love with the fabulous Ms. Scognamiglio.

August has brought a nice surprise. Dana is finally going to come visit, and she's gonna bring the family. I can hardly wait to see Maya. It's going to be so much fun watching that little doll go into that ice-cold ocean for the first time. I hope she's tougher than her mother because Dana is a big baby.

Gina and I discussed how to handle the Little family's visit. In most ways, it would be nice to have them at Gina's home, but since they're coming for the beach experience, it only makes sense to do it at my house. Lorna's not going to be at the house this weekend, so that's when Dana's going to come. Gina and I will stay in Lorna's room, and Dana will take my room. I've never seen Gina around a little child, but I bet she's good with the baby. I just hope Dana behaves this time. I've made it clear to her how I feel about Gina, and even though she didn't seem very happy with my news, she took it pretty well. For her part, Gina seems perfectly fine about the whole thing. For the first time since I've known her, she's taking Sunday off. It's so nice to see how willing she is to make things good for me. That's one of the many things I love about her.

❖

We got a good bit of luck. This weekend is supposed to not only be sunny, but also warm. Now that the Atlantic has had a few months to heat up, the baby might not actually turn blue if she wants to go in. Gina knows more than I do about being a good hostess because she took me to the store and we bought snacks for the adults and lots of treats for the baby. She says you have to have things for your guests to eat the minute they get to your house, and who am I to argue? Gina asked so many questions about Dana's and Renée's favorite foods that you'd think we were having them move in with us. But for first time, I'm really ready for guests to arrive. Elaine's going to be here this weekend, and Sheila's coming tomorrow. I bought enough to make dinner for all of us, including Elaine, so we're ready to rock.

As I suspected, Gina was fantastic with the baby. I'm supposed to be the fairy godmother, but Maya watched Gina walk around the house as though mesmerized by her. I don't know why that should surprise me since I'm mesmerized by her, but Gina's mine, so Maya better keep her hands off.

Dana was on good behavior, as was Renée, but that didn't surprise me since Renée is very well mannered. Elaine showed up fairly late, but she was pleasant and kept a good conversation going. It's very nice that I no longer feel that she's the spawn of the devil. I'm not even dreading seeing her around school this year.

Have I mentioned today how thoughtful Gina is? Just in case I haven't beaten this to death, here's another example. When we went to bed, she made some very subtle overtures toward having sex. If I didn't know her so well, I would have just thought she was kissing me goodnight. But I do know her, and I knew she was ready and willing if I wanted to go further. If we'd been at home, she would've been more forceful. I never doubt her intentions when we're alone. But because we were in the house with other people, she was much more subtle. I could tell she was a little worked up, so I whispered to her that we had to be quiet. She got a definite gleam in her eye at that, and we had a very nice time together making quiet love. I don't know if I want that to be part of our regular routine, but it was fun. It sure is fun being in love with someone who's not only a great partner, but also very considerate about your friends. That's a tough combo to find. Thank God I've found it.

We had a great time at the beach today, even though I missed Gina. But I couldn't expect her to take two days off. Not that it would be hard for her to take the time off, but that would mean having Case work double shifts two days in a row, and that's too much to ask of a kid his age. Dana and Maya took a long nap, and when they woke up, Gina was there making Maya very happy. We're going to go up to Montauk to have lobster rolls. I wonder if I'll be able to sit on Gina's lap and drive.

❖

Either I've gotten more comfortable with public displays of affection or I ignore my discomfort when Gina wants to be close. I think it's the latter. We got into the boat tonight, and Gina sat, as I expected her to, in the pilot's seat. I stayed on the dock until everybody else was in the boat, and when I jumped on, Gina smiled at me and patted her lap. Without pausing to think of how it would look or how it would make Dana feel, I kissed her cheek and snuggled in between Gina's legs.

It took a few seconds for Dana to comment. "Is it a good idea to be having Driver's Ed?"

Gina replied, calmly saying, "Oh, Hayden's very good. She's been driving all summer."

"Then why do you need to be there?"

"I don't need to be," Gina said. "I want to be. This is just a good excuse to have her sit on my lap."

"Like you need an excuse," I said, laughing.

"It hasn't been that long for us either, honey," Renée said. "You remember what it was like when we were falling in love." After a pause of a few seconds, Renée added, "That wasn't presumptuous of me, was it?"

"Not a bit." I rubbed my shoulders against Gina's breasts, settling in for a nice long ride with my best girl.

❖

It was still fairly early when we got home from our trip to Montauk. After Dana got Maya settled for the night, Gina suggested we go for a walk on the beach. Elaine didn't want to go, so she volunteered to listen for any disturbance from Maya's room. Both of the new parents seemed a little reticent to leave, but Elaine said she'd call if Maya woke.

So, the four of us went for a long walk on the beach. Gina was very voluble tonight, and she chattered like a little magpie. Renée seemed genuinely interested in the ferry business, and she asked many insightful questions. Before long, Renée was walking next to Gina, having an in-depth discussion about transportation and the benefit of ferries to cities like New York. Dana and I lagged behind, and she surprised me by putting her arm around my shoulders. "You've really fallen for her haven't you?"

"I didn't fall; I jumped. And you'd better keep an eye on Renée," I teased. "Gina's like a stealth virus. She gets in your blood before you're even aware she's there."

Dana laughed, but it wasn't one of her normal laughs. There was an edge of anger to it that I didn't like. "I don't think I have to worry about losing Renée to someone like Gina."

I moved away from Dana, letting her arm drop. I tried very hard to keep the anger from my voice, but I'm not sure I was successful. "Why don't you try to think back to how I treated Renée when you were first together? And don't forget the small detail that you broke up with me so you could take the best of all possible jobs. Also, don't forget that your job was more important than our relationship. Now, put all of those facts together and think about how gracious I was to Renée. Then do one of the things you're not best at, Dr. Little, and do a little introspection. You might see that a true friend would be not only happy for me, but would go out of her way to make Gina feel welcome. Renée is doing a great job; why not parrot her?" I started to storm away, but Dana caught me, grabbing the leg of my shorts.

"I just meant that Renée wouldn't give up our relationship for anybody. We promised each other that even if things got hard between us, we'd stay together to raise the baby. That's all!"

I scanned her features in the moonlight, wondering if I used to buy this line of bullshit when we were together. I probably did. "If that's what you meant, you would have said, 'I don't have to worry about losing Renée.' There wouldn't have been any reason to add the 'to somebody like Gina.' It won't fly, Dana."

Luckily, Dana still hated to get into trouble. She started backpedaling so fast she could've wound up back in Boston. "I meant like Gina or anybody. Really."

She looked at me with her big brown eyes, doing a good rendition of a sad puppy. But the puppy look didn't work for me anymore. I did, however, have some empathy for her. It's hard to see an ex-lover move on, even if you moved on first. "Let's drop it. We're having a nice weekend, and I don't want to spoil it by fighting."

In some ways, being with Dana had been like being with a guy. She hated to talk about our relationship, she hated to talk about her feelings, and after we had a fight, no matter how bad it was, she never mentioned it again. It hurt like hell when she broke up with me, but I think it was good for both of us. She seems happy with Renée, and they're very good parents to Maya. And if I were any happier with Gina, I might actually explode.

On our homeward walk, I took hold of Gina's hand and didn't let go. She kept giving me the most adorable looks, and I knew that if we didn't have guests she'd be propositioning me. But she was very well-mannered, and she kept her propositioning subtle enough for only me to be able to see it. I'd gotten to know her very well over the past few months, and one thing I knew was that she was always ready to go the week before she got her period. Our cycles have synced up, and we're both due next week. I think I was more receptive during this week, too, but since I wanted her nearly every minute, it was a little hard to tell.

❦

Gina went to take a shower while the rest of us slowly got ready for bed. Everyone was tucked away when Gina came into Lorna's room. I'd been lying there, thinking about how I was going to seduce her. I hated the fact that we had company, since that made us be respectful of everyone's comfort, but I'd learned last night that there was something kind of hot about making love when you had the possibility of being discovered.

I was still thinking about how I would signal my receptivity when Gina came into the room. Her damp hair was combed straight back, but a big hank of it had fallen forward, giving her a dashing look. She had almost no clothes stored at my house, so she was just wearing a bath towel. Few people looked good in a towel; luckily for me, Gina was one of them.

"Leave that on," I said, surprising her a little. She stood with her hand holding the towel where it overlapped between her breasts. "You look hot."

She grinned at me—her sexy "I'm gonna have you" grin. "Wouldn't I look hotter without this towel?"

I rolled onto my side and tilted my head so I could get a good look at her. "No, at the moment, you look very hot in that towel. I've been lying here thinking about how I wanted to have you tonight."

"So, you're having me tonight, huh?" She looked pretty darned happy at this development. Her eyes grew a little brighter and scanned across my body, giving me a thorough going-over. She did this often, and it made me feel very sexy. It made me feel like just looking at my body aroused her, and that aroused me. "Would you like to know what looks hot to me?"

"Hell, yes!"

Gina laughed, and it made me feel good that I could make her laugh so easily. "Okay." She moved across the room so she was at a right angle to the bed. Then she grabbed Lorna's desk chair and straddled it, bracing her arms across the back. "Take off your tank top," she said, losing the smile as a flame started to dance in her eyes. I did as she asked, lying there naked, staring at her, waiting for instructions. Yes, I did notice that my plan for seducing her hadn't gotten very far. But she was so much better at this than I was. Her voice grew softer. "Stay on your side and stretch your right arm out. Now bend your elbow and put your head on your hand. Nice." Her sexy smile was back, and I'm sure I had one, too. "Now move your left leg up. Yeah, that's it. Move your knee a little higher. Ah…that's perfect."

She rolled across the floor on the chair, looking at me from every angle. When her chair was behind me, she said softly, "You know why you look so hot?" I shook my head. "You have such nice womanly lines to your body. In this position, your breasts look so full. And I can see that beautiful curve to your hip. And when your leg's like that, I can see just the slightest hint of your sex. Just where your skin starts to turn a little darker. And I know what's right there, waiting for me, hungry for me."

Gina might be better at propositioning me, but I was a champ at accepting her proposition. I rolled over and grabbed her, pulling her and the chair so close to the bed that she almost toppled over. I held her head in my hands and started kissing her ferociously. She pulled away, cautioning, "We need to be quiet, baby."

"We need to have *sex*, baby." Have I mentioned that it was pretty easy to get me to make a detour from my goal? At this point, I didn't care if we knocked the walls down. But Gina, even though she was younger, was more of an adult than I. But she also had a playful side. She stood up, dropped her towel, and picked up Lorna's bedspread and a quilt. She wrapped the bedspread around herself and tossed me the quilt. "Follow me."

I dutifully followed her, hoping she was in control of her faculties. She opened the sliding door and then closed it after me. I thought she'd lie down on one of the chaises, but she pulled the bedspread up, so she didn't trip on it, and then tiptoed down the stairs. "Gina," I said, now that we were outside and away from the house. "What are you doing?"

She turned and smiled at me. "It's warm, the stars are shining, and when we're out here, you can scream at the top of your lungs, and the ocean will still overpower you. This is a great place to make love."

"Any place is great if you're there," I said, grinning at her like the love-struck fool that I was.

❖

A few minutes later, we were in a secluded spot by the sea grass. I figured Gina chose this spot because everyone who walked on the beach at night stayed close to the water. We were a hundred yards from the water, and the sea grass and sand dunes buffered us from any homes.

She put the bedspread down, and I sat down, holding my arms out to her. Smiling down at me, she bundled the quilt up to block any sand from blowing on us. "We're gonna have to take these to my house and wash them before Lorna comes out again."

"Stop thinking and start kissing," I said, shaking my extended arms at her. She obliged, wrapping me in her arms and starting to kiss me. It didn't take long before I was lying on my back, gazing dreamily up at the stars, while Gina used that talented tongue to drive me wild. We could moan and groan to our hearts' delight, and I'll gladly admit that Gina had the right idea to move outside. We would have woken Elaine, Dana, Renée, Maya, and any sand fleas that had snuck into the house. It took me a few minutes to recover, and I had to admit that post-conjugal bliss was aptly named. My whole body buzzed with feeling, particularly my love for Gina. Damn, she was a wonderful woman. And being with her made me feel like I was pretty wonderful, too. Funny how that works, isn't it?

✦

This weekend went so damned fast. It seems as if they just got here, but they're gonna have to leave this afternoon. It's been really nice seeing Dana and Renée, but for a number of reasons, I'm glad things didn't work out with Harvard. I think we'll all remain better friends seeing each other occasionally. As I said, Renée is a very well-mannered woman. I just don't think she'd like me to be in Boston full-time. Dana has a way of addressing me rather than Renée about anything to do with history. And since history is her job and her passion, the topic comes up a lot. Renée is a very bright woman, but English is her field. I can't say that I blame Renée for feeling left out, since it seems rather rude of Dana to do so. I made sure not to make that same kind of mistake with Gina this weekend. If it wasn't a topic that all of us could discuss together, I didn't bring it up. Well, that's not true. There are many things that Maya just doesn't get, and only talking about her toys gets a little old.

I'm going to make lunch for everybody, and Gina is going to walk Dana down to the store to pick up some extra diapers for the baby. I'd told Dana not to forget anything, and I'm pretty sure she will have learned her lesson after she sees how much a package of diapers costs on Fire Island.

✦

Gina and Dana had been back at the house for only a few minutes when Gina said, "Something came up at the dock. I've got to get over there and see what's going on." I stared at her as she walked over to Renée and gave her a hug, then shook Dana's hand, and then got down on her knees and hugged and kissed Maya. She stood up, dusted off her knees, and said, "It was nice to spend time with you guys. Next time, you can stay at my house and use the pool. It's a lot warmer than the ocean." Then she headed for the door, waved goodbye, and said, "Talk to you later. I've gotta run." Before I could even ask a question, she was gone.

Dana looked a little edgy, so I asked, "Did anything happen on your walk?"

"Like what?" she asked, looking and sounding guilty. "We just walked down to the store. She didn't come in with me, though, so maybe she got a phone call when I was inside."

I didn't believe her, but I didn't feel comfortable browbeating her like I would have if Renée hadn't been there. I helped them get ready to leave, and then all of us walked down to the ferry. We had to wait in a pretty long line, and I didn't know the deck attendants. I didn't have a ticket, and I didn't want to explain to the young men that I was their boss' girlfriend, so I didn't have the opportunity to go up and ask Case if he knew what was going on. I said goodbye to our guests and went back to my house. I tried Gina's cell phone a few times, but it went to voicemail immediately. So, I ignored the slight unease I sensed and went to work. I knew that Gina would call when she had things fixed, and knowing that let me concentrate.

The afternoon got away from me, and by the time I came out of my research haze, it was dinnertime. My cell phone didn't work well at my house, so I went down to the dock. It was a half hour until the next ferry, so I sat down on a bench behind Berries, a popular place to sit on the second-floor deck and watch the ferry come and go. This time, I didn't care that the guys working the deck didn't know me. I told them that I knew Case and just had to speak to him for a moment. They acted as if that was something they heard all the time, and they let me on. I went up to the top deck and found Case writing in a notebook.

"Hey, Case." He looked up, surprised.

"Hi." He snuck a quick look behind me. "Where's Gina?"

Now I was surprised. "I thought *you'd* know. She left a few hours ago. Said there was some emergency at work."

His dark brow shot up. "Really? I was just there twenty minutes ago and nothing seemed wrong."

I sat on the edge of a seat, flummoxed. "Could you call the office? She's not answering her cell."

He took his two-way radio and called, saying, "Office, pick up."

"Hi, Case. What's up?"

"Is Gina around?"

"No. She took today off. Hey, you're taking her shift!"

He rolled his eyes. "Yeah, I know Sheri. I just wanted to talk to her if she was there. See you in a few minutes."

"Bye, Case."

He put the radio down and looked up at me. "I'll look around when I get back to the dock. Want me to call you?"

It just took me a second to make a decision. "Mind if I ride with you? I'm worried that something's happened to her."

He nodded. "She always returns calls fast. Something must be up."

Feeling worse, I sat down and let my imagination run wild, seeing my sweet girlfriend in all sorts of peril. I knew the Coast Guard would have been notified if she'd had trouble with Taxi! Taxi!, but I was afraid to ask Case if he could contact them. If I couldn't find her, I had a list of things to do, and I didn't want to start on the list until I absolutely had to. When we docked, I walked past the office, but it was locked up tight. Gina didn't trust any of the weekend staff with the key, so she obviously hadn't been to the dock.

Her bike wasn't in its usual parking spot, and her car wasn't in the small spot by the office she reserved for herself. So, I got to make the long walk to her house. I wouldn't have minded if I wasn't so worried. But my heart was racing the whole time, and by the time I arrived, I was dripping flop sweat.

I went to the door and rang the doorbell and then rang it again. No answer. I knew I couldn't see the pool area from the street, but I went to the back of the house and called her name a dozen times. The garage was locked, and I stupidly hadn't brought the keys to her house with me. I called her cell again, and once again, it went to voicemail. I knew it wouldn't be fruitful, but I called her house, listening to the phone ring through the door. On the sixth ring, I heard her voice, but it wasn't her usual message. My stomach knotted at the first word and continued to somersault as she spoke.

I'm unavailable until Monday morning. If there's an emergency, please call Vince Scoggins at 631-555-1904.

Her voice was flat and hard, the way it sounded each time she'd been angry with me. And it had to be me she was angry with. Nothing else made sense. Nothing was wrong at work. She was using her father in case something came up, so it wasn't him. And she wouldn't return my phone calls. But what in the fuck did I do?

Just to make sure she was at home, I walked down to her dock and saw that Taxi! Taxi! was right where it belonged. But she'd gotten out in haste since she hadn't put the cover on her. Her kayak was where it belonged, so she was almost certainly at her house, unless she was out riding her bike. I trudged back to her house and sat down on the front step, leaning my head against her door. It took me a few minutes to figure out how to tailor my appeal, especially since I didn't know what my crime was. But I'd clearly been convicted. "Gina," I finally said, feeling stupid but not caring. "I don't know what happened today, but I assume Dana said something or did something to make you angry. I've been wracking my brain trying to figure out what could have happened, but I can't come up with a thing. She said nothing happened, but she was acting a little funny, so I can only assume that was the cause of whatever it is that's upset you."

I sighed, feeling so fucking helpless. I knew she was in there, but this fucking door might as well have been made of steel. Of course, Gina had a steel barrier that was damned hard to get through, too. Damn! I felt sick to my stomach. Just last night, we laid on the beach together, sharing our love. And there's no doubt in my mind that she loves me. So, why does she have to punish me like this? I felt like a dog who wets the carpet, gets whacked on the nose with a rolled up newspaper, and then thrown outside. I know I'm in trouble, but I can't for the life of me figure out why.

Disconsolate, I walked down to the dock and sat in her boat. I normally felt so energized when we were in it. We always had a great time, and being on her lap made me feel loved and cared for in a deeply intimate way. But today…today it was just a nice chair in a cute boat. There was no Gina magic to be found.

It was hot, and the sun was beating down on me. I hadn't put extra sunblock on, and I knew the moisture lotion I put on every morning wouldn't keep me safe for more than a half hour. Damn, I wish my parents had been swarthy. It sucks to be as fair-skinned as I am. If we have kids, Gina's got to have them. Kids. Listen to me. I can't get her to answer the damned door!

Partly to save my skin and partly because I got tired when I was depressed, I went down to the little cubby where Gina kept some safety gear. It was a small space, but it was, technically, a berth. There was a pop-up window or whatever it's properly called, but I didn't bother opening it. I must have a sadistic side, because whenever I'm depressed, I seem to go out of my way to make myself uncomfortable. And believe me, being in a little space at the front of a small boat on a hot day, with sun beating through the skylight, makes for an uncomfortable nap space. But it also let me fall asleep in seconds, probably from heatstroke.

✦

I don't know how I didn't hear her walking on the pier, but I slept right through Gina jumping onto the boat, starting her up, and pulling away from the dock. It wasn't until she gave it some gas—or diesel—that she got my attention. I woke up hot and sweaty and sick to my stomach, the latter from being in a little space that's bobbing up and down at tremendous speed. Gina must have been seething because she never drove the boat like this when I was with her. What am I saying? I *am* with her. She just doesn't know it. At the risk of barfing my guts out, I'm gonna stay here until we get to where we're going. Maybe, just maybe, she's going to my house, and I can revel in the experience of having an adult argument with her. Yeah, I agree. I'd better not hold my breath.

✦

I'd thought she was going fast at first, but she was being prudent when she was near shore. I don't know how fast the boat went, but that's how fast we were going. I hit my head on the ceiling a couple of times, and I was lying down! I finally braced myself against the sides of the boat using all of my limbs, just trying to avoid a concussion. I don't know how far we went, but it took a good, or I should say bad, half hour. The boat slowed dramatically, and then she cut the engine. I stayed where I was for a few seconds and then started to go up onto the deck. I stopped when I heard her start to curse—at me!

She opened and slammed something, and then I heard her say, "You think you can treat me like a goddamned mushroom! Keep me in the dark and cover me with shit! Well, you can't, Hayden Fucking Chandler! I'm a goddamned adult, and I won't fucking tolerate it!"

Gina was shouting at full voice. I mean really shouting. I'd never heard her be so loud or so angry. She honestly sounded like she wanted to hit me. I started to shake, feeling, for the first time, that she could be so out of control that she might be violent. I was frightened—something I never thought I'd be of my sweet, sweet girl. But she was another person when she was angry. A person I desperately wanted to get away from. But I was stuck. There was no way out, and I was so scared that I started to cry. I was shaking so hard and felt so frightened that I was afraid I'd wet my pants.

She continued ranting, going on and on about how I didn't respect her and how she'd make me treat her right or... "Who's there?" she demanded, jumping down into the cubby. "What in the fuck?"

I cried harder once I saw the look in her eyes. She looked absolutely wild—like she'd take a bite out of me and spit my flesh in my face. Defensively, I curled up into a ball, trying to make myself as small as possible in case she started hitting me. I was gasping for breath, waiting for the blows, when I heard what sounded like the wail of a wounded animal. I brought my head up just enough to see her drop to the floor and cover her face with her hands.

Tentatively, I started to sit up. Gina was crying now, crying twice as hard as I had been. I didn't know what to do. I was still so frightened of her, but she looked like her heart was breaking. My body warned me to stay away from her, but my heart wouldn't listen. I scooted off the berth and knelt next to her, wrapping her in my arms. She wrenched away, contorting herself into a position that looked impossibly uncomfortable. "Leave me alone!" she cried. "Just fucking leave me alone! Can't I have any peace? Isn't there anywhere I can be alone for two fucking seconds? What in the fuck do you want from me?"

Spit was flying from her mouth, and her nose was running, fluid draining her face. I was powerless. Powerless to think or to act. I just knelt there, not having a clue as to what I should do.

"Leave!" she cried, scaring me all over again. "Get out!"

"I can't!" I cried back, my tears returning full-force. "I'll drown!"

Now she started to moan, the keening sound freaking me out. "Why couldn't you leave me alone? Just leave me alone." She sobbed and sobbed, sounding as if she were breathing her last.

I would have given anything to get off that boat. In fact, I considered grabbing a life vest and bailing out. But I didn't have a death wish, and bobbing around in the Great South Bay on a Sunday afternoon wasn't anywhere near smart.

Gina made things a little easier when she climbed onto the berth and cried while murmuring to herself. It was breaking my heart to watch her, so I went outside, breathing fresh air for the first time in what seemed like hours.

The sun was starting to set, and there were boats and jet skis all around. I didn't know if we were safe or if there was anything I should do to let other boats see us. But after a moment of worrying about it, I decided I wouldn't complain if we were blindsided. This hurt so much— so much more than I could have imagined—that being obliterated didn't sound bad at all.

I sat in the pilot's seat and rested my head back against the soft, white vinyl. I tried to stop crying, but I wasn't having any luck. Gina's miserable cries were killing me, and for the first time in my life, that didn't seem like a metaphor.

I have no idea how long we held our positions, but it was near dark when she emerged and turned on some lights at the front and back of the boat. She looked as bad as I'd ever seen her—swollen eyes, red nose, blotchy skin. She flopped down on the bench at the back of the boat and asked, sounding exhausted, "Why couldn't you leave me alone?"

I turned in my chair and tried to figure out how honest I could be. All of the fight was gone out of her, but I didn't want to stir her up again. I didn't make eye contact, afraid of what I'd see in her eyes. "I thought you were hurt or something. I was worried about you."

"That's a lie," she snapped, and I could see a few embers of her anger come to life.

"No, it's not. I was worried sick about you, Gina. Ask Case. I walked to your house just to see if the boat was there."

"Then what? You knew I was safe when you saw it. Why not leave?"

"Because I love you," I said, not realizing I was crying again until I felt the breeze cool the hot tears on my cheeks. "I knew you were mad, but I didn't know why. I...didn't know what else to do."

"What you do," she said, enunciating each work with more volume, "is leave me alone! Goddamn it, Hayden. You can't have it both ways!"

"What ways?" I was shaking again, and this seemed to make her angrier.

"You don't want me to get angry and yell at you! You're the one who said my temper scared you! So, leave me the fucking hell alone!" She bent over and held her face again, sobbing.

I felt like I was approaching a wounded grizzly, and I knew it wasn't wise, but I didn't know what else to do. I had to comfort her, to take her in my arms and make it better. I sat next to her gingerly, waiting for a sign that I could touch her without her smacking me. "I didn't know why you were angry, honey. I didn't even know *that* you were angry. I was worried about you, Gina. I love you." I gently, very gently, touched her back. It was wet with sweat, and she was shaking. But she didn't pull away this time. She didn't lean into me like she usually did when I touched her, but I was reassured that she didn't pull away.

"You can't have it both ways," she repeated, softly this time. "I can't control my temper, so I have to get away. But you have to *let* me get away."

"Oh, Gina, my poor baby." It must have been my tone of voice. Maybe she could tell I truly felt empathy for her. Whatever it was, she propelled herself into my lap, crying like a child. I stroked her back, her hair, every part of her I could reach. She cried and cried, nuzzling into me. I cried, too. I could feel how deeply I'd hurt her, even though I still didn't know what I'd done. Hurting my Gina was the last thing I ever wanted to do. "I'm so sorry, honey. I'm so very sorry."

"I thought you didn't know what you've done," she mumbled, her voice muffled by my shorts.

"I don't. But whatever it was hurt you deeply. And I never, ever want to hurt you, baby. I swear I don't."

She turned to the side, letting me see her poor, battered-looking face. "Then why did you try to get a job with Harvard and then turn them down without even telling me about it? Am I so stupid that I can't even be a sounding board?"

"Oh, fuck!" Now I was mad. Mad at Dana. Gina flinched, and I put my hand on her back again, patting it. "Dana might just have ruined our friendship."

"Why? Because she told me something you wouldn't?"

"No," I said, now feeling angry with Gina. "Because she told you a lie. I would never turn down a legitimate job offer without talking to you."

She sat up, rubbing her raw-looking eyes. "Then what in the hell happened?"

I sighed. "Whole story. Dana arranged for me to have a quick lunch interview with the Harvard Classics department head. I was going to tell you about it, but we were in a funny place when it came up. You seemed worried about how attached to you I was, and I was pretty sure I'd take an offer if I got one."

I saw the tears fill her eyes again, but I kept on going. "I didn't want you to feel like you were on probation, baby. But I was still going to tell you."

"But you didn't."

"I didn't because it turned out that I could talk to the guy during that conference I went to. And after we talked, I knew I didn't want the quasi-job he offered. So, there wasn't any reason to bring it up. It was moot."

"What's moot?"

"Oh. It was over. Moot means…" I chuckled. "I don't know how to explain it. It's a legal term that I use when I want to say something doesn't matter."

For the first time in what seemed like forever, a little bit of a smile settled on her lips. "Around here we just say it doesn't matter."

"I'll try to change. I know it's pompous to use Latin terms when English ones will do."

"What's pompous?"

She looked so guileless that I searched my brain for a quick definition. But she was playing possum, the little rat. She stuck her tongue out at me and said, "I know that one."

"I thought you did!"

"So, tell me about this quasi-job."

"It was actually kind of insulting," I said, letting myself think back to the day it occurred. "I think that's part of the reason I didn't want to talk about it. The guy wanted me to quit my job, go to Boston, and teach at the same level I taught at when I was still in school! Then, if everything went well, in a year I might get the same level of job I have now. Of course, if they didn't love me, they'd just kick me to the curb, leaving me with no job at all." I was mad just thinking about it!

"Well, that sucks. What a dick!"

"Well, in his defense, he can get away with it. But not with me, he can't."

"That's my girl," she said, sitting up and draping an arm around me. Gina didn't smell particularly good, the combination of anger, heat, emotion, and more anger not creating a nice perfume. But I was so glad to have her arm around me that I cuddled up against her and breathed her in. "So, you told Dana about it—"

"Wrong," I interrupted. "I did not tell Dana about it. Actually, I lied to her. I told her he didn't offer me a job because he really didn't. Obviously, she did some digging and found out that he'd offered me this probation-kinda thing."

"So, she wanted me to work on you?"

"I have no idea, honey. She didn't mention one word to me. She obviously thought she could get me to change my mind by going through you."

"She doesn't know me very well," she said, laughing softly. "I told her she'd better never try it again."

I leaned forward and kissed her cheek. "Good for you. I'm really glad you told her to knock it off. And I'm really sorry she caught you by surprise. That must have hurt."

"Would have hurt more if she'd known I didn't know," Gina said, smiling slyly.

"You didn't let on?"

"Fuck no!" She stuck that cute little chin out, giving me the defiant look that was so sexy. "I'd never let somebody know you kept something from me. Our business is our business alone."

I hugged her so tightly that she let out a whimper. "Oh, Gina, I love you so much. You're such a good partner."

"No, I'm not," she said softly. "I could see how afraid of me you were. That broke my heart."

"Shh," I whispered. "You are a good partner. I was wrong to hide this from you, and I swear I wouldn't have done it if we'd been further along in our relationship."

"But you *were* afraid of me."

"Yeah," I said, nodding my head. "I was. And that's something we have to work on. I've never been close to anyone who had a bad temper, and it freaks me out."

"I'm trying, Hayden, I really am. But I can't—"

"Shh," I said again. "We have things to work out. This is just one of them. You don't get angry often, baby. We just have to work on how to deal with it when you do."

Her lower lip quivered when she said, "I never want to frighten you."

"I know, I know. And I never want to make you feel betrayed. I know that's how you felt, and I know that's a body-blow for you."

"Yeah," she said, "it really is."

"We can't walk into this and have a perfect relationship waiting for us, baby. Things will come up, but we'll work on them one at a time. We'll put this one to bed until neither of us is sensitive about it. Then, we'll work on it."

"We have time?" she asked, looking at me with those soulful eyes.

"All the time in the world." I kissed her, trying to put all of my love in one kiss.

She gazed at me, sending a basketful of love right back into me. We had some work to do; every couple does. But I couldn't dream of a better partner to fight through the stormy seas of love than the fabulous creature I held in my arms. I thought of the song I often sang while walking down to the dock to meet her. I'd had to butcher the words to make them fit, but singing it always made my heart swell.

Then I'll kiss her so she'll know. And both of us will be a little dreamy-eyed, living in our cottage by the ocean side. Where those salty breezes blow. Me and Ms. Scognamiglio.

The End

Publisher Website *www.briskpress.com*
Author Website *www.susanxmeagher.com*